PENGUIN BOOKS A

Assassin's Creed
Odyssey

Also in the Assassin's Creed® series

Assassin's Creed®
Odyssey

GORDON DOHERTY

UBISOFT

PENGUIN BOOKS

PENGUIN BOOKS

UK | USA | Canada | Ireland | Australia
India | New Zealand | South Africa

Penguin Books is part of the Penguin Random House group of companies
whose addresses can be found at global.penguinrandomhouse.com

First published 2018
001

Copyright © 2018 Ubisoft Entertainment
All rights reserved

Assassin's Creed, Ubisoft and the Ubisoft logo are
trademarks of Ubisoft Entertainment in the US and/or other countries

The moral right of the author has been asserted

Set in 12.5/14.75 pt Garamond MT Std
Typeset by Jouve (UK), Milton Keynes
Printed and bound in Great Britain by Clays Ltd, Elcograf S.p.A.

A CIP catalogue record for this book is available from the British Library

B FORMAT PAPERBACK: 978–1–405–93973–7
A FORMAT PAPERBACK: 978–1–405–93974–4
ROYAL FORMAT PAPERBACK: 978–1–405–94039–9

www.greenpenguin.co.uk

Penguin Random House is committed to a
sustainable future for our business, our readers
and our planet. This book is made from Forest
Stewardship Council® certified paper.

For my family

Acknowledgements

A big thanks to Caroline, Anthony, Anouk, Melissa, Aymar, Clémence, Stéphanie-Anne, Jonathan, Miranda, Sara and Bob Schwager, and everyone at Ubisoft and Penguin for giving me this chance to immerse myself in the world of Assassin's Creed. It has been a hugely enjoyable journey, and your expert guidance and support along the way have been greatly appreciated. An equally big thanks to my agent, James Wills of Watson, Little Ltd, for helping to make this adventure happen.

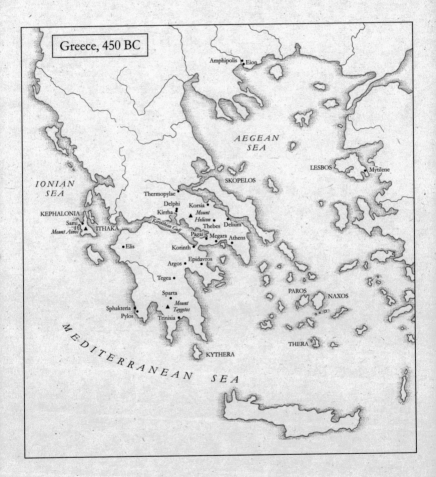

Greece, 450 BC

Amphipolis • Eion

AEGEAN
SEA

IONIAN
SEA

SKOPELOS

LESBOS • Mytilene

Thermopylae

Delphi   Korsia
Kirrha   ▲ Mount
              Helicon
KEPHALONIA   Thebes   Delium
Sami   Pagai • Megara
▲   ITHAKA   Athens
Mount Ainos

Korinthian Gulf

• Elis

Korinth

Argos • Epidavros

Tegea •

Sparta •
      ▲ Mount
        Taygetos
Sphakteria •
Pylos •   Trinisia •

PAROS   NAXOS

THERA

KYTHERA

MEDITERRANEAN   SEA

Prologue

For seven summers, I carried a secret inside me. A flame, warming and true. Nobody else could see it, but I knew it was there. When I looked up to my mother and father I felt it grow brighter, and when I gazed at my baby brother I sensed its warmth in every part of me. One day I dared to describe it to Mother. 'You speak of love, Kassandra,' she whispered, her eyes darting as if she feared that someone might hear. 'But not the kind a Spartan knows. Spartans must love only the land, the state and the Gods.' She squeezed my hands and made me swear her an oath: 'Never reveal your secret to anyone.'

One winter's night during a howling storm, we sat together in the hearth room of our home before a crackling fire, young Alexios in Mother's arms, I sitting by Father's feet. Perhaps all four of us carried that same secret flame within? It comforted me to think so, at least.

And then our warm, quiet sanctuary was pierced by the sound of nails scratching upon the door.

Father's slow, steady breathing halted. Mother clutched little Alexios to her chest and stared at the door as if she alone could see a demon standing in the shadows there.

'It is time, Nikolaos,' a voice like crackling parchment called from outside.

Father rose, sweeping his blood-red cloak around his musclebound body, his thick black beard masking any expression on his face.

'Wait, just a little longer,' Mother begged him, rising too and reaching up to stroke his thick, dark curls.

'For what, Myrrine?' he snapped, swiping her hand away. 'You know what must happen tonight.'

With that, he swung towards the door, picking up his spear. I saw the door creak open, the chill rain scourging Father as he stepped outside. The wind groaned and thunder grumbled high above as we stepped out behind him – for he was our shield.

And then I saw them.

They faced us in a sickle-blade arc. The priests, bare chested, wearing wreaths on their brows. The grey-robed ephors – men more powerful even than Sparta's two kings – holding torches that spat and roared in the tempest. The oldest ephor's long grey hair whipped in the wind, his bald crown gleaming in the moonlight as he beheld us with bloodshot eyes, his age-long teeth serried in an unsettling smile. He turned away, wordlessly beckoning us in his wake. We followed them through the streets of Pitana – my home and one of the five sacred Spartan villages – and I was wet to my skin and freezing before we even reached the outskirts.

The ephors and priests trooped on through the Hollow Land, droning and chanting up at the storm as they went. I used my half-spear as Father did his, like a walking cane, the butt end crunching into the shale with every step. It sent a strange thrill through me just to hold the broken lance, for it had once belonged to King Leonidas – the long-dead champion-king of Sparta. Every soul in Lakonia venerated our family, because Leonidas' blood ran in our veins. Mother was of his line and thus so was I, and Alexios too. We were the descendants of the great man, the hero of the Hot Gates. Yet it was Father who was my true

2

hero: teaching me to be strong and spry — as hardy as any Spartan boy. For all that, he never taught me the strength of mind that I would need for what lay ahead. In all Hellas, was there any tutor who could?

We took a winding uphill path towards the looming grey heights of Mount Taygetos, scarred by plunging ravines, the high crests shrouded in snow. There was nothing about our strange journey that made sense. Something felt very wrong. It had been like that ever since Mother and Father had travelled to Delphi in the autumn, to speak with the Oracle. They did not share with me the great seeress' words, but whatever she had told them must have been bleak: Father had been tense ever since, irritable and distant; Mother seemed adrift most days, her eyes glassy.

Right now she walked with her eyes closed for long periods, the rain streaking in rivulets down her cheeks. She held Alexios tightly, kissing the small bundle of rags every few steps. When she saw my anxious looks up at her, she gulped and handed the bundle to me. 'Carry your brother, Kassandra . . .' she said.

I roped my half-spear to my belt, took him and held him close to me as we climbed the now-precipitous path. The thunder found its voice, pealing somewhere nearby, and lightning shuddered across the sky. The rain turned to sleet and I made a little canopy with the edge of Alexios' blankets to keep his face dry. His skin — scented with sweet oil and the comforting smell of thistledown bedding — was so warm against my frozen face. His weak hands brushed at my hair. He gurgled and I cooed back at him.

At last we came to a plateau. At the far end sat an altar of blue-veined marble, scarred by weather and age. A sheltered candle guttered there next to a pot of oil, a krater of sleet-lashed wine and a platter of grapes.

Mother halted with a choking sob.

'Myrrine, do not be so weak,' Father snapped at her.

3

I could sense a fire rising within her. 'Weak? How can you call me that? It takes courage to confront your true feelings, Nikolaos. Weak men hide behind masks of bravery.'

'It is not the Spartan way,' Father hissed through his teeth.

'Gather before the altar,' said one of the priests, his bony cage of ribs running with melting sleet. I cared not for the sight of the ancient table . . . nor for the edge of the plateau and the night-black abyss lurking beyond—a well of shadow plunging down into the guts of the mountain.

'Now, the child,' said the senior ephor, his ring of hair dancing in the wind, his eyes like hot coals. He held out bony hands towards me, and now I understood, a dark mantle of realization settling upon my shoulders. 'Give me the boy-child,' he repeated.

The roof of my mouth stung with dread, all moisture gone in a heartbeat. 'Mother, Father?' I whimpered to each in turn.

Mother took a step towards Father, placing a beseeching hand on one of his broad shoulders. But he stood there, impassive, like a finger of rock.

'The Oracle has spoken,' the priests wailed in unison. 'Sparta will fall . . . unless the boy falls in its stead.'

Horror speared through me and I clutched little Alexios tight, stepping back. My baby brother was hale and strong—there was no justice in condemning him to the cruel fate that befell weak or deformed Spartan babies. This is what the Oracle had decreed on my parents' trip to see her? Who empowered her to doom him like this? Why was Father not spitting on this grim mandate, drawing his spear upon these wretched old men? And when he did act it was only to shove Mother away, casting her to the ground like a rag.

'No . . . no!' Mother wept as two priests dragged her back. 'Nikolaos, please, do something.'

Father stared into infinity.

One of the priests came at me from behind, seizing me by the shoulders. A second tore Alexios from me and handed the little bundle to the oldest ephor, who cradled my brother like a treasure. 'Mighty Apollo, the Truth-giver, Athena Poliachos, Great Protectress, gaze upon us as we bend to your will, humble, grateful for your wisdom. Now . . . the boy will die.'

He lifted Alexios over his head, stepping past the altar to the edge of the abyss.

Mother fell to her knees with a hoarse cry that tore my heart in two.

As the ephor's body tensed, readying to hurl my brother to his death, lightning struck across the heavens in time with a monstrous roar of thunder. It was as if the bolt had struck me: I felt the most tremendous surge of energy and injustice. I screamed with all my being, shaking free of the priest's pinning hands. I lurched forward like a sprinter, desperate, maddened, arms outstretched towards my brother. Time slowed, I caught baby Alexios' eye and he mine. If I could have captured that moment in amber and lived there for all time I would have done so, both of us alive, connected. And in that trice, I still had a hope of catching him, stopping his fall. Until I lost my stride, stumbled, and felt my shoulder crash against the wretched old ephor's flank, heard a sudden intake of many breaths, saw the ephor flailing, saw him topple out over the edge . . . Alexios too.

The pair plunged into the blackness and the ephor's cry faded like a demon's shriek.

And then . . . silence.

I fell to my knees at the precipice, shaking, as manic oaths of outrage rose behind me.

'Murderer!'

'She killed the ephor!'

I stared into the abyss, aghast, the sleet lashing across my face.

I

Runnels of water trickled across her cheeks. Behind closed eyes, she heard and saw it all again with vivid, terrible clarity. The line of Leonidas, shamed, tarnished. Twenty years was enough for some to forget their debts, come to terms with their flaws, or make peace with the past. 'Not for me,' Kassandra whispered, the broken lance in her hands reverberating. She stabbed the weapon hard into the sand by her side and the memories faded.

Her eyes peeled open slowly, adjusting to the bright glare of the spring morning. The cerulean waters hugging Kephallonia's eastern shores sparkled like a tray of jewels. The surf creamed in across the sand, fading to a gentle, cool gurgle that rolled up to where she sat and crept across her bare toes. The salt-spray came in soft clouds, condensing on and cooling her skin. A squabble of gulls wheeled and screeched in the cloudless sky, while a cormorant plunged into the waters in an explosion of crystalline drops. Due east, out near the hazy horizon, Athenian galleys moved in an endless train. They were like shades, gliding across the twilight-blue, deeper waters and into the Korinthian Gulf to aid the blockade of Megara. The bright sails billowed like the lungs of titans, and every so often the sea wind carried the groan of ropes and timbers and the throaty shouts of the many warriors on board.

Earlier this year, Kephallonia itself had been subsumed into the Athenian sphere, as had most of the islands. And so the war grew like a canker. Some small voice inside told her she should care about the colossal struggle that raged across Hellas, stirring the great cauldron of ideologies, bringing the once-allied cities to each other's throats. But how could she? Proud Athens, she cared little for. And on the other side . . . unswerving Sparta.

Sparta.

The mere presence of the word in her thoughts shattered the delicate idyll of the shore. She eyed the ancient half-spear of Leonidas askance. The winged iron head, the intricate workings around the tang, and the half-length haft, worn and discoloured from years of oiling. It had always seemed fitting to her that the one thing she had left from her broken past was a broken thing.

A shrill *screech* pierced her thoughts, and she looked up to see the cormorant emerging from the waves with a silvery mackerel in its beak . . . but speeding down towards it came a spotted eagle. The cormorant screeched again in terror, dropped its semi-masticated prize then plunged under the waves for cover. The eagle clawed at the discarded fish corpse, only for the morsel to slip under the waves too. With a mighty shriek of dismay, the great bird wheeled round and glided in towards the shore, settling with a gentle run across the sand, coming to a halt beside Kassandra. She smiled despite herself, for the damned spear was not the only thing that remained of the past.

'We talked about this already, Ikaros,' she chuckled. 'You were to bring me mackerel to roast for my afternoon meal.'

Ikaros stared at her, his buttercup-yellow beak and keen eyes giving him the look of a disapproving old man.

'I see.' She arched an eyebrow. 'It was the cormorant's fault.'

Her belly groaned, reminding her of the long hours since she had last eaten. With a sigh, she plucked the spear of Leonidas from the sand. For a moment, she caught sight of her dull reflection in the blade. Broad of face, with little humour in her hazel eyes and a thick braid of russet hair hanging across her left shoulder. She wore a dark brown exomis – a one-shouldered, man's garment – shabby and sad. Just holding the spear brought the memories alive again, and so she quickly tied the lance to her leather belt, rose and turned away from the shoreline.

But something caught her eye, halting her. It was a strange incident – the kind that is conspicuous for its irregularity, like a drunk man behaving himself: out there, amidst the sea haze, a galley cut through the waves. One of hundreds, but this boat was not tacking round the distant headlands and into the Korinthian Gulf. Instead, it was coming straight across the water, towards Kephallonia. Her eyes narrowed and beheld the white sail – or, more specifically, the staring, grimacing gorgon head emblazoned upon it. It was a most hideous depiction, discoloured grey-green lips peeled back to reveal fangs, the eyes glowing like hot coals, while the nest of snakes that served as the creature's hair seemed to writhe with every lungful of wind that buffeted the sails. She stared at the terrifying mien for a time, the legend of Medusa stirring from the depths of memory: once a beautiful and strong

9

woman, betrayed and cursed by the Gods. A morsel of empathy rose and fell within her, like a spark from a fire. But there was something else; she could not see anything of the crew on the strange boat, but she was sure – certain – that she was being watched from those decks. For a moment, the pleasant coolness of the sea spray and wind became unwelcome, chilling.

Spartan children must never be afraid of the dark, of the cold or of the unknown, a voice drawled from buried memory. *His* voice. She spat into the sand, turning away from the sea and the strange boat. The taunting memories of her father's teachings were all that remained of her once-proud family. Passing traders had brought with them bleak tales of the broken house of Leonidas. Myrrine, bereft, had taken her own life, they said, driven to death by the loss of not just one but both of her children. *Because of what I did that night*, she thought.

She strode from the beach, through the dunes and the wind-bent marram grass and picked her way up a rocky path. This brought her onto a small promontory over-looking the coast, and the simple stone shelter that was her home. The white-plastered walls shimmered in the sunlight, the poles and pegged rags that served as an awning of sorts creaked and flapped in the gentle wind and the lone olive tree nearby rustled and swayed. Green-finches pecked at a pool of lying water near a broken stone column, chirruping in song. A good few hours' walk from the shore town of Sami, days could pass here with little contact from passers-by. *The perfect place for a woman to live out her time and die alone*, she mused. She paused to twist back towards the sea again, gazing into the distance and the faraway blur of the mainland. *How might things have been*, she wondered, *had the past not been so cruel?*

She turned back to her home, ducking under the low lintel to enter, the constant sea breeze falling away to nothing. She glanced around the single room: a wooden bed, a table, a hunting bow, a chest of simple things – a broken ivory comb and an old cloak. There was no cage around Kephallonia's shores, nor shackles upon her limbs, but poverty was her keeper. None but the rich men of this island could ever hope to leave it.

She sat on a stool by the table, pouring a cup of water from a clay krater, then unwrapping the hide package she had prepared earlier. A small loaf of bread – hard as a pebble – a finger-sized strip of salted hare meat and a little clay pot containing three small olives stared up at her. A pathetic meal. Her belly howled in protest, demanding to know where the rest was.

She looked up and through the small window at the back of her home, seeing the recently dug hole in the ground. Until yesterday, her storage pit had held two sacks of wheat and a full salted hare, a round of goats' cheese and a dozen dried figs. Enough for five or six days' nourishment. Then she had returned from yesterday's fruitless fishing session to see two thugs stealing away into the distance with those provisions. They had a good half-mile head start on her and she was too hungry to give chase in any case, and so she had lain down to sleep with an empty belly last night. Absently, she ran the pad of her thumb along the edge of the Leonidas spear: honed to perfection. She felt the top layer of skin split, and hissed the name of her present tormentor – the one who had sent the thieves: 'Curse you to the fires, Cyclops.'

Turning back to her meagre meal, she took the bread, dipping it in a little oil to soften it, then lifting it to her mouth. A further belly groan stopped her – but not her own. She looked to the doorway. The girl standing there stared at the pathetic loaf as a man might eye a torc of gold.

'Phoibe?' Kassandra said. 'I haven't seen you for days.'

'Oh, don't mind me, Kass,' Phoibe said, examining her dirt-caked fingernails, tucking her dark tresses of hair behind her ears and fidgeting with the frayed hem of her grubby off-white stola.

Kassandra turned from the girl to the loaf to the sill of the window, where a dark shape fluttered into view. Ikaros gave her that same wide-eyed look of hope, his affections directed towards the sliver of salted hare. *Nor me*, she heard when Ikaros screeched.

With an unconvincing smile, she pushed back from the table, tossing the meat to Ikaros and the bread loaf to Phoibe. The pair were transformed into gannets at that moment, each devouring their meagre meal with relish. Phoibe, Athenian-born and orphaned, was just twelve. Kassandra had first come across the girl begging in the streets near Sami, three years ago. She had given her a few coins that day on her way into the town. On the way back, she had lifted the mite and carried her home, feeding her and letting her sleep in the shelter. Watching her reminded Kassandra of times past, of distant memories of that soft, gentle heat within, of that long-ago snuffed-out flame inside. *Not love*, she assured herself, *I will never be so weak again*.

She sighed, standing and slinging on her bow and lifting a leather waterskin. 'Come, let us eat while we walk,' she said, taking the olives and popping them into her mouth. The soft, salty flesh and rich oil were tantalizing, awakening her tastebuds but doing little to satiate her hunger. 'Unless we want this to be the last meal we eat, we should go to visit Markos.' *The scumbag*, she added inwardly as she strapped on her leather bracers. 'It is time to call in some debts.'

They headed south, following a sun-beaten track that hugged the coastal bluffs for a while, before bending inland. The heat grew strong as noon approached, and they cut across a meadow freckled with violas – the air rich with the scent of oregano and wild lemon groves. The long grass stroked her calves, butterflies flitted across their path in flashes of crimson, amber and blue, cicadas chirruped in the heat and for all the world the war and the past couldn't have been more distant, until they bypassed and overlooked Sami. The port town was an unwalled warren of shacks and simple, white-painted homes surrounding a raised mound of marble villas. Rich men chatted and supped wine on the roofs and verandas. Horses and bare-chested, sweat-slicked workers toiled in the tight lanes and bustling market, hauling olive crops and pine logs towards the docks. There, transport vessels jostled for space at the pale stone wharf where the materials were to be conveyed to the Athenian military shipyards and supply warehouses. Bells pealed, whips snapped, lyre music rose and so too did pale twists of scented smoke from the temples. Kassandra entered the town only when she needed to – for food or supplies she could not obtain in other ways.

And to carry out the jobs Markos lined up for her.

A misthios, they called her. A mercenary. Sometimes to carry messages, sometimes to escort shipments of stolen goods . . . more often though, to do what so few could. Her heart hardened as she thought of her most recent assignment – to a dockside den where a group of notorious bandits were hiding out. The Leonidas spear had been stained red that dark night, and the air fouled by the smell of torn guts. Every slaying was like a prickly seed of guilt that took root deep within . . . but nothing she had done for Markos compared to the twisted, gnarled oak sown on that night of her youth on the edge of the abyss, and the two deaths that had changed her life for ever.

She shook her head to prevent the memories from taking hold and thought instead of her empty purse. Markos had yet again wriggled out of paying her when she had returned to report her successful efforts at the dockside hideout. How much did he owe her now? She felt her hackles rising. *He's a scumbag, a crook, a filthy* . . .

Another memory staggered across her spiralling thoughts – her first moments on this green island, twenty years ago. The day Markos had found her on the stone beach north of the town, washed up beside her broken raft. She remembered his pitted, oily features and curly, greasy black hair as he beheld her. 'You *are* a strange-looking fish,' he chuckled, patting her back as she vomited gutfuls and lungfuls of seawater. He had fed her for a time, but seemed eager to be rid of her . . . until he noticed how nimble and strong she was. 'Who in all Hellas trained you to move like that? I could use someone like you,' he had remarked.

The thoughts faded as Sami fell into the distance behind them. Phoibe skipped ahead, looking up at the soaring Ikaros while 'flying' a toy wooden eagle of her own, making screeching noises. When they came to a fork in the track, Phoibe raced off down the rightmost tine. 'We're nearly there,' she chirped over her shoulder. Kassandra gazed after her, perplexed. That route led towards Mount Ainos. An imperious, sun-bleached statue towered up on those rocky heights: Zeus, God of the Sky, crouched on one knee, holding a thunderbolt in his raised hand. The soils ringing the lower slopes were enriched with minerals washed down during the rains and so terraced vineyards decorated the base of the mountain, each lined with green vines, silvery stone storehouses and small red-tiled villas. 'Don't be a goat, Phoibe,' Kassandra called after her, gesturing to the leftmost track. 'Markos' place is further on – near the southern cove and . . .' Her words trailed off when she saw Phoibe speed on into the nearest vineyard. The estate had always been there, but the figure down by the crops in a green-and-white cloak, had not. 'Markos?' she whispered.

'He asked me not to tell you,' Phoibe said when Kassandra caught up with her on the vineyard's edge.

15

'I'm sure he did,' Kassandra burred. 'Stay here.'

She stole past two workers pruning the crop on the lowest terrace. They didn't even notice her approach, or Phoibe – following in her wake, disobedient as always. As she crept through the vines, she heard Markos, bickering with a worker who clearly knew better.

'We,' he started, then paused to stifle a hiccup, 'we will grow grapes as big as melons,' he insisted, before throwing back his head and taking a long pull on what was evidently a skin of barely watered wine.

'You'll kill the vine, Master Markos,' the worker reasoned, tilting his broad-brimmed sun hat back. 'We can't allow the fruit to grow this year or the next, or the stems will bend and snap. The third year will be the time for the first harvest.'

'Years?' Markos spluttered. 'How in Hades am I supposed to pay back –' He fell silent when Kassandra emerged from the vines. 'Ah, Kassandra,' he beamed, throwing his arms out wide, nearly backhanding the well-meaning worker.

'You bought a vineyard, Markos?'

'Only the finest wines for us from now on, my girl,' he purred, spinning on the spot to gesture all around, nearly losing his footing. Phoibe, darting in and out of the vines nearby, tittered, then set off again after Ikaros. Ikaros began to screech, agitated, but Kassandra's mind was on other matters.

'I don't want your grapes or your wine, Markos,' Kassandra insisted. 'Phoibe and I need food, clothing, bedding. I want the drachmae you owe me.'

Markos shrank a little then, fiddling with the mouth of his wineskin. 'Ah, ever the misthios,' he chuckled nervously. 'Well, you see, there will be a short delay in getting those coins to you.'

'A short three years, by the sounds of it,' Kassandra said flatly. She shot a look up at the circling Ikaros, now screeching madly. A rising sense of unease nagged at her: the eagle did not usually become this agitated when playing with Phoibe.

'When the grapes become wine,' Markos interrupted her thoughts, 'I will have money aplenty, my dear. First, I must make sure I pay back my loan for this place. I'm, er, slightly behind on my payments you see.'

'Quite,' said the nearby worker absently as he returned to snipping and tying vines, 'and the Cyclops doesn't like late payments.'

Markos shot a wild, scolding look at the man's back.

'You borrowed from the Cyclops?' Kassandra gasped, stepping back from Markos as if he were riddled with a pox. 'This,' she gestured around them, 'was funded by *him*? You have bought yourself a nightmare, Markos. Are you a fool?' She glanced around at the shimmering green-gold slopes of Mount Ainos, concerned about how far her voice had carried. 'The Cyclops' men ransacked my stores last night. He hates me already. He's killed scores of men on this island and has put a price on my head. He knows you and I work together. To him, we are equally indebted. If you fall short of your payments then I will be one of the first to suffer.'

'Not quite,' a gruff voice said, behind them both.

Kassandra swung round to the forest of vines. Two strangers stood there, grins stretched across their faces. One, with a face like a stepped-on pear, held a fear-frozen Phoibe, clasping a hand over her mouth and holding a dagger to her throat. Kassandra now recognized the duo: the ones who had plundered her storage pit last night. *Ikaros, why didn't I listen to you?* she chided herself, seeing the eagle still circling, shrieking in alarm.

'Try anything and the girl's throat will be opened,' said the second man, patting a short sword against the palm of his free hand, his brow jutting like a cliff, casting his eyes in shadow. 'Markos has run up quite a debt, but so have you, misthios: you've holed one of my master's boats, you've killed a convoy of his men – friends of mine. So how's about you come along with us, eh? Settle matters to my master's satisfaction?'

Kassandra felt the blood freeze in her veins. She knew that to go with them would mean death for her and slavery at best for Phoibe. But to resist might mean death for them all here and now.

A tense moment passed and Kassandra did not move.

'Seems the misthios is not keen on coming quietly,' Shadow-brow growled. 'Let's show her we mean business.'

Kassandra's heart froze. *Watch your opponent,* Nikolaos hissed from the mists of the past. *Their eyes will betray their intentions before they even make a move.*

She saw the thug holding Phoibe roll his eyes down towards the girl, and his dagger-hand knuckles whiten. It all happened in a single, visceral reflex: she lunged forward, simultaneously clasping and pulling the roped spear

18

from her belt and lashing it forth like a whip. The flat of the ancient lance head licked up and whacked into the thug's temple. The man's eyes rolled in their sockets, blood trickled from his nostrils and he crumpled like a kicked-over stack of bricks. Phoibe staggered away, weeping. Kassandra yanked the spear rope, catching the lance by the haft this time, holding it like a true hoplite might.

Shadow-brow held her gaze, shuffled, feinting left then plunging right with a roar. Kassandra drew her weight onto one foot to let the foe hurtle past, and when he skidded and came back at her, she fell to her haunches and slashed her spear across his belly. He stumbled on a few steps, then glanced down, confused, as a writhing mass of blue-grey gut ropes slipped and slithered out into the noon light to slap down upon the dusty ground. He looked at the eavity that remained of his belly, then up at Markos and Kassandra with a perplexed grin, before falling face-first onto the ground.

'By the balls of Zeus,' Markos wailed, wringing his hands through his greasy curls and falling to his knees as he gawped at the two corpses. 'The Cyclops will kill me for certain now.'

Kassandra hugged the weeping Phoibe tight, kissing the top of her head, drawing her hands over the girl's ears to shield her from the discussion. 'We'll bury the bodies. Nobody will know what became of them.'

'But he will find out,' Markos groaned. 'You must learn: today you cut two heads from the beast, but four will sprout to take their places. And the Cyclops' rage will be tripled. Like any tyrant, you must either obey him utterly . . . or destroy him completely, don't you see?' He swiped a dismissive hand, 'I am no tutor. Perhaps one day you will find a better one.'

'And perhaps you had better set down that wineskin and let your head clear. You need to find a way to pay the Cyclops back.'

Markos' bulging eyes searched the ether before him, his face gradually slackening in despair. Then, as if struck by an invisible lightning bolt, he jolted, rising to his feet, stomping over to seize Kassandra by the shoulders, shaking her. 'That's it; there *is* a way.'

Kassandra shrugged him off. 'A way to earn a sackful of silver on this island? I doubt it.'

Markos' eyes tapered. 'Not silver, my dear. Obsidian.'

Kassandra stared at him blankly.

'Think. What does the Cyclops value most? His men, his land, his ships? No. His obsidian eye.' He tapped madly under one of his own eyes. 'It's even veined with gold. We steal the eye, we sell it – somewhere on the mainland, maybe, or to passing traders. *Then* we have our sackfuls of silver. Enough to pay off my vineyard, enough to pay you what I owe you. To feed Phoibe,' he yelped, delighted at having found an altruistic rationale at last.

'*We* steal the Cyclops' eye?'

'He never wears it. It's too valuable. He keeps it in his home.'

'His home is like a fort,' she said dryly, thinking of the well-watched den on a small peninsula that sprouted from the west of the island. 'Skamandrios was the last person to try to break in there. He has never been seen since.'

Both paused to reflect on the weasel-like misthios Ska-mandrios, thinking of the hundred possible fates he might have suffered. Burning, flaying and gradual dismember-ment were some of the Cyclops' preferred methods of despatching his foes. Skamandrios was hardly a great loss to society, but he had prided himself on his stealth and quickness. The Shadow, some had called him.

Kassandra shook her head clear. 'But getting back to the point . . . *we* steal his eye?'

Markos cowered a little and shrugged pathetically. 'You are the misthios, my dear. I would only slow you down. For this to work it is vital, *vital*, that you are not spotted.'

'I'm rather more concerned that he will catch me,' Kas-sandra said.

'He will not catch you, for he is not at his den.' Markos wagged a finger. 'As you know, almost every private galley on this island has been summoned to join the Athenian fleet. The *Adrestia* is one of the last vessels left. The Cyclops is out on the hunt, and that galley is his prey. He has some grudge with the ship's triearchos, I hear.'

Phoibe wriggled free of Kassandra. 'What's happen-ing?' she asked.

'Nothing, my young girl,' Markos answered first. 'Kas-sandra and I were just discussing how much money I owe her. She just has one last job to do for me and then she will have it all. Isn't that right, my dear?' he asked Kassandra.

'Then we can eat like queens, night after night?' Phoibe asked.

'Aye,' Kassandra said quietly, stroking Phoibe's hair.

'Excellent,' Markos purred. 'You will stay here tonight and enjoy a full meal: fried mullet, octopus, freshly baked loaves, yoghurt, honey and pistachios and several kraters of wine. And then, a comfortable bed and a good rest. Tomorrow, you can be on your way.' Then he whispered so Phoibe would not hear, 'And remember, you must not be seen or all three of us will be . . .' He drew a finger over his throat and stuck out his tongue.

Kassandra refused to let Markos out of her sour stare.

2

Despite the promised warm and soft bed, she slept not a moment, troubled by the task that lay ahead. She stared at the head of her lance, propped near the bed, illuminated by a shaft of moonlight, for what felt like hours before deciding to rise while it was still dark. Phoibe, pressed against her, did not stir. She kissed the girl's head before swinging her legs from the bed, dressing and slipping away from the vineyard and out into the night-chilled countryside. She stayed close to the western shoreline. In the pre-dawn gloom, she heard wildcats hissing and yowling, and kept one hand on her hunting bow as she went. The sun soon breached the horizon and spread its fiery wings across the island, combing across the hills and meadows. On one high point, she saw the neighbouring island of Ithaka, weltering in the rising heat. The remains of the ancient Palace of Odysseus stood on a hillside there, fingers of light streaking through that ghostly ruin. She gazed at the crumbling edifice as she always did. And who could not? It was a wistful monument to a long-dead hero, an adventurer who had travelled across the world and back, fighting in a great war with his wits as well as his weapons. She glanced around the brushland of Kephallonia with a renewed disdain. *Stop dreaming. I will never get off this damned island. Here I live and here I will die.*

On she went and soon she came to the root of the rugged western peninsula that struck out into the sea like a thorn. She crouched there like a hunter, sipping her water, the cicada song growing in intensity like the heat as she studied the land. The Cyclops' hideout sat upon a flat-topped, natural mound roughly half a mile ahead, near the peninsula's tip. The sprawling compound was a hideout in name only – for the Cyclops did not need to hide from anyone. A low wall closed off the estate, grass and pink geraniums sprouting from the cracks in the weathered stonework. Within, a villa stood proud, roofed with terracotta tiles, the pale marble façade and Doric columns painted in ochre and sea-blue. She counted six of his hired thugs upon the outer walls, walking back and forth along the crude parapets, watching the countryside. Two men stood statue-still outside the eastern gatehouse, and she could see a similar gateway on the northern wall too. Worse, Kassandra realized, the ground that lay between her and the estate walls offered little cover for her approach – just a few cypress trees and olive stands, but mostly low, thin brush – and four more men strolled to and fro across this open ground, wearing wide-brimmed hats to shield their eyes from the sun, watching for any movement, and all in plain sight of each other and the men on the walls. These outlying watchmen were effectively a border, sealing off this thorn of land as if it were the Cyclops' own country.

No way through.

There is always a way, Nikolaos spat.

And so she looked north, down the brush and rock

slopes leading to the shore. The deep-blue waters lapped gently upon the thin strip of shingle down there. One edge of her lips flickered in loathing acceptance as she realized that Nikolaos was right. Thumbing the cork from her waterskin, she tipped it upside down and let the precious water trickle away into the parched golden earth.

Keeping low and watching the closest of the four outlying sentries, she picked her way carefully down to the shore. There, she wrapped her spear and bow in oiled leather and strapped both across her back, before wading into the bracing shallows. When the waters rose to her breasts, she launched herself prone, stretching out with her arms, kicking back with her legs to corkscrew through the water, westwards, along the peninsula's coastline and towards its tip. Weeds and tiny fish stroked and brushed at her legs and belly until she was out in the deeper sections. With every second stroke of her arms, she glanced up at the shoreline on her left. No sign of the nearest outlier. Suddenly, dolphins leapt and chattered, out in the deeper waters. She heard the scrape of boots on the shore and saw the tip of a wide-brimmed hat coming to investigate. With a full breath, she plunged under the surface. Through the undulating blue, she saw the dolphins speeding along like her. Looking towards the shore, she saw the shins of the guard, wading into the shallows for a better look. Up through the water's surface, she saw the distorted outline of the man, the shape of his spear held across his chest. But he waded no further than knee-deep: he had seen nothing but dolphins at play, and he seemed quite happy to stand there and bask in the sunlight . . . all while the breath in Kassandra's lungs grew stale and then fiery. If she surfaced now she was as good as dead. If she did not, the same fate awaited. Black spots burst and spread around the edges of her vision as the spent breath escaped from her lips in a flurry of bubbles like rats fleeing a sinking skiff. The cold hand of panic tried to seize her, yet calmly, she took her thumb from the mouth of her air-filled drinking skin, sucked in a deep and full breath and swam on, revitalized.

He had watched her from afar, seeing how she had taken time to judge her approach to the Cyclops' den. Now he watched her surface gracefully, just downhill from the peninsula's tip and the estate's northern gateway, and not too far from his vantage point either. So far, she was living up to her reputation.

'And soon we will see if she is as skilful and deadly as they claim,' mused the watcher, folding his arms and letting a grin rise across his face.

Kassandra levered herself from the water and onto a flat, sun-warmed shelf of stone. She picked her way up the rocky hinterland, keeping low behind bushes as she went. Within a stretch of a hundred strides or so, she was almost dry from the sun. Nearing the estate's northern walls, she settled down behind a boulder then peeked up to gauge the two guards flanking the gateway. They wore leather corselets and one sported a red headband. One gripped a good spear diagonally across his chest and the other carried a small axe in his belt. Through the gates she saw no movement around the villa itself, none patrolling the rooftop terrace or standing at the entrance vestibule. The Cyclops had taken most of his men with him, she realized. The outer walls were the key. If she could slip by the watch here . . . she would be into the unguarded interior. These gate sentries had to be dealt with, but how to do so without alerting the dozen or so others strolling the parapets? A gentle shuffling sounded right beside her and her heart almost leapt from her mouth in fright. 'Ikaros, by all the Gods!' she hissed. Ikaros gave her a hood-eyed look, then lurched up into flight. Kassandra ducked down, one eye peeking over the boulder to see the spotted eagle glide towards the gate. The two sentries didn't notice until he was close, and with a flap of his wings, he sped up and over the head of one guard, talons extending to snatch the red headband.

'*Malákas!*' the guard yelped, grabbing at his own scalp and howling at the bird as it sped on inside the estate. The pair lumbered inside after Ikaros. A few of the men on top of the wall laughed and heckled as they watched the spectacle.

Kassandra's eyes stayed on the backs of the distracted two as she rose and sped low, cat-soft on her feet. Just as she slipped through the gateway, the pair gave up their chase of Ikaros and turned back towards her. As if caught by the swing of an invisible boxer, Kassandra threw herself to her right and from their line of sight, landing in a tangle of wild gorse sprouting near the base of the walls. The bush settled and she held a burning breath in her lungs, watching through the undergrowth as the two guards walked right past her . . . and back to their places at the gateway. The other men on the walls turned to face outwards too. She was inside, unseen.

Heart thumping, she rolled her eyes towards the villa. The main entrance beckoned like a shady maw, the twin red pillars flanking it like bloody fangs. She picked her way across the compound, ducking behind wagons, strewn barrels, piled hay and wooden outhouses until she was a short arrowshot away. Her legs shook, primed to sprint inside. It was only bitter experience that chained her there, on her haunches. *Can't see a damned thing in there*, she mused. *There might be a dozen of the Cyclops' men standing in those shadows.* She looked up instead – the roof terrace sported a doorway into the upper floor. Creeping forward, she seized an ivy vine and walked herself up the villa wall. A foot slipped, kicking a terracotta tile on the porch roof. The tile cracked and slid, spinning away towards the ground. Kassandra let go of the vine with one hand and caught the tile, exhaling in relief.

Stealth, Nikolaos hissed in her head. *A Spartan must be nimble and silent, like a shade.*

'I am not a Spartan, I am an outcast,' she growled to chase away the voice, then hopped up over the marble balustrade.

The arched doorway leading into the villa's upper floor was just as shady as the main entrance. Sucking in a deep breath, she edged inside, one hand poised near her spear haft, the other extended for balance should she need to roll or leap clear of an attack. For a moment she was blinded by the darkness, her head flicking in every direction and her braided tail lashing like a whip. In her mind's eye she saw grim-faced sentries rushing her, silvery blades chopping down . . . and then her eyes adjusted and she saw just a quiet, deserted bedchamber. The pale-washed walls were licked with bright paint, depicting a scene of battle, with a one-eyed champion triumphing over many smaller foes. A grand bed lay at one end of the room, laden with plush silk blankets. *Nothing in here*, she decided . . . until she turned round and saw the plinth of Parian marble by the chamber hearth. The trophies resting upon it chilled her to her marrow.

Three desiccated heads, mounted on wooden stands like prize battle helms. Kassandra paced over towards them guardedly, as if they might sprout bodies and attack her. But these three were long dead. One, a bad-toothed man with long hair, had clearly died in pain, judging by the death rictus fixed on his face. The next was a young lad who had had his nose sawn off to leave a ragged mess at the centre of his now-peaceful face. The third, a middle-aged woman, was locked in a sightless scream, mouth ajar as if crying out, *Behind you!*

A floorboard groaned.

Kassandra spun round, part-drawing her spear, fright lashing her like a tongue of fire.

Nothing.

Her heart thundered against her ribs. Had the noise been her imagination? She returned her spear to her belt and flicked a glance back at the heads. None of them was Skamandrios, she was certain. Perhaps the weasel had stolen whatever he was after and escaped – fled to the north to live the life of a rich man? The thought instilled a bravado in her, and she crept to the bedchamber door-way with a degree of confidence. Edging her head out onto the landing to look around, she saw nothing to the left, nothing to the right and then, straight ahead . . . *two guards!*

She went for her spear again, only to realize the 'guards' were in fact ancient suits of armour. Bronze cuirasses, helms and greaves probably robbed from the ruins of the old palace on Ithaka. Webs had gathered inside the helms like sagging faces.

Scowling, she paced across the landing, eyeing the two doors ahead. One was surely the Cyclops' strongroom. Most on the island said he slept on his gold, but this was the next closest thing. Edging to the leftmost door, she twisted the handle slowly. With a clunk, it relaxed and the door whined as it floated open. The noise sent a thousand cold-footed rats scampering through Kassandra's guts. She held her breath for a moment . . . but nobody outside had heard the noise. Relieved, she peered into the room. Nothing – just stark stone walls, unpainted or plastered, and a plain wooden floor. Not a jot of furniture except for a shabby old cupboard on the right-hand wall. Its doors were missing and it was empty.

Stepping to her right, she gently turned the handle of the second door. It opened silently to reveal a vision of gold. A finger of sunlight shone in through a narrow oculus in the ceiling. Dust motes floated lazily in the gilt light, illuminating a trove of plunder: ivory chests of coins and charms; a bench laid out with silver circlets, tokens and cups too; a shelf bedecked with lapis lazuli stones of the most mesmerizing blue. Opals, sardonyx, emeralds, necklaces of amethyst beads. An ornamental war bow chased with electrum. And there, to the rear of the chamber, just where the shaft of sunlight became dark shadow again, sat the eye. She licked her dry lips. It rested on a cedarwood plinth, fixed so as to stare at her with its golden pupil. This was the greatest treasure of them all, more valuable than a pocketful or even a sackful of coins or gems. All she had to do was step across the room, past the other riches . . . and take it.

Take it!

She took a step forward, then halted. It was the slightest of sensations that stopped her: a smell of something incongruous. Behind the odour of metal and polish a scent of . . . death, decay. Her eyes rolled left and right. The stonework just inside the left edge of the doorway was scarred, as if a mason had been chipping at it to make a grid of dots. The right edge of the doorway was clad in cedar wood, not stone. Her eyes narrowed. Dropping to her haunches, she held out her bow and reached over the threshold of the room carefully. With a gentle *dunt*, she pressed the bow's tip down upon the first floorboard inside the room.

With a *whoosh*, the cedar panels to the right of the doorway suddenly exploded with movement and a gust of disturbed air. She fell back, snatching her bow to her chest as a mass hurtled across the doorway and crashed against the stone on the left with a metallic *clank* and a shower of sparks. As she rose, she beheld the contraption: a bed of iron spikes, the full height of the door, that would

31

have ripped her apart had she set foot on that floorboard. She stared at the forlorn corpse of Skamandrios, entangled in the spikes. He was more skeleton than flesh, just leathery rags of skin dangling from the bones. A spike had pierced his temple, another his neck, several his chest and limbs. 'At least it was quick for you, Shadow,' she said flatly.

The trap was wedged in place and the way into the strongroom blocked. She stepped back, vexed, then heard the dull chatter of two guards outside, drawing closer to the villa.

'The sun grows strong. I'll tend to the horses in the stable, you lock up the villa,' one said to the other. 'Master will be back tonight and he'll not be happy if the rooms aren't cool enough for him.'

A moment later she heard their footsteps on the lower floor and the steady clunk and click of doors and windows being closed over and locked.

No time, Kassandra realized, her breath quickening. She had to get out, but she could not leave without getting the eye. She closed the door to hide the sprung trap, then looked all around the upper landing. No other way into the strongroom. She thought of the oculus on the ceiling — perhaps she could climb up onto the roof and drop into the chamber that way? No, the opening was too small even for a child to fit through. Her thoughts spun in a thousand different directions until they settled on the first room again. *Why would a rich, power-hungry thug like the Cyclops have a bare room in his villa?* she mused, glancing around to confirm that every other part of the place — upstairs at least — was bedecked with trophies and finery. She came before the first room's open door and tapped her way in with her bow. No traps. Inside, she turned to face the wall shared with the strongroom and eyed the shabby, doorless cupboard with suspicion. Placing a hand on either side of it, she edged it as quietly as she could to one side, and stared at the wooden hatch it revealed. Heart surging with anticipation, she twisted the handle and crawled inside the golden room, racked with suspicion that every movement might bring a hidden blade scything down upon her or send her toppling into a concealed pit of spikes. But there was nothing more. She reached out to pluck the obsidian eye from the plinth, feeling the cold weight of it in her hand, knowing that it would pay off both her troubles and those of Markos. As she moved back out into the landing and towards the bedchamber and the climb back down the ivy, elation began to swell in the pit of her stomach, and then she heard a sigh.

'Just the bedchamber and that's the upstairs done,' the guard mumbled to himself through the opening in an old leather helm that covered most of his face.

She pressed her back to the wall, hugging the shadows, watching as the guard ambled into the bedchamber before she could. She heard a clatter of shutters being closed then a thick clunk of a locking chain. The guard emerged from the chamber again and wandered back downstairs.

She paced along behind him like his shadow, creeping down the stairs in time with him to disguise her footsteps, edging up to the main entrance as he did. If he locked it while she was still inside . . . her stomach twisted as she imagined a fourth head on the marble mantel upstairs.

Just then, the guard dropped his keys. As he stooped to pick them up, Kassandra took a further step. The boards creaked, the guard bristled, then leapt up and round in one motion. His face curled into a baleful sneer as he swung his axe level, his lips parting to shout for his comrades. The cry never came as Kassandra in one stroke grabbed and threw the small knife tucked into the lip of her bracer. It flew straight and pierced the man's throat. He fell, pink foam bubbling from the wound. Kassandra caught his body to reduce the noise. She eyed the man for a moment, his keys, his garb, the door, the way to freedom.

The watcher stared as the guard ambled from the villa and strolled across the grounds, draped in a black cloak. He heard a few words being exchanged as the guard said something to the other posted at the gateway of the outer walls, before the guard continued on out into the countryside. A thrill of anticipation crawled through him: she was everything, everything they hoped she might be. He craned forward from his vantage point like a crow, unblinking.

Kassandra heard her own breath crash like waves within the confines of the visored leather helm. Worse, the guard she had killed and taken it from had clearly been munching on raw garlic for a year, going by the stink. She did all she could to walk in a carefree – almost bored – manner, away from the Cyclops' estate and off out into the brush, patting the flat of the stolen guard axe upon her palm.

Her excuse had been simple: 'I'm going to scout around outside. I'm sure I saw something out there while I was on the villa's top floor.' The other sentry at the gate had been too weary from the midday heat to pick up on her questionable attempt at a low, gruff voice.

She walked into a stand of fir and juniper and felt the shade in there drape across her – blissful invisibility and coolness. The air was spiced with the tang of pine and the soft carpet of fallen needles felt pleasant to walk on. Up ahead, she saw a clearing with a splash of blue waves beyond. The shore. Giddiness rose in her breast like scented smoke, intoxicating her with the oh-so-close promise of success as she stepped into the clearing.

The slow, steady sound of a pair of hands clapping halted her in her stride, sending the fear of all the Gods through her.

'Excellent, *excellent*,' a voice said.

Kassandra turned her head towards the figure sitting on a fallen log in the clearing's treeline. He was a gull of a man, sporting thin brown hair combed forward, his body swaddled in a pristine white robe, streaked with a vivid silver stripe, his scrawny neck and wrists dripping with bracelets. A rich man, she realized instantly, and not of this island.

'The Cyclops of Kephallonia is seldom relieved of his hard-won treasures,' he said, his chest shaking with a chuckle.

Kassandra shivered. There was something about his tone – overly familiar, assuming. And the way he looked at her, his eyes combing her body. It was not a carnal look, but it was desirous and lustful all the same.

35

'Rest your hands from your axe. You have nothing to fear from me.'

Kassandra did not let her gaze waver, refused to blink, and certainly did not set down her stolen axe. Ikaros swooped down just then to perch on her shoulder, shrieking at the stranger. Like a hunter, she took in every scintilla of her peripheral vision. There were no others in the tree-line, she realized. But she noticed something else: downhill, at a small inlet, a boat was moored just off a timber jetty. The hideous gorgon head on the sail stared up at her as crewmen on board hoisted it up to the spar.

'Who are you?' she said through clenched teeth.

'I am Elpenor of Kirrha,' he replied calmly.

Kirrha? Kassandra thought. *The gateway to Delphi, the home of the Oracle.* She felt a great urge to spit.

'I came looking for you because I heard great things about you – the misthios of Kephallonia,' Elpenor continued.

'You have the wrong person,' she growled. 'There are several mercenaries on this island.'

'None with your skills, Kassandra,' he said with the timbre of a tombstone rolling into place. 'Preternatural speed of mind and body.'

She reached up to prise the stinking leather helm from her head and tossed it into the nearby grass, her hidden braid of hair spilling loose across her chest. 'What do you want with me? Speak plainly, or I will lodge this axe in your chest.'

Elpenor laughed, his bony body shaking with amusement. 'I want to offer you a vast sum of wealth, Kassandra.

More than twice the value of that obsidian eye you took from the Cyclops.'

She moved a hand to her purse, checking the eye was still there. It was. *Twice as much again?* Such riches would allow her to pay off the Cyclops, then buy a good home for Phoibe. More, it would break the chains of poverty that kept her on this island. She could go anywhere, do anything. The notion thrilled her with terror and wonder. Then, when she saw how he rapaciously eyed her bare arms again, she stiffened and stared down her nose at him. 'I do not lie with men for money. Besides, you are old and I might break you.'

Elpenor cocked an eyebrow. 'It is not your body I want, not in that way, at least. I come to offer you a bounty, in return for a head.'

'You already have a head of your own,' Kassandra sneered.

Elpenor half-smiled. 'The head of a warrior. A Spartan general.'

Kassandra felt the world shift under her feet.

'They call him the Wolf,' he said.

Kassandra steadied herself, ignoring the streaks of sweat stealing down her back. 'Generals bleed like all other men,' she shrugged. 'Spartans too, despite their misplaced conceit.'

'So you accept the contract?'

'Where is he?'

'Across the sea. In the most coveted land in the Greek world.'

Kassandra's eyes narrowed. She followed his gaze, past her shoulder and off to the east. She thought of the haze out at sea and the constant train of Athenian galleys, tacking round into the Gulf of Korinthia, to bolster the siege of . . . 'Megaris? He's in Megaris?'

Elpenor nodded. 'In the tug-of-war between Sparta and Athens, the city of Megara and its narrow strip of land is the rope. Athens wants the twin ports to complete its naval noose around Hellas, Sparta wants the land to use as a bridge into Attika.'

Kassandra took a step back and spluttered. 'So he's *inside* the Athenian blockade?'

'The Wolf and his troops marched overland from Lakonia, and are now headed for Pagai, Megaris' western port.'

'Why do you want him dead?' she asked.

'The war rages and . . . the Wolf is on the wrong side.'

She shot him a cold look. 'How do I know you are on the right side?'

He lifted a purse from his robe and shook it. The thick clunk of drachmae sounded from within. 'Because I am the one paying you. Here –' He tossed the bag of coins towards her. She plucked it from the air, pleasantly surprised by its weight. 'Do as I ask, misthios, and you shall have ten times this.' He smiled in a way that drained all humour from his eyes.

She glared at him. 'I'll need a boat to run and pierce that blockade. Give me yours and I will accept,' she said, flicking her head towards the gorgon-head galley. In truth she had only once before been to sea as a misthios – circling Kephallonia in a rotting old trade cog to bring stolen hides to one of Markos' contacts.

'My sails cannot be seen in the vicinity when it happens, misthios,' Elpenor said with an air of finality.

'But without a boat, the contract is void. Athens wore down all of her allies' fleets years ago – forced them to pay into the treasury of the Delian League so she could swell her own navy. There are few seaworthy galleys left in private hands, and none on Kephallonia that would be fast enough to cut through a blockade.'

Elpenor's nose wrinkled. 'Is it too much for you, misthios? Have I overestimated your skills?' When she hesitated to answer, he rose and turned from her, taking a step towards the trees and the track leading downhill towards his boat.

'Nothing is too much for me, old man,' she called after him. 'You'll have the Wolf's head in good time.'

He halted, looking back over his shoulder with hooded eyes. 'Good. Come and find me at Pilgrim's Landing in Kirrha, once it is done.'

She trekked along the shoreline, heading back towards Markos' vineyard. The strange Elpenor's parting words danced around in her thoughts like a falling sycamore seed. Right now, that all seemed misty and unreal. Kirrha, she had never been to. The Wolf, she had never met. Beyond Kephallonia's coastal waters, she had not ventured. Not for twenty years. *What a fool*, she chided herself. *Why can't you learn to say no to suspect contracts? Markos and his wretched schemes and now this death-trap of a job.* She laughed aloud and the sound surprised her. 'This Wolf is safe. I will never get off this damned island.'

She trudged on for a time. After a while she rounded a rocky cape and came to the pale sand of Kleptous Bay. She took her drinking skin from her belt to slake her thirst, but it never reached her lips.

'I swear I uttered not a word of a lie. Please do not take her from me!'

The cry sailed across the bay, the voice ragged and desperate.

She fell to her haunches and shielded her eyes from the sun. At first she saw just white foaming breakers, wheeling seabirds and a few wild goats chomping on marram grass. It was only on a second sweep that she spotted the trireme lodged on the shoreline, further up the bay, the stern in the sand and the fore bobbing in the water. It was smaller than the Athenian war galleys and Elpenor's gorgon-head boat, but it looked slender and well crafted, painted black near the keel and red around the rails. The stern rose into a curving scorpion-tail and the rostrum sported a glinting bronze ram, eyes painted on either side.

'The *Adrestia* is everything to me,' the voice wailed.

'*Adrestia*,' Kassandra whispered. The Goddess of Retribution . . . and the name of this ship? Shivers streaked down her back as she cycled the name over and over in her head. *The* Adrestia, *the* Adrestia, she mouthed, clicking her fingers, unable to recall why the name seemed familiar.

There was movement too, all over the decks. Tiny shapes of men. Bandits, tying kneeling crewmen, beating those who tried to rise. There was one older man, bent double thanks to the giant holding his head over a large clay pot. The pinned fellow writhed and struggled in vain. She heard the gurgling, forlorn cry again. 'Gods, spare me, spare my ship!'

The cry ended in a frantic gurgle as the giant plunged the wretch's head into the pot, water and foam spewing up from the edges. Now her vision grew eagle-sharp, and she saw the giant for who he was, and realized where she had heard of the *Adrestia* before. Markos' words echoed in her mind: *The Adrestia is one of the last galleys left on the island. The Cyclops is on the hunt, and that ship is his prey.*

3

Barnabas cried out in vain, bubbles roaring past his ears as his breath escaped, the dull moan of his underwater pleas sounding strange and otherworldly. His hands, bound behind his back, were hot with blood where the ropes had chewed into the skin. The water surged up his nose and flooded his mouth, pushing into his throat like a serpent. This was the worst part: when the air was gone from his lungs, when his body screamed for him to suck in a fresh breath, while the Cyclops' vice-like, meaty hand held him here, denying him. Flashes of white were followed by black splodges like squid ink, growing, spreading, joining, stealing away his vision. This was it, he realized. This time, the Cyclops would not bring him up for air. Charon the Ferryman would have him. Inside, he wept, and from the pits of memory, his well-lived life played out in flashes, like a sputtering torch. He saw the sandy island on which he had been marooned as a young sailor – saw the swell of the ocean that morning when he had been dying of thirst . . . saw the glistening, gargantuan *thing* that had arisen from the waves. Sun-madness, his rescuers had claimed, dismissing his tale.

Suddenly, it all changed. The water roared and then fell away as the meaty hand wrenched his head up. His soaked tresses of long hazel, white-shot hair and beard swinging like octopus arms, spraying water in every direction. The crystal clarity of the air seemed deafening, and his head ached at the brightness of the sunlight. Blinking, retching and gasping for air, he stared up at the giant holding him, the lone eye staring down at him in return.

'Your loose lips are turning a little blue, Barnabas,' the Cyclops rumbled with laughter.

'What I said,' Barnabas coughed, 'was meant as no affront to you. I swear to the Gods.'

'Too much talk of Gods,' the Cyclops sneered, his grip on the back of Barnabas' head tightening again. 'Time for you to *go* meet one of them, old man. Hades awaits you!'

'No –' Barnabas' half-plea ended with a splash and a mouthful of water. Back into the briny abyss, the darkening vision, the burning lungs. This time he saw his first mission as a triearchos, when he had led his crew to an island in search of an ancient treasure. They had found nothing but a labyrinth of caves. They wandered for days in those dark underground passages, lost. They found no treasure. But Barnabas had seen something, one night, while all the others slept. It was a . . . creature. Well, it was a shadow at least: of a huge beast, broad of shoulder, with horns, watching them as they slumbered. As soon as he had seen it, it vanished. The mists of his dreams? That's what his men had said when he tried to tell them about it, but later he had found the faint tracks and the markings of cloven hooves. He sucked in a lungful of water, felt his body slacken as the life seeped from him. The struggle was almost over. Then . . .

'What's wrong, you old bastard?' the Cyclops hissed as

43

he ripped Barnabas back from the pot again. 'Are your Gods silent? Or did they tell you to go away?'

The bandits watching the tied crew exploded in laughter. 'Finish it!' one cheered.

Barnabas felt the Cyclops' hand tighten on the back of his head again. He did not bother to suck in a breath, knowing it would only make his end more lasting and painful. 'Why did you not come to my aid?' he whispered skywards. The next thing he saw was the water in the pot rushing up towards him . . .

'Let him go,' a voice struck across the bay.

The Cyclops' hand froze. Barnabas stared at the pot water, his nose a finger's-width from the surface. With his head locked like that, he rolled his eyes to the side. What he saw sent a shiver of awe through him. She walked across the bay with a swagger, tall, lithe and strong, wearing a hunter's bow, an axe and a strange half-lance. Her chiselled features seemed to be set hard, her eyes shaded under a baleful brow; and on her shoulder sat the most wondrous sight. An eagle. A bird of the Gods. Tears gathered in Barnabas' eyes. Who was this daughter of Ares?

'I will not ask you again, Cyclops,' she boomed, loose sand swirling around her like a mist.

The one-eyed giant shook with rage, then a low growl spilled from his lips, before he tossed Barnabas aside like a used rag.

The Cyclops of Kephallonia stared down at her from the boat's stern, his long-ago mutilated face and the pitted hole that once housed his right eye pinched in a look of permanent anger. His oak-like limbs were tensed, glistening with sweat, his torso bulging beneath his bronze-studded leather thorax.

'Misthios?' he called, his scooped-up tail of black hair whipped in the wind like a living flame as Kassandra came to a halt twenty paces from the boat. '*Misthios!*' he shouted in disbelief.

Kassandra shuffled to stand, feet apart, shoulders square, Ikaros bracing on her shoulder. *Radiate power*, Nikolaos growled in her mind. What she hoped the Cyclops and his men could not see was that her hands shook like the plucked strings of a lyre. But she had to face him – after years of avoiding this brute and his thugs, she *had* to face him, to end his stranglehold over her, Phoibe and Markos . . . over all Kephallonia. And to get that damned boat.

'What are you doing here?' the Cyclops boomed. 'I asked my men to bring you to me in ropes.'

'They are dead. I came alone, to face you . . . *Cyclops.*'

The Cyclops bashed a fist upon the rail there. 'Do not call me that,' he roared, then waved four of his men towards her. They vaulted over the rail and landed on the shore, spreading out on either side of her.

As they paced towards her, Kassandra's mind whirred. 'Have you only one ear as well as one eye, Cyclops? I said I came to face *you*, not your thugs.'

The Cyclops' lips twitched, then he flicked a finger to direct his four men. 'Tear her legs off so she can never walk again, then drag her aboard and I will take her head once I have finished drowning this old sot.'

As he half-turned back towards Barnabas, she plucked the obsidian eye from her purse and lifted it up to catch the sun. 'Look what I found in your home.'

The Cyclops swung back to face her, his single eye growing moonlike. He rumbled with an evil, low laugh. 'Oh, you will pay dearly for that . . .' He and his remaining six men dropped down from the boat, stalking out around her like a noose. Ten men *and* the Cyclops? *Bravery and folly oft ride in company*, Nikolaos hissed. *Fight wisely, never overcommit.*

A rough bleating sounded behind her, and the next step of the plan was born. She turned to the goat cropping on grass behind her. 'Perhaps I should stow the eye for safe keeping?' she suggested, motioning towards the goat's rear, lifting its tail.

The Cyclops froze, aghast. 'You would not dare!'

Kassandra smiled by way of reply, popping the eye in her mouth to moisten it, then shoving it deep into the goat's anus. The goat's head rose with a startled bleat, confused, before she slapped its rump, causing it to bolt between two of the Cyclops' men, off up the bay and over the horizon.

The Cyclops howled. 'Catch the damned goat, get my eye,' he screamed. Three set off after the creature.

Three fewer bastards to deal with, she thought.

The Cyclops and the remaining seven now crouched like hunting cats, facing Kassandra. 'A bag of silver to the one who rips open her throat,' he offered.

She took the guard's axe stolen from the Cyclops' den in one hand and the Leonidas spear in the other, watching,

46

waiting for the first to move. The meanest-looking of the thugs, bald with heavy gold earrings and a leather kilt, wriggled a little. When he lurched forward, she threw up spear and axe in an X to block, but the blow sent her staggering back towards those behind. She pivoted mid-stride to meet the expected attack from that direction, only to see the streaking shadow of Ikaros, swooping down to claw at the eyes of the brute behind her, saving her from his wicked-looking sickle. She swung to face her next attacker, parrying then chopping the axe into his shoulder, cleaving deep and bringing a gout of black blood. The foe fell away and she saw the next coming for her. She bent her body around his sword thrust and jabbed the Leonidas spear into his face. He fell with an animal moan, his head ruptured like a melon. Two more lunged at her now. One scored her breastbone with a swipe of his spear, and the other nearly crushed her head with a heavy iron mace. Too many . . . and the Cyclops himself was weighing up his moment to strike the killing blow. *A Spartan must have the eyes of a hunter, see everything, not just that which lies before them*, Nikolaos berated her. From the edges of her vision, she saw something on the *Adrestia*'s decks: the ship's spar and the rope holding it in place – one end knotted by the rail. As the two oncoming thugs screamed, she ducked, avoiding their twin strikes, and tugged the axe from the cloven chest of the first she had killed. Rising, she hurled the axe towards the ship. She did not wait to see if her aim had been good, turning to block another attack. The next thing she heard was the *thunk* of the axe biting through rope and into timber, the groan of wood, the roar of the Cyclops charging at her, his heavy blade tensed and ready to slice across her belly. Then the shadow of something passed overhead. The spar – freed – pivoted around on the mast, the rope flailing past. Kassandra leapt up to grab the brine-wet rope and clung on for dear life, just as the Cyclops' blade cut through the space she had been occupying. The rope dragged her through the air, and she kicked out at the Cyclops, smashing his nose with her heel, then swept round like a stone in a sling, shooting free of the ring of thugs and towards the ship. She let go of the rope and slammed against the vessel's rail then levered herself onto the deck. She ran to Barnabas and sliced through his bonds, then those of the nearest crewmen. They leapt up, panicked.

'Be ready,' she berated the crew, turning towards the stern and the shore. She heard the Cyclops' breathy rage, seeing the ropes tossed up from the shore snagging on bolts and timbers then tensing as the brute and his thugs climbed. The crew tossed hooks and poles to and fro, then rushed to the stern rail to batter at the climbing men, knocking some off like limpets. But the Cyclops was too strong. He reached the rail, slashed up and ripped open the neck of one crew member, who toppled into the shallows. He and three thugs managed to reboard. When the one-eyed giant lunged towards Kassandra, the fretting, unarmed Barnabas staggered into his path, and the Cyclops tensed his blade, ready to slice the man out of the way. Kassandra grabbed a fishing pole – affixed with a spike on the end – and launched it across the deck at the giant. The makeshift javelin hammered into the Cyclops'

48

chest, threw him backwards and pinned him to the mast. The brute's eye flared in anger and disbelief, before a gout of dark blood leapt from his mouth, followed by a rattling breath. Finally, he slumped into death.

The few thugs still fighting now backed away, gawping, all confidence gone. They leapt from the boat and sped up the bay.

'The Cyclops of Kephallonia is . . . dead?' one crewman stammered.

'The island is free from his terror,' croaked another.

Barnabas, still soaking and somewhat bedraggled, came before Kassandra, stared at her, then fell to one knee like a dropped cloak. He gazed up at her in awe and veneration. Just then, Ikaros swooped in and landed on her shoulder. 'Daughter of Ares?'

'Kassandra,' she replied, waving him up then casting an eye over the strewn bodies and the clay pot. 'I had heard of some grudge between the Cyclops and the triearchos of this boat. I didn't realize how severe it was.'

Barnabas rose with a deep sigh. 'What happened with the Cyclops was a misunderstanding, shall we say. I was in Sami recently, enjoying a meal in the dockside tavern there. When I say a meal, I mean a bucketful of wine. I grew rather merry and decided to tell the locals a tale of a past voyage, about a thing I saw out in the islands – while I was hideously drunk, admittedly . . . but I *did* see it: a horrifying creature, ugly beyond description. I mentioned the words "one-eyed monster" and our friend back there rises, kicking over his table. He thinks I'm talking about him, you see, and chases me from the place. We were

49

lucky to escape the Sami docks before he could catch us. But it seems he watched for my next landing, because as soon as we put into shore here, he and his men pounced.'

'Yes, the Cyclops tends . . . tended to take that kind of thing personally.' Kassandra half-smiled.

Barnabas' sun-darkened face slackened in relief as he beheld the Cyclops' body and then the clay pot. 'After spending most of my life at sea, it would have been absolutely shameful to drown in a pot. I owe you my life. We all do. Yet I can never repay you but with my loyalty.'

'The use of your ship for a time would be payment enough,' she said.

'A journey?' he asked. 'I will take you anywhere, misthios. To the edge of the world, if needs be.'

The *Adrestia* left Kleptous Bay behind and sailed around the island to the harbour of Sami. There it remained at anchor for several days while Barnabas' men gathered provender and supplies for the journey that lay ahead, the crew trooping back and forth across the gangplank laden with sacks of provisions on their shoulders. Kassandra rested one elbow on the ship's rail, her mind already at sea, the babble of the docks, the screeching of gulls and the clack of cups from the nearby taverns incessant around her.

Light footsteps rose behind her, rattling along the jetty. 'I'm ready,' Phoibe panted. 'I have packed all my things.'

Kassandra's eyes closed tight, and she fought to douse the flickering flame within. 'You're not coming,' she said coldly.

The footsteps slowed, behind her. 'If you're going, I'm going,' Phoibe said in a clipped tone.

'Where I'm headed is no place for a child,' Kassandra said, turning slowly to face her, crouching to her eye level. Now she could see the clipped tone was but a mask. Tears quivered in Phoibe's eyes. 'You must stay on this island. The Cyclops is gone now and so you and Markos will be safe.' She shot a look over Phoibe's shoulder. Markos stood on the jetty, locked in discussions with some boss-eyed trader, trying to sell him a mangy donkey with a bald back. 'A battle horse,' he crowed, 'fit for a general.' He stopped for a moment, and returned Kassandra's look, offering her a half-nod in farewell. *Look after her*, she mouthed to him. Another hurried nod like a scolded child.

She felt something being pressed into her hand then. Phoibe's toy wooden eagle. 'Then take Chara with you,' Phoibe said. 'Wherever you go, Chara will be with you, and so will I – in a way.'

Kassandra felt invisible hands squeezing her throat, and a sob pressing through the gap. But she wrapped her fingers over the toy eagle and stifled the emotion with a cold sigh. 'And I have something for you,' she whispered, slipping the Cyclops' obsidian eye into Phoibe's palm. It had been a deft sleight of hand back at Kleptous Bay: she wondered for a moment if the poor goat had now evacuated the pebble she had shoved up its backside. 'Keep this for yourself. Don't let Markos know about it. If you run into trouble, sell it and use the coins wisely.' Phoibe stared at the eye, agape, then tucked it in her purse.

'Farewell, Phoibe,' Kassandra said, rising.

'You will come back, one day, won't you?' Phoibe pleaded.

'I cannot promise you that, Phoibe, but I hope we will meet again.'

Shouts echoed across the boat as the last of the supplies were brought onboard and the gangplank was readied to be drawn up. Phoibe backed away, smiling, crying. She hopped from the boat and down towards Markos. Kassandra turned away from her, clutching the toy eagle tightly.

The *Adrestia* pulled out to sea under oar. Barnabas strode to and fro across the deck. Unlike that day when she had saved him, he no longer resembled a drowned cat. He wore a pale-blue exomis with white shoulders, his long, thick locks swept back from his face and his beard combed to forked points. He was handsome in an avuncular way, stout and strong. After a time, he called out to his men: 'Ship the oars, set sail.' The crew were like squirrels, speeding up the mast, tugging on ropes. With a rumble like faraway thunder, rolling closer, the cloud-white sail of the *Adrestia* tumbled from the spar to reveal a crimson blazon of a soaring eagle. The sail caught the stiff wind, billowing like a giant's chest, and the boat lurched eastward at speed, spray soaking all those aboard in moments, a trail of white foam churning in its wake.

Barnabas came to Kassandra's side, hair rapping in the wind of the voyage. 'When the Cyclops forced me underwater, I prayed to the Gods. And then you came . . .'

Kassandra laughed dryly. 'You called, and I answered.'

'And you fought like an Amazon queen, like a sister of Achilles! All while Zeus' eagle flew around your head,' Barnabas continued. Ikaros, following the vessel, screeched in acknowledgement. Barnabas' eyes grew glassy, sparkling with wonder. 'On my travels, I've encountered people who claimed to have blood of the Gods in their veins. But claims are cheap and easy . . . I find the true measure of a person lies in their deeds.'

Coyly, she glanced away and around the deck. It was bare and tidy, with a small cabin just below the scorpion-tail stern and a number of nooks and high nests that the crew seemed to favour, men sitting on the spar with their legs dangling. Some slept in the shade near the prow, using rolled-up cloaks as pillows, others sang as they scrubbed the timbers and some played games of knuckle-bones by the rail. Thirty men altogether, she counted.

'Each of them is a brother to me,' he said, noticing her gaze. 'And you can rely on them utterly. But I must ask: why, of all places I could take you . . . why Megaris?' He gazed off to where the ship was headed: the wide waters of the Gulf of Korinthia.

'At the Megaran port of Pagai lies a great prize.'

'And the heart of the war, misthios,' Barnabas countered. 'The Megaran lands crawl with Spartan phalanxes, and the waters are ringed with Athenian galleys. The latter will pose no problem, for although the *Adrestia* is small and aged, she is fast and swift to turn . . . and she sports a sharp beak. But even then, we will make shore at a time when rumours thicken of Perikles leading an Athenian land army into Megaris to face and destroy the Spartan regiments. What prize could possibly be worth setting foot on such a war-torn land?'

'The head of a Spartan general,' she replied.

The crewmen nearby gasped.

'I have been hired to kill the one they call the Wolf,' she said, her confidence growing as the trireme sliced across deeper waters.

Barnabas blew air through his lips and laughed without humour, as one might when surveying a sheer-sided cliff smeared with oil that they have been asked to climb. 'The Wolf? You have taken on a tall task, misthios. They say Nikolaos of Sparta has shoulders of iron, sleeps with his spear in hand and one eye open. And his bodyguards are like demons too . . .'

Kassandra heard Barnabas' words fade into a deafening ring. She heard herself mutter: 'What did you say?' and saw the looks of confusion on the captain's face and on the faces of the crew nearby who came to her aid when her legs weakened. She shook them off, grabbing the ship's rail and leaning over to stare down into the water.

The Wolf is Nikolaos of Sparta? I have been sent to kill my father?

As he watched the Adrestia *drift out to sea, spearing towards the Korinthian Gulf under power of sail, Elpenor stroked the strange mask in his hands, chuckling quietly to himself. He saw the small figure of Kassandra at the stern. Proud, brave, mighty, at first. Then he almost felt the crushing blow as it was delivered, seeing her fall to one knee, waving the men away.*

'She knows . . .' he purred. 'It has begun.'

4

'Hoist the sail!' Barnabas yelled. As the great blazon of the eagle was tucked away, twenty men settled on the padded leather benches running either side of the ship, each taking a fir-pole oar, lifting it up and threading it through a leather loop and thole pin. With a rhythmic splash, the oars met the waves.

Megaris was in sight. The journey was all but over.

Kassandra, perched at the prow, stared at the forest of Athenian galleys ahead. Flapping striped sails, fir masts and pitch-painted hulls. Every one of the mighty vessels was packed with glinting hoplites, archers, slingers, peltasts. Some were even laden with Thessalian steeds, their heads shrouded to stop them becoming panicked at the sight of the ocean. A floating army stood between the *Adrestia* and the hazy Megaran hinterland beyond, and the port of Pagai itself.

'I have to face him,' she whispered to herself. It was a mantra that had echoed in her thoughts for the past two days of the voyage as she came to terms with the Wolf's true identity. 'But there is no way through that blockade.'

The ships were serried in banks, four or five deep. She saw the knots of white-tunic'd peltasts aboard the two nearest triremes turn from the blockaded land to behold the tiny vessel speeding towards their flotilla like a mouse charging a pride of lions. They shouted and pointed, their commander barking at them to lift their javelins and take aim. Kassandra looked back at Barnabas and his men, ready to tell them to turn around, that it had been a mistake. Maybe they could swing north or south and land on one side or other of the Korinthian Gulf. From there it might take them a only month or so to pick their way overland to Pagai and –

'*Kybernetes*,' Barnabas roared before she could say a word. 'Turn . . . turn . . . *turn!*'

Under the shadow of the galley's scorpion tail, the coal-skinned helmsman named Reza grabbed onto the twin steering oars, his mighty shoulders shaking with effort, leaning left to edge the boat to the right. He roared with the strain, until two crewmen rushed to add their weight to the mix.

With a *hiss* of churning water, the galley tilted sharply to the right, slicing through the waves. Kassandra grabbed hold of the rail for balance. A sheet of water leapt over her, soaking the deck too, and she saw the loosed javelins of the Athenian peltasts sail harmlessly into the churn of the *Adrestia*'s wake. The galley rolled level once more and Kassandra gawped at the lone Athenian trireme ahead, side on to the *Adrestia*'s prow. Barnabas had spotted it through all the other boats: a weak spot in the blockade.

'Aaand: *O-opop-O-opop-O-opop* . . .' the keleustes chanted faster and faster, passionately punching a fist into his palm as he strode along the spine of the deck. Every repetition of the sound saw the oarsmen draw back, brought the *Adrestia* up to ever-more incredible speeds . . . the bronze beak speeding towards the flank of the lone Athenian galley. Kassandra's eyes widened, and the Athenians' faces dropped. 'Brace!' Barnabas roared.

The world exploded in a roar of crumpling timbers. Kassandra felt her shoulders nearly leap from their sockets as the *Adrestia* lurched, and the sky darkened for a moment with clouds of kindling. Through a chorus of screams the *Adrestia* cut, the two halves of the broken Athenian galley swinging open like doors, the great mast falling, the crew clinging on to timber poles for dear life. The commotion fell away as rapidly as it had risen.

Kassandra gazed back at the chaos of foaming waters and groaning wreckage, sure the rest of the Athenian fleet would fall upon them.

'They won't follow,' Barnabas said. 'They won't risk getting too close to the shore to catch one small boat.'

The shore, she thought, looking towards the shingle bay and bluffs of Pagai. A flurry of icy thorns pricked her heart as she realized there was no excuse now. She was here . . . and so was he. She scoured the coastline, heart thumping. Nothing.

The ship drew into a deserted stretch of shore, sliding onto the shingle. Kassandra leapt down onto the bay, staring along the deserted hinterland. *Where are you, Wolf?*

A desperate gasp nearby sent a jolt of fright through her. An Athenian warrior, from the ship they had halved, scrambled through the shallows and onto the shore, panting, spitting, his blue-and-white exomis sopping wet. All along the coast she saw more – hundreds of them, swimming in from the wreckage. Some used their shields as floats, and most were armed too. Those on the other boats out in the blockade raised a distant cheer. For a moment, it seemed that the Athenians had an unlikely foothold on the bay.

Until, from the pine woods, a crimson pack poured forth.

Kassandra dropped down behind a thicket of gorse and watched as a Spartan lochos – a regiment of some five hundred men, one-fifth of the ever-rarer purebred Spartiates – emerged from the trees. They went with their crimson cloaks flowing, their beards and hair tied tight in braids, jostling like ropes as they marched in barefoot lockstep towards the shoreline. Their helms dazzled in the late-afternoon sun, their bronze-coated shields streaked with blood-red lambda icons, their spears levelled like executioner's fingers, pointing accusingly at the washed-up Athenians.

They fell upon their prey in silence, faces bent in malice, spears licking out to pierce chests, bursts of blood misting above the fray, screams rising from the stricken. Those Athenians still swimming in or crawling through the shallows on all fours were mercilessly bludgeoned with the bronze butt-spikes on the base of the Spartan spears. When a band of seven or so Athenians dared to put up a fight, there was one amongst the Spartans who moved like a nightmare unleashed. Kassandra saw only glimpses of him, his whipping red tribon cloak, his head and face obscured by an old-style Korinthian helm, his spear flashing in the sunlight. Every one of the seven fell to him, riven. Within moments, the hundreds of survivors of the rammed ship were but a flotsam of cadavers, bobbing in a bloody soup. Silence befell the bay, leaving just the sound of the waves lapping gently on the shore.

She saw him in full at last, and knew it was the Wolf, for he wore the trappings of a general: a transverse plume – blood-red like his gore-sodden cloak. She stared at the T of shadow at the front of the helm, seeking out the face, memories of the past scourging her like whips of fire. Her heart hammered, the Leonidas spear seeming to shudder and vibrate in her grasp.

The men around the Wolf raised their spears to him. 'Aroo!' they boomed once, solemnly.

The sheer aura and number of these warriors doused her in cold reality. Now was not the time to strike. She let go of the spear and drew her cloak over it, and the fire within settled. She watched as the Wolf moved towards a younger officer and clasped a hand to his shoulder. 'You fought well, Stentor,' she heard him say. With that, the Spartan general, her father . . . her quarry, turned and left the bay, heading towards a path that wound up the coastal bluffs, a few men walking by his side.

Kassandra looked back over her shoulder, seeing Barnabas watching anxiously. *Wait here*, she mouthed to him, then rose from behind the gorse and approached the Spartan soldiers. The one named Stentor noticed her first and stepped over to block her path.

He was a little older than her: at least thirty, she guessed, given that he seemed to be an officer. He stared at her, impassive, his inky beard ringing thin lips, his nose like a blade. He was strong and lean . . . perhaps too lean – the tolls of battle and hunger? His mouth twitched, loaded with acid words of challenge, until he noticed the *Adrestia* moored nearby, then glanced to the dead Athenians, and then across the water at the floating remains of the ship. 'You . . . you halved that galley?' he concluded, the statement punctuated by the nearby stretch and snap of sinew as a vulture plucked an eyeball from a dead Athenian's head.

'It was in my way,' Kassandra replied, matching his laconic tone.

She noticed a glint of respect in his eyes, and followed his prideful glance up to the top of the coastal bluffs: up there, the Wolf now stood, looking over the bay, his cloak fluttering in the fiery light of sunset. He rested his weight on a bakteriya staff.

She realized she had been staring at him just a little *too* long. And so did Stentor.

'What do you want with the Wolf?' he snapped, his voice suddenly dripping with suspicion.

Kassandra feigned nonchalance. 'I come to . . . serve him.'

'So you are a misthios. And you think that we need help? Did you not just witness what happened to these Athenian fools? Is Megara not still in Spartan hands?'

'For now,' she replied. 'Though I have heard that Perikles of Athens plans to mount a major land offensive on these parts.'

Stentor's top lip arched at one end.

'I am sure you will win most battles,' she replied before

he could curse her, 'but could you not use a mercenary for certain tasks? I ask only for a place in your camp and safe harbour for the men of my boat while I am here.'

Stentor snorted in dry amusement. 'You want to serve us? Do you really think I would let a hired blade anywhere near my father?' He shot a look up at the Wolf as he said this.

'You are the Wolf's . . . son?' Kassandra said, her voice breaking up.

'He adopted me not long after both of his children died,' Stentor explained. 'He mentored me and trained me. It is thanks to him that I am a lochagos, leader of this regiment. He is everything to me, and he is everything I want to be. I would follow him to the gates of the underworld.'

'I ask only the chance to do the same,' she said.

He looked at her askance, eyeing her from head to toe like a merchant evaluating a nag, before chopping one hand into the palm of the other, decision made. 'No. No misthios will enter our camp or set foot near the Wolf,' he insisted. 'Enough of your kind lurk inland as it is, working for the Athenians . . .' His nose wrinkled. 'Hyrkanos and his hired rogues have been smashing up our supply wagons, denying our men their bread. Others seek my father's head and the purse it will bring. Too many thorns in the Wolf's paw already. No more. For all I know you could be one of them – here to kill my father.' He stared hard at her for a time. 'So go, sleep on your boat and be grateful that I let you keep your head, stranger.'

A gentle clanking of spears being levelled behind her told her it was time to leave. She half-bowed and backed away, towards the fragile sanctuary of the *Adrestia*.

Having eaten a meal of salted roasted sardines and bread, washed down with well-watered wine, Kassandra lay down to sleep near the boat's prow. An eerie silence descended over the bay. She could not find rest, despite her aching muscles and foggy mind, and so she sat up on the rail, hugging her knees to her chest, Ikaros preening himself beside her in the light of a sickle moon that illuminated the waters. She watched the ring of torchlight out on the Athenian galleys, and the glow of orange up on the bluff, where the Spartans were camped. Here in this netherworld of the beach, she was surrounded by a deckful of snoring sailors, and the still, stinking corpses of the Athenian dead a stone's throw along the sands. They had been stripped of their armour but left unburied.

Her heart froze when she heard a lapping of oars out on the water. A night attack? But she saw just a small rowboat coming towards the shore from the blockade, and watched keenly as two unarmoured Athenians disembarked and headed up towards the Spartan camp. Brave men, *dead* men, surely, she thought. But they returned a short while later, and then a larger team of unarmed Athenians rowed ashore to join them and helped dig graves in the sand and bury their dead, granted amnesty to do so by their fiercest enemies.

Kassandra stared up at the Spartan camp. The Wolf was at the bluff's edge again, looking down upon the burials, framed by the inky sky and a silvery sand of stars. *You no doubt congratulate yourself for showing such a crumb of honour*, she mouthed hatefully. *Yet where was your honour that night on the mountain?*

For the next moon, the *Adrestia* remained beached near Pagai, and Kassandra set about winning the Spartans' trust. By day, she shadowed the ranks as they marched to and fro, defending the few good bays and docking sites whenever the Athenians tried to land, or driving off the infantry assaults from the north. Twice, she helped turn the fray. First, by perching on a rock near the shore and sending blazing arrows over the heads of the waiting, battle-ready Spartans and into the sails of the approaching Athenian triremes, the vessels going up in flames before they even reached the shore. Stentor had glowered at her like a vulture robbed of his corpse. Then, a few days later, she had entered the edge of battle again, springing from the woods to defeat an Athenian champion. Stentor had rewarded her with a tirade and a quarter-drawn blade. 'Stay away from my soldiers. Stay away from my father,' he had spat. But she could see the black rings under his eyes, and the flagging steps of the Spartan soldiers. Despite their pride and reputation for laughing in the face of hunger, the missing supply wagons meant many had not eaten solids for nearly half a moon.

Spartan trust was like a thick iron lock. Grain was the key, she realized. She rose, slipped silently from the boat and headed inland.

*

Up on the bluff, a circle of torches delineated the Spartan camp. Sentries stood, watchful and expressionless, the butt-spikes of their spears dug into the earth so the shafts stood upright like pickets. A few Skiritae – expert javelin marksmen and outlying night watchmen, not purebred Spartans, but soldiers held in some esteem nonetheless – sat in trees and on elevated ground in the surrounding countryside. Inside the camp, Spartan soldiers sat by fires rumbling with deep laughter, slurping painfully thin black broth from their kothons or whetting their spears. A few stood naked, their Helot slaves carefully oiling their gaunt bodies and scraping them clean with strigils.

Stentor sat by the fire at the heart of the camp, tired, famished and irritable. Unable to rest, he had risen in the darkness and brought a few other insomniac warriors with him to the fire to while the hours of night away. 'Sing the verses of Tyrtaios for me,' he grunted. 'One of his war songs.'

The two Spartiate warriors sitting across from him coughed and shuffled, then began a dreadful rendition of a song written some three hundred years previously by Sparta's greatest poet. Stentor's face melted with dismay. 'Make it stop, before the shade of the great man rises and rips your tongues from your mouths.'

He gazed down at the *Adrestia*, clinging to the shore like a limpet. The irksome misthios had been here for nearly two moons now – all throughout the stinking hot summer. Her interference in recent battles had tarnished their victories, and once with her use of the bow – such an un-Spartan weapon! One day he had walked down to the bay to watch his men training on the sand. They had lined up in opposing phalanxes and marched at one another in mock battle. He had laughed gruffly and applauded as one by one the lines picked each other apart, knocking their opponents down or scoring 'kills'. In the end, one soldier remained standing after an imperious display, the rest dazed and groaning. He had roared in ovation as he approached the champion . . . until he saw that underneath that red Spartan robe and bronze helm was no man of Lakonia. It was her. *Her!*

He had berated his men like a vengeful titan for letting her train with them, for giving her a Spartan spear and shield. 'But she merits them, sir,' one soldier had countered. 'She has been expertly trained in the Spartan ways, by whom she will not say.'

One of the men she had beaten later tried to woo her, by way of grabbing her and trying to kiss her. That one now sat in the corner of the camp, still nursing a broken jaw and bruised testicles. More strangely, in the last moon, the Skiritae had reported her odd night movements – roving far inland under darkness. *What are you, misthios?* he wondered.

In any case, there were darker troubles approaching. The girl's claims had been accurate: Perikles of Athens *was* moving a strong force of hoplites south in an attempt to break the Spartan hold on this land, and so the Spartan lochos would soon be marching north to intercept them – indeed, the allies had already been summoned. He wrung his fingers through his hair: talk of Athenian heroes, of vast enemy numbers, of what many whispered was sure to be a famous Spartan defeat, gnawed at the edges of his morale, just as the hunger clawed at his empty belly.

Crunch-crunch-crunch. Footsteps, fast, coming through the tents towards him.

His head whipped up. 'Guards!' he snapped.

A shadow appeared near the fire, striding purposefully towards him. He rose, reaching for his short sword, when the shadow halted and tossed a heavy object in his direction. The object landed near the fire and burst open. Precious wheat spilled from the sack. All eyes fell upon the wheat as if it were gold. Stentor looked up as the shadow came into view. Kassandra wore the look of a huntress, her brow dipped and her eyes fixed on him.

'Misthios?' he growled.

'Hyrkanos is dead. For the last moon I have tracked him down. Tonight, I infiltrated his camp, killed him and his men. A dozen more wagons of stolen grain lie there: you and your men can eat and regain your strength – in time for the arrival of the Athenian land assault.'

He stood, elated and enraged. 'So you bring us salvation again?' he seethed. 'You wish to have us bow and praise you?'

'I ask for nothing other than an audience with the Wolf,' she said quietly.

Stentor's ire faded, and a sparkling jewel of an idea began to glimmer in his mind. They needed every spear they could gather. 'Very well. There is one way to secure such a meeting. When we march north to face the Athenian phalanxes,' he stabbed a finger at her, 'you, misthios, will march in my enomotia, my sworn band. I will vouch

66

for you. You trained well on the bay. But mock-fighting on the sand is no way to measure a warrior. You must prove your worth as a hoplite, as part of the wall of steel, in *true* battle.'

The two Spartans sitting by the fire rumbled with laughter at the idea.

Stentor willed her to crumble at the prospect of true battle. *Run, misthios, be gone!*

Kassandra held his gaze. 'Give me a spear and a shield, and I will fight as a Spartan should.'

Stentor's sneer faded into a cold glower.

Dust clouds rose over Megaris like rival serpents drawing closer as the two great armies marched towards battle. Barnabas had been like an old hen that morning, trying to give Kassandra extra bread and making sure she had enough water.

Now, a half morning's march north of Pagai Bay, she wondered if she would ever see him again. Inside the helm, the blood thundered through her ears, her breath crashed like waves and the stink of sweat laced the air. The bulky shoulders of the Spartan on her left brushed against her arm with every step, the shield roped across her back chewing into her shoulders and the haft of the hoplite spear grating on her palm. She had left the Leonidas spear on the *Adrestia*, knowing that she could not be seen with it lest the Wolf recognize it and her. She glanced along the front of Stentor's enomotia: thirty-one bearded men with faces set like stone. The Wolf marched with them too. The rest of the bands marched like the trailing tail of a great crimson snake. Reinforcements had been summoned from the Peloponnesian allies: Thebans, Korinthians, Megarans, Phocians, Locrians – swelling the Wolf's force to nearly seven thousand strong. The Skiritae roved ahead like a vanguard, along with a contingent of Boeotian horsemen. The rolling countryside ahead peeled away as they marched mile after mile. Rocky hills, wooded uplands.

And then they saw the iron wall awaiting them on the great dust bowl ahead.

Steel, bronze, blue-and-white robes and banners. Athens' brigades stretched out like the horizon itself. Nearly ten thousand, Kassandra guessed. They erupted in a din of cries and songs of derision.

Terse commands rang out along the Spartan column. The tail of the column swung forth, forming a broad front to match the Athenian line, leaving the Wolf's Spartans on the right, the allies in the centre and the Skiritae anchoring the left. The din of boots faded away, replaced by a *shush* of wood and metal as every man brought his shield forward to present a wall of bronze and bright-painted emblems – the Peloponnesian allies with blazons of thunderbolts, snakes and scorpions. Kassandra swung her shield from her back likewise, slipping her left forearm through the bronze porpax sleeve on the inside and grasping the leather strap at the cuff end. It felt like part of her body now.

Suddenly there was silence, broken only by a gentle sigh of wind. Then came a strained bleat. A white-haired Spartan priest dragged a goat through the lines, stopping in front of the Wolf. Kassandra stared at the withered old man: the laurel wreath wrapped around his head and the bony, bare shoulders. Memories of that night came streaking back. He chanted to the sky, holding a blade to the terrified animal's neck, beseeching the Gods for their favour, before yanking his arm back. The goat thrashed and fell, blood leaping from its gaping neck in spurts.

When the animal was finally still, the priest declared that the Gods were pleased. The Wolf raised a hand, and every single spear was levelled, like iron fingers pointing across the plain at the Athenians.

An unarmoured Spartan behind Kassandra lifted a set of auloi – forked pipes that jutted down from his mouth like the tusks of an elephant – then sucked in a breath and blew. A low, dreadful moan poured from the pipes and across the plain. Kassandra's flesh crept, the sound of the 'Hymn to Castor' shifting the earth from long-buried memories: of childhood feasts, of better times. As she looked over the field to the Athenian lines, she realized her mouth had drained of all moisture, and her bladder had swollen to the size of an overripe melon. She knew she could face and defeat any of the men there, one to one. And, damn, had the Wolf not trained her endlessly in the art of phalanx fighting during her childhood, showing her how to stand, how to be strong and immovable, when to push, when to strike? Had she not shown those Spartans training on the bay just how skilled and worthy she was? Yet true warfare like this was new to her, strange . . . unsettling.

'Afraid, misthios?' Stentor asked, posted by her right side.

She did not look at him.

'Marching into battle is like running with chains on your ankles. You cannot turn and run, lest you covet shame. You cannot dodge and duck as you might when you fight a lone foe. You are part of a wall, part of the Spartan machine. And part of the wall you will remain. This is no mere training bout. You will fight and win on this field . . . or fight and die.' He sighed and chuckled. 'But you should rejoice, for those who live on the edge of death are the ones who live the most.'

'You want me to run,' she hissed back. 'I will not.'

'Perhaps not. But maybe you will learn something by watching me – for today I will seize glory for the Wolf. I will be his champion. It will be *I* with whom he seeks audience once the day is done!'

She eyed him sideways, wondering if it would be best to say nothing more. But she could not help but wonder at what might have been. Had that night on the mountain never occurred, would Stentor even be here? Might it be her instead? Or perhaps Alexios? Her next words slipped out before she could catch them. 'The Wolf . . . if I fall today I will never meet him. Tell me about him.'

Stentor flashed her an iron glower. 'About his guards, his routines? You'd like that, wouldn't you? You think I have forgotten that you are a misthios?'

She sighed, turning her head to him. 'No, I mean . . . what is he like, as a father?'

Stentor's iron shell crumpled. She saw for the first time a boy within the man's eyes. She understood him in that one look. He said nothing in reply. As quickly as his visage had changed, it returned to that cold, hateful mien. On and on the pipes blared, and Kassandra knew there would be no more talk. So she almost leapt when he did at last reply.

'He is strong. Caring too. A good father, I would say. Yet there are times where it seems that he does not believe so. Times when a distant look overcomes him. A sadness descends like a cold mist.' He laughed once – his Spartan demeanour slipping again. 'But we all have regrets, I suppose.'

'Aye, we do,' Kassandra replied, her heart hardening, glancing over at the Wolf. *And some will be set right soon enough.*

The dreadful moan of the pipes fell away. The Athenian jeers and bawdy cries settled too.

Many hundreds of officers on both sides cried for the advance. Like a great arm sweeping across a tabletop, the Spartans and their allies set off at a pace that surprised Kassandra. It was a lockstep walk, yes, but a rapid one, and in utter silence too. While the allies sang or shouted, the Spartans were mute, staring, hateful. The distance between the two lines shrank rapidly. Kassandra saw the Athenian taxiarchy coming for them – a band of hoplites in cloud-white tunics, the right shoulders sapphire blue. Their taxiarchos was bedecked with a plumed attic helm and an ancient bronze thorax and white leather boots chased with gold, and he led a trilling war cry as they drew closer.

'*Elelelelef! Elelelelef!*'

Kassandra's heartbeat sped like a runaway horse. Now

the answer to Stentor's question – *Afraid?* – was most definitely *yes*. She stamped with every footstep, determined not to give in to the prickling dread as the Athenian spear tips drew closer, closer, and then . . .

Crash!

The lethal points scraped on her shield, driving the breath from her, some speared or swished near her head, some going for her shins. All along the lines, a mighty din of iron and bronze rang out, like metallic fangs gnashing. Some men thrust their lances to displace an opponent's shield, allowing the comrade by their side to spear the foe in the ribs. Hundreds fell in those first few moments like this, gurgling wet cries and the slap of freed guts hitting the ground ringing out over the deafening fray. A spear scored across Kassandra's cheek, slashed free a loose lock of her hair. She felt her own hot blood sheet down her face, smelled and tasted it on her lips. The Athenian taxi-archos speared rapidly at her, seeing her as a weak link. Fixed in the wall of Spartan hoplites, all she could do was stay behind her shield and lance back at her opponent.

'Look – the Spartans bring a bitch to the fight!' the officer roared gleefully just as a horrific stink of loosened bowels wafted across the battle lines, accompanied by a hot mizzle of blood. The man's spear snapped thanks to his efforts, and so too did many hundreds more on both sides. With the gnashing fangs broken, the opposing lines surged together until the shields clashed with a dull thunder. Kassandra found herself nose-to-nose with the Athenian officer, she and every other Spartan now locked in a shoving match against their numerically superior foe.

'I'm going to cut off your dugs, Spartan bitch,' the Athenian officer snarled, his spittle flecking her face. 'Then drag your corpse behind my horse for a mile.'

Stentor was right by her side, his face black with blood.

'Draw your sword, misthios,' he snarled, doing so himself and ramming his short blade into the throat of the Athenian against whom he pushed. Kassandra saw the taxiarchos move to strike her first, but her lightning-sharp reactions won out: she drew the small curved blade given to her that morning and rammed it hard into the bragging taxiarchos' eye. The man's boasts became a pained shriek and then he was gone. Another Athenian quickly took his place and the two sides remained locked, pushing and shoving for their lives until, with a series of wet, dying howls, the moment came. The Athenians slipped back a step, then two. The brave songs of war turned to screams of despair. Their numbers had failed to overcome the famous Spartan will. The lines disintegrated, great swathes of Athenians speeding away, throwing down their shields. Kassandra felt the great pressure fall away. Stentor laughed as the Boetian horsemen raced in from one flank to ensure a rout, while peltasts streamed along the other flank, raining javelins on the few Athenian regiments that still held fast.

'The dance of war is almost over,' Stentor boomed triumphantly. 'See how the Athenians fear us? Perikles flees to cower in his Parthenon, surrounded by playwrights and sophists. He knows Athens' days in Megaris are numbered. And Athens itself will be next!'

But as the bold projection rang out, Kassandra saw

something just along the Spartan line: the Wolf, injured and separated from his kinsmen and surrounded by four hardy Athenians. *No, he is mine!* she roared inwardly. Without a moment of hesitation she lurched forward, bringing her shield down on the back of one Athenian's head, stabbing a second in the flank. He fell like a stone. The third Athenian leapt and tensed to thrust his spear at the Wolf. The spear never left the Athenian's hand as Kassandra hammered her sword into his ribs, cracking through his exomis, skin, gristle and bone, plunging into one lung. He fell in paroxysms of agony, taking the blade with him. The Wolf finished the final attacker with a blow of the shield boss to the face – breaking the foe's nose, then sending a swift and expert swipe of his spear across the man's throat. The Athenian fell away, head jerking, tongue lolling.

Kassandra flopped to her knees, panting, her hands devoid of weapons and the Wolf right in front of her. He stared at her for a moment before his men surrounded him. In that solemn, eerie way, they once again lifted their spears and made the dust-bowl battlefield shake with a mighty '*Aroo!*'

While the allies exploded in continued celebrations, the Spartans fell silent, that one cry their only extravagance. They merely planted their spear butts in the dust and took quiet drinks from their waterskins, a few speaking in muted tones.

To kill or die for our homeland, Nikolaos had once told her, *that is our job. We do it without pomp or spectacle.*

One group calmly stripped a few Athenian dead of their armour, digging spears into the dust in an X-shaped frame, then decorating it with the enemy breastplates, helms and shields. In the end, it had the look of a four-headed Athenian hoplite. A simple, silent stele of victory. Flies gathered over the carpet of ripped corpses in a growing drone, and carrion hawks began to descend.

A soldier emerged from the Wolf's circle of men. 'You are the misthios?'

She looked up, nodding.

'The Wolf was impressed by your efforts today. When we draw back to the Pagai camp, he requests that you come to him,' he said.

She saw Stentor watching from the corner of her eye, his face dark with fury.

That evening, the air was thick with that sulphurous stench that precedes a storm, and the skies began to crackle and groan, eager to explode. Kassandra said little as she returned from battle and climbed aboard the beached *Adrestia*. Shrugging off Barnabas' attempts to examine her cuts and bruises, she simply snatched up her half-lance, tucked it away in her belt and turned to stare up at the coastal bluffs, the Spartan camp and the nearby promontory to which she had been summoned.

'I will return soon,' she growled. 'Be ready to sail at haste . . . our lives will depend on it.'

With that, she hopped down onto the bay and strode towards the rising cliff path, her black cloak flapping in the growing wind and her tail of hair whipping in her wake. Atop the bluffs, she came to the promontory . . . and froze.

There he was, standing with his back turned, staring moodily out into the dark and choppy ocean as if it were an old foe. She edged towards him, her heart beating hard. The sight of his wind-writhing, blood-red cloak threw a flash of memory at her. *The walk uphill*, she thought. *To Taygetos . . .*

She noticed strands of white in the black curls of hair that hung from his helm, and the short stretch of shin visible below the hem of his tribon cloak hinted at knotted, age-worn legs. Strong but tired.

She made not a sound as she drew closer, but he sensed her presence, his head tilting down and to one side just a fraction.

Of course he heard, she hissed to herself. *He is a Spartan, trained in stealth from birth.*

She stopped.

He turned to her, slowly.

Thunder growled overhead.

He regarded her through the T-shape visor on his helm with the same laconic stare that Stentor had obviously learned from him. His body, naked under the cloak, was laced with scars, including a freshly bandaged gash earned against the Athenians in the dust-bowl battle. The years had not been kind. *Nor will I*, she raged within.

'So you are the shadow that has been following my army for months,' he began. 'Come, tell me of yourself, of why you fight so well and all for no purse.'

His voice was as deep as she remembered, but it had loosened a little with age.

She stared into his eyes, sparkling in the first burst of

lightning – a jagged thorn that lit the bay. *Why don't you remember me? After what you did?*

'My trust is hard earned, as you will have realized. But now that you have it, there will be many future purses for you to earn and –'

The wind howled, blowing Kassandra's cloak back like a war banner, revealing her belt . . . and the half-spear of Leonidas.

The Wolf fell silent. Another shudder of lightning, behind Kassandra, betrayed his eyes in full now: wide, staring, disbelieving. 'You . . .' he croaked.

Kassandra's hand went for her ancient spear, and as soon as she touched it, the past seized her in its claws.

I stared into that inky abyss, hoping against all hope that this was not real. The cold sleet bulleting down upon me said otherwise. Alexios was dead.

'Murderer!' The priest's shrill cry cut through the wintry storm like a scythe. 'She killed the ephor!'

'She has cursed Sparta, condemned us all to the doom predicted by the Oracle,' shrieked another.

Silence . . . then: 'She must die in retribution. Nikolaos, throw her over too – make her pay for her dishonour.'

I felt icy fingers crawl up my back. Turning from the abyss, I saw Mother thrashing, still held from behind by one old man, and Father, mighty shoulders rounded, face torn with horror.

'She. Must. Die,' keened a skull-faced priest. 'If she lives you will be cast into exile, Nikolaos. Shame will follow you like a spirit. Your wife will loathe you.'

'No!' Myrrine shrieked. 'Don't listen to them, Nikolaos.'

'Even Helots will spit on your name,' the priest continued. 'Do as a true Spartan would.'

'For Sparta!' many others howled.

'No!' Mother rasped, her voice all but gone.

At that moment I wanted nothing more than to be with them all, by the fire in our home, for this all to have been a wretched dream. Father stepped towards me, the barrage of wicked demands raining down on his shoulders, Mother's pleas fending them off. I opened my arms to take his embrace. He would protect me, shield me – I knew this just as I knew Apollo, God of the Sun, would rise from the east every morning. He halted before me, sighed deeply, and stared not at me, but through me and into eternity. At that moment I swear I saw the light in his eyes gutter and die.

Father seized my wrist, his hand an iron claw. I gasped as he lifted me. He took a step towards the abyss and I felt my feet scrape at the edge and then at nothing.

'No . . . no! Look at me Nikolaos,' Mother cried. 'It's not too late. Look at me!'

'Father?' I whimpered.

'Forgive me,' he said.

And then he let go. My father, my hero, chose to let me go.

My hands clawed the air. I plummeted into blackness, seeing his face vanish, hearing Mother's soul-tearing final cry. For a few breaths, there was a weightless fall, in time with the sleet, and a roaring wind around my ears, and then it was all over.

And from blackness I awakened. A high-pitched squeaking stirred me first, and then a gentle pecking at my face. I opened my eyes. First, I could see the flickering of the storm high above, the few icy blobs of sleet that penetrated this far down pattering on my face. On the floor of this sheltered abyss, all seemed eerily quiet. Were these the first moments of my eternity as a shade?

Then a tiny bird's head craned over me. Coated in white down with grey-ringed eyes. A pathetic specimen. I ducked out of the way as it pecked at me again. A dry clunk of something shifting beneath me and a horrendous pain through my shoulders and one leg told me I was no shade. I was alive. Somehow, I was alive. I sat up. The bird waddled clumsily up onto my thigh. A spotted eagle hatchling, I realized. I lifted the mite, cradling it in my palms, weeping, longing to wake from this nightmare. My eyes began to adjust, and I saw the dry rubble upon which I lay for what it truly was: a pool of bones. Grinning skulls, smashed and cracked, rib cages hanging from gnarled outcrops, rags of clothing too. With a cold, rampant horror, I realized that almost all of them were the skeletons of infants. The unwanted progenies of Sparta. Too weak or imperfect, the elders had deemed.

'Alexios?' I whimpered, knowing he must be down here too. Even to cradle his body would have meant something. 'Alexios?'

Nothing.

I set the eagle hatchling down and rolled onto my knees, keeping the weight from my damaged leg, crawling over the ossuary pit, feeling with my hands where the darkness would not allow me to see. Then I felt it: something soft and still warm. 'Alexios?' I wept.

A streak of lightning high above revealed the staring, smashed corpse of the ephor — his face locked in a shriek and the back of his bald pate burst like an egg. I leapt back, horrified, grabbing a bone — as if I would need a cudgel to protect myself from that dead wretch. Yet I lifted up before me not a bone, but the Leonidas half-spear.

I stared into the blade, hateful, bereft, lost. I staggered around the pit of bones, searching for Alexios' body in a daze . . . until I heard the sound of bones shifting in a rocky corridor nearby, saw a tall *shadow. Someone was coming. If they found me here, alive after all that had happened, they would strike me down. And so I took up the eagle chick and ran . . . from Sparta, from the past and all its horror.*

The Wolf of Sparta braced, hands raised to halt his onrushing daughter. 'How can it be?' he gasped.

Kassandra answered with a lightning attack, her lance streaking round for his throat. It was only his Spartan instincts that saved him, yanking a short sword from a biceps belt and blocking her strike with it. He swayed, his heels on the precipice, his eyes darting to the Spartan camp behind Kassandra as the thunder raged above.

'Zeus roars for me,' she growled, 'and so none will hear if you cry for help.'

The Wolf's arms shot out for balance and Ikaros swooped in to steal his blade. He gasped, pitching out into a death drop onto the bay below.

Kassandra reached out to grab him by the throat, the lance tip poised at his side, holding him on twin horns of death. 'Now, *Wolf*,' she spat, edging him out a little further, 'justice can be done.'

'Kill me, then,' he said with a throaty crackle. 'But before you do, there is something you must know. I loved you and your brother as if you were truly my own . . . but you were never mine.'

The storm raged around her and a tempest rose within too. 'What do you mean?' She jerked the spear tip a little, drawing blood on his flank.

'That is something you must ask your mother.'

Kassandra felt her soul freeze. 'Mother is . . . alive?'

Nikolaos nodded as best he could. 'She is lost to me and I to her, but she lives. She fled Sparta that very night. To where, I do not know. Find her, Kassandra, and be sure to tell her that I have never forgiven myself for what happened. But with every step you take you must beware,' he rasped, his eyes maddened. 'Beware the snakes in the grass.' He grabbed her spear hand, pushing the lance tip a little deeper into his own flesh. 'Now . . . end this.'

At the last, lightning shivered across the sky and in his bronze Korinthian helmet she saw her own face reflected. Ice crept across her heart, her throat grip slackening to let him fall, her spear arm tensing to run him through. The key to twenty years of caged injustice lay in her grasp at last.

5

The port-town of Kirrha sweltered in the June heat, the glare of the sea blinding, the pale mountains rising behind it dazzling. The tracks veining those slopes were dotted with pilgrims trekking into the heights to visit Delphi and its famous inhabitant: the Oracle, the Pythia, the keeper of the wisdom of Apollo, the seeress of all Hellas.

Kirrha's dock was a riot of stenches and garish colours. Not a single patch of harbour water could be seen, thanks to the hundreds of bobbing rafts, skiffs and small private boats crammed there. Sailors scampered around the decks and scurried up the masts of one boat, tied at a private mooring, tying up its hideous gorgon-head sail. Pilgrims swarmed over gangways and onto the wharfside, jabbering and singing, looking around in wonder. Merchants yapped and bleated, offering their 'sacred' statuettes and trinkets to the passers-by. Local children leapt from raft to raft, peddling cool drinks to the thirsty visitors. Smoke columns rose and bells clanged constantly as the crowds waded through the packed streets and onto the pilgrims' path.

Cutting through the swarms from the private mooring, like a boat moving upstream, was a gold-draped litter. Elpenor, its occupant, was a cruel man – the kind of man who enjoyed watching his friends fail. He weighed the sack of coins resting beside him. Perhaps he would divert these funds to his growing fishing business. 'I could buy three new boats for my fleet,' he purred, 'or . . . I could pay the toothless crooks at the harbour to scuttle twelve of Drakon's ships.'

Drakon had been his best friend since childhood, and his wife and daughters even called Elpenor 'uncle'. In the early days, Drakon's family had been poor – almost beggars – and Elpenor had enjoyed giving the family a few coins from his business earnings. The enjoyment came not from helping them, but from the feeling of control. Without his small donations, they might not eat. It thrilled him at the time. But Drakon had been overly loud about his gradual change of fortunes: finding a sea-bream nesting area out at sea, and using his pathetic little skiff to bring in bounteous catches for months on end. On and on Drakon had bleated about his new boat, then his burgeoning fleet and the wealth he had acquired through it, and no longer did he need Elpenor's charity. 'Decision made.' Elpenor grinned with a venomous twitch. 'I hope you are a good swimmer, Drakon.'

His nostrils flared in disgust as a waft of onions and unwashed nether regions rose from the bare-chested pilgrims standing outside the tavern, braying crudely at their own gutter humour. *Get into the hills, pay your dues and begone*, he inwardly cursed them all. He clapped his hands once to quicken his carriers. 'Move. I want to be in my villa before noon, before the stink becomes intolerable.'

They cut through a maze of tight lanes and at last came to the edge of town, passing through the iron gates of his estate. The litter was set down and Elpenor rose, hearing the gentle gurgle of the fountain, smelling the sweet camomile of his gardens. Stepping inside, he slipped off his expensive leather slippers and enjoyed the feel of the cool white marble floors on the soles of his feet. He heard the two litter slaves shuffling away and turned to one of them, clicking his fingers. 'You, pour some sweet oils into the bathing pool,' his gaze grew carnal, 'and wait on me in there. You had better please me this time. I don't want to have to hurt you again.'

The slave stared into space, nodded once, and did as he was told.

Elpenor stepped into his office, well-appointed with busts and plush seats, a hearth on one side and a colonnade on the other, open to the gardens to allow the blissful song of nature to spill inside. Moving over to the black and burnt-orange krater on the table, he poured himself a cup of wine and chilled water. It slightly disappointed him that the krater was not empty, for it robbed him of a reason to whip the girl whose duty it was to keep his home stocked with fine drinks and foods. 'Now, to the business of the day,' he mused to himself, sipping the cool liquid with a contented sigh. He swung on his heel towards the polished ash-wood bureau where his tokens and tablets waited. But he took just one stride towards it and froze.

A Spartan officer's helm sat upon the desk, staring back at him, the transverse crimson crest spread like a peacock's tail. One-half of the helm was gleaming bronze, the other half encrusted in dried blood.

'First, you will pay me,' a voice spoke from the shadows behind the colonnade.

He snatched in a breath, seeing her now. She paced into view, her face dark. She seemed different from that moment on Kephallonia last spring. Leaner, taller, more confident in her stride.

'And then you will tell me why,' she continued in a breathy drawl.

'Why?' Elpenor said.

'Don't play games with me. You knew when you sent me on that mission. You *knew* you had sent me to take my Father's head.'

Elpenor beheld her with hooded eyes and a creeping smile. 'If you had known, misthios, would you have taken the contract?' he said, sliding open a drawer under the table and lifting a small sack of coins, never taking his gaze from her. He plunked the coins down on the bureau dismissively.

'I believe some evils are best left undisturbed,' she replied, stalking wide towards the bureau as if wary of a trap.

'Yet once a hornet's nest has been shaken, the swarm must be faced,' Elpenor said in a conspiratorial whisper. 'He wasn't your *real* father, was he?'

Kassandra's lips twitched, betraying a bestial grimace. 'You will tell me everything, you snake. Why did you send me to kill him?'

Elpenor shrugged, sinking back onto a cushioned bench with an affected sigh, sipping his wine, stroking a standing marble statue of Ares by the bench's end, the war god clutching a bronze spear. 'The Wolf was a brilliant general. He would have unpicked Athens' strategies and defences before long . . . and there's no profit in a quick war, is there?'

'How did you know about his past and mine?' Kassandra hissed, taking the coin purse and stepping towards him.

'I love theatre. A great general throws his own children from a cliff on the say-so of the Oracle . . . it is a tragedy for all the ages,' he chuckled.

'You find amusement in the strangest of places,' she said. 'Perhaps you will laugh one last time when I sink my spear into your chest?'

'Now, now, misthios, let me explain,' Elpenor lifted his cup to drink again. His eyes obscured momentarily, he glanced to the colonnade. His eyes met those of a guard, and the guard quickly saw what was going on. *Excellent*, he thought as the leather-clad brute crept in from the gardens, coming for Kassandra unseen like a leopard stalking a gazelle. 'The Wolf told you about your mother, I presume? And that you were fathered by another man.'

She nodded once, staring down her nose at him as she drew close.

'Then it is simple,' he said. 'They will be your next two targets.'

She recoiled. 'What did you say?'

'You heard me, misthios. You have proven yourself a parent-slayer already. Why the misgivings now?'

'I thought you a soulless cur at first, now I know you are far worse,' she croaked. 'Why? Why would I do what you ask?'

'Then the answer is no?' Elpenor said, leaning forward on the bench, eyes wide as if awaiting a revelation.

'Never,' she said through gritted teeth.

'Such a shame, you could have been of use to me,' Elpenor said, then nodded once to the creeping guard behind her.

In a single movement, Kassandra bent round from the hips, drawing, nocking and loosing her bow. The arrow took the guard in the eye just as he lurched in an attempt to run her through. The man flailed and crashed head-long into the unlit hearth, where he lay, feet twitching.

Elpenor snatched the bronze spear from the marble hands of Ares, swishing it round towards her. He heard a clean chopping noise and saw both his hands and the spear spin through the air, Kassandra's half-spear flash-ing in a shaft of sunlight. He stared at the perfectly hewn stumps below both wrists: white bone, marrow, blood . . . then lots and lots of blood. He fell to his knees, wailing. 'What have you done?'

She clamped a hand over his mouth and pressed him back against the bench. 'You will bleed to death in moments. I can save you, but I want answers.'

Elpenor felt fiery agony in his forearms at first, then the hot wetness of the soaking blood. Then . . . a growing coldness. He nodded weakly, she slid her hand from his lips. 'You are a fool, Kassandra. You only left Kephallonia alive because of me. The Cult wanted you dead. I said you would be more use alive.'

Kassandra's face grew pinched and hateful. 'The Cult? . . . What is –'

But Elpenor sensed a final victory in the onset of death. He would be her master, at the last, ridiculing her with his dying breath. 'Go, as the Wolf once did . . . and ask the Oracle,' he cackled, before he slipped into a cold black infinity.

Kassandra stumbled back from his greying corpse, numb. Absently, she snatched a few more coin purses from a drawer in his desk, then opened a wooden chest to find a silk robe that would no doubt fetch a good price and a wicked-looking but probably valuable theatre mask. She put them both in her leather bag. As she crouched to make her escape before any more guards arrived, she saw the slave kneeling by the indoor pool, white with fear, staring at her, having seen it all. She tossed him one of the coin purses. 'Go,' she said, 'far from this place.'

She heard the slave and the few other poor wretches of the household scampering away towards the docks. She, however, turned inland, towards the rising mountains and the streaming crowds of pilgrims flooding up into those heights. Soon her thighs ached as she climbed with them, her head bowed, neck scorched by the sun, mind heavy with mysteries. All throughout the past winter, spent hiding in the islands with Barnabas and his crew, she had rehearsed her confrontation with Elpenor. Now it was over, and she had nothing but a few coin sacks and a pair of fine garments – worthless compared with the answers she needed.

She glanced over her shoulder in the direction of the cur's villa, behind and far below. Kirrha town was now but a shimmer of activity – the warren of streets and alleys like a tessellated promenade, hugging the green waters of the Korinthian Gulf. Up here the heat was dry and choking, the dust sticking to the back of her throat and stinging her eyes. She felt like a fool: climbing towards Delphi and the Temple of Apollo and its damned Oracle as if she would truly find any answers there. But there was no other way. The Wolf had not told her the whereabouts of her true father or her mother; her only clues were Elpenor's dying jest and whatever perennially abstruse words the seeress might offer.

Ikaros shrieked, banking and soaring up above. Kassandra squinted upwards. He wheeled and sped across the pale rock and greenery ahead. A wreath of cloud obscured the higher parts, and the heat began to ameliorate with freshness. Here, a high green valley yawned, the sides veined with streamlets and dotted with pine and cypress trees.

On a plateau overlooking the valley floor, like an eagle in its eyrie, was perched the Temple of Apollo. The home of the Oracle. Silvery Doric columns supported a red-tiled roof, and starlings swooped to and from their nests in the brightly painted architraves. This, some claimed, was the centre of the world, the neutral heart of all Hellas. The sanctuary of the Gods where Spartan and Athenian alike were but mortals.

The great train of pilgrims wound all the way up around smaller temples and shrines, snaking towards the grand entrance. Peddlers lapped against the sides of the column like waves on a causeway, holding up ivory plaques and beaded necklaces. When the hawkers crowded around her, she ignored them all, instead staring up at the ancient temple, thinking of what had happened on Mount Taygetos all those years ago. *All at your behest,* she mouthed sourly, thinking of the Oracle upon whose poisoned words her brother's murder had been carried out. *You will give me answers today, seeress, or I will sheathe my spear in your heart.*

Her growing ire faded when she bumped into the man before her.

'Apologies,' she muttered, realizing the queue had come to a halt. She looked up the three-times snaking path onto the plateau. A painful hour passed, with just a few shuffles forward.

Those queueing near her were full of grumbles and conspiracy: 'This place has changed,' one moaned. 'They say some are being turned away with no explanation,' complained another. 'Guards everywhere too. Something's going on,' cursed a third.

Just then she heard a colourful and familiar voice, up on the plateau and nearer the front of the queue. She tilted her head back to look up. 'Tell them. *Tell them!*' Barnabas chirped. The captain had come up here while she had headed to Elpenor's, and it seemed he had found a friend – someone his own age in an ankle-length exomis, with a tangle of brown hair held back from his weathered face by a blue band. He seemed aghast at Barnabas' prompts. 'Will you keep your voice down?' the man groaned.

'But you've travelled even further and wider than I,' Barnabas persisted. 'All across Ionia. You've even seen a phoenix, aye?'

'No,' the other fellow said, waving his hands to

disappoint those in the queue who were listening in. 'It was merely a seagull with its tail feathers ablaze.'

Barnabas' face fell, and he climbed upon a stone bench to address the queue, jabbing a thumb into his own chest. 'Well, *I* saw a phoenix once, I swear I did. From a burning city she rose, swept high overhead and –'

'Shat on your bald spot?' one strapping, horn-voiced pilgrim laughed. 'What next: were you chased by the Sphinx? Or perhaps wooed by an over-amorous Minotaur?'

Barnabas' eyes widened and he clicked his fingers, pointing at the man in excitement. 'The Minotaur, yes! There was a set of caves where I was looking for treasure . . .'

But his hurried explanations were drowned out as the mocking man put his fingers to his head like horns and ran in circles around the bench, making 'mooing' noises. Laughter exploded all around. Barnabas' face turned a shade of puce. His new friend tugged him down from the bench to spare him any further embarrassment.

Kassandra pushed up through the snaking queue, ignoring the curses and yelps as she went, until she reached Barnabas. He was only a few dozen spaces from the entrance of the great temple.

'Misthios.' He bowed to her, a few tresses of his sweat-slicked hair stuck to his still-red face. 'I thought you were going to visit someone.'

'I went. I saw him.'

'But I didn't expect to see you until I got back to the ship. When I asked if you wanted to come to the Oracle with me, you told me to travel a short distance and make love to myself . . . or words to that effect.'

'Things changed. I must speak to the Oracle,' she said, holding one arm level as Ikaros glided down to land on her bracer.

'Then you can join me in my place in the queue, of course,' Barnabas said, shifting to one side to let her in, 'assuming my friend allows it too?'

The other man waved a hand, beckoning her in with minimal fuss.

'Kassandra, Herodotos,' Barnabas introduced them. When Herodotos stared intently at Kassandra, Barnabas tried to clarify: 'You know, the misthios I was telling you about?'

'I see,' Herodotos said, his tone guarded.

'While I'm a traveller, Herodotos is a historian,' Barnabas explained. 'What a life he has lived: led the revolt against the Tyrant of Halicarnassus, then sailed to almost every corner of the world before making his home in Athens. Somehow, he finds the time to write his adventures down – titled with the names of the nine Muses, no less.'

'You did not tell me she was a Spartan,' said Herodotos. Kassandra arched an eyebrow.

'Oh I can tell.' Herodotos half-smiled. 'The proud stance and the arrogant, iron stare.'

As he examined her, Kassandra could not help but notice his eyes widening, the pupils shrinking, as he caught sight of the half-spear, partly hidden under the fold of her cloak. His face paled like a man who has just seen his own shade. She pulled her garment round to hide it. 'I am a child of nowhere,' she said, clamming up.

'We are all born somewhere, my lady,' he said, his face

lengthening to exaggerate the lines of age. 'And do not assume that I am biased against the Spartans. There is much to both admire and loathe in the ways of the proud warrior race of Lakonia *and* the Athenians alike. The thing that troubles me most readily is that their differences have broiled into war. For all the glory of the days when both sides stood together, fought and won against the innumerable Persians, it has come to this.' He eyed the shady portico of the temple and the towering doorway: two guards stood watch before it, armoured in black leather vests, black-painted shields and matching helms. 'At least here we have a haven of neutrality,' he said.

Kassandra's eyes narrowed. For all the world it had sounded like a question.

Just then, Reza the helmsman shouted up from the valley floor. 'Triearchos,' he called, waving his hands. 'Trouble at the Kirrha harbour – they're looking for a toll for our mooring. We need you back there.'

Barnabas sighed. 'After a whole day of queuing? Really?' He slumped and sighed again. Kassandra gave him a handful of drachmae from Elpenor's sack of coins. 'Most generous, misthios.' He tipped his head in appreciation. 'I will see you back on board,' he said, trudging back down the queue, leaving her alone with the old historian. Kassandra set Ikaros off in flight with him.

The queue shuffled forward. 'Kings travel to these parts to consult the Oracle. She can start wars or end them,' Herodotos mused. 'What do you seek today?' he asked.

'Resolution,' she replied, placing a hand on her chest.

93

He smiled sadly, nodding. 'Me, I seek . . . the truth. Though I fear I will not want it when I possess it.'

'Next,' one of the guards snapped.

Herodotos half-bowed. 'I feel that you should go before me, my lady.'

She tilted her head a little to one side in acknowledgement, noticing how he glanced once more at the fold of her clothes covering the Leonidas spear, and stepped forward. The eyes of the two black-shelled guards slid round, following her stride. She entered the shady interior to find the air thick with a cloying sweetness. From low, wide copper sconces mounted on tripods, ribbons of myrrh and frankincense smoke rose like ghosts.

When she came to the adyton chamber at the heart of the temple, it was nearly night-dark. Marble likenesses of Poseidon, Zeus, the Fates and Apollo himself glared down at her, uplit by the eldritch gloom of the sconces. She almost flinched when she saw two 'statues' which were in fact more of the dark-garbed sentries. But more disconcerting was the slumped figure that sat on a three-legged stool in the centre of the chamber. She was draped in a long white gown and strings of beads, her wreathed head lolling, lost in the pillars of scented smoke rising from glowing pots set on the tiled floor around her.

Kassandra peered at the Oracle, hatred building in her heart. Perhaps there would be no answers here, but there could be resolution of some sort, for the guards had been foolish enough to let her enter with her weapons. Now the snake-woman would pay for the cursed words that had shattered her life and . . . Her spiralling thoughts ground to a halt when the woman's head rolled back. She was young – years younger than Kassandra – not an old hag as tradition dictated. She actually reminded her of an adolescent Phoibe. The hatred ebbed quickly. The Oracle who had dictated the bleak demands all those years ago was now long dead, it seemed.

'Enter into the light of Apollo, the light that illuminates shadow,' the girl sighed throatily, gesturing to the gentle glow of the burning pots. 'What do you wish to know, traveller?'

'I . . . I seek the truth about my past. Perhaps my future too. I want to know of my parents, their whereabouts.'

The Oracle's swaying head slowed a little. 'Who asks Apollo for such wisdom?' she boomed, belying her small frame.

Kassandra stared at the seeress, knowing how foolish this was, sickened that she would have neither answers nor even the satisfaction of revenge now. 'I was born in the land of Sparta. My brother was cast from the mountains and so was I. Now, I have nobody, nothing.'

The Oracle stopped swaying altogether. Her eyes rolled up to meet Kassandra's. She seemed different now, as if wakened. But when her eyes flicked towards the nearest guard, she lapsed back into that trance-like state, head swaying again. 'You will find your parents . . . on the other side of the river.'

Kassandra's senses sharpened. Her mind spun with what little knowledge she had of this region. The River Pleistos ran near here. Her parents were there?

'When your days draw to an end and you pay Charon

the Ferryman to cross the Styx, you will be reunited with them on the far banks.'

Kassandra's heart plunged as hope crumbled away. A silence passed. The guards shuffled impatiently. 'Your time is up,' one grunted.

'I bid you farewell,' she said to the Oracle.

Just as she turned to leave, a shout echoed through the temple from outside, and the sound of a smashing vase.

'Trouble!' a guard's voice grunted from out there. The two in the chamber looked at one another, then rushed outside.

Kassandra made to follow them, but a voice stopped her.

'Wait,' the Oracle whispered.

For a moment Kassandra did not recognize her voice – weak, frightened, shorn of the affected and theatrical tones of a moment ago.

'They hunt the child who fell from the mountain . . .' the Oracle whispered.

Kassandra's flesh crept. She stepped back towards the Oracle. 'What did you say?'

'The Cult hunt the she-child who fell.'

Kassandra's mind reeled. She grabbed the Oracle by the shoulders and shook her. 'Who, where are they?' She saw the tears in the girl's eyes now, and realized all was very much not well here. She slackened her grip. 'I can help you if you help me.'

'I cannot be helped,' the Oracle croaked. Her eyes grew moon-wide as the clatter of footsteps sounded behind Kassandra. 'They're coming back, you must go.'

'You, get back,' one of the guards snarled.

'The Cult plan to meet tonight, in the Cave of Gaia,' the Oracle started as Kassandra backed away a half-step. 'There, you may find the answers you seek.'

'I said *get back*!' One guard grabbed Kassandra's shoulders and hauled her away towards the entrance. She did not struggle. Another seized the Oracle and dragged her into the shadows at the rear of the temple.

Kassandra winced as the stark light of day fell upon her again. 'The Oracle will see no more supplicants today,' the guard boomed over her head as he shoved her outside. A great groan arose from the queue. As the noise settled, Kassandra heard a rhythmic yelp, and spotted the tall, horn-voiced man who had mocked Barnabas in the queue. He was now pinned to the ground by one temple guard while a second tirelessly volleyed him in the groin over and over. The poor fellow's eyes and tongue were bulging from his face.

'Burst the other one and then we're done,' the guard pinning the man chuckled evilly.

'Seems the clumsy oaf smashed a votive amphora,' Herodotos said, sidling up next to Kassandra and guiding her away. 'Tsk!' he added with a mischievous glint in his eye.

She looked from Herodotos to the pinned man to the smashed amphora and back to Herodotos again. 'He . . . no, *you* –'

'Yes, yes, keep your voice down. I am allowed the occasional lie – I am no Persian, after all. I smashed that vase because I thought it might give you a chance to talk plainly with the Oracle.'

She noticed how he glanced at her spear again, and once again she covered it up with her cloak.

'The priests and protectors in there have a reputation for interfering and chanting and generally getting in the way,' Herodotos continued.

Kassandra's brow furrowed. 'Priests, protectors? There were none. Just those beetle-black temple guards.'

Herodotos' face drained of colour. 'Go on.'

'The Oracle spoke mindless, trite platitudes and vague possibilities until the guards left to deal with the commotion, and *then* she began to tell me things that seemed significant.'

'Began?'

'Before she was finished, the guards came back in and hauled her from her stool, dragged her like a slave into the temple's recesses.'

Herodotos' face sagged until he looked more like a man of seventy summers. 'Then the rumours are true. They *do* have the Oracle under their control.'

'They?' she asked.

'I told you I came here in search of truth,' he said. 'Well, I have found it, and it is a black truth. Do you not understand? All Hellas pivots around the word of the Oracle. Sparta and its hundreds of allies in the Peloponnesian League. Athens and its many supporters in the Delian League. Every single neutral city-state. *All* do as the Oracle advises. War might rage between the two great powers, but if *they* are in control of the Oracle, then *they* will be the victors. Imagine what power *they* will have, if *they* control the words that come from her mouth.'

'Herodotos, for the favour of all the Gods, please tell me who *they* are?'

His eyes darted to check nobody was too close. 'The Cult of Kosmos,' he said, his voice little more than a whisper.

A shiver shot up her spine as if stroked by cold, dead hands. 'The Cult.'

'They are like shadows. Nobody knows who the members are, for they meet in secret and wear masks to protect their identities. I have only seen a Cultist once, and on a dark night. In his mask he looked like a fiend and –' His face fell agape when he saw Kassandra pulling from her leather bag Elpenor's wicked-looking wooden theatre mask, the nose hooked and sharp, the eyebrows bent in a scowl, the mouth locked in a sinister grin. 'Apollo walks!' he hissed, shoving the mask back into her bag and glancing around once again. 'Where did you get that?'

'I think I have already met a Cultist,' Kassandra said. 'And I need to meet the others. The Oracle told me only fragments of information.' Her mind spun, then she clicked her fingers. 'She said the Cult are to meet tonight, in the Cave of Gaia. Where in all Hellas is that?'

Herodotos looped an arm through hers and steered her away from the temple, down the steps and along the long winding path leading from the plateau. 'The Cave of Gaia lies somewhere underneath this very temple mount – which is riddled with a honeycomb of natural caverns, vast and maze-like.'

'Then I will come back here tonight,' Kassandra said, seeing the dozen or more small, dark openings in the mountainside. 'All I ask is that you keep watch for me while I'm in there.'

Herodotos sighed deeply. 'Very well. But you must promise me one thing: that you will come out of there alive. I like you, Child of Nowhere. Do not make me regret this.'

6

Crickets sang in the cool night air. Somewhere in the wooded parts of the high valley, bears grumbled and boars foraged. The valley floor was nearly deserted. The many thousands of pilgrims had dispersed and just a few remained, camped and singing gently around fires. Up on the temple mount, slaves and attendants shuffled around quietly, cleaning, sweeping and tidying in the torchlight. Dozens of black-armoured guards strode to and fro watchfully.

Kassandra levered herself up onto a small shelf of rock, and then threw a rope down to Herodotos. The man belied earlier complaints about having a bad back to pick his way up onto the shelf beside her. They turned to the low cave opening in the rock face. Inside was pure blackness. 'This has to be a way in,' she mused, then twisted to Herodotos. 'Don't you think?'

The historian shrugged. 'It is a honeycomb in there, misthios, that is all I know.'

She weighed the leather bag holding robe and mask. If this tunnel did lead to the Cave of Gaia then she would have to wear them in there if she was to remain anonymous. Her bow, spear and bracers would be too conspicuous, she realized. Grudgingly, she peeled off her bracers and belt and slid her bow and quiver from her back, feeling naked without the equipment. Herodotos took her bow without fuss, but when she gave him her spear, he gulped and refused to touch it, holding out a leather bag of his own instead for her to drop it in.

She said nothing of it. 'If I'm not back by dawn, you leave, yes? And tell Barnabas to leave too, and to forget about me.'

Herodotos nodded and Kassandra ducked down to scuttle inside the tunnel. It was a cramped space and so she bent double, but even then, hanging stalactites scraped her back. It became warren-like after a while, forcing her to worm along on her belly. No way of turning back. Very little air. For a moment, she imagined Herodotos gaily strolling back down to Kirrha to sell her spear while she wriggled into a dark grave. Then, without warning, the floor fell away and she slid down a pile of scree. She found herself at the edges of a bubble of orange light, and heard the guttural echoes of many strong and confident voices. Shadows moved, somewhere beyond a natural column of stone. She hurriedly threw Elpenor's embroidered cloak around her shoulders and slid the mask on, just as a pair of figures walked past. It looked as if they were floating, thanks to their trailing robes.

'Do not tarry over there,' said one, his mask – exactly like Elpenor's – staring foully at her. 'The artefact has been brought out. Hurry, or you will miss your chance to hold it.'

'I would not miss this chance for anything,' she replied, her voice muffled behind the identical mask's mouth slit.

The pair glided on past her, chattering about hiring

regiments and placing mercenaries for the work that lay ahead. She let them walk on for a while before following them through a stony corridor. Torches crackled and spat and every so often she passed chambers that had been hewn from the bedrock. Some bore beds or furniture, but all appeared empty. Then, from the doorway of one just ahead, a puff of steam spat out, along with a scream that twisted her stomach into a tight knot. She slowed, certain she did not want to see what had caused the scream, but as she edged past she could not help but look. A brute of a Cultist was in there, his breathing heavy behind his mask, his shoulders bulging from his sleeveless robe and his arms thick with black, curly hairs. In one meaty hand, he held a poker over a crackling brazier until it glowed white at the tip. Before him was a withered, broken wretch tied to a vertical frame, head hanging forward, a patter of fluid dripping from his hidden face. 'We hired you to kill Phidias of Athens,' scowled the masked brute. 'We paid you well. You botched your work and nearly ended up in the stinking Athenian jail for it. Well, you would have been better off in there, you fool,' he said, grabbing the tied man's hair and yanking his head back to reveal a face half-ruined: the right side a mess of bloody runnels, the eye socket a gaping black hole. The brute lifted the poker and moved the white tip towards the man's remaining eye. The man's eye bulged and darted as if trying to escape his head, but there was no escape. With a sizzle and a stink of charring flesh and then a *pop*, the eye burst in a splash of white liquid and blood that sprayed across the room and showered Kassandra in the doorway. It took everything she had not to flinch or retch. The masked brute turned to see her and shouted over the tortured man's screams: 'Apologies. I will saw off this bastard's head and then I will have one of my slaves clean your robes.'

'Very good,' she said, 'but be quick – the artefact is on show.'

Pleased with her composure, she shuffled on down the rocky corridor until it opened up into a wide chamber, the stone floor polished and etched with symbols. A few Cultists stood here, all wearing the same wicked-looking theatre masks, deep in discussion. She dared not break up a group of them. But there, kneeling alone before a stone altar at one end of the room, was one whose hair was long and black, with a distinctive white streak.

Approaching and watching, she nearly leapt from her skin when a voice spoke behind her shoulder: 'Do not be shy: pray with Chrysis,' said a masked man who resembled a beanpole. 'She does not mind company.'

Kassandra nodded her thanks then mimicked the one called Chrysis' gestures, kneeling and bowing at the altar beside her, hands clasped across her chest.

'Ah, yes, you feel it too?' the female Cultist said huskily from behind the mask. 'All we have achieved pleases the Gods. We have won so much control. Prayer is tradition. Tradition is control. The masses bow their heads in prayer to a higher power . . . and *we* are that higher power. Does it not make you feel proud?'

As Chrysis spoke, the rasping of a saw and a final wet scream sounded from the brute's torture chamber, some way behind, followed by the dull thud of an object landing on the ground.

'I am a mere novitiate, but my pride flows over,' Kassandra purred, finding that the only way she could hope to be believed was to act as they did, to pretend the horrors going on in the torture chamber were not real.

'Then I shall instruct you, child. The Oracle is our key to greatness,' Chrysis continued. 'For generations now, her voice has been ours.'

The words pealed through Kassandra's mind like the song of a bell struck with a hammer. *The order to throw my baby brother from the mountain came not from the seeress ... but from these abominations.*

'Through her we have gained so much,' Chrysis continued. 'Soon, we will control all Hellas. Let the two sides have their war, while we rule them both. Yet the Oracle is nothing compared to –' She paused, shuddering as if touched by the hand of an invisible lover. 'The artefact.'

'The sacred artefact,' said three masked passers-by who had overheard.

'The sacred artefact,' chanted Kassandra dutifully.

'And our champion will be here soon,' said another. 'The one who can unlock its power – to see past, present, future.'

'It will be a fine moment,' Kassandra said, then rose and walked slowly across the room, trying to discern some sense from the seven or eight chattering voices. Two were bickering passionately, a man and a woman. She picked up their names quickly: Silanos and Diona.

'Forget the mother,' Diona said, swiping a hand through the air. 'She is old and useless now.'

'But I almost have the mother in my grasp,' scoffed Silanos. 'It *must* be her we focus on.'

Silanos' mask swung to pin Kassandra. 'You. What do you think? Should we hunt for our champion's mother or his sister?'

Kassandra's throat turned as dry as sand. 'I . . .' she croaked.

'Pah, the answer is neither,' said a third, somewhere behind her. 'Both are elusive. Perikles of Athens is not – he wanders around wearing his plumed helm like an archer's target. Let us cut out his heart and cripple the Athenians and their chaotic and orderless ways. Or perhaps install a leader in his place who more suits our aims.'

These three now began arguing amongst themselves, and Kassandra slipped away.

On she went, passing through a doorway that led into an antechamber. The rock of the far wall had been hewn into a glorious and terrifying form of a hooded horned snake, rising from the ground, mouth open and fangs bared, its niche-eyes picked out by two glowing candles. A masked man stood before it. Kassandra edged closer to see what he was doing, then trapped a gasp as she saw him lifting his wrists to the fangs and running the skin across the tips. Blood coated his skin and dribbled into a stone trough under the snake's mouth and the man tilted his head back and gasped in pleasure. His euphoria slid away and his head rolled round towards Kassandra. His eyes – one dark and the other misted – darted behind the mask's eye holes, searching her. 'Do not let the fangs grow dry, go on, give offering,' he said, stepping back, bandaging the two jagged cuts on his wrists.

'Not today,' she said firmly.

'Go on, and give thanks that it is only blood we must offer. Deimos will be demanding we cut off our hands next. The sooner we capture the rest of his bloodline, the sooner we can dispense with our champion and his chaotic, crude ways.'

Kassandra's silence seemed to evoke suspicion.

'You had best not be thinking of telling Deimos,' he said, stepping closer. 'If he knew, he would turn completely to his animal side. He is a living weapon. A fiery steed that cannot be tamed. Power and chaos in one body. He is everything the Cult needs and everything it stands against. If he knew we were about to capture his mother . . .' He trailed off with a dark chuckle. 'Well, let's just say I do not wish for my nightmares to come to life.'

'Nor I,' Kassandra agreed, suddenly feeling the air in the underground vault turn chilly. She left the antechamber and followed Chrysis, Silanos and Diona, all now moving deeper into the complex. A thousand voices screamed in Kassandra's head: talk of lands being controlled by the Cult of Kosmos, men offering their own blood, the Oracle of Delphi herself in the palm of these creatures. She wandered in a daze into a great chamber, and felt a low reverberating hum penetrate her very marrow. It was the sensation she felt whenever she touched her ancient – and absent – Leonidas spear. But this was something else, something stronger. *Much* stronger.

Huge stalactites hung from the cave's high ceiling, and a circle of polished stone in the centre of the floor was studded with several dozen cloaked, masked figures: the torturer brute ambled into place with them, as did the one called Chrysis and the one with the bandaged wrists too. Three more hurried in behind Kassandra and took a place in the circle. Each of them sang long, deep notes in a constant drone, and only when it faltered slightly and some of them looked back at her, did she realize she was expected to join them. Striding over to vacant space she stepped into it, making up the ring. The endless chant filled the cave and sent shivers scampering across her skin, and her eyes beheld the plinth of red-veined marble in the centre of the circle, topped with a small golden pyramid.

The artefact.

The misthios in her instantly valued the piece and imagined what it might buy. The warrior in her wanted to stride forth and challenge every one of these masked whoresons – murderers of her baby brother, destroyers of her life – to a death fight. Her hands clenched into fists under her robe, cursing Herodotos for convincing her to leave her weapons behind. But then she realized that it was the pyramid itself that was resonating, causing the chamber to shiver, sending those strange impulses through her.

One of the Cultists stepped forward, reaching out in great reverence to place a hand over the pyramid. The rest muttered and sighed in envy, some shuffling impatiently, eager to take their turn. Kassandra was sure that it must contain a candle or lamp within, for it glowed gently with a golden light. 'I see it,' intoned the worshipper. 'Invisible chains around the necks and ankles of every man and woman. The dying of the chaotic light. The narrow corridor of thought, of pure devotion, pure *order*.'

The rest rose in a babble of appreciation. Three more approached, one at a time, to speak of what they saw, before Chrysis whispered to Kassandra. 'It works fully only when the champion touches it at the same time as one of us – he sees our thoughts and allows us to see further. But it is still a wondrous thing to place your hand upon it alone. You, you must take a turn.'

Kassandra gulped, grateful for the mask, then stepped into the circle's centre. She reached out, her hand hovering over the pyramid's tip. Her heart thundered, the buzz of voices shook the air around her, sweat stole down her back despite the chill, and then . . .

Crash!

A door at the back of the cave smashed back on its hinges, pins and screws flying loose and the door sagging, broken. A tall, sculpted vision lunged into the chamber and fell into a swaying crouch, like a maddened animal. His legs and arms were hewn with muscle and he wore a white breastplate dripping with golden pteruges and a white cape. His thick waves of dark hair were held back in a topknot, draped down his back. He wore no mask, and his handsome face was spoiled by a look of uncaged anger. A warrior. A champion. *Deimos?*

'There is a traitor in our midst,' he snarled. 'Forty-two of us there are, and I count forty-two here. Yet how can that be when one of our number lies cold and dead in Kirrha?'

He lifted a severed head and tossed it across the floor.

Kassandra stared at the head as it rolled to a halt, horror rising from the soles of her feet and through her like an icy tide. *Elpenor?* But she had not cut off his head. This animal must have desecrated the corpse to make a point.

'Who is it?' he raged, his voice like a war drum. 'Remove your masks!'

Kassandra's mind sped, terror rising in her heart.

'That is not our way, Deimos. We choose to remain anonymous to each other,' spoke one Cultist.

Kassandra's alarm eased a fraction, and then Chrysis stepped forward. 'Let us each show our devotion to the Cult by laying a hand on the artefact along with our champion, as has always been the way. Deimos will see what they see, and will discern any secrets they harbour.'

Deimos lumbered down the steps from the door and barged into the circle. 'Very well,' he snarled, looking at Kassandra – already by the pyramid – up and down. 'You, go ahead. Touch it and tell me what you see. You cannot lie, because I will see it too,' he said, placing his hand on one face of the pyramid.

Kassandra stared at the champion. His tawny-gold eyes were ablaze with hatred. For a moment, she saw her own doom in them. But what could she do? She let her palm drop and rest on the opposing face of the pyramid. Nothing. For a moment, she felt a strong urge to laugh at these fools. What happened next was like a mule's kick to her head.

Her neck arched and white light flashed through her mind. It was not like those moments when the spear conjured memories of the past. This was real. She could taste the autumnal air, smell the damp bracken, hear the chirruping of birds in the Eurotas Forest.

She was in the lands of Sparta.

I creep through the ferns under a bruised afternoon sky, watching the plump boar ahead, thinking of the delicious meal it would make — and of how strong they would think me, only seven summers old — were I to fell it myself. I kneel, draw back my spear, holding it on an outbreath, lining up the tip with the boar's flank. But then doubt creeps into my thoughts: should I wait, should I loose, or should I . . .

With a flash of silver, another lance flies over my head and spears down into the dirt, startling the boar. The beast squeals and bolts. I leap up and round to face the mystery thrower. 'Who's there?' I yell. 'Come out!'

Mother emerges from the trees, cradling baby Alexios.

'Hesitation only hastens . . .' Mother begins.

'. . . the grave,' I groan, realizing I have failed her lesson. 'I know,' I reply. 'Father will be disappointed when he hears I am still not ready.'

'Your form is improving, and you are tenacious. But the greatest skill is knowing when to act.' She paces around, setting Alexios down on a fallen tree, then plucking from the earth the lance she has thrown. 'Perhaps it is time for you to have this.'

I take the spear. It catches the grey light and dazzles me. Such a fine weapon. The haft is broken, but it is a perfect length for me.

When I touch the leaf-shaped blade, I feel an odd shiver, a fluttering inside. 'I . . . I felt something.'

'Oh?' says Mother, smiling.

I touch it again and again it sends a strange sensation through me. 'This is no ordinary spear.'

'No, it isn't. It carries with it a long line of power. A bloodline of

heroes — the same blood that runs in you and me, in our family. And once, long ago, in King Leonidas.'

'This is . . . was . . . King Leonidas' spear?' I croak.

She smiles, stroking my face. 'Leonidas had great courage, and he made a great sacrifice at Thermopylae. You share in his blood, and the strength he possessed. We are able to feel certain things happening around us. We are quick as lions to react to danger. That is our family's gift. But not everyone understands that. Some recognize the power we bear, and want it only for themselves. They will try to take it from us.'

'I won't let them,' I say then, with the carefree courage of a child.

'I know,' Mother says. 'You're a warrior.'

I carefully wrap the spear in a leather roll, sensing that I should treat it with great care. I place it in my quiver. When I hear the sky growl, I look up.

'A storm's coming,' Mother says, lifting Alexios.

It is a strange thing, for it has felt that way to me ever since Mother and Father returned from their visit to the Oracle in autumn. Mother senses my unease, and places baby Alexios in my arms. I feel instantly calm, kissing his forehead and gazing into his gleaming tawny-gold eyes . . .

Her hand shot up from the pyramid and she gasped. As the memory faded, she stared at Deimos. He was staring back at her, the tawny-gold eyes now wide as moons. There was no mistaking it . . .

Alexios? she mouthed, stupefied.

His head shook in disbelief, his lips barely moving: *Kassandra?*

She took a step backwards, her legs numb.

112

'Well?' screeched one Cultist. 'What did you see, Deimos? Can we trust this one?'

Silence.

'Answer the question, Deimos,' another one pleaded.

Nothing.

A heartbeat later and another Cultist bustled forward, sighing. 'Then let me take my turn, I have nothing to hide.'

This seemed to snap Deimos from his trance. With a roar, he grabbed the back of the Cultist's head and rammed the masked face onto the point of the pyramid. With a thick *clunk*, the mask snapped. Blood puffed, the body jerked then slumped. The pyramid was pristine and golden, completely undamaged, but the Cultist's face was a crumpled mess. Some of the other Cultists backed away, wailing, but a handful surged forward. 'What are you doing, Deimos?' they screeched, clustering around him.

Kassandra backed away, stumbling all the way to the chamber entrance, then turned . . . and sped like a deer, stunned, shaken. She felt nothing as she hurtled back to the secret tunnel and scrambled through it in a blur. She barely even noticed Herodotos' words when she emerged into the night and onto the rocky shelf outside, gasping, doubling over and slumping back against the bluff face.

'My dear, what happened?'

She gazed up at the historian, eyes wide. 'He's in there. He's their champion.'

'Who, my dear?'

'My brother. Alexios.'

*

In the blackness of night, the *Adrestia* sailed from Kirrha. Reza and the few other crew members manned the sails and the steering oar. Barnabas stood on the prow, one foot on the rail, eyeing the dark as if it were an old foe. Every so often he looked back towards the stern, seeking a decision from Kassandra, to whom he had offered both his life and his livelihood, the *Adrestia*, in gratitude, but still she was lost in thought. She sat by the small cabin, clutching the hand that had touched the pyramid, staring into space. What she had thought of as reality had been cast down and shattered into a thousand pieces.

Herodotos, sitting beside her, carefully cut slices from an apple, lifting each into his mouth slowly and methodically. He again offered her a piece, which she again refused, and so he tossed it to Ikaros instead, who poked and prodded at it with mild disdain.

'There were many of them, all masked,' she said quietly. 'The Oracle is theirs, and the Gods speak to the people through her, and the pyramid is at the root of it all. They have an army of spies and warriors. They control nearly all of Hellas. Everything.'

'Then it is worse than I thought,' Herodotos mused. He stared off into the night for a time. 'If Perikles is in danger, as you claim, we must make for Athens.'

She slid her eyes towards him. 'Of all the things I saw and heard in there, why should I care about him? My brother lives, yet the Cult has turned him into something . . . *horrible*. They are out to kill my mother. This is my boat and Perikles is nothing to me – just another greedy and blood-thirsty general.'

'Bloodthirsty? You do not know the man,' Herodotos chided. 'This war was thrust upon him.'

Kassandra eyed Herodotos sourly. 'A general who doesn't relish war? Unlikely.' She thought of the hearsay and rumours she had heard in the filthy taverns near Sami. 'Some say he engineered this conflict under a guise of peace, so he could muster and flaunt Athens' invincible navy and bask in its glory. Those boats go unchallenged by the pathetic Spartan navy, yet the Spartan hoplites rule the land, peerless and unafraid of the feeble Athenian infantry. But as long as Perikles receives adulation for what happens at sea, who cares about the interminable war?'

'Perhaps. Or maybe he saw that war was inevitable and guided affairs to make the best of them,' Herodotos shrugged.

'You are not convincing me. Why should I care for this distant King of Athens?'

Herodotos laughed, loud and long. 'Athens has no king. Perikles serves the people. And his position is hardly splendid: there are plenty who lurk in Athens' shadows, eager to take his place. If the Cult are colluding against him, it could turn what has been a fraught but noble war into a chaotic and bloody disaster for all.'

Kassandra stared at him, still unconvinced.

'Very well,' Herodotos continued. 'But ask yourself this: if you are running *from* your brother, then you must be looking *for* your mother?'

She nodded.

'And where will you go to find her? Hellas is vast.'

'I presume you have a suggestion,' she said tersely.

'And you know what it is,' he replied. 'Athens is the hub of our world, my dear. Unlike Sparta, with its closed borders and backward-looking ways, Athens seeks traders, merchants, travellers like me. Great minds preside over affairs there. Minds in the possession of much knowledge. If there is to be a clue as to your mother's whereabouts, it lies within the streets of –'

'Athens,' Kassandra snapped, loudly enough for Barnabas to hear.

He saluted her and bawled the order to his crew. The *Adrestia*'s sail groaned and the boat tacked round, altering its course to head out to sea for a long voyage around the Peloponnese, towards Attika.

Herodotos lay down to sleep. Kassandra rose and stood at the stern, watching the churn behind the trireme fizzle away in the boat's wake. In the silvery moonlight, the rest of the sea was an unbroken sheet of gentle peaks and the sky a canopy of deep indigo, freckled with myriad stars. She stared for what felt like an eternity. When her eyes were growing tired, she blinked. One wave had seemed larger, higher, different, as if something was cutting through the water way back there. *Another boat?* She heard distant whalesong, drawing her gaze in a different direction. When she looked back in the *Adrestia*'s wake, the phantom boat was nowhere to be seen. She shook her head, knowing tiredness was playing with her senses.

When she turned away from the stern, Herodotos was awake and sitting up again. He was staring at Kassandra's bow and spear, stowed upright against the cabin.

'You eye my spear as if it is a shade,' she laughed.

He looked up at her without a trace of matching humour. 'The Lance of Leonidas. As soon as I saw you with it at the temple queue, I knew you had been drawn there just as I had.'

She sat across from him with a deep sigh. 'I am of Leonidas' bloodline. Some say I *shamed* his bloodline.' A memory of the Cultist's voices snaked through her mind just then. *The sooner we capture the rest of his bloodline, the sooner we can dispense with our champion and his chaotic, crude ways.* She held up the spear, examining it. 'It speaks to me sometimes, like nothing else . . . until tonight.'

'That thing you described, in the Cave of Gaia. The golden artefact?' he said, his eyes looking up and around the night sky as if to check for watching wraiths.

She nodded. 'It threw shackles around my mind and my heart, cast me back to times past in a way I've never experienced before. So sharp, so visceral.' She set down the spear and shrugged. 'What makes the golden pyramid and my spear so special?'

His face lengthened and paled. 'The spear and the pyramid are special, Kassandra . . . but not as special as you.'

'I don't understand.'

He gazed off to the prow, beckoning Barnabas over. 'Soon, you will.'

Under a cloud-streaked summer sky, the *Adrestia* drew into an ancient coastal pass, overlooked by towering mountains of dark rock, lined with green woods. Kassandra's spine tingled as she looked up at the heights. *Thermopylae. A place of ancient heroes.*

117

'You're happy with this extra stop, misthios?' Barnabas asked.

'You trust Herodotos, thus so do I. We will continue on to Athens soon enough.' She smiled, then leapt down onto the wet sand. Herodotos climbed down with the aid of a rope ladder.

She and the historian walked up the shore, taking a winding hill track that led into the mountains. 'This is the track along which Ephialtes led the Persians,' Herodotos mused, his eyes narrow, misted with moisture. He brought her to a small overhang that looked out onto the bay again. A little further up the mountainside, weak trails of sulphurous steam rose from cave openings. The Gates to Hades, some said. The Hot Gates, said others. 'Here, the Persians fell upon the Spartans and their allies. Here, it ended for your great ancestor.'

They came to a weathered statue of a lion, clad in cream-and-yellow lichen, the beast's features worn smooth by buffeting coastal winds. The Spartan king's name was still visible, carved on the stone plinth underneath. 'Take out your spear, hold it, let it speak to you,' he said.

Kassandra lifted the half-spear and clasped it with both hands. Nothing. 'This is nonsense. It only speaks to me when it wishes to, there is no point in trying to force —' *Bang!*

Arrows rain like hail, the sky dark with them. All around me, hoplites pitch over, riddled with shafts, screaming. Red-cloaked warriors fight like wolves, shouting at their allies to battle on, to stay strong. So few of them, and so many of the darker-skinned pack pressing in on them from all sides — flooding down from the hill track, spilling along the bay, a moving wall of wicker shields and sharp spears. The Spartan piper playing the call for a last stand falls, torn by a Persian lance.

'Send forth the Immortals!' a strange, jagged cry sounds from the Persian command. They come in their thousands, slashing and spearing the defenders down, breaking open that slender route south into the heart of Hellas. At the last, there are but a knot of the red-cloaked Spartans left. On they fight, lost in the dance of battle. I see him then — older than I had imagined, his body laced with cuts and wet with blood, carrying the weight of a nation on his weary shoulders . . . and the unbroken spear in his hands.

'Leonidas?' I whisper.

Through the final moments of the fray, the hero-king stares through the ether and at me. Right at me. A fresh storm of arrows falls. Three strike him, yet on he fights, blocking and beating away a crowd of Immortals — his lance shattering into two halves as he does so. Another two shafts punch into his neck, pushing him onto one knee. Then a final one plunges into his breastbone. The battle-field falls silent, and King Leonidas of Sparta rolls onto his side, dead.

She blinked, the calm, deserted and rugged coastline before her free of bodies and blood, just old Herodotos smiling sadly at her.

She dropped the spear. 'Why did you bring me here?'

Herodotos sighed. 'Because you spoke of shame, and being unworthy of your lineage. That is not true, Kassandra. You are every bit his heir, despite what might have happened in your past.' He stooped to pick up the spear using the leather bag again, so he would not have to touch it. He handed it back to her. 'This lance and the object you saw under the Oracle's temple . . . they were not crafted by our kind.'

'So they were made by Persians?'

Herodotos laughed quietly.

'Then by the Gods?' she said.

Herodotos' laughter faded. 'Not quite. They were fashioned by a people who came before. Before Hellas, before Persia, before the Trojan War, before the flood . . . before even the time of man.'

Kassandra stared, uncomprehending.

Herodotos motioned for her to sit. He brought out a loaf of bread and broke it in two, handing her half. 'I have not written of this in my histories lest men think me mad – and already some do – but I have found things, Kassandra, strange things,' he said as they ate, gazing out over the ancient pass. 'One summer I came across a wandering man. A short, round little fellow by the name of Meliton who spent his days sailing the Aegean in a tub of a boat, with no home and no destination. He told me of his adventures – some even wilder than Barnabas' tales! I let most of the stories wash over me, but there was one that snagged my attention, for unlike all his other stories, he told this one without a glint of mischief in his eye, and with a hushed and fearful voice.'

Kassandra stopped chewing and nodded for him to continue.

'He had been shipwrecked in his youth on the shores of Thera, that broken husk of an island, blown apart by a volcano long, long ago. Now that island is barren and bleak – naught but ash and decay. But he managed to survive there for many months eating grubs and molluscs. One night he was awoken by a strange tremor in the ground.'

'The volcano?' Kassandra whispered.

'No, the volcano is long dead like everything else on the isle. It was far stranger than that, misthios,' Herodotos replied, his eyes growing dark. 'As the ground shook, he saw a bright light, glowing in the night, somewhere up in the black heights of the island. It could not have been the fires of a volcano, for the light was pure and golden. He stumbled through the darkness towards the light. Dawn broke before he could reach the spot, and when he got there he found just a plain black rock face. It took him a few moments to notice the markings.'

'The markings?'

'Carved into the black rock, etched expertly, were strange symbols and sequences. I asked Meliton to describe them to me as best he could, so he drew them out in the dirt.' As he spoke, Herodotos used a finger to trace out geometric shapes in the dirt where they sat. 'This,' he said, tapping the dirt, 'is the wisdom of Pythagoras.'

A thrill raced up Kassandra's back.

'Aye,' Herodotos nodded, seeing that she understood the magnitude of it, 'the philosopher, the political theorist, the geometrician . . . one of the most brilliant minds to have graced Hellas. He was one of the few who understood the things that came before man.'

'But they said Pythagoras' wisdom was lost,' she said, recalling a drunken conversation about the topic in a

Kephallonian tavern. 'That it died with him, more than sixty years ago.'

'I too thought it was gone.' Herodotos gestured to the spear. 'And this etching is a mere fragment. But do you know what it might mean if his wisdom were to be recovered in its entirety? If the people of today could obtain the knowledge to craft things such as your lance, or the artefact you saw in the Cultist cave? And what if I were to tell you that the Cult has been searching for Pythagoras' lost writings.'

The thrill on Kassandra's skin turned into a chill shiver. 'By all the Gods, it cannot happen.'

'Leonidas said the same. He knew only pieces of it all, but enough to realize that people seeking to harness this ancient knowledge and use it like a sword had to be fought. You are of his line, Kassandra, and that is why you and your family must be saved. In this dark game that so few understand, our world itself is at risk.' He stepped away and walked slowly back towards the *Adrestia*, motioning for her to stay when she tried to follow. 'Take some time, think over what I have said.'

She stayed there for an hour, sitting by the lion and staring down at the bay, wondering how many bones lay underneath the sands. She absently fed Ikaros crumbs of bread, eating a little herself. Thrills of unease and wonder rose within her as she tried to comprehend Herodotos' words. *But damn, historian, your answers come in the form of a thousand questions*, she thought with a tired laugh. 'Time to head for Athens, for some real answers,' she sighed, rising.

Thrum . . . whack!

At once she leapt back and fell into a crouch, staring at the arrow quivering in the earth by her feet. Her eyes combed the heights behind her. Nothing. Then she saw him, staring down at her like a god from a high shelf of rock.

'Deimos?' she croaked. That strange feeling on the boat, the choppy peaks in the night. Her instincts had been right: they *had* been followed.

He said nothing, simply turning and walking away from the edge and from sight. She stared at the high shelf, then threw herself at the rock face. A moment later and she was halfway up the mountainside, scaling towards the shelf. She hesitated for a moment before hauling herself up and onto her knees. Deimos was there, waiting for her, back turned. 'You followed me all this way?'

'I remember you,' he said. 'I was a babe, but I remember you holding me.'

That long-dead flame sparked to life in her heart, flickering within the steely cage. 'And I have never forgotten what it was like to hold y–'

'My parents condemned me to be thrown from the mountain,' he cut in dispassionately. 'But it was you . . . *you* who pushed me and the old ephor to our deaths. I saw it. The golden artefact showed me.'

'No,' she started. 'I tried to save you, you must believe me, Alexios. I had no idea you survi–'

He swung to face her, the sea wind casting his dark locks across his baleful face. 'Alexios died that night. Deimos was the name given to me by my *real* family.'

Kassandra tilted her head back in disdain, the flickering flame in her breastbone dying. 'I learned from your wretched cave-symposium we're doing the same thing. Looking for our mother.'

Deimos' head tilted a little to one side. 'If you're looking for her, that means she abandoned you too.'

'Even if we were abandoned, we survived. We can go back to the way things were. We just need to find her.'

'I don't need her.'

'Your Cultists think differently,' Kassandra said flatly. 'Myrrine's their next target.'

He remained silent for a time. 'The Cult wants us because we are special,' he rasped. 'But you know that now, don't you?' He gestured back down towards the lion.

'Then you will not join me to find her?' she said, taking a step back.

'Nor you me?' he countered.

'I will not be part of the . . . *Cult*,' she spat.

A tense silence passed.

'Yet you cannot run from them. You are headed for Athens,' he said at last. 'Or so your route would suggest. Well, the Cult is already there. When you go, tell Perikles and his elitist scum they're next.'

He backed away into a small cave opening, vanishing into a cloud of sulphurous steam.

'Alexios?' she called after him.

'Do not follow me, Sister,' his voice rang out from within. 'Be thankful I let you live . . . for now.'

7

The air over the harbour of Piraeus was tinged with the stink of sweating sailors and dung, the aroma of baking bread and roasting bream, and the heady scent of wine. So many people, Kassandra thought. Voices called out from every direction, dogs barked, gulls screamed, people bartered and chatted, soldiers in blue and white trooped to and from the serried war galleys, while wagons heaped with grain sacks swayed as they rolled down from supply cogs and onto the white-flagged wharf.

She stepped off the *Adrestia* and onto the quay, her gaze drawn like one enchanted by the sight of treasure, across the many heads, to the view some two miles inland: the famous city of Athens. A sea of red-tiled roofs, from which the acropolis rose like an island of marble topped with breathtaking temples and monuments the like of which she had never seen before, not in Kephallonia, not on her travels and certainly not in Sparta.

The Parthenon shimmered, the silvery stonework and lustrous paintwork blinding in the sunlight. The high, bronze statue of Athena glistened like flame, her face solemn and imperious, spear held like a sentinel.

The way to the city from this harbour was an odd thing: a narrow promenade that stretched for all of those two miles like an arm reaching out from the city proper to clutch and keep hold of this nearest piece of coastland and its wharf. Stonemasons and slaves swarmed like ants, settling the final blocks into place atop strange walls lining either side of the promenade, their chisels tapping in an incessant rhythm.

'Come, misthios,' Herodotos beckoned her as he set off along this promenade.

She glanced back to see Barnabas, Reza and a few crewmen from another boat engaged in a bet of sorts – that Ikaros could not snatch a ring from the finger of the other boat's captain. Ikaros hopped from foot to foot, as if highly motivated to win the bet for the *Adrestia* men.

She smiled and left them to it. They went along the road, the long walls casting them in pleasant shade. An old beggar crooned at anyone who might listen: 'Have we not learned of old Troy and of the Hittites and the Assyrians? Great walls bring mighty destroyers.'

Kassandra now noticed how crude the promenade walls were – hurried and ramshackle, composed of paving stones, rubble, broken pieces of architrave and the like, contrasting starkly with the shining marble splendour and fine battlements of the city proper that awaited at the far end.

Herodotos noticed her observations. 'The Long Walls, as they are called, are ugly, yet beautifully expedient,' he explained. 'They keep the Spartans – so unskilled at siege – out, and allow the grain to keep flowing in from the ships and to the city. You thought Perikles shrewd? Well, he is, in that sense. Sparta can neither break Athens nor starve her.'

'That is Perikles' strategy?' she mused. 'Where is the glory in that?'

'Glory? Ah, ever the Spartan,' he laughed.

They reached a stretch of the promenade where either edge was thickly lined with shanty villages of shacks and tents, thronged with grubby-faced, staring people. Soon they were stepping over the prone forms of sleeping men, picking their way through packed crowds of families and whole communities. 'I have never seen this many people crammed inside walls before,' she muttered.

'The countryfolk,' Herodotos whispered. 'It is they who struggle most to follow Perikles' wisdom. They had to abandon their homes out in the fields and valleys and come in here to live like paupers.'

The promenade steepened as it reached Athens proper, into wards of brightly painted villas, rising around the acropolis like worshippers. There was the sprawling agora, centred around a statue of Eirene and Ploutos – Peace and Wealth, an unlikely dream as things stood. This market hub was thronged with stalls, cattle, hawkers selling painted ostrich eggs, spices and one even holding up a blood-wet cow's liver as if it were a prize. Everywhere, the streets were jammed with sweating bodies, the air thick with the odour of the unwashed, and the general hubbub sounded tense, hovering on the edge of argument. She noticed the sentries atop the high battlements of the city's fine curtain wall: Athenian hoplites, just like those she had faced and vanquished in Megaris. They seemed occupied, pointing and discussing goings-on out in the countryside. *What lay out there that caused them such concern?*

She had absently wandered off to one side of the agora. Herodotos stopped her with a firm hand. 'Not that way, misthios,' he said, looking in the direction she had been headed with a mien of disgust. She saw the sad, shadowy compound resting at the far end of the agora. From within, a forlorn moan sounded. The cry of a man starved of hope. 'That is the jail. That is where souls are sent to be forgotten.'

The look on his face as he eyed the place caused her to shudder. But he quickly guided her in a different direction, affecting a cheerful smile. 'No, this way. Up, onto the famous Pnyx, *misthios*.' Herodotos ushered her towards the white marble stairs that led up to the acropolis heights. 'For that is where we will find our answers.'

The steps themselves were lined with guards and people too, bickering, arguing amongst themselves. The squabbling became louder – like a drone of hornets – as they reached the plateau at the top. They were greeted first by the silent glare of the bronze Athena statue, Kassandra almost cricking her neck as she gazed up in wonder at the colossal monument. Next, in an open square in the half-shadow of the Parthenon, the Assembly was in full sway. The whole thing seemed so un-Spartan, so alien to Kassandra: thousands of men dressed in expensive robes, many bald heads gleaming in the sun, waving their arms in the air, howling in protest at one another. No . . . at one man. One poor man standing upon a plinth.

'There is the man we seek,' said Herodotos. 'Perikles, General of Athens.'

Kassandra gazed up at the man. He certainly was no

king, dressed simply in a plain robe, with wings of grey hair, a neatly trimmed beard and a broad nose. He was near Herodotos in age, but he carried himself like one who had not let his body go to seed quite as quickly.

'How long will we carry this fraud upon our shoulders?' roared the loudest objector – a red-haired younger man with dark eyes and a pointed beard, who strode around the plinth's base, punching a fist into his palm with every stride, intermittently throwing an accusing finger up at Perikles. 'Just as in the Korkyraean standoff, Perikles again excels as the master of deliberation, of hesitation, of unsatisfactory compromise. He sees merit in injuring allies and emboldening foes.'

Herodotus pointed towards the heckler. 'And that one marching around him like a scalded pig is Kleon the demagogue. He tells the people what they want to hear, even if it is fantasy. For all the enemies Perikles has faced in battle and in debate, he has never quite come up against a foe like this.'

Kleon raged on. 'He has stripped all the island cities of their fleets, extorted from them their silver, and now treats the treasury up on this mount as his own! Look at how he favours the building of the Temple of Athena Nike over the welfare of his people. Is that not the behaviour of a *king*?' He spat the word as if it were poisonous. When the people erupted in agreement, Kleon flicked his hands up as if to fan the flames, nodding and yelling himself.

'I want the temple works to continue to maintain morale,' Perikles replied calmly once the clamour had settled. 'I seek to build no king's palace here. Did I not order the stripping of gold from the shrines and villas – mine included – to fund our fleet?'

Kleon's answer was merely a derisive snort as he sought to change tack. 'Our fleet? Our *mighty* fleet which drains the treasury with its pitiful efforts – no more than nibbling at the coastline of the Peloponnesians? Following your calamitous efforts in Megaris, you avoid true, noble battle on land, while our farms and our ancestral homes are reduced to nothing. We, born of the soil, must now watch it turn to ash.'

'To ash?' Kassandra frowned. Herodotos noticed, placed a hand on her shoulder and guided her gaze round, to look out from the acropolis and over the summer haze of the Attikan countryside. There, in the buckling heat, she saw the sheer silvery mountains that dominated most of the land, but in the precious stretches of flat, arable ground, she saw terrible things. She blinked twice to be sure her eyes were not deceiving her. They were not. In place of what had once been estates and granges of wheat, orchards of lemons and olives, there were black stains of fresh ash and recently toppled marble and brick. Dotted out there were patches of red – like pools of blood. Then she saw what they truly were.

Red-cloaked Spartans, camped and blocking landward access to the city. Watching, waiting, their spears winking in the glaring sun. Conquerors of the countryside now just seeking a way to beat the walls and overrun the city. *Stentor?* she mouthed, wondering if he was out there, leading the siege in place of the Wolf.

'I take no pleasure in seeing our countryside ravaged,'

Perikles snapped back. 'It is a necessary sacrifice. Don't you see? We must not offer peace to the Spartans, for they will treat any such move like the bleat of a cornered lamb and it will only embolden them. Yet we cannot charge headlong into battle with them. Have they not proved time and again that their phalanx goes unmatched? The answer lies in stone. The Long Walls will save us: the boats will ferry in fish from the northern sea and grain from the coastal kingdoms. Let Sparta beat her fists upon our walls. They *cannot* win.'

Kleon's face widened in utter delight, slapping the back of one hand into the palm of the other with his every word: 'Nor. Can. *We!*'

The assembly exploded in a storm of agreement. Perikles weathered it all like a statue. 'Kleon is right,' one man jeered. 'Our city is in stinking squalor, and there is no end in sight for this damned war.'

'Quite,' Kleon agreed. 'And is this not the first time in months . . . *months!* That the mighty Perikles has deigned to actually attend our sacred gathering? Does he believe he is not subject to your scrutiny?'

More abusive cries.

Uninvited, Kleon stepped up onto the plinth. He swung a loose fold of his sapphire robe over his arm and continued his diatribe, chopping his free hand through the air like an axe as he spoke. Quietly, Perikles stepped down to allow his rival to rant. It went on for an age, and only when the crowd grew tired of the matter did the Assembly turn its attentions to the next topic of debate: an ostracism. 'Anaxagoras, a friend of Perikles, stands before you today accused of impiety.' Kleon pointed to an ancient man in the crowd.

Rumbles of disgust rang out.

'He claimed the sun was not Apollo himself . . . but some blazing ball of matter!'

The rumbles rose into shrill jeers now.

Anaxagoras tutted and swiped a hand at the air as if angrily swatting away bees, then gestured up at the sun as if the truth was evident to anyone with eyes.

A fellow came round, holding a sack. Each man in the assembly dropped in it a piece of broken vase to mark their vote. Perikles deposited his piece just as Herodotos led Kassandra over towards him. As they approached, she saw that his statue-hard expression from the plinth was gone, replaced by one of dejected weariness.

'Old friend?' Herodotos said.

Perikles looked up, and his face lifted again, like a man seeing the sun after days of rain. He and Herodotos embraced. She noticed the historian whisper something in his ear. Perikles' face dropped for a moment, before he nodded and thanked his friend. When they parted, he beheld Kassandra. 'And this is?'

'Kassandra. A friend,' Herodotos said. 'I heard from the men on the docks that you intend to hold a symposium tonight. She seeks the wisdom of your closest comrades. Perhaps she could attend?'

'After what you have just told me, old friend,' Perikles stopped him, 'I would be a fool to invite a stranger – a misthios, no less – into my home.'

Herodotos leaned in to whisper in his ear again.

Perikles' stared at Kassandra for a time. Whatever Herodotos had said had changed things in her favour. 'You may attend,' he said. 'You cannot bring your weapons . . . but you would be best advised to come armed with your wits.'

The marble-walled andron was a forest of polished columns, blazoned in bands of fiery red. Emerald vines hung like drapes from the pillars and the ceiling, and pots of purple bougainvillaea and lemon trees hugged the corners. The floor was a riot of colour: a tessellated scene of Poseidon lurching from a teal sea along with a school of silvery sea creatures, all dappled with an archipelago of sunset-red, honey-gold and lapis-blue Persian silk rugs. The air was thick with the scent of baked fish, roasting meats and most of all, rich wine.

Citizens stood in clusters, locked in discussion and heated debate. Laughter and gasps of surprise floated through the room like waves. Men leaned on the columns, hung over balconies, swaying, shrieking with laughter, faces ruddy from the wine. A lyre and a lute combined to fill the hall with a sweet but lively melody, and every chorus seemed to be marked by the raucous laughter of groups and pairs falling from one side room to the next, or the *crash* of a dropped amphorae and a mighty cheer.

At one such sudden din, right behind her, Kassandra instinctively made a grab for her belt, her spear . . . then smoothed the thigh of her azure Athenian stola – cursing the absent mercenary leathers and weapons. 'You're supposed to be the symposiarch, aye?' she said with a roguish look. 'The one *stopping* them getting too drunk?'

Herodotos, by her side, shrugged. 'In theory. A task somewhat akin to grabbing a rabid wolf by the ears.' He tilted his as-yet unfilled cup towards her, showing her the hideous, boil-ridden creature painted on the inner base. 'The idea is that they will drink more slowly so as not to be first to see the monstrosity at the bottom of their cup – bad luck, apparently.'

Kassandra gazed around. Everybody seemed rather keen on this bad luck. She saw one fellow tilt his cup back to drain it and frowned at the thing painted on the vessel's underside. 'Is that . . .'

'A massive, angry, swollen penis?' Herodotos finished for her. 'Aye, Priapos would be proud. Supposedly the statesmanlike types here should be too reserved and cautious to tilt their cups back so much as to reveal the image. But . . .'

He needed to say no more as the drinking man held the cup over his groin as if the penis image was his own. He danced a jig, a dozen others exploding with laughter.

'It seems wrong, aye?' Herodotos remarked. 'The countryside burns, the streets are crammed with refugees . . . and up here men who should be leading this city to safety guzzle on wine and pickle their minds? But you have seen how it is outside the city. The Spartans are here and we are trapped within these walls like dogs. At the end of the world, who is to say how one should behave?' he said, then threw his head back with a throaty laugh. 'I verge onto the dramatic – something best left to the experts on such matters.' He gestured to some of the attendees. 'In truth, Perikles hosts these gatherings not because he's a lover of crowds, but to keep Athens' loudest voices speaking in his favour. And not every mind in here is ablaze with wine. Go, speak with the ones who are not staggering or vomiting. They are the ones Perikles truly trusts – the ones upon whose shoulders Athens' fate rests.' He handed her a krater of wine and another of water. 'Take this, and before you ask anyone for information, fill their cup. If they ask for a good amount of water to dilute the wine then they're worth speaking to.'

Herodotos wandered off to talk with a cluster of hoary old men and Kassandra suddenly felt the walls of the villa close in on her. Every one of the men here seemed gull-like and intimidating. Long of tooth and reeking of experience. She felt like a girl, out of place. What a fool, thinking she could mine these haughty types for information. Some shot her arch glances, looking away again as soon as she caught their eye. She took a deep breath and stepped into the sea of strangers.

He watched her arrive as twilight cast Athens in a dark veil. The wretched historian walked as her chaperone. What a wonderful and unexpected turn of events, he mused, tracing the contours of his mask. Now, he would not have to hunt her through the squalid city streets. Now, he could deal with her – and the damned historian – right here in Perikles' villa. He snapped his fingers, and the four shadows with him scuttled away into position.

She saw one short, pug-nosed, dark-bearded and incredibly hirsute fellow grinning at her, and turned away from him. Spotting another, a hawk-faced type – a man who looked like he oozed knowledge and seemed somewhat trustworthy – she edged over in his direction. 'Wine?' she said. He stared through her, then slid gently, silently down the wall to a sitting position, his head lolling forward and a great serrated, wine-fuelled snore pouring from his nostrils.

'Appearances can be deceptive,' a voice spoke, right by her shoulder. She started, turning to see nothing, then looking down to see the short, hairy, grinning homunculus from moments ago, who had now sidled up to her. He wore a himation – an old-style garment that left half of his chest bare – and walked with the aid of a stick. She eyed him askance.

He smiled, straightening up and setting his stick to one side. 'Yes, I am too young to need this stick, but I like to play with people's perceptions. Assumption is the basis of ignorance, like shackles on the mind. Break them and a wondrous road opens up: from illusion, through belief, beyond reason . . . to pure, golden *knowledge*. And is knowledge not the one true good in this world?'

Kassandra looked at him blankly for a time. 'And you are?' she asked, extending the wine krater to refill his cup. He nodded towards the water krater.

'Ask anyone and they'll tell you Sokrates, but a name gives you nothing. Our actions determine who we are, and every action has its pleasures and its price. With that said, then, whom do you claim to be?'

Her eyes narrowed. 'Kass–'

'Kassandra,' he finished for her. 'Perikles explained you would be here tonight.'

Kassandra noticed Herodotos and Sokrates exchange a warm and earnest look across the room. Her doubts eased a fraction. 'And where is Perikles?'

Sokrates chuckled. 'He rarely attends his own parties.'

'I imagine he is upset by the ostracism of his friend,' she said. The results had been announced just before dusk. Poor Anaxagoras had been exiled for ten years.

'Quite to the contrary,' replied Sokrates. 'He was singing like a lark about it earlier.'

Kassandra turned the wine krater towards her own cup, filling it and taking a deep glug. The wine was sour and punchy. 'I don't understand. Why would he wish his own friend into exile?'

'Things are rarely as they seem, Kassandra. Anaxagoras is my friend too. Indeed, he was my tutor – planting the first seeds of light up here.' He tapped his temple and supped on his wine. 'But I too whispered a prayer of thanks to the Gods when the result was announced. I understand your confusion. But ask yourself: what use are succour and shelter in a nest of vipers?' He leaned a little closer to her. 'Anaxagoras was in danger here. *Grave* danger. Most in this room likewise.' He pointed to a tall fellow in yellow robes, streaked with white dust. He was stacking ornaments on a table like a tower, enthusiastically describing the proportions of his 'construction' to a gathered circle of people. 'Phidias there is the city's chief sculptor and architect, the creator of the great bronze statue of Athena and the unfinished temple. Yet he too is not safe and hopes to be next to find safe passage from the city.'

'Fleeing . . . from whom?' she asked guardedly.

Sokrates' playful look faded. 'Take your pick. This city is a pit of snakes, Kassandra.'

When her face fell and her eyes grew watchful, he noticed this, placing a hand on her shoulder and squeezing. 'But there are many good sorts too, especially here. Look around you; amongst the inebriates you might see some of Athens' finest minds: Thucydides, a fine soldier and an even better leader of soldiers ... although he envies Herodotos and one day wants to write histories like him.' He pointed at a young, balding and stern-faced man surrounded by military types, going by their scarlaced bodies. Then he pointed to a trio locked in heated debate. 'Euripides and Sophocles over there – the pair of loving old goats that they are – masters of poetic tragedy. And Aristophanes, who loves to insert a dose of comic wit into their works, and would love to insert something else into Euripides, I'd wager.'

A chap with a pinched face and dark sprouts of hair either side of a bald pate waddled past Sokrates, swiping a dismissive hand. 'Pour him some wine then move on,' the stranger advised Kassandra. 'Lest the infuriating airbladder start waffling with his usual perplexions, telling us night is day and day night – and that we are blind because we cannot see it is so!'

'Ah, Thrasymachos, my old sparring partner in matters of the mind,' Sokrates replied in an entirely contrasting tone.

Thrasymachos halted and stared at Sokrates. He balled his fists and his lips moved as if to say *rise above it*. He glanced at Kassandra: 'If you seek wisdom, then speak with someone else.'

'Quite,' Sokrates agreed. 'There are many golden minds in this room. Sophocles is wise, Euripides is wiser . . .'

'But of all men, Sokrates is wisest!' chirped a roaring drunk man from nearby.

Thrasymachos' face was a picture, shooting red-hot daggers at the oblivious drunk.

'Come now, Thrasymachos. Perhaps *you* are now the wisest? Have you finally seen the light on the matter of justice?'

Thrasymachos took a step past Sokrates as if to storm away . . . but he halted, shook slightly, then swung back to face him, hooked like a trout. 'This, *again*?'

Kassandra disguised a chuckle by taking another gulp of wine.

'We were discussing the nature of rulers, and the administration of justice,' Sokrates explained to Kassandra. 'There is no better place to do so than in Perikles' home, wouldn't you agree? I simply asked my friend here, and I'll ask him again: would you agree that the act of ruling is an art?'

Thrasymachos snorted in derision. 'Yes, it is an art, as are all the undertakings of man. That is not a matter for argument.'

'Very well.' He let a moment pass – enough for Thrasymachos' guard to drop, then: 'Yet, medicine is for the betterment of the patient and not the physician. Carpentry improves the building, not the builder. Thus, is the art of ruling not for the betterment of the ruled rather than the ruler?'

Thrasymachos stared at Sokrates agog. 'What? *No!* Have you been listening to nothing that I say?'

Sokrates countered the man's brimming ire with a placid half-smile.

Kassandra threw back another mouthful of wine. 'Justice is only good if it serves freedom,' she ventured, confident . . . or perhaps slightly drunk.

'Yet, is justice not a set of rules by which we must all abide?' Sokrates posed the question to both of them. 'Is it not, by definition, *opposed* to freedom?'

Thrasymachos answered first. 'No, because without rules there would be anarchy, and only the powerful would be free.'

'And are we to see that as different from the world in which we live?'

'Of course not!' Thrasymachos seethed.

'Wait . . . what are you trying to say?' Kassandra said, her mind in knots, now understanding the frustrations of Thrasymachos.

'I never *try* to say anything . . .' Sokrates began.

'No, he never does,' Thrasymachos agreed testily.

'. . . I am only exploring your ideas,' Sokrates finished.

Thrasymachos wrung his fingers through his twin tufts of hair, issued a half-expletive then swung on his heel and stormed off for good this time.

Sokrates giggled like a boy. 'I am sorry about that. I cannot help but tease him. He seeks answers instead of questions.'

'So do I,' Kassandra said firmly. 'I'm looking for a woman who fled Sparta.'

Sokrates glanced at a polished bronze mirror on the wall nearby, drawing Kassandra's eyes to it also. She stared at her own reflection. 'There she is,' he grinned.

'Very perceptive. But I'm looking for another woman. One who fled some twenty years past.'

'Have you any idea how many strangers have come through Athens this last moon, let alone in the past twenty years?'

She sighed. 'No, and I don't know if she even came here.'

Sokrates shook his head, pinching his bottom lip in thought. 'If she went north, overland, then her route would have necessitated a passage through the Argolid.'

Kassandra's heart sank. She didn't even know if her mother had gone on foot. 'The Argolid is vast.'

'It is,' Sokrates agreed. 'But it is also mountainous and riddled with bandits. Travellers rarely veer from the one well-worn route – a route that passes Epidavros and the Sanctuary of Asklepios. The priests there are famed for the shelter they offer wanderers and those in need.'

'Priests? Given what this woman had been through, I doubt she and they would have got along.'

'Ah,' Sokrates whispered, 'but there is another in those parts. My friend, Hippokrates – a physician – practises there. He is no priest, and he has a memory for details, faces. He once nearly had Thrasymachos in tears, so easily could he debunk the man's arguments with his lightning-fast recollections. He more than any other will recall those who passed north from Sparta. Especially a woman – travelling on her own?'

Kassandra nodded quietly. 'Then I will seek out Hippokrates,' she said, thankful but dismayed too at the vagueness of the lead. Sokrates made his excuses, citing the need to use the latrines . . . only to head over towards the relaxed-again Thrasymachos and begin torturing him with his questions once more.

Alone again, Kassandra edged through the crowds. Hawk-face was now drenched in his own vomit, two others were drinking straight from amphorae and another was arguing with a wall. She stopped near the trio Sokrates had pointed out earlier: Euripides and Sophocles the poets and lovers, and Aristophanes, the comic wit, standing like an axe between these two sheepish types, his gums flapping and nearby listeners roaring with laughter.

'You must have seen me doing my impression of Kleon? I call it, "The Orange Ape". Tell me, what did you think?'

Those nearby brayed and cackled in praise as Aristophanes hopped from foot to foot grunting and swinging his arms. Then all fell silent and looked to Euripides, who had not given his verdict. Instead, he looked at his sandalled feet.

Aristophanes clapped a firm hand on Euripides' shoulder. 'Good men lead quiet lives, as old Euripides likes to say, don't you, Euripides?'

Euripides opened his mouth but said nothing, nodding shyly instead.

Aristophanes blared on exuberantly with a glowing review of his own dramatic works, while Sophocles shifted and shuffled behind him, trying to make eye contact with his lover. But Aristophanes was set on having Euripides for himself, it seemed.

'All three love each other really,' said a light voice from behind Kassandra.

Kassandra swung round.

A doe-eyed girl stared up at her, biting her lip, face wrinkled with guilt and a dash of defiance.

'Phoibe?'

Phoibe threw her arms around Kassandra's waist. 'I missed you terribly,' she wailed into Kassandra's stola. 'After you left, Markos looked after me well enough, but then he found out about the eye. He convinced me to lend it to him so he could invest it, and promised to double its value.' She sighed.

'Phoibe, you didn't . . .'

'He lost it all.'

Kassandra's teeth ground. 'Of course he did.'

'He was distraught for days on end. It was only new and more dreadful business ideas that brought him back to his usual self. He wanted to steal a herd of cattle from the estate north of Mount Ainos. It was a ludicrous plan that involved me wearing a cow suit.' She shook her head. 'Anyway, it has been a year since you left, and I knew I had to come in search of you. I sneaked aboard one of the supply ships bringing timber to the Piraeus harbour. I now work for Aspasia, wife of Perikles. I am a servant, yes, but at least I don't have to wear a cow suit. I knew you would come here eventually. Everyone does, they say. Tonight, when I saw you, I . . .' She fell silent, her eyes brimming over with tears. Kassandra held her tight, kissing the top of her head, enjoying the familiar scent of her hair, stamping down on the deeper wells of emotion that tried to rise from her heart.

'Tell me why – why did you not return to Kephallonia,' said Phoibe, 'even just to let me know you were well?'

'Because the quest I set out upon has grown horns, tentacles and talons,' Kassandra sighed. 'My mother lives, Phoibe.'

Phoibe's eyes grew moonlike. 'She lives? But you told me –'

Kassandra placed a finger over her lips. Phoibe was one of the few who knew everything. 'I told you what I thought was true. I was wrong. She lives. Where, I don't know. That is why I am in this place. Someone here tonight might know.'

'Aspasia will help you,' she said confidently, straightening up. 'Everyone here knows something, but she knows nearly everything. She is as bright and shrewd as Perikles himself. Brighter, even, say some.'

'Where is she?' Kassandra asked, seeing no women present.

'Oh, she is here,' Phoibe smiled knowingly.

Thucydides and his military men called Phoibe over, waving their empty wine cups. Phoibe rolled her eyes then hurried over to tend to them.

Kassandra moved to the edge of the room, rested a shoulder against a locked door and tried to work out whom to approach next. From behind the door muffled voices spoke. Her ears pricked up and every half-formed word she heard was like a shiny coin landing in her purse. *Anything*, she willed herself to hear, *even the smallest clue.*

'Wider, wider. Yes . . . *yes!*' A squeal of delight. A sucking noise and then a popping sound, quickly followed by a gasp of pleasure and a joint cry of delight from a group of voices. Instinctively, she jolted upright, as if the wood itself were part of this debauched tryst. The door rattled from the force of her movement.

Footsteps, then the door swung open. A golden-haired vision stood within, chiselled and young, standing proud. He was pale-skinned and blue-eyed, wearing just a leather cord around his neck and a diaphanous silk scarf around his waist. *Standing proud in all senses*, Kassandra realized, cocking her head to one side then looking up again. Behind him, the room glowed with the light of a few oil lamps and weltered with sweet incense smoke, steam from a sunken bath and the heat of naked bodies. Men and women writhed on the beds and couches, all across the floor, under the table. Glistening buttocks and bouncing breasts – all of varying standards – moans of pleasure and tangles of limbs.

'Ah, another participant?' the golden-haired man grinned.

'Possibly,' she said, seeing an opening.

'Alkibiades. Perikles' nephew.' He bowed, taking and kissing her hand, his eyes drinking in her body's every contour.

'I'm looking for a woman,' Kassandra said.

Alkibiades' grin widened and he extended a hand, gesturing towards a voluptuous older lady who was sitting on her own by the side of a sunken bath. The woman shot Kassandra a lustful glower, running her tongue across her perfect teeth, her raven hair spilling in coils across her shoulders as she slid her legs apart.

Kassandra arched an eyebrow. 'No, that's not what I meant.'

'A man then?' he suggested, his waist-scarf twitching.

'It depends on what that man can tell me.'

'I can tell you anything you'd like to hear. Come, come.' He beckoned her in.

Kassandra set down her wine and water kraters and stepped inside. 'I seek a woman called –'

Alkibiades shot a hand across her front, like a barrier, halting her and swinging the door closed with a click. With his other hand, still across her front, he traced her breasts. She balled a fist, feeling a strong urge to break his jaw as she had done with the opportunistic Spartan in Stentor's camp ... but then she saw the glint of opportunity.

She relaxed her fist, stepped towards him and pressed her lips to his. He chuckled softly as they kissed, his lips hot and wet, his tongue venturing into her mouth. He wrapped his musclebound arms around her and she felt him guiding her towards a rare free couch, but she halted him with a hand on his broad chest, pulling back, knowing she had the fish on the hook. 'I'm looking for a woman who fled Sparta a long, long time ago,' she said.

Alkibiades whimpered, face still contorted for more kissing, eyes still half-closed. When he realized the tryst was on hold until he answered, he shook his head as if to clear away the haze of desire. 'Fled Sparta? No one *flees* Sparta. And alone?' He blew air through his lips. 'But, let's pretend she did. Come to Athens without a male chaperone and she'd be arrested. Thebes, Boeotia, all the rest, it would be the same. If she was smart, she'd go to the one place where women can be free and independent.'

Kassandra stared at him, her hard eyes demanding the rest.

'Korinth,' he said. 'The Hetaerae of the temples are the heart of that city. Aye, they lie with men for money and gifts, but only because it is the will of the Gods. They are strong, free . . .' His eyes grew distant, his lips quirking with some debauched memory. 'Imaginative.'

She clicked her fingers a few times in front of his eyes, breaking the spell.

He shook his head. 'Anthousa is the one you should speak to. Korinth is in her care as much as Athens is in Perikles' . . .' He sighed, glancing over her shoulder at the door. 'For now, anyway.'

Outside, she heard a muffled voice. Someone speaking in strained, panicked tones. *Herodotos?*

She stepped away from Alkibiades, deliberately brushing his groin scarf. 'Thank you, Alkibiades. Perhaps when next we meet I can show you a thing or two.'

He looked her over once more with a sigh, realizing now that she would not be his conquest.

'If you see Sokrates out there, send him in, will you. I've had my eye on him for an age, and he keeps wriggling out of my grasp with his words – he's like an oiled cat.'

She slipped from the orgy room and back into the andron. No Herodotos. She swung her eyes in every direction. That was when she saw *him* instead. He was no different from the others in his appearance: dressed well, if simply, in an exomis and leather sandals, mutedly chattering with Thucydides' companions. She overheard the name: Hermippus. He wore a squared beard, his thin, greasy dark hair swept back without a parting. She would have thought nothing of him, had she not noticed the one misted eye . . . and the markings on each wrist: jagged, pink scars – only recently healed over. Her mind flickered with images of the last gathering she had attended – a far darker affair – and the masked cur who had sliced his own skin at the snake statue to give an offering of blood.

Do not let the fangs grow dry, go on, give offering . . .

Frozen with indecision for a time, she watched him. Did he know she was here? Was he here to attack Perikles? Phoibe, what about Phoibe? Her heartbeat grew rapid, galloping like a runaway horse. She backed away into a corner of the room, lifting a krater from a table there and pouring herself a full cup of wine. *Let them gasp at how I drink it unwatered*, she scoffed inwardly, *I need this.* As she raised the cup to her lips, a hand caught her elbow.

'Pretend to drink, but do not,' a voice said, soft but strong. 'Hermippus laced that wine with poison. Drink it and you will be unconscious within a trice. One of two things will happen after that. You might never awaken – and that would probably be for the best – or you will come to in a black cave somewhere, chained, at the mercy of Hermippus and his ilk.'

Her flesh crept, but she did as the voice said, 'sipping' on the wine. Hermippus' odd-eyed glances over towards her continued like a slow, steady heartbeat. When he saw her 'drink', the dimples above his beard deepened and a look of great satisfaction spread across his face.

Kassandra stepped behind a polished red-veined marble column, into a colonnade of shadow. There, hidden from the eyes of the room, she turned to the voice. A woman in a purple stola and a golden pectoral. She was older than Kassandra, a beauty too. She wore dark tresses of hair piled atop her head, her face powdered and painted. Although her lips were marked in ochre with a kink of a smile, Kassandra saw how they were in fact set straight, humourless. Her eyes – like dark, inky wells – searched Kassandra's, probing deep within.

'Aspasia?' she whispered.

Aspasia nodded gently. 'Phoibe told me you might need my help. Well, now you have it. Hermippus is here and you can guarantee that so too are more of them. He'll quickly realize that his poison hasn't worked, and whatever gambit they have as a backup plan will befall you next. You need to leave this villa, leave Athens . . . *now.*' Her words were soft and gentle, but at the same time hard as a smith's chisel striking stone.

'But I came all this way to speak with these people. I seek my mother's whereabouts, yet still I have gathered only a few loose pieces of advice: to speak with a healer in Argolis and a temple prostitute in Korinth. Perhaps tomorrow I will leave but tonight I must speak to . . .' Her words tapered off as she saw – down an unlit corridor – a pair of shadows moving into place, filling that passage like sepulchre doors.

'Die tonight and your quest is over,' Aspasia hissed, grabbing her by the biceps. 'Go with what you have. Find out what you can, then return here at a safer time.'

She glanced down the corridor in the other direction. There, two more shadows moved into place.

'Come with me,' Aspasia whispered, guiding her speedily into a small antechamber and closing the door. She moved over to a panel in the wall and cranked the lever beside it. The panel slid away, revealing a web-draped stone stairway that vanished down into the acropolis' bedrock. 'This passage leads to the lower city. I have a man waiting there, he will guide you safely back to the Piraeus docks.'

'But Herodotos –'

'– is already with my man.'

'And Phoibe?'

'She will be safe here,' Aspasia barked, shoving her into the tunnel. 'Now get to your boat and put to sea . . . *Go!*'

8

The masked circle talked quietly. The lone lamp in the centre cast their shadows on the chamber walls: titanic, crooked, inhuman. 'Deimos has served his purpose. He is strong, yes, but he thrashes like a roped bull. Where is he now? None have seen him since he left the Cave of Gaia, when he smashed one of our number's faces to a pulp.'

'He is far more valuable than the one he killed,' another snapped. 'He will return to our heel when we call him.'

Footsteps echoed through the cave. Each of them looked up. Their masks were already locked in unsettling grins, but behind them, each of the Cultists grinned for real as the old messenger came in and slid to one knee, panting.

'It is done?' a Cultist whispered. 'News from Athens. The sister has joined us . . . or she is dead?'

The messenger looked up, his wide, age-lined eyes giving away the answer. 'She escaped,' the old fellow croaked. 'She fled Athens on her ship. Hermippus and the other four of your number who were there to intercept her gave chase aboard two Athenian galleys but . . .' He stopped to gulp. 'The sister's galley was like a shark, smashing one boat in half and setting the second ablaze.'

The Cultist who had spoken stared at the elderly messenger for a time. All heads turned to the gaps in their circle. 'So she has sent five of our members to Hades?' he said with an edge of respect.

The messenger nodded. 'All aboard those galleys perished.'

The Cultist stepped forward, nodding and tapping a finger to the lips of his mask in thought. 'You have done well, old man,' he said, cupping the messenger's jaw in one hand. 'You did as you were asked without fault. You whispered not a word of whom you were working for, I trust?'

The old man nodded pridefully.

'Excellent work.'

He gently placed his other hand on the back of the old man's head, then twisted it all the way to the right . . . then even further. The messenger's head locked up and he yelped. 'What . . . what are you doing?' But the Cultist's hands grew white, shaking with effort. The old messenger slapped and clawed at the masked man's hands, but the Cultist strained and strained until, with a *crack*, the messenger's head snapped round to face backwards. The Cultist stepped back. The messenger's head loosely rolled back to the front and then lolled – the neck hanging at a sickening angle and a shard of sheared vertebrae poking at the underside of the skin. The body flopped forward as the Cultist turned back to his circle.

'The sister's capture has only been delayed. Where is she headed now?'

The Argolid hinterland shimmered in the summer heat. All Argives with their wits about them were indoors, sheltering in the shade of their homes or under trees. Some, however, could not afford to pass up this chance to be here at the broad bay, not while *he* was here. A man, slight and bald with a single surviving lock of brown hair curled at the front of his pate, walked amongst the hundreds who sat or lay: simple countryfolk, heads propped on their robes or on rocks, weeping, moaning; soldiers of Sparta and of Athens, clutching grievous wounds, heedless to the proximity of their foes; mothers cradling silent babies, praying, wailing. He hitched the folds of his purple exomis, set down his wicker basket and crouched by one youth – an apprentice carpenter, he guessed, going by the cuts and callused whorls on his hands. The youngster gazed into the sky, pale and lost, his lips moving slowly, trembling. His face was dotted with red sores.

'My mother and my dog wait on me back on the island of Kea. They said you would fix me,' the youngster whispered. 'Travel to Argolis and the bay near Epidavros, they said. The great Hippokrates is there. He can heal anyone – bring the dead to life again.'

Hippokrates' face creased in a tortured smile. The lad had all of the symptoms.

'All the way here I dreamt of only one thing. Of returning to them, of holding Mother in my arms again, of kissing my dog on the head, letting him lick my face.'

Hippokrates' vision blurred with tears. There was no way home for this lad, not at this stage of the sickness. All that awaited him was a slow, horrific slide into the Ferryman's clutches. 'Here, lad,' he said, stroking the boy's hair and holding a small vial to his lips. 'Here is the cure.'

153

The lad shook with the effort of raising his head, then drank it gladly. Hippokrates stayed there, stroking the boy's head, whispering comforting words to him about the journey home, about his mother and his hound. Hours passed, and the henbane numbed the boy's body, easing his suffering. But it was no cure. Eventually, the lad's eyes – brimming with fondness – slid shut for ever.

He stood, the invisible burden on his shoulders another man heavier. All around him, dozens reached out, moaning weakly for his attentions, many with the same symptoms as the boy. So few amongst them could be saved, he realized. *But I have to try. Please*, he raged inwardly, glancing up to the skies, *let me find a cure*. The Gods did not answer.

He turned towards a woman whose bones showed through her sagging skin, and made to move towards her, when a pair stepped across his path and halted there like gates. He knew instantly they were not patients – neither war-torn soldiers nor countryfolk riven with the strange sickness. In their eyes he saw not hope of salvation but cold malice, glinting like jewels. One, his shoulder-length hair held back from his brow by a bronze circlet, smiled – the expression massively at odds with his eyes.

'Hippokrates,' he chirped. 'We were surprised when we didn't find you at the sanctuary inland. Is that not the place where all healers should practise?'

'Healers should practise where there are sick to heal,' he replied calmly.

The pair shared a look. He knew there and then who they were, even before he saw the lone figure watching from a hillside inland. A woman, black-haired with a white streak near one temple, her expression wintry.

'Why don't you come with us, Hippokrates,' said the second man – a fellow with a head like a misshapen turnip. The hard look that followed underlined that it was not a question.

They led him away from the bay and inland, towards the hill. The track took them through a low dell, ringed with poplars and tinged with the musty odours of ferns and fungi, frogs croaking as they went. Charged with hubris, he had dismissed Perikles' warnings about coming back here alone. Sokrates had implored him too. *Take an escort!* But to bring even a knot of active Athenian hoplites into this land would have been to spread the war here – Argolis, a treacherous, age-old enemy of everyone, perched on the shoulder of Spartan lands and spitting distance across the Saronic Gulf from Athens.

He saw the shapes of masks under the pair's cloaks, and of swords too. *Even take a hired thug*, Thucydides had beseeched him. But no, he had known better.

'How will it end for me?' he said, annoyed by the tremor of fear in his voice.

'Chrysis will decide,' said the turnip-headed one.

The long-haired one added: 'There is a hornet hive up on the hill where she waits. Have you seen a man die from the stings of an angered swarm?' He laughed.

Hippokrates clenched both hands into fists, fighting off his rampaging fear. There would be a short time of pain, then the release of death. That was all. Or . . . he glanced down at his basket. One vial of hemlock in there, enough to end things on his own terms. His heart crashed as he lifted it, breaking the clay seal, moving it towards his lips . . .

And then a thick splash of dark-red matter blinded him.

With a yelp, he staggered backwards, the vial and his basket falling. He pawed the filth from his eyes, realizing it was all over his face and clothes too. He stared at the long-haired one's swaying body: the neck was a wet, red stump and the head was gone. The turnip-headed one was crouched like a cat, head switching this way and that until he saw the shape in the trees, heard the burr of the sling, and launched himself to one side to avoid the next missile.

With a growl, Turnip-head threw up one arm – strapped with a small bronze shield. 'You'll die for that, brigand,' he yelled into the woods. Another bullet spat forth but Turnip-head was swift, angling his arm to catch the missile on the shield. 'You'll run out of bullet-stones before long, and I'm going nowhere!'

That was when she emerged. Like a tigress slinking from her den, draped with worn leathers, a bow across her back, the sling in one hand, hanging slack. She dropped it, then took out a strange half-lance and fell into a poise that matched Turnip-head's.

Kassandra watched him circle, and could tell that he had been a warrior before he had been a Cultist, as lithe as he was ugly. He mock-jabbed a few times, chuckling at her reactions. 'You?' he purred. 'Well, I came for the healer, but I might just have secured an even greater prize today.'

'The same prize Hermippus crowed about before his boat became two smaller boats?' she shot back. 'Before he drowned, screaming?'

'Hermippus was an oaf. A lumbering elephant. I am a scorpion,' he hissed, dropping low and spearing out with lightning speed. Kassandra, having seen his intentions at the last moment, planted a foot on a boulder and sprung over his attack. Sailing over his misshapen head, she speared down, the Leonidas lance splitting his crown and cleaving deep into his brain. A thick soup of black blood and pinkish matter spewed from the cloven skull, and Turnip-head slumped onto the dell floor with a final sigh.

She landed with a side-roll, leaping up to face the corpse, only trusting that he was dead when she saw the ruined head for herself. A snap of ferns behind her brought her swinging round to face the healer. He stumbled and made to run.

'Stop! Sokrates sent me,' she called after him.

He slowed and turned back. 'Sokrates? My friend sent you?' he started, only to grow wide-eyed, looking up and past her shoulder.

Kassandra's head swung too: on the hillside above the dell, Ikaros swooped and darted. The woman with the white streak up there swiped at him as he attacked her, and then she fled.

'Chrysis?'

'You know her?' Hippokrates asked warily.

Kassandra's top lip twitched as she remembered the Cave of Gaia and the praying masked one. 'I know she must die. Where did she flee to?'

Hippokrates held up both hands as if to calm a runaway horse. 'I will tell you, but first we should talk. Come.'

They returned to the bay and walked for a time amongst the injured and sick, Kassandra bathing and bandaging soldiers' torn legs and shoulders while Hippokrates dealt with the less obvious ailments. She tended to a girl of Phoibe's age who had an infected wound on her leg from an animal bite. She tied off the bandage then squeezed the girl's arm and pinched her cheek. The girl giggled. Kassandra smiled briefly, but then thought of Phoibe on her own in Athens, felt a spike of concern and a spark of flame in her heart. Wiping away the smile and caging those emotions – weaknesses that could be the death of her on this quest – she turned to the next patient: a gaunt, groaning man, riddled with sores and drained of strength. There was no wound to clean, no snapped bone to splint. She held his hand for a time, listening to his weak words as he told her about his life as a fletcher. After a time he fell into a light sleep.

'There is something strange arising in Hellas,' Hippokrates said quietly as he stroked the man's forehead.

'The Cult,' Kassandra agreed.

Hippokrates laughed dryly. 'Something else. This sickness. I have not seen its like before. It seems to have arisen in cramped places – settlements with too many bodies inside. And from there it has been carried to the ports, even across the open countryside.'

'If there is a cure, you will find it,' she said firmly.

'For I am the great Hippokrates.' He sighed.

They took a break in the late afternoon light, sitting on

a knoll overlooking the stricken – strewn on the beach like washed-up fish. The sea wind stroked their skin as Hippokrates tore a loaf of bread in half, offering her one part along with a cut of fatty mutton and a boiled egg. She ate quickly, realizing how she had neglected such basic needs during the flight from Athens – eating just scraps here and there. She tossed some mutton to Ikaros. They ate an apple each then washed the meal down with a skinful of cool brook water. Hippokrates flicked a finger towards the small shape anchored up the coast.

'Ah, I see your boat now. And my friend Herodotos is aboard?'

'Much to his dismay,' she said, nodding. 'My captain, Barnabas, is somewhat excitable around him. He begged me to come ashore but I couldn't risk bringing him. I wasn't sure what I might find here.'

'You didn't come here to kill Chrysis, did you?' he said, his eyes searching hers.

'No, but I will kill her,' she said. 'I came to ask you something. I'm looking for someone.'

Hippokrates' lips lifted at one end. 'I remember your mother,' he said.

A thrill raced across Kassandra's skin. 'How . . . how did you know?'

He held up his apple core. 'The apple does not fall far from the tree. I saw her in you the moment you emerged from those trees.'

'So she *did* pass through here?'

Hippokrates' gaze fell to his feet. 'I was so young then – I didn't know how to help. I turned her away. But her look of determination remained – burned into my mind. It has never left me and it never will. Myrrine was fire in the shape of a woman!'

'Do you know where she went?'

Another sigh. 'I do not. But there is a man who might.' He flicked a finger over his shoulder, inland. 'The Sanctuary of Asklepios – where I used to practise – is not what it used to be. Their standards and mine have . . . diverged, shall we say. They seem to think the sick can be cured simply by sitting in their temples and libraries; good for the soul, perhaps, but not so useful when your arm is hanging off.' He shook his head as if to ward off a building diatribe. 'Go there. Speak to Dolops the priest – he lives by the library. Tell him I sent you. He and his forefathers have kept a record of every soul who has passed through these lands. Myrrine was here, and so her name will be amongst them – her name, her ailments, where she went next . . .'

As he described where she would find him, Kassandra felt the flickering flame within, the mere thought of Mother bringing it to life. She caged it, clasping a hand to Hippokrates' shoulder and standing. 'Thank you.'

'Go in good health, Kassandra,' he called after her as she headed inland. 'And be wary. The light is fading and –'

'And the countryside of Argolis is not a safe place to wander,' she finished for him.

'Quite. But there's something else I didn't tell you. This Dolops . . . he is Chrysis' son.'

Night fell as she forged through the woods to the song of chattering crickets, hooting owls and a lone wolf howling somewhere beyond. She spotted the spoor of a lion too, and heard the deep, throaty call of the beast, somewhere nearby in the trees. Taking care to stay downwind of the calls, she picked her way on until she saw an end to the woods ahead.

She parted a wall of ferns to peer across the grounds of the great, weathered sanctuary: even clothed in night's shroud, the landscape was wondrous. Three low mountains stood like sentinels around the area, one bearing the majestic Temple of Apollo, another the birthplace of the legendary Asklepios himself. In the clearing between the mountains, houses of marble were dotted, linked by broad avenues and fine, peaceful gardens. There was a long, majestic portico, within which hunched old priests shuffled; a gymnasium, a small temple, a library, and the abaton itself – the hall where the sick lay – uplit by gently crackling torches; a theatre cut into the hillside and a smattering of simple priestly residences. A low Orphic chant came and went in the night air, sailing from within one temple.

She quietly stepped out into the clearing and made for the priest's home near the library building. Dolops nearly fell from his chair when she entered. She had half expected him to yell, but he did not make a sound. Instead, he stared at her, his face grey and drawn, his wispy hair unkempt. Glancing around his room, she noticed strange writings on the walls, brushed on crudely, the same words over and over: *Why, Mother, why? Let them live!* But no sign of Chrysis?

Still feeling a creeping sense of unease, she sat opposite

him and explained why she had come, who had sent her. His alarm faded a little, especially when he heard Hippokrates' name.

'I'm looking for any clue at all about a woman named Myrrine, please,' she repeated.

His throat bulged as if he were swallowing a plum stone. But after a time he rose, took up a torch and beckoned her, ever silent, into the night. They came to the open ward near the portico. Here, stone tablets were piled high or serried in ranks like hoplites. She frowned, horror-stricken, when he gestured to one. What was this, a tombstone? But he handed her his torch and gestured for her to crouch. She fell to her haunches and passed the torch across the face of the stone. Not a tomb slab, but a record of a patient – just as Hippokrates had claimed. She scanned the inscribed words.

DIODORIS CAME HERE IN THE SPRING WITH ONLY ONE EYE. IN THE NIGHT, AS HE SLEPT IN THE ABATON, THE GODS CAME TO HIM, APPLIED OINTMENT TO HIS EMPTY SOCKET AND THUS HE AWOKE IN THE MORNING WITH TWO HALE EYES!

She arched one eyebrow, just managing to halt a laugh of disbelief. The next stone read:

ALAS! THYSON OF HERMIONE WAS BLIND IN BOTH EYES . . . UNTIL THE TEMPLE HOUND LICKED HIS ORGANS AND HE REJOICED, BLESSED WITH SIGHT AGAIN.

'Organs?' Kassandra mused over which organs these might be.

On and on the colourful stones went: men who swallowed leeches whole so the creatures would eat away their inner diseases; the man who was bitten by a wolf and cured by the fangs of a viper; Asklepios' inventive treatment for dropsy – which involved cutting off the patient's head, draining it of the built-up fluids then setting it back in place.

She felt her eyes grow dry and tired as she read the ever-more ludicrous treatment records. Eventually, she noticed the night veil lighten in the east. Had she been reading for so long? She made to rise from her haunches, when she caught a flash of a word on a nearby tablet that changed everything.

Sparta.

She fell to her knees, eyes scouring this stone. Most of the surface had been hurriedly scratched out.

. . . of Sparta . . . . came here with child. sought . . . pity from the Gods.

She rose. 'Who defaced this stone?'

Dolops' face paled in fear again, as it had done when she had first stepped into his home.

Tired and sore, her patience snapped. 'By all the Gods, will you just tell me. I have travelled across Hellas and this half-ruined stone is all I have. Please, *tell* me!'

His lips parted. The breath halted in her lungs . . . and she saw why he did not speak. The gnarled, ragged stump of grey and black was all that remained of his tongue. It had been recent too, she realized, going by the rawness of the cauterization wounds. 'I'm sorry, I . . . I didn't realize. Look, I need something, something more than this half-message. Help me, please.'

He stared at her, eyes wet with tears, then gazed past her shoulder.

Kassandra's heart thumped as she turned. Nothing. Just the southern border of the Asklepion vale. Then, out there, far beyond . . . she saw it. A pinprick of light in the wooded darkness there.

'The answer lies there?' she asked.

He nodded once, sadly.

She turned away from Dolops and fell into a speedy run. Ikaros swooped down from the portico roof, shadowing her. She plunged into the trees, surged through the undergrowth and barely blinked as she went, lest she lose sight of that strange beacon. At last she saw what it was: a small round, forgotten shrine – dedicated to the healer Apollo Maleatas. It was topped with a cone of red tiles and ringed by columns clad in lichen and moss, some listing and cracked. From within, she heard the gentle crying of a baby. Confused, she crept over to the temple entrance and felt the heat of the orange bubble of candlelight on her skin as she stepped through the doorway. Inside, a woman was crouched, back turned, the crying baby in her arms, before an old drape and an ancient stone altar. Flower petals were scattered across the floor. For a moment, Kassandra's heart flame rose and touched every part of her. It couldn't be, could it? 'M . . . Mother?' she croaked.

The woman rose and turned to her. 'Not quite,' Chrysis

said through a cage of teeth and a shark's smile. She held a dagger over the baby's chest.

Kassandra's heart froze.

'Though I *could* be your mother, if you so wished? My real son, Dolops, is an idiot. I presume it was he who betrayed me?'

Kassandra said nothing.

'Your real mother came here – I realize you've worked that out now,' Chrysis continued.

'With a child,' Kassandra panted, seeing Chrysis, the dagger and the baby in an even bleaker light now. 'What did you do to them? What did you *do*?'

'The baby lived, and this you know also,' Chrysis purred taking a step towards her. 'Deimos is. *my* boy now – despite some of my group complaining about his animal behaviours.'

'And my mother?'

Chrysis' smile deepened. 'I still remember the night she brought me my child. The sad, pathetic thing, crying in the rain. Ah, had I only known then that Myrrine had two children ... but, here you are. My family is complete.'

Kassandra stared at her, head dipped like a bull ready to charge. 'Where. Is. My. Mother?'

'I let her go. Bereft, she was, that I could not save little Alexios.'

'But you said ... but ... you *lied* to her? You told her Alexios had perished?'

'She entrusted him to my care, you see. Alexios was a

remarkable child. The Spartans tried to kill him, but I saved him, raised him. Gave him all the best teachers in art and war. He is mine, as are all the children Hera brings to me.'

Kassandra's veins flooded with ice. 'What are you?'

Chrysis set the baby down on the altar by the candles and took another step towards her. 'You know what I am. You know what my group are. Now, for the puzzle to be complete, we just need you to join us as Deimos has. So, Kassandra . . .' She leaned in to whisper in her ear, the breath hot and wet. 'Will you let me be your mother?'

Kassandra's entire body convulsed in horror, she thrust Chrysis back. Chrysis flailed, then brought her dagger round to point at Kassandra. But when Kassandra drew her spear, Chrysis' eyes flared and she backed away. With a roar, she swept an arm across the altar, knocking the candles and the now-screaming baby to the ground. The hanging drape went up with a *whoosh*, as did the petals and dry bracken on the shrine floor. Chrysis backed out of the rear exit, laughing. 'You cannot catch me, Kassandra, else the babe will die in the flames. You wouldn't want another baby to be lost because of your poor choices, would you?'

Kassandra stood there, torn in two by the dilemma. But a trice was all it took for her to know what was right. The monster, Chrysis, could wait. She plunged into the flames, scooping up the baby, throwing the folds of her exomis around the mite then staggering from the rear exit herself. Coughing, retching and spitting, she fell to her knees, smoke-blackened, eyes stinging. Chrysis would be long gone, she realized. So when she looked up and saw the Cultist standing just a pace ahead, back turned, she froze.

And then Chrysis fell onto her back, her face cleaved with a woodsman's axe.

Dolops walked silently over to the shuddering corpse of his mother and plucked the axe free. He moved his lips silently, speaking to her one last time: *I'm sorry, Mother . . . but now you are gone, the young ones can live.*

With that, he took the babe from Kassandra in his free arm and wandered quietly back through the woods towards the Sanctuary of Asklepios.

9

The masked man stormed across the centre of the chamber, his robes flailing in the wind of his stride. He reached the centre of the circle and hurled the garment down. All stared at it – torn crudely and stained dark brown with dried blood.

'Chrysis was found in the woods. The wolves had ripped most of the meat from her body and so we can't tell how she died. The two posted there with her, however,' he gestured at the fresh gap in the Cult circle, 'died by spear and sling.'

'The sister,' dozens rumbled.

'We should raise one of our silent regiments, send them to Argolis to hunt her. She may be fast and strong, but nobody can fight one thousand spears.'

'She is no longer in the Argolid,' the man in the centre snapped. 'Her boat remains moored there, but she has moved off overland, alone.'

'Then where –'

He threw up a finger for silence, then stepped over to a tessellated section of the floor, showing a map of Hellas. With the toe of his soft leather slipper he traced a line from Argolis, moving north across the countryside and to the collarbone of land bordering Megaris, halting at the dark tile on the coast, underlined by one word.

Korinthia.

One Cultist let a dry laugh spill from his lips. A moment later two more joined in and soon all were enraptured. One – built like an ox and breathing heavily like one too – stepped into the centre and revolved on the spot, arms outstretched in glory. 'There, her journey will end. It is time for me to return home.'

Kassandra felt her lungs working harder than usual as she strode through Korinth's streets. The city was enveloped in a yellowish haze of temple smoke and dust, and the garishly painted and too-high tenements and villas loomed over the road. She had heard much of this city: bustling, Spartan-allied and wealthy. But today the streets were deserted.

The market was but a carcass of empty stalls, untended carts and stockpiles of the region's famous pots and vases – some bare clay, others etched with black-and-orange images of gods and ancient heroes. The taverns were a sea of empty benches and stools. No citizens, no traders, no children at play, no voluptuous and purring *pornai* – for which Korinth was well-known – whoring in the tight alleys. The steps to the high Temple of Aphrodite were bare too. Every so often she heard the creak of a shutter or a snatched whisper, her head swinging to catch sight of pale faces ducking from sight. The people *were* here, but they were in hiding. Terrified, as if fearing an approaching storm. *The war?* she wondered. The war had not scarred this place yet – Korinth was the naval superpower upon which Sparta heavily relied to fend off the Athenian navy, but as of yet, the city's high, grubby walls were intact. She spotted a tavern keeper then. His eyes grew moonlike and he ducked behind a barrel. Unfortunately for him, he was about three times fatter than his screen. She stomped over to him and kicked the cask. 'Out,' she demanded.

The fleshy tavern keeper rose, pretending he had only just seen her, wiping at the barrel top with a cloth. 'Oh, greetings. Wine, food?'

'Anthousa,' Kassandra replied.

The man winced and glanced at his feet again, as if contemplating a second concealment.

She leaned across the barrel, grabbing the man's tunic collar and pulling him over so they were nose-to-nose. He reeked of onions and his skin was riddled with oily black pits. 'I have walked for a day and a night all the way from Argolis to get here. Where is Anthousa, she who leads the Hetaerae?'

Just then, Ikaros swooped in through the tavern's open front, landing on a counter with a shriek, pacing up and down, kicking over a few empty cups.

Another whimper, and then the man answered at last. 'The Hetaerae are all gone. They have abandoned the High Temple. They could not risk staying here.'

Kassandra's brow furrowed. The Hetaerae were held in great esteem. Temple-endorsed mistresses, blessed by the Gods, highly educated and often living in luxury. If anyone was to be chased from the city, the Hetaerae would surely be the last.

'Where?' she squeezed his collar.

'They're at the Spring of Peirene,' he croaked, pointing off towards the south.

'Why?'

'Because he . . . he's supposed to be returning to the city today.'

'Who?'

'The giant – the Monger. He runs the streets where once Anthousa did. Anthousa is cold and cruel at times, but nothing compared to . . . *him*. Many have felt his wrath. He took every coin I had stored in here and I was sure he would take my head too.'

Her eyes darted. *I don't care who this brute is. I must find Anthousa.*

She released him and clicked her fingers, beckoning Ikaros. Ikaros kicked over one last cup and jutted his head aggressively in the tavern keeper's direction. The tavern keeper fell into a ball, covering his head and wailing, before the eagle hopped from the counter and took flight.

Out through the city gates she went. In the hazy light, she thought she spotted the guards up on the gatehouse walkway eyeing her carefully. Or was it just a trick of the light? She cared little and turned her gaze to the high, dusty bluffs about four miles inland and the imposing rocky mount rising from them. The ancient Spring of Peirene lay up there, if the tavern keeper's directional sense was anything to go by. She and Ikaros trekked across the flats, the first winds of autumn scudding across their path, blowing dust onto her sweat-soaked skin as they rounded the many gaping clay pits dotting the plain.

When she reached the bluffs, she climbed the track that

wound up the mount, her head pounding with the effort of the at-times treacherous scramble. One section was a sheer climb with a deadly drop, and she felt the high winds claw at her as if trying to pull her from the fingertip-shallow handholds. When she reached the top, she slung a thankful arm onto the flat ground and began to lever herself up . . . only to stare into the tip of a well-honed sword.

'Another step without my say-so and I'll slit you from neck to groin,' the hard-faced woman spat. Kassandra heard the creak of drawn bows from either side of her, saw two more women training their weapons in her direction, arrows nocked.

Kassandra rose slowly, hands outstretched, palms upwards to show she held no weapon.

The woman flicked her head to the right. Kassandra edged onto the plateau mountaintop in that direction, guided by the sword point. Ikaros screeched and seemed set to come in at a dive, but Kassandra shot him a look and he pulled back. She looked around the windswept heights, dotted with a few cypress and fir trees, but otherwise barren. Then her gaze halted on the low, ancient and gold-painted edifice near the centre. Ashlar blocks and caryatid pillars closed off a small square space inside. In the shade of the columns, women mended clothing, worked wood and carried caught game around on poles. When they saw Kassandra, many froze or backed away. That same look as the Korinthians. She saw a young girl squatting beside a cat, stroking the creature's belly. The grubby stola, the unkempt hair . . . for a moment, she was almost tricked into saying *Phoibe?* But the girl turned, saw her, and scuttled away. The Spartan bars around Kassandra's heart shuddered as her fears for Phoibe tried to escape once more. She dug her nails into her palms to quash such feelings of weakness.

The woman guided Kassandra into the golden building. The wind fell away, there was darkness for a few steps before she emerged into its interior: the centrepiece was a smooth basin of snow-white marble filled with water of a wondrous teal hue that bubbled up through a small natural vent in the pool floor. Some said the ancient spring was born of the eponymous founder's shed tears, others claimed it was created when Pegasus' hoof struck the ground. Scenes of Odysseus' travels adorned the enclosing walls, and some of the women were busy repainting the flaking sections.

The guiding woman halted Kassandra by the poolside. 'Beautiful, isn't it? Well, the most recent of his mercenaries who came up here drowned in that pool.'

'His? You mean the Monger?'

'Don't play the fool,' she said, jabbing the sword into Kassandra's back.

'I do not know and do not want to know the Monger. I come to speak with Anthousa.'

'You have found her.'

Kassandra's mouth dried up. 'I, I am seeking my mother,' she said, trying to turn and face Anthousa. Another jab of the sword kept her facing the pool.

'Who sent you?' Anthousa barked.

'Alkibiades.'

The sword pressure lessened a little. 'He stopped rutting long enough to speak? Impressive.'

'My mother fled from Sparta, long ago. She may have gone by the name of Myrrine.'

'Myrrine?' The sword point fell away completely now. Kassandra dared to turn to her captor. Anthousa's granite features had softened, a faint glow of fondness in her eyes.

'She was here, wasn't she?'

'Aye,' Anthousa said quietly, 'and she left again all too soon.'

It all changed in the blink of an eye, and the sword point rose again. 'She taught me to be who I am now: forged in flames, unbending. A businesswoman. I do not deal in emotions any more. You want to know where she went, I presume?'

Kassandra nodded.

'Then you must do something for me.' She flicked her eyes towards the enclosure opening and the distant, hazy smudge that was Korinth. 'The Monger is rumoured to be returning to the city and his harbour warehouse. Free my home. Kill the Monger.'

Kassandra gazed at the distant city with her. 'I will do anything to find my mother. But tell me: who is the Monger?'

'He is a bloodthirsty fiend. As big as a bull and even stronger.' Anthousa's face crumpled in disgust as she spoke. The women nearest her shrank away at the words. 'He has killed three of my girls already, and holds two more – Roxana and Erinna – hostage. Do you know what he does to his victims? He melts off their flesh, piece by

174

piece, with a hot poker. Only one Hetaera has ever escaped his den.' She looked over to the poolside. A young woman sat there, head bowed. Kassandra could just make out the featureless mesh of scar and the two hollow eye sockets.

Kassandra's mind shot back to the Cave of Gaia – recalling the excitable brute who had been burning out a poor wretch's eyes with a white-hot brand. She realized she knew exactly who and what the Monger was. 'I will kill him, or I will die trying.'

Erinna held out a hand and clasped Roxana's. Both held on tight as the heavy footsteps approached. They stared at the gaunt man sitting opposite them. He was as filthy, bruised and as scared as they were. The footsteps were joined by heavy breathing. Louder, louder . . . and then it all stopped. The cell door clicked and groaned open. The two girls hugged one another, closing their eyes tight, wanting to make these last few moments together count, waiting on the Monger's meaty hands to snatch one of them away.

But it was the man who screamed. They blinked and looked round just in time to see the fellow on his front, clawing at the floor, aghast, the Monger's oily hand wrapped around his ankle, dragging him like a toy. 'Time to burn,' the giant brute grunted as he hauled his latest victim into the dock warehouse's main chamber.

The cell door clicked shut.

'There is no one else,' Roxana whispered, looking round the filthy cell at the places where others had been sitting until one by one each had been dragged away like that. 'Next time, it will be one of us. We will never see Anthousa again.'

Both of them jolted in fright when the cell door clicked again. They stared, seeing the reed that had been skilfully wedged in the door's bolting mechanism – preventing it from locking – floating to the floor, then gawping at the woman standing in the doorway, draped in leathers and weapons. She paced over to them and crouched, her eyes like flint as she waved them up. 'Go, stay low and head for the main doors. Make haste for the spring in the mountains.'

'Will you guide us?'

'I cannot,' said the woman. 'My business here is not done.'

The chamber at the heart of the warehouse was a world of darkness, the air warping with heat and flying orange sparks and rife with the stink of smoke. The Monger stoked the crucible and lifted an iron rod from it, delighting in the white-hot soup that dribbled from the end. The scrawny man tied to the table convulsed and screamed as the rod moved over his face. A single droplet of molten iron landed on the man's cheek, sizzled through his flesh and made its way deep into his skull. His screams grew inhuman. The Monger gripped his head. 'Shut up, dog – you make my head throb with your whimpering.'

'Please, please. No more. I'll do anything, I'll –'

'You'll tell me where in those cursed hills Anthousa and her girls are hiding?' the Monger finished for him.

A silence passed.

Then the chained man sobbed. 'I cannot. That is the one thing I simply cannot do. Nor can any in this city. To betray her is to betray Aphrodite, to offend all of the Go–' His voice rose into a scream as the Monger raised his poker like a cudgel . . . then brought it swishing down breaking the man's bonds and tossing the poker to the floor. For a moment, the fellow was free. He gawped in disbelief.

And then the Monger grabbed the table at one end, tilting it.

'No . . . no . . . *Nooo!*'

Kassandra was crawling along the top of a high pile of grain sacks, watching the gruesome spectacle, when the sweating, hulking giant tilted the table towards the crucible. The scrawny man scrabbled like a cat on a polished floor, before sliding into the molten soup with a piercing death cry. The giant watched, his gleeful face uplit by the glow. It was a mercy that he wore a mask when with the Cult, she thought, for without it, he looked like an ogre – heavy-jawed with no front teeth, his thick bottom lip and dark beard wet with saliva. Suddenly, he switched his head towards the sack pile. Whips of fright struck through her, and she dropped down through a small gap in the pile before he spotted her, into a deep, dark niche. There was a gap through the sacks ahead, affording a view of the crucible and the goings-on. She watched as the Monger edged round to stoke the crucible again, staring at his back and seeing the opportunity to leap through the gap and deal him a clean strike – right between the shoulder blades. She reaffirmed her grip on her spear. The gang of thugs standing in front of the grain sacks, between him and her, numbered twelve in total. They bore cudgels and maces. *They can be tackled*, she told herself. *Don't be a fool*, she concluded moments later.

'Fun's over all too quickly. Who do I burn now, eh? One of the whores?' the Monger snarled, then stared at one of his men. 'Or maybe one of you!'

The man emitted a high-pitched yelp and then pointed at one of his comrades, who gawped in horror. The Monger grabbed the other and dragged him over to the crucible, pushing his face towards the surface, only to stop at the last moment, releasing the guard. 'Ha!' he roared at his joke.

She watched as the Monger briefed them on their business for the next day: their extortion rounds, the muscle that needed to be shown to those who had not coughed up enough . . . and another scouting party into the hills in search of the Hetaerae's leader, Anthousa. On and on for what seemed like hours he droned, and Kassandra felt her eyelids growing heavy. She had not slept the night before in her haste to reach Korinth. Her limbs were sore and her belly untended. She pinched her fingernails into her palm to waken herself. Her mother's voice echoed from memory: *Hesitation only hastens the grave! You have to act, you will only grow weaker. Twelve guards or not, it's now or never.*

She settled into a sprinter's crouch, wiggled her hips a few times, and set her eyes on the Monger's back. He was her target. Kill him and the rest might scatter. *Might.* She gritted her teeth to chase her doubts away, then tensed, ready to lurch from the sack pile . . .

. . . when a cold blade touched the small of her back.

She half-gasped.

'Don't be a fool. Make a move and we're both dead,' a man's voice rumbled.

She rolled her eyes round to see a young dark man in here too, just behind her. He was broodily handsome, bearded and with long hair. She noticed his red cloak. Not one of the Monger's men.

'Aye, a Spartan, and an enemy of the Monger, just like you,' he hissed, reading her mind.

'Who in Hades are you?'

'I am Brasidas,' he whispered.

She had heard the name – spoken in the talks of war she had overheard on her travels. 'The adviser, the officer?'

'A spy, for now. When messengers stopped coming to Sparta from this place, the ephors sent me to be their eyes and ears here, to find out what is going on. I *have* found out – that massive bastard has taken this city for himself. Anthousa was a scheming wretch, but the Monger is far more trouble than she ever was. I have not yet even been able to send word back to the ephors about all of this.'

'Why not?' she hissed as if she was a reprimanding ephor.

He frowned angrily. 'Because I have been hiding amongst these bags for six damned days.' He caught his voice just as it threatened to rise beyond a whisper. '. . . Waiting for the chance to catch that sack of ordure alone.

This is the closest I have come so far, then *you* turn up and ruin it.'

She noticed a faint air of mushrooms wafting from him. 'You've been hiding in here for six days, you say?'

'I made this space inside the sack pile. There's a hole in the floor I've been using as my latrine, and a purse of salted meat and a few flasks of water have kept me strong.'

'Strong indeed.' She sniffed the air again.

But he did not reply. Instead, he was staring at her Leonidas spear, having just noticed it. 'I guessed from your accent that you were from my homeland, but now I *know* you are ... and that you are no ordinary Spartan.' He lowered the blade from her back as he said this.

'I am not a Spartan, not any more,' she whispered in reply.

He made a guttural noise of disgust. 'How can you say that? Do you know how many hold your family in esteem?' he said, gesturing at the lance.

'Held,' she said. 'My family is broken, like my spear, and scattered across all Hellas.'

Brasidas' broody look took on new depths as he pinched his bottom lip in deep thought, then shook his head. 'I never believed what they said about that night ... on Mount Taygetos.'

'So you believe in me, the famous blood that runs in my veins?'

He hesitated, then straightened. 'Aye.'

'Then let us work together. We wait for his guards to disperse, then we strike – kill this monster.'

They settled in silence. Hours passed, and eventually

the Monger dismissed all but three of his men. With the remaining trio, he dragged out a planning table and started to go over the approach they should take into the mountains the following day. 'Across the bluffs, from edge to edge, agreed?' he asked the man nearest to confirm.

'Yes, Master,' said the guard.

'Agreed?' he looked to the next nearest.

'We'll find Anthousa and those Hetaerae bitches. They will work for you or they'll burn.'

'Agreed?' he asked the third.

'It will be done.'

Then the Monger looked up, towards the grain sacks. 'Agreed?'

Silence.

Kassandra felt an awful twist in her stomach.

'I asked you a question, Brasidas. Do you approve of my plan?'

Kassandra felt ice slide across her flesh. She and Brasidas shared a look, just before the sacks forming a roof over their small hide were torn away, the Monger's other nine men grinning down at them, bows nocked and trained.

'Well, well, well,' the Monger growled, seeing Kassandra in there with Brasidas, 'it seems that my prize has doubled.'

The shackles were heavy – and strong enough to hold a bear. The Monger wrenched them tight, drawing Kassandra's last free limb taut and pinning her to the table in the same way the poor man had been bound a short while ago. The close heat of the crucible by the table's side seared her skin.

Nearby, the Monger's guards held the kneeling Brasidas in a maw of spears, his wrists roped together.

'You think I did not know you were in there, Brasidas?' the Monger chuckled, flicking a finger at the now-dismantled sack pile. 'I could smell you, I could hear you. Why didn't I have you killed earlier? Well, I like to let my victims build up a little hope before I put them to a terrible end. Makes it all the more distressing for them, you see. I will rope you by the ankles and dip your head in the molten pool tonight. By all the Gods, I cannot wait to hear you begging for my mercy,' he said, smacking his lips together and rumbling with laughter.

He turned to Kassandra, lifting a poker from the crucible, grinning down at her. 'For you, it will be much, much slower. I knew all along you were coming here. I thought I might have to hunt and catch you, but no, you walked right into my lair. I will burn and peel you until you cry out – not for mercy, but with an oath to serve me, to serve my group.'

'Fuck you,' Kassandra said flatly.

The Monger's face fell, and he lowered the glowing poker onto her thigh. The pain was indescribable. White-hot agony consumed her. She heard a shrill scream and barely realized it was her own. She heard the shackles clanking even tighter as her body convulsed, smelled the horrific stink of her own flesh cooking, and tasted blood as she bit deep into her tongue.

The warehouse shuddered once again as he pressed the

182

rod into her, this time against her flank. She felt the blackness of unconsciousness rise up as if to save her, but shook
her head to stay awake, knowing that if she lost conscious-
ness she would waken in the den of the Cult, or never
again. As she thrashed, she saw the Monger draw a freshly
heated spike from the molten cauldron, and bring it
towards her face. The heat stung her cheeks and nose
even from a hand's width away. When he brought the
sharp, white tip to a finger's width from her eyeball, she
felt the surface of her eye shrivel, a blinding pain shooting
through her head. 'Listen . . . listen. Here comes the pop!'
the Monger purred in glee.

That was when she saw the vision. In the white blur of
heat, she saw something moving, behind the Monger's
dozen. Two more figures, creeping. Erinna, Roxana. Scar-
faced, tear-streaked. She saw them rise and strike like
leopards, one running a guard through from behind,
another braining one with a cudgel. They struck down
two more of the twelve before the rest reacted, and it was
clearly enough to buy Brasidas a breath of hope. The
Spartan leapt up from the mouth of spears, slitting his
wrist ropes on the way, grabbing one lance and tearing the
throat of the holder, then kicking another away.

The blinding white faded, and the heat too, as the
Monger swung away from Kassandra to face the threat.
Half-blind, she heard a thunder of fighting, heard the
Monger roar, then felt the dull *clunk* of her chains being
sheared. 'Up!' Brasidas roared, dragging her from the
table by her wrist, pushing her recovered half-lance into
her hand. She took it all in in a trice: Roxana and Erinna

had not fled as she had told them to. Instead they fought with the fire of wronged souls. Six guards remained with the Monger. Kassandra leapt over to spear the flank of one guard who was locked in combat with the nearest girl, then spun to chop clean through the shin of another.

'Go,' she shouted at the girls, stabbing a finger towards the warehouse doors. 'Get back to Anthousa.'

The girls blinked through tears, nodding and scrambling away at last, mouthing words of gratitude.

Brasidas slew two more guards, before pressing back-to-back with Kassandra, facing the last four thugs and the enraged Monger.

'My sword has sheared,' Brasidas gasped.

'One weapon against five of us,' the Monger growled. 'This will hurt, be assured.' He flicked a finger to his four men. 'Kill them.'

As the four lunged forward, Roxana – racing towards the main doors and freedom – yanked on a rope. From above two of the oncoming guards, a cargo of grain burst from an overhead silo. They vanished under the almighty purge. Kassandra blocked the strike of one of the remaining pair, then rammed her spear into his belly before turning to face the last, who tossed down his weapons and sprinted away.

Brasidas and Kassandra turned to face the Monger now. The brute stood like a bull ready to charge, a spear in each hand, murder in his eyes. Kassandra shot Brasidas a look, holding up a wrist with a trailing length of chain dangling from the shackle there. At once, Brasidas understood, grabbing the broken chain end. The Monger charged at them and together, they rushed for him. Before he could strike, they leapt, the drawn-taut chain catching on his neck, hauling him backwards. He stumbled back two, three, four steps, before his heel stubbed on the base of the brimming crucible. He pitched over and into the molten soup with a strangled cry that turned into an animal moan which filled the night along with the stink of searing meat and burning hair. The ruined mess of flesh and molten metal rose twice, like a drowning man, before the noise faded to nothing.

The citizens of Korinth woke to a dark pall of smoke. They emerged from their homes for the first time in months, nervous and shy, then confused when they heard the rumours: the dockside warehouse had burnt to the ground the night before. More, all had been summoned to the theatre that day. The venue had been closed ever since the Monger had taken the reins here. Slowly, they began to trust the heralds who repeated the summons. By noon, the theatre was packed, with many more on the nearby rooftops and higher streets, peering in at the stage.

Kassandra stood amongst the masses, exhausted, her flank and thigh wrapped in white linen bandages, the seared flesh underneath dressed with a cooling ointment. Brasidas had left as soon as the warehouse had been set alight – returning to Sparta to carry news of the whole affair to the two kings. He had implored her one thing: *Throw the Monger's bones into the water. Let that be the end to it.*

She smiled dryly. *I like you, Brasidas, but too much valour is a weakness. You don't know the full horror of the Monger and his Cult.*

Just then an orator paraded across the stage, telling all that the city was once again free. Voices rose in confusion and disbelief, many looking around for confirmation that this was not some elaborate ruse by the brute to weed out dissenters.

Kassandra waited, waited, waited. And then . . .

Swoosh, judder!

A collective and horrified intake of many thousand breaths brought silence. All stared at the grotesque meld of man and metal that had fallen from the lintel above the stage. It swayed for a time then slowed and hung at a standstill.

Now the masses surged into wails of joy, weeping, prayer, explosions of gratitude to their unknown liberator. Kassandra felt not a crumb of pride. She noticed a shape moving through the crowd towards her.

'Your mother sailed from here on the *Siren Song*,' said Anthousa, 'a boat painted like living flame. She travelled to the Cyclades.'

10

The masked man threw down an iron poker – cold and bent. 'The Monger failed.'

All others in the dark chamber stared at the iron rod.

'He was the strongest of our circle,' one dared to utter.

'The strongest of arm, perhaps, but not of mind,' said another.

'Are we forgetting that we have another, fiercer than the Monger, with blade-sharp wits too?'

'Deimos is not truly one of *us* though, is he? And he is too unpredictable. He roams like a rabid hound, snapping and howling.'

'Exactly,' said the first Cultist. 'So this is our opportunity to use him to the greatest effect . . . or replace him. The sister received some information in Korinth, it seems. She has spent the winter sailing through the Cyclades, fruitlessly searching that archipelago for her mother. Myriad islands, countless towns, confederacies, pirates. She still does not know of Myrrine's whereabouts . . . or that we have her trapped. At this very moment she returns to Athens seeking the wisdom of Perikles and his retinue on the matter.'

'Athens?' said another, as all the rest fell silent.

'Yes,' said the first. 'And are we not now agreed that it is time for a change of the guard in that famous old city?'

'Aye,' rumbled the others in unison.

'So let us send Deimos to change Athens' fate. While he is there, he can greet the sister. She cannot defeat him. Nobody can. She will join us as his replacement, or breathe her last . . .'

Throughout winter, silent snowfall tumbled across the Aegean as the *Adrestia* searched the Cyclades islands. Nights spent shivering in bleak bays, days hailing islanders – none of whom knew anything of Myrrine's whereabouts – and outrunning pirates. But winter was gone and now, in the depths of summer and on the way to Athens, it had shocked the crew to waken and find the seas clouded in a heavy bank of fog – like a hot, wet shroud. Kassandra leaned over the rail of the speeding ship to peer into the grey, her eyes like slits.

'Do not look too long, misthios,' Barnabas advised her. 'Once, I stared into the mist for fear of hitting rocks. Three days and nights, I was awake. Not a blink of sleep. I saw them then: draped on the very rocks I feared. But damn they were beautiful . . . and they sang to me – the sound as sweet as honey. I very nearly lost my wits and steered my boat towards those damned rocks . . . just to hear their sweet song in full and drink in the sight of them . . .' He gazed into the ether dreamily as he spoke, his eyes misting with tears.

Just then, Reza wandered past. 'Ha – I remember that. You nearly steered us into the rocks because you fell asleep!'

Barnabas shot him a sour look, but Reza was already scampering away up the mast.

Kassandra smiled, then turned back to the fog. For a moment the grey parted and they caught a glimpse of the Attikan countryside. She stared: as before, there were the patches of ash and toppled stone where farms and estates had been razed . . . but the crimson camps were nowhere to be seen.

'The Spartan siege is over,' Herodotos whispered.

'For now,' Kassandra mused, knowing Stentor would not relent.

A short while later, Reza cried from somewhere up on the fog-shrouded mast. Barnabas relayed the call to the rest of his crew, and the galley jolted and fell still.

Kassandra feared they might be in the clutches of one of Barnabas' apocryphal sea demons, but the drifting, cool fog parted to reveal the stony towers and wharf of Piraeus harbour. Kassandra, Barnabas and Herodotos stared across the wharf. Near-deserted from what little they could see: no bustling traders and hurrying slaves; no noise either, bar the sad pealing of a distant bell. Wagons sat parked at all angles as if abandoned hastily. Some were on their sides, the contents spilled and part-pillaged. Then came the smell – a stink that hit them like a slap, an insidious and potent stench of decay.

'Gods!' Barnabas croaked, pulling a rag over his nose and mouth. 'What happened here?'

Kassandra paced down from the gangplank first and gazed around the harbour. There was nobody to be seen in the drifting fog. She glanced up at the harbour walls. The few sentries up there each wore rags around their faces too.

'Move on into the city,' one barked down at her, gesturing towards the promenade running inside the enclosing sleeve of the Long Walls. 'Don't touch anything, or anyone.'

Kassandra's flesh crept. *Phoibe?* she mouthed, struck with a sudden need to know that Phoibe was unharmed amidst this strangeness. The cage around her heart began to tremble, the flame within rising. 'Stay with the ship,' she called back to Barnabas, watching from the rail with Ikaros sitting next to him.

Herodotos stepped over by her side. 'I've been on that boat for long enough. I'm coming with you. Besides . . . something is badly wrong here.'

'We speak with Perikles and Aspasia and then we leave,' she agreed as they set off through the grey mist and along the promenade. In the thick fog, she thought she could see the ethereal outline of bulky shapes lining the roadsides ahead. The shanty huts of the refugees, she guessed. There was a strange mix of sound coming from that direction: a drone of flies and a plaintive chant. Weeping too. 'One of them has to know where in the Cyclades I should look for my mother. If I was to search every one of those islands it would take me many years. I couldn't ask Barnabas and his crew to do th—'

She fell silent and stopped in her tracks, Herodotos too. Ahead, the mist swirled and parted: the roadside shapes she had seen were not shanty huts. Those ramshackle shelters were gone. In their place were serried piles of dead, as far as the mist would allow them to see. Hundreds . . . no, *thousands* of cadavers. Some were soldiers, but most were simple people and animals: children, old ones, mothers, dogs and horses too. Grey, staring faces, eyes shrivelled or pecked out by crows, jaws lolling; skin broken, part-rotted or riddled with angry, purulent sores; a dangling detritus of limbs, hair, dripping pus, blood and seeping excrement. The further they went, the higher these piles became, like earth ramparts – almost as high as the Long Walls themselves – and they lined the way as far as the eye could see. The drone of the flies grew deafening. Carrion hawks picked their way across the feast, pecking and tearing stinking, putrefying flesh from the topmost corpses.

'The Spartans found a way inside the walls?' Herodotos croaked.

'No,' Kassandra realized, seeing the sores on some of the dead. 'Much worse. It is the sickness. Hippokrates foresaw this.'

They edged carefully along the way, wary of every out-stretched, rotting arm or leg.

'A sickness, aye, that makes sense,' said Herodotos sadly. 'The Spartans could not break down Perikles' mighty walls. But this pestilence rose within. Too many people crammed in such a small space for so long. The Spartans are gone, but the true enemy now runs riot in the streets.'

They came to the city proper and found more grim corpse-heaps in each corner of the agora. Men and women shuffled past with cloths on their faces, bringing fresh dead to add to the piles. The reek here was overpowering, and now Kassandra had to draw her cloak round to cover her nose and mouth, Herodotos doing likewise.

A hunched woman dropped the body of a young girl on the pile then staggered away, sobbing.

Phoibe! Kassandra gasped inwardly, momentarily mistaking the corpse's face for that of her dear friend.

'How many?' Herodotos croaked to the hunched lady, gesturing to the piles.

'Nearly one in every three now rests upon these towers of bones,' she said. 'I am the last of my family . . . and I feel the fever rising within me. I have asked my neighbour to place me on the heaps when my time comes, but then he too is weak and wracked with delirium. Our armies are crippled by this sickness, and now even the mercenaries and allies are refusing to come here for muster. This plague spares no one,' she sighed.

A troop of citizen hoplites hurried past nearby, cutting across the market square.

'Trouble?' Kassandra asked the woman.

'Always. Kleon seeks to use this plague like a lever, to make the acropolis hill his own. While his people die around him, he gathers militia and buys the loyalty of citizen soldiers.'

The mention of the acropolis brought the eyes of Kassandra and Herodotos to the Pnyx hill, silhouetted by a sad grey finger of light that barely penetrated the fog. The mighty Parthenon and the towering bronze statue of Athena were counterbalanced by the jagged, unfinished walls of the Temple of Athena Nike. Worse, they saw clouds of flies and vultures up there too, hovering in the air above more corpse-heaps. They wished the woman well then climbed the rock-cut stairs to the acropolis plateau and approached Perikles' villa.

'No guards?' Kassandra mused.

'Apart from the few at the harbour and a handful patrolling the city walls, I have seen no armed men at all,' Herodotos agreed.

Still no Phoibe, Kassandra fretted.

They slipped from the drifting fog and inside the villa. All was so different from that night of the symposium. The place was devoid of life, the air thick with the cloying scent of sweet wax, melting on burners to hide the odour of death. Their footsteps echoed as they passed through the andron, then climbed to the second floor. At last, they heard a whisper of life – but a weak and fading one. It was coming from a bedchamber.

'The walls *should* have been our . . . salvation,' the weak voice whispered.

Kassandra beheld the one who had spoken: an emaciated sack of bones lying on the bed. Mist rolled in from the balcony's open shutters, and in the pale light she saw he had a puff of thin, patchy hair and a bedraggled beard. She wondered why Sokrates sat with this stranger, and why Aspasia was sitting with this diseased man, stroking his head lovingly.

Realization fell like a butcher's axe.

'Perikles?' Kassandra uttered.

Aspasia jolted. Sokrates yelped. Perikles' eyes – bulging from his haggard face – rolled to meet hers and Herodotos'. 'Ah . . . misthios, Herodotos,' he croaked. 'I regret that you have to see me this way. It is an embarrassment that I have been . . . stricken with the malaise. The people . . . elected me as a general to lead them. My manifesto was clear: to tell people plainly what needed to be done for the good of them all, to love my homeland and to remain incorruptible. I did these things, but the advocates for peace grew to detest me. Kleon and his war-party loathe me too. And here I lie . . . broken and useless.' His body convulsed with a violent coughing fit. Aspasia held a rag to his lips. When she brought it away, it was stained red. 'The truth lies out in the streets in grim piles: Athena has abandoned Athens and me. I have failed.'

'That's not true, old friend,' Sokrates said calmly. 'If a man grows ill with his efforts to save something he loves, is it failure, or testament to the strength of his love?'

'When this wretched plague claims me, I will miss our chats,' Perikles said, patting Sokrates on the hand.

Aspasia rose and made to leave the room. As she went, she made eye contact with Kassandra. Reading the signal, Kassandra followed her. Outside in the corridor, they were alone.

'Tell me Phoibe has not been stricken with the sickness,' Kassandra blurted out.

Aspasia placed a calming hand on her shoulder. 'Phoibe is well. She is playing in the villa grounds.'

Kassandra felt a great whoosh of relief pour through her like a cooling wind. 'Good,' she said, adopting the calm, aloof demeanour of a misthios once more.

'Did you find Hippokrates?' Aspasia said.

She nodded.

'Did he speak of a cure for this malaise?'

Kassandra's non-response was answer enough. She

expected to see tears in Aspasia's eyes, but she remained impassive, staring. *Some people cage grief in the strangest of ways*, Kassandra thought.

'What of your mother? Did you find her?'

The question surprised Kassandra, who had been unsure whether raising the matter of her own personal problems would be appreciated, given the circumstances. But the distraction was probably a welcome one, she realized.

'No. My journey to Argolis yielded nothing but a fight with a bitch of a Cultist. Korinth too – but at least there I did find a solid clue. It seems that my mother sailed from there in a boat called the *Siren Song* – a ship painted in flames. She went out into the Cyclades.'

Aspasia's eyes narrowed. 'The Cyclades? A ship can sail around that archipelago for years on end and still find new islands.'

'Aye, and that is why I came back to you as you asked me to. I thought you might be able to help guide me?'

Aspasia's head shook slowly. 'I am afraid I cannot. But there is a woman who lives on the Pnyx slopes who once sailed those parts. Xenia is her name. She may know the ship of which you speak. I will talk to her.'

Kassandra nodded in thanks. For all Perikles' fame, it was clear that Aspasia was as wise and shrewd as he. *Perhaps even wiser?* she mused.

Soft footsteps sounded as a slave approached bearing a basin of steaming water and a pile of cloths, quarter-bowing to Aspasia then entering the bedchamber. Herodotos and Sokrates made quick excuses and left.

'Bath time?' Kassandra guessed.

'Aye. I will help bathe him. It is one of the few things I can do for him. You should rest. Most of our workers have perished and so the villa is tired and untended, but treat it as your own, help yourself to wine or bread from the pantry. I will have a proper meal prepared for tonight. You will eat with us, yes?'

Kassandra nodded. Aspasia entered the bedchamber and closed the door with a click, leaving Kassandra to trudge around the villa in a daze. She found a bare room on the upper floor and slumped on a cushioned bench in there, letting her head loll. Some time passed as she thought of all that had happened in these last two years. And then she heard the sweetest sound of laughter from somewhere outside. She ran to the bedchamber's balcony and peered out into the fog, her eyes combing the untended gardens below. Through a spiral of hedgerows Phoibe ran.

'Phoibe!'

The girl stopped and stared up at Kassandra, agog. 'Kass?'

'Wait there,' she called down, 'wait there!'

She turned and sped from the bedchamber and downstairs, then outside and into the gardens. Staggering to a halt before Phoibe, she began to stammer: 'I . . . I . . .' her heart cried out with sweet words of love, yet the long-ago fused bars of the Spartan cage around it kept them prisoner there. Her efforts ended when Phoibe sprung forward and leapt into her arms. Both laughed and Kassandra rose, lifting and swinging the girl round.

'Chara kept me safe,' Kassandra said as they parted, bringing the toy wooden eagle from her purse.

'Perhaps you do not need her any more . . . if your journey is over?' Phoibe said hopefully.

Kassandra smoothed her hair fondly. 'My journey is not over.' She saw Phoibe's face crumple. 'But let us not think of the future. Let's play!'

Phoibe's face lit up again.

They larked around the gardens, Phoibe hiding in the mist and behind the hedgerows, Kassandra catching her with a lion's roar, their shared laughter rolling across the bleak acropolis. When night came, they gathered in Perikles' bedchamber and ate a meal of bread, olives and baked bream with Sokrates, Herodotos and Aspasia, who fed the bedridden Perikles a thin broth. In the candlelight, Herodotos told stories of his travels with Kassandra, Phoibe snuggled into her side, drinking in every detail. Kassandra kissed Phoibe's head as they settled down to sleep in a bed in the slave quarters.

'Tomorrow, we can play again?' Phoibe said, her voice muffled in the pillow. 'We can act out the moment when you fought the army of sheep in Argolis.'

Kassandra smiled – Herodotos had added a few fanciful details to keep the girl entertained. But the smile faded and she stared into the darkness. Aspasia had arranged to speak with her friend Xenia in the morning. With any luck, she would have her answers soon after. *Tomorrow, I must leave.* But there would be time for some fun before setting sail. 'Aye,' she replied, hugging Phoibe tight.

'I love you, Kass,' Phoibe whispered as they lay together.

In the darkness, Kassandra's lips moved to reply, but the words remained unspoken, chained within.

They woke the following morning to an even thicker shroud of fog. After a light breakfast of yoghurt and honey, Phoibe headed out into the gardens while Kassandra sat with the others around Perikles' bed once more. He talked of unfinished business, and his friends tried to comfort him and assure him. But there was one matter he was adamant about. 'There is something I must do: take me to the unfinished temple, aye? Perhaps there I can speak with Athena, ask her for guidance.'

'You are not strong enough,' Aspasia snapped.

'Athena will give me strength.'

Herodotos and Sokrates helped Perikles to rise. He was little more than a skeleton, his nightshirt hanging from him like a sail and his soft slippers too big. They led him from the bedchamber at a shuffle, his arms around their shoulders. Aspasia threw on a cloak and met Kassandra's eyes. 'I will go to speak with Xenia. Wait for me here. If there are answers, I will find them.'

Alone, Kassandra sat and sighed. She felt the gloom of the fog and the state of Perikles tug on her heart like lead weights, dragging her spirits down with them. But then she heard the light patter of footsteps outside, just as she had yesterday. Giggling, the rustle of hedgerows and Phoibe's cry: 'You'll never find me this time, Kass.'

The sound was enough to shear the twines holding those lead weights. Kassandra's heart soared at the promise of another short spell of playful abandon. She rose and flitted downstairs, jogging outside into the mist-shrouded gardens. She darted into the hedgerow maze, ducking and making low lion-noises that had tickled Phoibe so much yesterday. No laughter this time? *She must be well hidden*, thought Kass. She stalked on, grabbing and shaking an overgrown branch. Usually this was enough to send Phoibe into a fit of giggles, falling from whatever nook she had hidden in. But . . . nothing.

She saw something ahead – the mist swirling. A shape. A tall shape.

'Phoibe?' she called, straightening up, stepping towards it. But the shape faded into the fog as she approached it. Then she halted, staring at the small body on the ground before her. So much blood. It oozed from the grievous cleft in Phoibe's chest. The girl's eyes stared lifelessly at her, one hand outstretched.

Kassandra fell to her knees, her soul tearing in two, the bars around her heart bending and shattering, the caged love within turning grey, souring, transformed into rampant sorrow.

'No. No. No . . . no . . . no!'

She passed her shaking hands around Phoibe's body as if desperate to caress her but afraid that touching her would make this terrible vision real. 'Who did this to you?' She wept, clasping Phoibe's hand at last. The hotness of tears on her cheeks felt so strange: the first time she had cried since her childhood.

A few strides away, the tall shape appeared in the mist again. Kassandra's eyes rolled up to see the Cultist standing there, grinning mask staring at her. He held an axe, still wet with Phoibe's blood. Two more masked brutes rose from behind the hedges to flank this one.

'You have a debt to pay, misthios,' screeched the central one. 'You have murdered many of our group, and so you must pay with your service . . . or with your life.'

They paced towards her with the confidence of men who counted victory as a certainty. She stared at them, the tears drying. Rising, she raced towards them with a fire of fury in her heart. She threw up one hand, the small knife in her bracer shooting into the eye slot of the leftmost one's mask. He shuddered then fell like a stone. She leapt to kick the axe from the hands of Phoibe's murderer, then plunged the Leonidas spear into his collarbone, sinking the lance deep down. He fell to his knees in spasms, vomiting black blood. She swung to catch the mace blow of the third on her bracer, then rammed her spear up under his jaw, the point bursting from the top of his head with a spurt of brains. She ripped the lance back, kicking the corpse into the hedges, then fell to one knee by Phoibe once more. Panting, she lifted the body and cradled it. Fumbling in her purse, she brought Chara out, pressing the wooden eagle into Phoibe's still-warm palm then closing the small fingers around it. 'I'm so sorry I wasn't there to protect you.' She bent over to kiss the girl's forehead, then licked her dry lips and – with great difficulty – summoned the words she had long ago been sworn never to speak of. 'I . . . I love y–'

A cry cut across the grim fog, drowning her out. It was the wet gurgle of a man being slain somewhere else up on these heights. Kassandra's every sense sharpened. She lowered Phoibe to the ground, covering her with her cloak, then rising.

'Perikles is in the temple!' a rapacious voice hissed. The voice of a killer. More Cultists? The thud of boots rang out. Kassandra's heart froze. She sped low across the acropolis, seeing one of the few acropolis guard hoplites lying on his side, twitching, his guts torn open. Then another, a strangler's rope still knotted tight around his bruised neck. She came to the unfinished Temple of Athena Nike. Through the half-built ashlar rear wall and the skeletal timber scaffolds, she saw inside: the three finished, blue-painted walls and crackling braziers keeping the fog at bay. Sokrates and Herodotos – Aspasia too – stood around the kneeling Perikles. The Athenian leader gazed up at the statue of the goddess – stripped of gold to fund the war. Two burly guard hoplites stood inside the temple's main doorway. Kassandra breathed a sigh of relief.

'Misthios?' Sokrates asked, spotting her. All twisted to behold her.

She stepped inside through the unfinished wall. 'There are killers on the loose. Phoibe has been murdered and –'

Two pained gasps sounded from the main entrance. All heads now swung that way. The two guard hoplites posted there spasmed, spears working clear of their breastbones from behind, then ripping back violently. The pair fell with wet sighs.

And then Deimos stepped over their bodies and into the temple, glowing in white and gold, his face bent in malice, twirling his twin lances before tossing them down and drawing his short sword with a hiss of iron on leather. He paced over to Perikles, the blade held level like a cursing finger, driving Sokrates, Herodotos and Aspasia back. A handful of masked men filed into place behind Deimos, brandishing spears in support. Deimos sank to a crouch and wrapped a mighty arm around Perikles' neck. He looked up to meet the eyes of Herodotos and Sokrates, Aspasia and finally Kassandra. 'I'm going to destroy everything you ever created,' he whispered in Perikles' ear, placing his blade-edge on the Athenian general's neck.

'Alexios, no,' Kassandra croaked, taking one step forward.

Deimos' arm jerked. Blood spouted and soaked Perikles' gown. His wan body turned grey in a trice. Deimos released the corpse and stood, his white and golden armour streaked with blood.

Herodotos and Sokrates croaked in horror. Aspasia stared in disbelief.

'Now, Sister, I must deal with you as I should have done when last we met,' said Deimos. 'You have been busy since then. But now it is time for a long, long rest.'

He lunged for her. His sheer speed was terrifying, and she could dodge the strike only by throwing herself backwards. She rose in time to leap from a sweeping cut of his blade.

'Go, go!' she yelled at Sokrates, Aspasia and Herodotos, putting herself between them and Deimos and the Cultists. As they fled through the gap in the temple's unfinished wall, she and Deimos circled.

'You are by far the weaker sibling, Sister,' he growled as she tried to fumble her spear free of her belt. 'It will end for you here.'

His sword swung and streaked down her shoulder and lower back, slashing open her leathers and tearing through her triceps, her side suddenly hot with blood. She cried out and staggered backwards, levelling her spear at last.

'You cannot win,' Deimos spat, coming for her again.

He lashed his blade in a flurry of strokes, and it was all she could do to parry. When she saw a glimpse of his calf, she stabbed out – a cut across it would bring him down. But, like a viper's tongue, his blade stabbed down to block, then licked up to slice across her forehead. Her eyes stung as blood rolled across them. Her strength began to ebb as the blood-loss worsened.

Kassandra knew Deimos was right. She could not win. She backed out of the half-built wall, Deimos striding to keep pace with her, then swung her spear with all she had at one of the timber poles holding up the scaffold. With a crack of wood and a rumble, the whole structure of platforms and struts came crashing down, bringing great chunks of stone with it. Grey dust puffed up in a cloud even thicker than the fog, and Kassandra heard Deimos's roar of anger as she turned and ran. A break-neck dash, down the Pnyx steps, leaping from a high wall and onto the rooftop of a market building, plunging down onto the corpse-heaped agora and then all the way along the long road to Piraeus before finally scrambling aboard the *Adrestia*, Herodotos helping her on board, Aspasia there too.

'Put to sea,' she implored Barnabas. '*Now!*'

The ship groaned as it pulled away from the wharf under oar. As it was leaving, she saw a rare break in the fog, and it afforded her a brief sight of the Pnyx hill. A force of men was marching up the marble steps, a regiment of silver and white. Their leader was visible even from this distance, his flame-hair like a torch.

'A new power takes Athens?' Reza gasped, squinting to see.

'Kleon,' Herodotos groaned as the force spilled up and across the acropolis. 'Of all the people to seize upon Perikles' demise, why did it have to be that war-hungry, red-eyed ape?'

Kassandra's mind raced with all that had happened. Then she spotted a lone figure on the jetty. 'Sokrates?' She swung to Barnabas. 'We must turn back.'

'Keep about your present course, misthios,' Sokrates called back from the harbour. 'More than ever, Athens needs me now. I will see that young Phoibe is buried . . . and I will try as best I can to limit the damage of Kleon's rule.'

Kassandra stared at him for a time. 'And you must promise me something else: stay alive!'

He held up one hand in farewell. 'What is life, but an illusion!' he replied, brief for once before the distance and the fog soon stole sight of him away.

For an age, she remained at the ship's rail, gazing into the ether. Only after a while did she realize that Aspasia was doing likewise, staring back at the fading shape of her erstwhile home. No tears, just a cold, solemn glower. The cage of grief within was obviously strong. She edged over to the widow, rehearsing words of comfort. But Aspasia spoke first, without turning to or looking at her.

'I found out what you wanted to know. I can tell you exactly where your mother is.'

11

Kassandra perched alongside Ikaros, high up on the *Adrestia*'s spar, her skin sun-burnished and her lips cracked. The boat's ropes and timbers creaked and groaned and the wind furrowed her loose hair. A year had passed since their flight from Athens – a year of living like prey, the *Adrestia* like a hare and the pursuing Cult galleys like wolves. They had chased hard for months, driving the *Adrestia* north into distant waters, along the Thessalian coast and almost to the distant Hellespont. It was only when winter came that the Cultists realized they could never outpace Barnabas' ship. That was when they had tried to trap and ambush the *Adrestia* instead – once when she put into shore for fresh water, and another time in a narrow strait near Skopelos. Both traps failed. By the time spring came, seven of the Cult boats rested on the sea bed, along with at least eight more masked demons. Now, in the height of summer once more, it seemed that they had finally, *finally* thrown off their pursuers. And so they tacked south again and into more familiar waters. The Cyclades . . .

The island of Naxos.

She eyed the isle: a sun-washed paradise of woods and silvery rock, a gemstone against the sapphire silken sea. Aspasia was in no doubt: Myrrine had gone there from

Korinth. Kassandra stamped upon every flicker of hope that tried to rise. There had been too many false leads, too many grim surprises . . . and another one rose into view as they drew closer.

Boats. No, galleys. Scores of them – all bearing green sails, circling the isle slowly, watchfully. She edged along the spar and hurriedly climbed down the mast.

'Another blockade?' Reza said as she came to the prow alongside him. 'Those boats are from Paros,' he said nodding towards the neighbouring isle just a short way west. Paros was a stark contrast to Naxos, stripped of most of its trees, and the bare hills addled with quarries, great white gouges that looked like the bitemarks of a titan.

'Why would Paros be blockading Naxos?' said another crewman. 'Naxos and Paros are part of the Delian League, allies and both under the protection of Athens.'

'The marble trade drives a wedge deep between these two proud islands,' Herodotos sighed. 'See the quarries? The marble from these parts is famed. Phidias demanded that his materials for the acropolis works were sourced from here. But when one island chews through its own supply and begins to run short –' he gestured towards the many chalky white pits on the bleak hills of Paros, then nodded to bountiful Naxos '– jealous eyes turn towards neighbouring isles.'

'Well,' Barnabas growled, 'I've not spent all this time playing cat and mouse with Cultist vermin and bringing you here just to turn away from a damned blockade.' He caught the eyes of Reza and the nearest crewmen.

Kassandra watched as they leapt into position, as the sails were hoisted and the oars met the water, the keleustes taking up the chant she had first heard on her approach to Megaris.

'*O-opop-O-opop-O-opop* . . .' he boomed, striding up and down the boat's length, passionately punching a fist into his other palm, spittle flying.

The *Adrestia* picked up into a terrific speed, spray lashing Kassandra, the prow pointing at the nearest Parian galley. 'Hold on to something,' she called over to Aspasia and Herodotos.

They did as she said, knuckles white, eyes wide. And then . . .

Nothing.

The ship they sped towards tacked out of their path, and the one behind it had halted, leaving a wide opening in the circle through which they slipped.

Kassandra saw a man by the rail of the stopped galley, draped in a white cape, with a mop of blonde hair and a fleshy face. He smiled at her as the ship passed. It was not a welcoming expression.

'He knows better,' Barnabas chuckled proudly as the *Adrestia* slowed into normal rowing speed and headed on towards the shore.

Unconvinced, Kassandra stared at the man for a time. When they drew closer to the shore, she scanned the sandy beaches. Further along the coast she spotted a pair of the blockading boats coming in to land. Gripped by the sight, she watched as Parian soldiers leapt out, onto the bay. They swarmed like ants past the marble portico of an unfinished bay temple, on towards an old stone fortlet perched on a rocky cape. Herodotos, Barnabas, Reza and the others joined her to watch this swift taking of what was surely a key Naxian shoreholding. Suddenly the grove of carob trees at the top of the shore shuddered. The Parian invaders hesitated, glancing back at the woods . . . just as a knot of Naxian horsemen exploded from them. They lay flat in the saddles, encased in baked brown leather helms and breastplates, holding long pikes, and they exploded into a trilling cry of war. There were only about twenty of them, charging for nearly one hundred Parians. The lead Naxian rider was swift and majestic, carrying a spear high as if in example to the rest, wearing a leather helm and a cage of iron covering the face. This rider ducked a thrown Parian lance and hurled a javelin into the thrower's neck. An instant later the Naxian cavalry wedge plunged home into the invading Parian mass. Men screamed and fell, and Kassandra and all watching knew the cavalry counterattack would be victorious even as the fray fell from sight when they drew closer to the shore.

The sea turned pale turquoise as they reached the shallows, and they passed over a vivid mosaic of colour on the sea bed – a crescent of coral in orange, gold, deep blue and pink.

The hull ground over white sand and the ship came to a rest. Kassandra eyed the thickly wooded hills inland.

'Phoenix Villa,' Aspasia said, pinpointing a settlement on one promontory.

'Go, find her,' said Barnabas, clasping a hand to her shoulder, his eyes wet with tears.

'Aye, misthios, you have struggled long enough to come this far,' agreed Herodotos. 'Waste no more time.'

She moved as if she were on one of her old stealth jobs for Markos, slipping uphill into the island's interior, through lush woods of mulberry and juniper. At one point she heard the thunder of hooves and ducked into the undergrowth, watching as the score of riders from the bay battle galloped along the open track from the beach, their brown armour glistening with semi-dried blood. Victory indeed. When she reached the vicinity of the Phoenix Villa, she found an unwalled town, of which the villa was the centrepiece. In truth, the 'town' was almost part of the woods – trees and outcrops rising beside homes, rope bridges linking sections of the settlement that lay across a narrow ravine, and a waterfall splashing down into an opal-blue tarn. In the glorious sunshine, women carried urns of goats' milk, men carefully lifted shards of honeycomb from bees' nests and children and dogs herded sheep, goats and oxen. She threw a stick into the nearby trees, drawing out the two men guarding the villa's main door, then slipped inside the ancient and grand villa and soon found herself creeping along the wide hallway on the upper floor. That was when she heard the voices.

'Archon, the Parians have crippled our fleet, stolen our trade, silenced our messengers, captured Navarchos Euneas. We are being strangled out of existence,' said a man's voice. Kassandra edged her head around the doorway to see the high, wide council chamber, with polished dark-timber floors and aged rugs. One wall was arrayed with open shutters allowing the sultry air and sunlight to bathe the room. A wide table sat in the centre of the chamber, upon which was pinned a hide map of the islands and nearby waters. Two officers stood, wearing the bloodstained brown cavalry armour of the twenty from the shore battle. They had both prised off their helms to address someone across the room, out of Kassandra's view. Both were disconcertingly young – one more adolescent than adult.

'Still, we drove them off today, Archon,' added the older of the two, 'with you riding at our head, as always. The fortlet on the Ferryman's Finger remains ours – despite the ring of Parian boats, they have no foothold on our shores. Since the day you first came to these shores and drove off the tyrant king, you have been our leader and our shield.' His voice brimmed with pride and veneration and he beat a fist against his chest in salute.

'Do not lose heart,' the archon replied. 'There will be a way to break the noose, to find freedom again.' The sound of the voice was like the note of a golden lyre, stirring up a thousand memories in Kassandra's heart. She began to tremble. When the archon walked into view, armoured like the two officers and holding the cage-visored helm underarm, Kassandra gripped the edge of the doorway, suppressing a gasp, unable to blink or look away.

Mother? she mouthed. There could be no doubting it: her dark hair threaded with silver and held in a braided ring around her crown, eyes edged with age-lines, body hugged with well-scarred armour. Kassandra watched numbly as Myrrine directed the two officers' attentions to the map, giving them clear and firm instructions on where the island's soldiers were to be posted, which landing sites were to be watched and what resources needed to be harvested for new ships, arms and armour.

After a time, Myrrine dismissed the two officers. Kassandra ducked into the shadows as they strode from the room, then edged round the doorway again. Myrrine, alone, had strolled out onto a balcony, shaded from the sun by a striped awning. This was it. This was the moment. Kassandra stepped softly into the room and over to the balcony door behind her. Then a floorboard groaned treacherously and Myrrine swung to face her like a warrior.

Their eyes met for the first time in over twenty-three years. Myrrine stared for an age, frozen in disbelief, then her gaze fell to Kassandra's waist . . . and the Leonidas spear.

'How . . . how can it be?' Myrrine whispered, dropping her helm.

Kassandra drank in the sight of the woman before her. 'Mother,' she whispered in reply.

They came together like gloved hands clapping and remained locked like that for what felt like a glorious eternity. Spikes of emotion rose and fell within Kassandra. It had been the first time she had embraced another since she had cradled poor Phoibe's body, the first time she had let her heart swell like this ever since it had nearly burst with grief that day.

'How? How can it be?' Myrrine croaked. 'Every night, for more than two score years, when I close my eyes I still see you falling.'

They parted just a little, noses a finger's width apart, both faces wet with tears. 'I have so much to tell you, Mother. That night –'

Myrrine placed a finger over her lips. 'No. First, I just want to feel you in my arms again,' she said with a sob, hugging Kassandra even tighter than before.

After an age, they sat together and Kassandra began to tell Myrrine everything: about the night on Mount Taygetos, about Kephallonia, about dear Phoibe, the mission to Megaris and the confrontation with Nikolaos ... and then the bleak dealings with the Cult ever since.

'They have been there all throughout our lives, Mother. It was the Cult of Kosmos – *not* the Oracle – who was behind the foul order to toss little Alexios from the mountain that night.'

Myrrine's hard, unflinching expression told her this was not a surprise. That was when she realized she had not actually told her mother everything. The hardest part of all remained unsaid.

'In Argolis, I uncovered a dark secret,' she said, her body tensing. 'I know you visited the healer's sanctuary.'

'I took Alexios there,' Myrrine said quietly. 'He did not die on the mountain, you see.'

Kassandra smiled sadly. 'I realized that. And that it was you I heard coming through the bone pit that night. I ran when I heard the noise, thinking it was someone coming to finish me off. If only I had possessed the courage to wait.'

Myrrine clasped and squeezed her forearm. 'You are here, after all that has happened to you. You have courage in your marrow, Kassandra. Perhaps if the healers near the Asklepios Sanctuary had managed to save Alexios then he too might have grown to be like –'

'Mother,' she interrupted, eyes closed, tears building. 'Alexios lives.'

Silence.

'Mother?' she said, opening her eyes to see Myrrine staring, haunted.

'I have rebuilt my life from ashes . . . I lived with the shades of you and him on my shoulders. And now you tell me that he too still walks the earth?'

Kassandra nodded sadly.

'Where is he?' she said, then caught her last word as if it were a secret. Her face paled even further and she began to tremble. 'They . . . have him, don't they?'

Kassandra faced Myrrine and they clasped hands. 'The Cult use him as their "champion". They call him Deimos.'

'Deimos? They named my boy after the God of Dread?' Myrrine's eyes searched every patch of the balcony.

'Mother, he is not the boy he might have been had he been raised by you. The Cultist bitch, Chrysis, poisoned his mind, feeding him with hate and anger.'

'Then she will pay,' Myrrine drawled.

'She already has. She took an axe in the face as punishment.'

'Good,' Myrrine snapped, her face twisted in malice, her top lip lifting like a hound satisfied it had driven off a rival . . . then sagging as a deep sob arose from within. 'But my boy . . .'

Kassandra guided her back inside, whispering tender words in her ear.

Months passed. Kassandra and Myrrine ate together, slept in the same bed, walked everywhere as a pair. Kassandra felt her revelation about Alexios was eating at her mother's conscience but she could not help herself from enjoying this precious time with her. She learned of Naxos' troubles and advised where she could. Barnabas, Herodotos and the crew came to the village and were afforded good homes in the leafy paradise. Barnabas even took a fondness to one of the local women, Photina, allowing her to tattoo his back and braid his hair. Reza and his closest crewmen went spear fishing every day on the coast, catching bream then flicking obscene hand gestures at the Parian blockade or standing knee-deep in the shallows, roaring and swinging their genitals at the enemy boats. Herodotos immersed himself in his writings, cataloguing the flora and fauna of this wonderful island, and jotting down local folk tales and making sketches of old ruins. Ikaros spent the days soaring across the forest, finding rich pickings amongst the dense woods. Aspasia withdrew into herself, spending much time alone. Kassandra visited her often though, just to be sure she was well. She was taciturn but never sad. She always seemed to be lost in thought, her eyes bright, her mind engaged in some deep contemplation.

One day Kassandra and Myrrine sat on the balcony again, wearing soft linen robes, looking down the green wooded hill to the shore and the sparkling waters, the sun bathing their bare feet and legs, the awning shading their faces.

Neither spoke for an age, and the silence was blissful. But it did not last.

'We have to find him, to cut him free,' Myrrine said.

Kassandra turned to her mother.

'Whatever Alexios has become,' her mother continued, 'we have to try to save him.'

In truth, Kassandra had known this moment was coming, that those words hovered behind Myrrine's lips and hers, that these few months were but a passing calm. She sucked in a deep breath, preparing to become a misthios once again.

'But . . .' Myrrine gazed across the shore and the sea, 'there is no damned way off this island.'

Kassandra eyed the Parian boat ring, drifting silently round like a school of sharks. 'We got in easily enough.'

Myrrine's eyes grew hooded. 'They let you in, Kassandra. No one gets out. That is why I came here today, to watch, to see if my best remaining sailors might prove me wrong.'

Kassandra followed Myrrine's outstretched hand, the finger pointing to a sleek galley setting sail from the stony turret at the Ferryman's Finger. The boat's hull was emblazoned with yellow, orange and deep red – tongues of flame. The *Siren Song*, Kassandra realized, having seen the wondrous boat in the Naxian harbour. A knot of brown-armoured Naxians were aboard. 'You send your best ship at them?'

'It has to be this way. All my other boats have failed.'

The ship's sail bulged as it sped towards the blockade ring. Myrrine grasped the balcony edge, her nails scraping as she watched. The galley made excellent way, spearing towards a gap between two boats . . . and then the nearest two green-sailed Parian triremes tacked round, scenting blood. They came together upon the *Siren Song*, one ramming the aft through and the other raining arrows on the crew. The Naxian ship pivoted up on its rear as the water frothed and gurgled. Men and timber pieces spread out from the disaster, the Parian archers picking them off with ease. The sounds of distant screaming gradually thinned and ended.

Myrrine slumped. 'Another fifty good soldiers lost. Men I could not afford to lose. I have fewer than one hundred spearmen left on the island.'

Kassandra watched as the Parians roped in one thrashing Naxian. She saw a figure in a white cape aboard the archer ship and realized this was the smiling man from the day they had arrived. He seemed to be directing his crew as they stripped the Naxian survivor naked, then slashed at him with knives. The man screamed, his pale body laced with red lines. Then they roped his ankles and tossed him back in the sea. The blockade continued silently, the roped man being dragged behind the archer ship, leaving a red trail in the water. A short time later, fins broke the surface and the man's screams rose once more as sharks tore him apart.

'The bastard on that boat, who is he?' Kassandra asked.

'The Archon of Paros,' Myrrine replied dryly. 'Silanos.'

'*Silanos?*' The sound of the name was like a bell struck

with a gong. She thought of the eldritch gathering in the Cave of Gaia, the words of the masked one with that same name ringing through her head: *I almost have the mother in my grasp, it* must *be her we focus on.*

Myrrine nodded.

'Mother, Silanos is a Cultist.' She grasped Myrrine by the shoulders. 'Don't you see, this blockade was never about marble or money. It's about *you*, the Cult hunts *you*.' She gazed out over the sea, breathing rapidly. 'We have to get off this island.'

'You've just seen what happened to the last people who tried,' Myrrine said. 'Our only hope was Euneas, my navarchos. He had a theory that there might be a flaw in the blockade pattern.'

'Then summon him,' Kassandra said.

'He vanished at sea, months ago, before you arrived.'

'Where?'

'On a scouting voyage to test his theory about the blockade flaw. He sailed for the Sound of Paros – the narrow channel between the islands.'

'Nobody has found wreckage, or his body?'

'Nothing.'

Kassandra rose. 'If he is our only hope, then we must find him.'

'Misthios, I do feel that this is a bit of a demotion,' Barnabas moaned as he rowed the tiny skiff. His face and arms ran with sweat and the back of his tunic bore a dark circle of perspiration.

'If you still have the breath to moan, then you're not

trying hard enough,' she panted, working the other oar. She glanced over her shoulder to where the rowing boat was headed. There it was, just as they had spotted from the mountain on the island's south-western corner: just off the saltmarshes on the coast was a lone galley, sails hoisted. One of Myrrine's men had confirmed it was Euneas' boat.

The turquoise waters all around them lapped and glinted as they drew closer.

Kassandra dropped her oar and stood to face the vessel, then called out through hands cupped around her mouth. 'Navarchos Euneas.'

The galley bobbed silently, no reply.

'Bring us closer,' she urged Barnabas.

'Navarchos,' she tried again.

With a shriek, Ikaros swooped down and landed on the ship's rail in a flurry of wingbeats. He seemed to be shrugging, confirming Kassandra's suspicions: the boat was deserted. She climbed aboard to find it was so. No signs of a struggle, no blood, dropped items or scrapes on the timbers. Just a forgotten ship, drifting silently in this halo of water between the Naxian shore and the Parian blockade. There were sacks of grain, vases of vinegar and oil, stocks of arrows, tools, all neatly stacked.

She dropped down onto the rowing boat again. 'So why would Euneas bring his ship around here? Mother said he was a bold type.' Her eyes scanned the Naxian coast as she mused, then swung to the Parian cliffs on the far side of the sound. 'Perhaps he drew too close to the enemy isle?'

'You may just be right, misthios,' Barnabas said, leaning forward, peering at the clifftops. 'See how the sun catches on something up there?'

She squinted and saw flashes of metal. Armour? Weapons? Moving too. She cupped a hand to her ear in that direction and heard the soft sound of a man's pleas. Desperate, ragged.

'During our time on Naxos,' Barnabas continued darkly, 'I have heard chilling tales about how Parians execute their captives . . .'

Euneas coughed and spat the mouthful of dust from his lips, only for another spadeful to land on his sun-blistered face. He wriggled his several-months undernourished limbs but found no purchase – buried now almost to his neck. 'Coins, I can get you coins,' he croaked. The two Parians roared with laughter at his continuing attempts to broker a deal and win his freedom.

'The sooner you die,' one said, 'the quicker Naxos falls, we get our hands on your bitch leader . . . and then there will be nothing Silanos cannot do. Why would we trade all that for some petty bribe?'

The second man patted the spade around Euneas' neck, compacting the dust there. Next, he uncorked a pot and tilted it over Euneas' head. Euneas jolted when viscous honey splatted on his hair and rolled down his face in thick streaks.

'Yum,' said the guard. The second guard then walked over to a knobbly pillar of earth nearby and kicked it. Euneas stared at the pillar for a moment, then fell agog at the sudden explosion of glistening black ants that poured from the nest. They scurried and swirled, angered. The two guards hopped up on a rock, chuckling, watching as the ants swarmed towards Euneas, the scent of honey intoxicating. He screamed, and could not bring himself to end his scream and close his mouth as they raced for him, surged over his face, into his mouth, his ears, across his bulging eyeballs, up his nose, through his hair. Each bite was like a droplet of fire. *Gods, no, this is too horrible a way to perish . . .*

Smash!

All of a sudden, the fury of biting fell away. A stench of vinegar curled up Euneas' nostrils and the shards of a broken amphora skidded before him, the liquid inside driving the ants back like a breaker might chase timid bathers from the shallows. He watched as the lithe woman strode before him and faced the pair of guards. One rushed her and fell, jaw ripped off by her strange spear. The second was toppled by a wicked blow to the side of the head, stunned.

Myrrine accepted the gentle words of veneration offered by the Naxian villagers as she walked through the Phoenix Gardens. The scent of summer jasmine, thyme and lemon mixed in the sweltering air as her people chattered and enjoyed the game, fruits and wine she had provided for this feast. It was all she could do, in such dark times – to distract them from the fact that their jewel of an island was a prison to Silanos . . . to the Cult.

'Kassandra is right,' Aspasia whispered, walking by her

side. The Athenian beauty mirrored her own expression: a smile of polished teeth, desperately trying to distract from the troubled eyes. 'The Cult are here for you. Every day you remain here, you are in danger – your people too.'

'I prayed last night,' Myrrine said. 'For the first time in years. I asked the Gods to spirit me from this place, Kassandra by my side.'

'No,' Aspasia whispered. 'Don't you see? That would make things easy for the Cult, for then you and she would be combined as one target.' She linked an arm with Myrrine and pulled her a little closer – ostensibly like two old friends falling into a fond recollection of shared memories. 'You must come away with *me*.'

Myrrine frowned. 'I have spent twenty-three years alone, thinking my daughter dead. I cannot, *will* not, part from her again.' A clack of cups and a refrain of tuneful laughter rose from those around the babbling fountain, and the tanner and his family raised their drinks to her as she passed. 'Archon!' they hailed her. Sanguine, trusting, *good* people. Talons of guilt scraped across her heart. 'Talk of leaving is fanciful. These people, they need me. I could not bear to abandon them. They have been my family for all these years.'

A gasp sounded, a cup fell, heads swung to the low gates of the villa gardens.

Myrrine and Aspasia looked that way. The two brown-shelled guards there parted, dropping their spears and helping the hobbling trio that entered. Myrrine shook free of Aspasia and rushed to them.

'How? Where?' she wept, cupping poor Euneas' swollen red face as Kassandra and Barnabas set him down on a marble bench by a statue of Apollo.

'I tried to . . . explore the Parian . . . cliffs . . .' he panted as helpers came and began dabbing at his angry wounds with wet rags and pastes. 'They beat me, starved me, flayed me for months. I was to die today – my head was to be stripped of flesh by ants. She killed one of my torturers. And the second one . . .'

Kassandra rested her hands on her hips, glancing archly back towards the western stretches of the island and the Sound of Paros. 'The ants did not go unfed.'

Myrrine held her by the shoulders, prideful and elated. But Kassandra's eyes were troubled. 'Daughter?'

Kassandra took her to one side of the crowd around Euneas and handed her a scroll. 'I found this on one of the guards.'

Myrrine frowned, unfurling the hide document. Her eyes widened as she beheld the strange cipher. It was not at all Greek. Dark clouds rolled across her heart as she realized she had seen this before. 'Cultic script,' she said. 'You were right about Silanos.'

'That was never in question,' Kassandra said. 'But when I planted the second guard in the ground, I asked him from whom Silanos took such orders. He said the scroll came from one of the kings.'

'I don't understand. Kings? Which kings?'

Kassandra's eyes rolled up to meet hers. 'One of the two Spartan kings.'

Myrrine's eyes grew distant. 'Once, they had the ephors under their control. Now, it is a king. But . . . which king?'

Kassandra absently shook her head. 'I barely remember King Archidamos. And King Pausanias rose to power after that night – he is but a name to me. The guard certainly did not know: I thought he might confess when the ants rushed for him, but he said that all Cultists retained their anonymity. The traitor king goes by a moniker: the Red-Eyed Lion.'

Myrrine rolled up the scroll, causing the two halves of the broken red wax seal to meet again. Upon the wax disc, the image of a lion's face was stamped. 'Despite all that happened to us in Sparta, we cannot let the wretched king remain on his throne,' Myrrine said through a cage of teeth, shaking. Then she threw her hands in the air, in the direction of the coast. 'Yet we cannot leave this island.'

'Archon,' said Euneas as he edged over towards them, his face now a patchwork of white unguents. 'Kassandra told me how things are. Well, you should not despair, for just before I was captured, I confirmed my suspicions about the Parian blockade pattern. There is a way out. The chances are slim indeed, but if we time it well . . .'

The tanner, the woodsmen, the guards and the herders and all their families had gathered around now. She met the eyes of every single one of them. At last, she smiled sadly. 'It matters not. I shan't be leaving this island.'

'Myrrine?' Aspasia gasped.

'Mother?' Kassandra added. 'The Hollow Land is calling. Can't you hear it? It is time to return to Sparta.'

Myrrine straightened, her chin jutting defiantly. 'I will not slip away and leave my people in the clutches of Silanos. *If* we were to escape, then he would find out eventually. It would be these people who would suffer for it.'

Kassandra glanced at Euneas and flicked her head towards Myrrine. 'Tell her.'

'Tell me what?'

Euneas managed a semi-grin. 'Remember the time I shot two curlews with one arrow, Archon?'

12

Silanos gripped the edge of the ship's rail, his eyes widening with glee. 'By all the Gods, they're coming at us,' he yelped in excitement as a speedy galley cut out towards his vessel from the Naxian shore. It was the *Adrestia* – that ship they had allowed to enter Naxian waters some months back – the one with the sister on board. He stared at the approaching ship's decks, sure he could see her there once again – perched on the rail and holding one of the ropes. And was that . . . 'The mother too!' he gasped. This would be the greatest feat imaginable – to capture and deliver both to the next Cult gathering.

'They're building up to ramming speed,' one of his crew said, a twinge of fear in his voice.

'Let them draw close,' Silanos replied, seeing that the vessel was indeed speeding towards their ship's side, the bronze beak glinting in the sunlight. 'Then signal our boats fore and aft. Bring them round to smash this hulk like pincers.'

'It will be done, Archon,' said the crewman.

'The sister and the mother will be kept in chains,' Silanos enthused to a nearby hand. 'As for the other survivors, we will rope them to lead ingots and toss them into the water, making sure that the rope is long enough for them to kick their way *almost* to the surface – so they can claw at the air with their fingers but not reach it with their mouths. Ah, to watch a man drown is a fine thing. To have him drown within reach of hope makes it all the finer . . . and for the drowning man, those few heartbeats it takes to slip into death must feel like a lifetime!'

A hubbub of confusion from his marines and soldiers arose behind him. 'What's wrong?' he snapped at them, twisting round. He saw for himself before they answered. Where were the trailing and leading boats? Behind his ship, the waters were deserted. The boat following them was trailing somewhere behind the headland of cliffs. And ahead: nothing – the lead boat had already tacked past the hilly coastline there and out of sight. They were alone. His confidence crumbled like a pillar of wet sand hit by a wave as he visualized his ring of blockade boats, then saw this stretch of the Naxian coast for what it was.

'A blind spot . . .' he croaked.

He looked up just as the oncoming Naxian vessel sliced through the waves at an incredible speed, cleaving like an axe for his flagship's side. He saw the malicious glares of the crew, the sun-burnished old captain, the sister perched on the rail and staring right at him, heard the frantic chant of the keleustes *O-opop-O-opop-O-opop!* Faster and faster and faster.

'Brace!' cried one of his crew over the roar of foaming water.

The cry did Silanos little good. The *Adrestia*'s ram plunged into the flagship's timbers, smashing through the rail. Silanos wailed as the deck disintegrated below his feet. He flailed wildly as he plummeted onto the *Adrestia*'s bronze beak, his belly hitting the sharp edge and his body folding over it. He felt a dull snapping sensation, and a sudden weightlessness. A moment later, he plunged into the cold, roaring waters. In the gloom and through the storm of bubbles, he kicked his legs to make for the surface. Oddly, it did no good. Then he noticed ribbons of red rising from below. He looked down to see the ragged mess of skin and intestines – trailing like the arms of an octopus – and the complete absence of the lower half of his body. Bemused, he then spotted the missing half, a short distance away: legs twitching, drifting slowly towards the sea bed. Up above, the great shadows of the two boats parted, the *Adrestia* cutting onto the open sea, leaving behind the smashed remains of his flagship.

He felt a sharp yank at the rags of skin and guts and looked down again to see a school of fish chewing and pulling on the bloody treat. The numbness of it all suddenly faded, and he felt the first waves of white-hot fiery pain surge through his halved body. And he realized he was right: the last few heartbeats for a drowning man to slip into death did indeed feel like a lifetime.

The masked ones stood in silence for a time, their eyes silently counting the many gaps in their circle.

The door to the dark chamber boomed open and another masked Cultist stormed in. His slapping footsteps and heaving shoulders suggested all was not well. 'She's escaped. The fucking *whore* has escaped again. The mother too.'

'But Silanos?'

'Silanos' body lies at the bottom of the sea!'

They rumbled in dismay, before one snapped: 'Where does she head now?'

'Into the snakepit,' said the messenger. 'Sparta.'

The dismay rose into a buzz of enthusiasm. 'Then we should inform the Red-Eyed Lion . . .'

The *Adrestia* cut through the waves, spume puffing on the chill autumnal breeze. Reza dangled on a waist-harness rope from the prow, plucking the remnant splinters of Silanos' galley from the timbers and chiselling at the baked-dry remnants of the enemy crew who had fallen in front of the ram.

Kassandra stood with Myrrine at the stern, under the shade of the scorpion tail. She felt her mother's tension. 'Silanos is dead, the Parian blockade will crumble. More, Aspasia is wise and strong. She will tend to the Naxians faithfully.'

Myrrine nodded slowly in a way that suggested she didn't really want to be reminded about the matter. Aspasia – a refugee fleeing Kleon's Athens – had volunteered to take her place as archon, overseer of Naxos. 'I will always fret over the Naxians, Kassandra, but it is not they of whom I think now: it's what lies ahead.' She scoured the growing, dark outline of land: the first of the three rocky fingers that jutted from the Lakonian coastline. 'The maps say that we look upon Lakonia. But my heart sees a land of ghosts.'

Kassandra felt a stark shiver rise from her toes to her scalp. It brought her thoughts to the one matter she and her mother had not yet broached: Nikolaos' revelation.

'Before we land, there is something I must know,' she said.

Myrrine stiffened.

'Who am I? The man I thought was my father was but a guardian.'

Myrrine's bottom lip quivered. She tried to speak, then broke down in sobs.

Kassandra caught her, held her tight and kissed her head. 'The question has been asked, but you need not answer me now. You can tell me when the time is right.'

Myrrine nodded, locked in Kassandra's embrace.

Footsteps interrupted the moment.

'The coastline is well watched,' said Barnabas, stalking around the ship's edge for the best vantage point. 'See the turrets and beacon fires on the hills? We dare not try to put in near any of them: if they do not rain fire missiles upon us, then the red cloaks will soon descend upon us just as they did to those Athenians at Megaris.'

'You are telling me we cannot land?' Kassandra asked.

Barnabas winked. 'There is nothing the *Adrestia* cannot do.'

Later that day they rounded the second of the three jagged capes. A gale picked up, whistling and choppy, conjuring the sea into a restless, roiling cauldron. Herodotos spent the afternoon at the rail, retching, uttering oaths for mercy in between each purge. They came to a stretch of black cliffs, shining wet and sheer, the sky above bruised and swollen. The coastal tides crashed in upon the rocks with a terrible din, sending foaming jets of spray high into the air. There were no Spartan watchtowers here. Understandable, given that no boat could hope to land in these parts. Yet here, Barnabas gave the order to turn in for the 'shore'.

'You have brought us to the darkest part of the darkest kingdom to land?' Kassandra cried over the howling winds.

Barnabas, hauling on ropes as his men worked the oars and Reza guided the steering paddles, laughed. 'Just wait – you will see.'

The *Adrestia* rolled in towards the black wall. Herodotos wailed in a rather high-pitched fashion, Kassandra and Myrrine both backed away up the deck, fearing that they were to be shredded against the bluffs . . . Until the wall of black seemed to slide apart.

Suddenly, the screaming gale fell away. The boat's flapping, loose ropes fell limp and the lurching vessel settled into a calm drift. Now she saw it: the illusory cleft in the black wall, barely wider than the ship. It led into an oval inlet about an arrowshot wide, ringed by the black heights.

'Few know about this cove,' Barnabas said, his eyes growing distant, his voice falling into an echoing whisper. He looked up at the wide oculus of angry sky above, raised his hands and moved them slowly apart, his face etched with a look of wonder. 'I like to call it "the eye of the Gods".'

Kassandra, Myrrine and Herodotos gazed around the place.

Reza casually ambled past, coiling up a loose rope. 'I call it Kronos' arsehole.'

Deflated, Barnabas called out to his crew to prepare to dock. They disembarked onto a long strip of black rock that served as a natural wharf. As darkness fell, they made a fire in the shelter of an overhang, while the gale raged high above and the sea slapped and gurgled at the cove entrance.

Kassandra chewed on a chunk of bread, dunking it in a pot of Naxian honey every so often. Barnabas and Herodotos were locked in debate, parts of which she overheard.

'It is a fake!' Herodotos scoffed.

Barnabas, affronted, gasped. 'It is *not*! Look!' He held up the medallion to the firelight, unhooking it from his neck and shoving it under Herodotos' nose. 'A *real* piece of Pythagoras' wisdom!'

Kassandra listened keenly now, recalling her chat with Herodotos by the lion statue at Thermopylae, and the talk of the dead legend and his lost knowledge.

'You acquired it on Naxos?' Herodotos quizzed.

'Aye.'

'How much did the peddler charge you for it? What price do they ask for naïveté these days?'

Barnabas leaned back, grumbling a low oath. 'I did not *buy* it,' he said. 'Photina gave it to me.'

'Ah, your Naxian mistress,' Herodotos chuckled.

'Aye. It was a sign of our brief love. It used to belong to her husband, Meliton, before he went missing.'

Kassandra's ears pricked up, the name triggering more memories of the chat at Thermopylae: *One summer I came across a wandering man. A short, round little fellow by the name of Meliton who spent his days sailing the Aegean in a tub of a boat . . . He had been shipwrecked in his youth on the shores of Thera . . .*

Herodotos sat up straight, frowning, now snatching the piece and scrutinizing it carefully.

Kassandra caught a glimpse of the medallion now: it was a shard of black rock, etched with a strange symbol. Herodotos' eyes rolled up from studying the piece to meet hers. She read a thousand questions in his gaze and a thousand more rose in her thoughts.

'How long are we to stay here?' one crewman asked her, breaking the moment.

Kassandra turned to the man, and tried as best she could to recall the lay of the land between here and her old home. As a child she had travelled from Sparta to the coast once with Nikolaos to learn to swim in the rough seas. It had seemed like a colossal journey then, although it had probably taken only a day or so.

'We'll set off tomorrow. I will go alone with my mother.'

Herodotos, Barnabas and the rest of the crew looked up, troubled.

'At least allow some of us to come with you as an escort,' pleaded Barnabas.

'No, it must be Mother and I. Nobody else. We may be gone for some time.'

They had become used to that tone of hers and knew there was no point in persisting.

'Then we must conceal the boat while you are gone,' Barnabas conceded, looking up. 'As well hidden as this cove is, the Spartans send land patrols along these cliffs from time to time. If they glance down here and see a boat, they'll slaughter us.'

'How do you hide a galley, exactly?' Herodotos chuckled.

Barnabas flicked his eyebrows up twice, then nodded to Reza. The helmsman and two others rose and set to work. They lowered the mast, strapped down all the loose fixtures. Next, one man positioned an iron piling against the hull and Reza took up a great hammer and swung it down upon the piling's end. A mighty crunch of timber echoed throughout the cove. As the noise faded, a rushing gurgling sound rose in its place.

'Gods!' Herodotos gasped, the bread falling from his mouth as he watched the *Adrestia* slip calmly under the surface, all but the rail submerged. The two with Reza took turns diving into the cove waters with ropes. Gradually, the galley sunk entirely from view into the inky waters.

'They tie rocks to the hull, to take the galley firmly to the bed of the cove. Her timbers will be preserved down there. None will see her from above. And as long as we stay from sight, none will know we are here. When we need her again we can cut the ropes and seal the hull.'

Herodotos already had his wax tablet out, stylus scurrying across the surface as he tried to capture this odd and intriguing practice. Reza and his two companions came back to the fire and settled down to towel themselves dry. Next, they opened a vase of wine and soon the crew were lost in ribald stories of past adventures, ruddy-cheeked and warm.

Kassandra sat with one arm around Myrrine, drinking

in the sight of her rag-tag band. When a chill lick of wind stole into the cove and touched her neck, she looked up at the dark circle of night sky and the scudding clouds, and thought of the days to come.

They bought a pair of sorrel-red geldings from a Messenian stable, paying double to buy the man's silence when he started to ask questions. The sullen sky cleared and they travelled under a perfect winter blue, trotting across rocky hills, swaddled in woollen blankets against the crisp air and the dogged easterly wind.

After a time, the hills peeled away to reveal the colossal rift ahead: the Hollow Land – a long strip of flat country walled by the Parnon sierra in the east . . . and the Taygetos range in the west. Kassandra felt her emotions rise like a sickness as she stared at the looming heights of Taygetos, hearing the screams and the curses of that wretched night afresh. Ikaros, soaring high above, erupted in a diatribe of shrieking, all seemingly directed at the range. It was only Myrrine's hand on her thigh that scattered the dreadful memories.

Kassandra let her gaze fall to the plain between the mountain ridges, veined with brooks and tributaries, all feeding the silvery artery that was the River Eurotas. Amongst the green-gold cloak of thick forest and swaying wheat, the minor villages lay – houses of timber and brick. The five largest villages were clustered near the heart of the plain, gleaming with the famous blue-veined marble of this land.

Sparta, she mouthed.

She and Myrrine kept good time as they rode, but each felt a tightening in her belly, and neither could help but balk at the growing closeness of their old home, of the past. They entered the Eurotas Forest mid-afternoon, falling under its shady canopy of olive and gnarled oak. All around them the golden branches rustled and whispered conspiratorially, the wind spreading gossip of their return. Drifts of fallen leaves crackled and swirled as the breeze followed them, and every pocket of shade ahead seemed to be in league and packed with spies. But on they went, and they saw neither man nor beast.

Until they heard the deep, menacing growl of a wolf and the panicked screams of children.

Kassandra threw a hand across Myrrine's chest, halting them both. Her eyes grew sharp as blades, seeing through the forest of shadows ahead. Movement. Boys. Three youngsters, heads shaved to the skin, naked bar grubby red cloaks. They leapt and rolled, narrowly avoiding the gnashing jaws of the most immense grey wolf. They were no match for the creature. Two of them were thrown back by the beast's great swishing head, then it leapt upon the third, took him by the throat.

She felt herself slide from the saddle, heard Myrrine hiss for her to stop. 'Kassandra, what are you doing? We are in Sparta and this is Agoge training territory.'

But on she went, until she was at the edge of the clearing. The wolf was shaking the boy like a toy. His face was turning grey, his eyes met Kassandra's . . .

She stepped into the clearing, brandishing her spear, streaking it across the wolf's flank. The wounded creature howled in fright, dropped the boy, then turned and ran. She sank to one knee and cradled the fallen lad. His neck was clearly broken.

'Mother?' the boy croaked, his pupils dilating.

'I'm not your mother,' Kassandra said quietly.

'Tell her that she . . . she should be proud of me. I faced the wolf. I was not afraid.'

Kassandra understood all too well.

'I am so cold,' the boy whimpered.

She lifted a fold of her cloak around him. Within a few final, rattling breaths, the light left his eyes. She set him down.

Just then, a new voice spoke. 'What are you doing here, stranger?'

She swung to see an adult, red-cloaked Spartiate, bearded and wearing his hair in long black ropes. His glare was like copper rods. 'I was passing through. I saw the boys in trouble and tried to help.'

'She lies!' one of the other two boys squealed gleefully. 'She tried to slay the wolf and steal the glory for herself.'

'You interfered with Spartan training and then lied about it?' the adult Spartan hissed. 'There is more honour in that dead boy's heart.' He made a throaty noise to beckon the two surviving lads. One of them picked up the corpse, he and the other muttering in unison: 'Never leave a comrade's body unburied.'

The boys shuffled off past the man, who then offered Kassandra a parting threat. 'You should return to wherever you came from, or you will soon find out just how unforgiving we Spartans are . . .'

She backed through the woods to where Myrrine was saddled. Myrrine glowered at her in a way that made her feel like a seven-year-old again. 'You should not have interfered. These woods are used to harden the boys, make men of them, as well you know.'

'They are no good to Sparta if they end up in a wolf's belly,' she snapped back.

'They are no use to Sparta if they are too weak to kill a wolf!' Myrrine rasped.

They rode on in awkward silence for another hour. At last, Myrrine spoke again. 'It is this place,' she said with an apologetic sigh. 'The air, the smell, the colours, all of it. I feel the oppression, the demands of what it was to be a Spartan when this was my home.'

'But you were right, I should not have tried to save that boy,' Kassandra countered.

'Why? What are you?' Myrrine asked with a tired sigh. 'A Spartan? A Greek? A wanderer?'

'A child of nowhere,' Kassandra finished for her. She met Myrrine's gaze. 'Part of me is Spartan, and I can never change that. But the rest of me? Who am I to deny myself feelings of love, of compassion, of grief?'

Myrrine's lips bent in a reluctant and sad smile. 'You and I think in similar ways. We left our old home as Spartans,' she said after a time. 'We return as very different creatures.'

The pair rode on.

Finally, the trees thinned and they came to Pitana, one of Sparta's five main settlements and Kassandra's birth-town. Like all Spartan towns, it had no walls. *The men of*

Sparta are her walls, their spear tips her borders, one of Nikolaos'
old sayings came back to her.

They emerged from the woods and stepped onto a
broad flagged way, edged with white-walled, red-tiled
homes and workshops. Woodsmoke rose, the sweet scent
mixed with the coppery stink of Spartan black broth, and
the *tink-tink* of a smith's hammer lent a rhythm to the low
priestly chant floating from a small temple at the heart of
the village. Kassandra recognized it all: the meat-smoking
rack by the well where she used to play, the armoury with
the bronze-strapped door, the tavern with the winged-
horse statuette above the entrance lintel. So little had
changed.

They rode, staring straight ahead, hiding all expression, burying the welling memories and emotions inside.
Helot slaves scampered to and fro, backs bent beneath
their burdens, wearing dogskin caps to denote their lowly
status. Red-cloaked Spartiates sat around near the long,
low barrack houses, whetting their spears. Not one of
them went without his weapon.

A woman sat on the porch of her home, grinding grain,
draped in a dark peplos that covered her from neck to
ankle . . . apart from the slit in one side that showed her
leg all the way up to the thigh. A boy – her son, to judge
by his features – crept up behind her, reached out and
plucked one of the small bags of flour from the table by
her side. As he edged away, his face splitting in a grin, his
mother rose and swung round in one motion, the grinding mill, grain and raw wheat spilling everywhere as
she seized him by the throat, lifted him and struck him

backhanded across the face. Kassandra heard the boy's nose breaking. The mother dropped the boy to the ground. 'You clumsy fool! You oaf! You cannot even steal a bag of flour. You will never be strong or skilful enough!'

As the boy endured this verbal barrage, another – the lad's brother, Kassandra realized – stole up and filched two of the scattered flour bags, running away unseen. A few of the watching Spartiates laughed in low rumbles of appreciation, slapping their hands on their thighs in applause.

The pair came to a fork in the road. Right led to Sparta's marble centrepiece – an unwalled citadel on a low mound where the five most ancient villages convened and where the kings were to be found . . . including the treacherous 'Red-Eyed Lion'. But both looked instead to the left, to the sad, forgotten home on Pitana's outskirts. Wordlessly, they guided their horses that way and came to a halt before the iron gates, long since chained shut. Kassandra remembered the innocent beginnings of that night: sitting with Father, Mother and Alexios by the fire. Ikaros, though he had never been in this home, seemed to sense Kassandra's sadness, and he cried plaintively through the gates and towards the door.

'It is ours by rights. It shall be ours again,' said Myrrine, 'once we have rid Sparta of the parasite king.'

'This estate is Stentor's,' a voice spoke, behind them.

Kassandra swung round, seeing the shape of a tall, strapping Spartiate. For a moment she wondered if she might have to fight. Then she saw the man's brooding expression, framed by his smooth, collar-length hair. 'Brasidas?' she whispered.

Myrrine threw a hand across her chest when she tried to step towards him. 'No, Mother, Brasidas is a friend. He helped me kill the Monger.'

Brasidas' brow bent. 'Well, I like to think *you* helped *me* to kill him, but anyway.' He nodded over their heads at the forgotten villa. 'The state holds the house for Stentor. He is ever away at war and so it has lain like this, ever since the Wolf disappeared.'

Myrrine and Kassandra did well not to flinch or look at one another.

'But I know who you two are. I know the place is yours as much as it is Stentor's. The thing is, it's not me you have to convince.' He shot a quick look over his shoulder towards the low marble citadel.

'We came to see the kings, anyway,' Kassandra said.

Brasidas tried to read her for a moment, then quarter-bowed. 'Then perhaps I should introduce you. It has been some time, after all . . .'

The citadel region was nothing like Athens' acropolis. The mound was no higher than a single storey, and the slopes were gentle, paved or blanketed in grass and cypress stands. They walked by an open gymnasium, where naked men raced around a track. Women stood at the side, swearing at the slowest, spitting upon them as they passed. When one stumbled and fell, a woman cursed in derision, vaulted the wooden fence and tore off her robe, then broke into a sprint. Her face bent with effort as she caught up with the males, who looked momentarily ashamed and searched for more speed from their tired limbs. The onlookers roared in delight, cheering as the woman runner kept pace and challenged for the lead. Off to one side, men were having their bodies oiled by Helots, while an already-gleaming pair tied each other in knots in a bout of pankration. They passed a theatre, the pale stone steps dotted with Spartiates who cheered and drummed their fists in applause as an actor played out the legend of Kadmos. The man leapt and rolled in a display of martial excellence around three Helots draped in a gaudily painted costume that was supposed to be the Theban dragon. From another direction they heard the pained bleating of a sheep, rolling down from a nearby hillock. Up there, the sheep sighed its last on the altar to Venus Morpho, as a bloodstained priest held up the beast's shining heart to the skies and sang some ancient prayer.

When they came to the base of the central mound, they passed by two young, shaven-headed men lashing their bakteriya staffs at a poor, grounded Helot. Kassandra's stomach twisted. The two were of the krypteia, she realized: graduates from the Agoge, not yet allowed to grow their hair or beards, but permitted to terrorize the slave underclass, to keep them in a perpetual state of dread.

'Look me in the eye, would you, dog?' one screamed in the downed Helot's nearly pulped face. Other Helots stood nearby, heads bowed, doing nothing. When the beaten slave fell unconscious, the perpetrator strode over to one of the nearby Helots and thrust out an expectant hand, not even looking the slave in the face. The slave handed him a towel without hesitation, and the Spartan wiped his hands of blood then threw the towel at the Helot's feet. For all the Cult was responsible for the terrible things that had happened here in her youth, Sparta herself was a cruel and unforgiving creature, red in tooth and claw.

As they climbed the mound, they passed an old ashlar shrine. Kassandra had almost forgotten about its existence until she felt her spear whisper to her, saw the flashbacks from Thermopylae again. A thrill chased over her as she looked at the old tomb and mouthed the legendary name etched on the entrance lintel: *Leonidas*.

'He walks with us,' Myrrine encouraged her. 'His bloodline is good, true, strong.'

They left the tomb behind and the top of the mound rolled into view, the centrepiece being a rectangular royal hall topped with a red-tiled roof and supported by pale-blue Doric columns. A warlike statue of Zeus Agetor stood over the high doorway, glaring down at their approach. A song of muffled chaos sounded beyond the tall doors. Two guards stood watch before this entrance. They were encased in decorative ceremonial armour – or as decorative as Spartans could be. They wore highly polished Korinthian-style helms and moulded leather thoraxes, bronze bands on their biceps and blood-red cloaks. Both held fine spears – the blades patterned like the Leonidas lance – and carried not lambda shields but stark black ones. The Hippeis, she remembered – the few hundred chosen men who formed the royal guard. They would not move aside for just anyone. Kassandra saw

243

their eyes dart in the eyeholes of their helms as they drew closer, noticed their bodies rock forward just a fraction, ready to challenge.

Brasidas stepped before them and threw out a hand in salute. '*Khaire*. I bring friends who seek counsel with the kings.'

The guards threw their hands in salute. 'Lochagos Brasidas!' they boomed in unison and parted without question.

'Lochagos?' Kassandra whispered as the doors opened. 'You now lead one of the five sacred regiments?'

'You are not the only one who has been busy, misthios,' he said with the barest quirk of his lips.

The doors swung open and the muffled song of strife hit them in full like a dragon's roar.

Hundreds of men heckled and jostled, roaring, punching the air, spittle flying. Two brawlers rolled across the floor, each bearing a spear. For a moment as they stepped inside, Kassandra thought she had been led to a Kephallonian tavern. But then she got a better look at the two on the floor: a young, pleasant-looking man and an older, hoary one, with a mane of dry grey hair and bloodshot, furious eyes . . . *King Archidamos?*

Just then the two rolled apart, Archidamos leapt up and whirled his spear overhead, bringing the point expertly down to rest on the still-floored younger man's throat. 'Yield, Pausanias?' he snarled through clenched teeth.

Pausanias, chest rising and falling, face etched with a similar malice, growled like an angered mastiff, then waved a derisive hand. 'Aye.'

The spear was lowered, the crowds cheered and both

kings' faces changed. Archidamos cackled in delight, Pausanias took his offered hand and rose, grinning. 'Archidamos' edict stands,' he conceded. 'We send a levy of Messenians to support the effort in Boeotia.'

Kassandra blinked to be sure of what she had seen. She had never set foot inside this place as a child, but she had heard rumours. She had even heard one drunken Athenian at Perikles' symposium mocking the Spartans' primitive means of voting. *They opt for the proposal of whoever garners the loudest cheer*, that old goat had scoffed. If only he had seen this: opting for the wisdom of whomever could kick more shit out of the other.

The wild audience retreated then, like a wave drawing back from shore. They settled on tiered benches lining the hall. Kassandra recognized the biggest group: the Gerousia – twenty-eight ancient things, hunched and bald, but rumoured to be laden with wisdom. When the two kings took their plinth chairs at the far end of the hall, the Gerousia stamped their walking canes on the ground in veneration. She also recognized a smaller group: five men in grey robes who stood on the plinth behind the kings' seats and made no such gesture of adoration. The ephors. Kassandra's heart turned to stone as she eyed them all, remembering the vulture-like one amongst them who had thrown Alexios from the mountain ... before taking the plunge himself. But her hatred eased as she saw five faces of men in their thirties and forties. None had been part of what happened that night. The ephors were not an evil force. *It was the Cult*, she reminded herself. *It has always been the Cult, working their way into any gap in the stonework.* Yes, the ephors owed the kings no adoration, but that was their purpose – to keep the monarchs in check. *Sparta: the two-headed dog, chained around the neck by a five headed master!*

'Brasidas,' Pausanias boomed, extending his arms in greeting. 'What do you bring for us today?'

Brasidas led Kassandra and Myrrine to the foot of the low plinth upon which the kings sat. As he began to introduce them, Kassandra noticed that for all Pausanias' eagerness, Archidamos sunk back into his throne, his mane settling on his shoulders, his face melting into a look of suspicion and disdain, and those blood-veined eyes searching Kassandra and Myrrine like a butcher judging a cut of meat.

'. . . they come to lay claim to an ancestral estate. One that lies unoccupied.'

'Who are they?' Pausanias asked, intrigued. 'What line, which estate?'

Just then, Archidamos' bloodshot eyes flared as he at last recognized Myrrine. 'You,' he roared, rising, the legs of his throne scraping on stone. His glower turned upon Kassandra, seeing the resemblance, the puzzle clicking together. *'And you!'*

With a guttural roar, he snatched up his spear and took a lunge down the few steps towards them. It was only Pausanias' swift reactions that halted him.

'Unhand me or by Zeus Agetor, I will skewer you,' Archidamos snarled.

'I don't understand. Why do they anger you so?' Pausanias complained.

'Because they are of the line of Leonidas . . . the shamed bloodline.'

Pausanias' face paled. He stared at Kassandra and Myrrine. 'The Taygetos disaster, all those years ago?'

Kassandra said nothing. The glassy film that rose across her eyes was answer enough.

'And they dare to return,' Archidamos confirmed. 'I thought you both dead, and better for you had it been that way.'

Pausanias stepped down between the malevolent king and the two women. 'Yet they come humbly before us. Brasidas vouches for them, yes?'

Brasidas nodded once. 'Kassandra has performed unsolicited and heroic acts for Sparta in these years of war. She helped me free Korinth from the brigand who had seized that city.'

Pausanias turned back to Archidamos. 'And they are of the line of our most famous king. Perhaps we should not be so quick to turn upon them . . . aye?' He reasoned further with the older king, cagey and respectful. It took an age, Archidamos' eyes still blazing over his shoulder at Kassandra and Myrrine. But, at last, the elderly monarch stepped back, slumping once more in his throne. 'If you want your estate back,' he grunted, 'then you will have to do something for me. Chase away your past shame. Prove to me you are worthy.'

Kassandra waited, watching as the fire in his eyes rose, a grin of yellowing teeth spreading across his face.

'Travel north in the spring, aid the effort in Boeotia, help secure that land for Sparta.'

The onlooking Gerousia gasped at this – surely a measure of the task.

Pausanias pounced on the sliver of accord. 'That seems to be a fair balance, aye? And while you winter here in wait of spring, I will arrange a place for you to stay.'

He clapped his hands. A Helot hurried to him with a wax slab. He muttered something to the slave, who scratched the arrangement onto the slab, before Pausanias pressed his ring into the wax to approve the requisition.

A signet ring! Kassandra's breath halted and her senses sharpened as she and Myrrine stared at the ring. It bore an emblem of . . . a crescent moon. *No lion seal?* she thought. *Then it must be* . . . Her gaze rolled towards Archidamos, who continued to glare back, eyes hooded. She glanced down at his callused hands, folded, covering his own seal-ring.

'It is a small home, but one I think you will find comfortable,' Pausanias continued, snapping the tablet closed. 'And over the cold months, you can help our champion, Testikles, to prepare for the coming Olympics. He needs as many training partners as he can find.'

'So, scion of Leonidas,' said Archidamos, his grin growing, 'you accept my task?'

He unfolded his hands and Kassandra stared as the seal-ring was exposed. Her heart thumped . . . and then she saw that it bore the image of . . . a soaring hawk. *What? How?*

'Is something wrong?' Archidamos chuckled.

Kassandra had never been certain of anything in her

life. But here, now, she felt an iron assurance that Archidamos was the traitor-king – that she was being sent north into Boeotia to die. If a trap awaited there, then so too perhaps did evidence of his Cultic ties.

She sensed the Gerousia, the ephors and the Hippeis guards all staring at her, awaiting her answer.

'I will do as you ask.'

13

'Come back!' Testikles roared. 'Oil me!'

Kassandra lifted her cloak and slung it over her naked body. 'Oil yourself. You're drunk . . . and in terrible condition.' She paced away from the gymnasium, leaving the wayward champion rolling around in the dust where she had knocked him for the third bout of pankration in a row. He was an idiot, but she liked him – possibly because he was a rather un-Spartan Spartan, fond of humour and pranks . . . and wine.

It had been a long winter, marked with drunken nights of epic Spartan poetry, games, races and craft. She had even managed to convince Pausanias to allow Barnabas, Herodotos and the crew to come here from their grim cove, and now they lived as guests of the young king. The citadel ward was cloaked in a thin shell of frost, but the first snowdrops sprouted on the meadows around the temples, and birds sang in the cypress trees. Spring was all but here. Tomorrow, she would set off for the north – a misthios once more – to turn the struggle in distant Boeotia. One thing she had learned in winter was just how ensconced the Spartan and Athenian forces were in those lands. She felt like a fool for agreeing to Archidamos' demands. One thing she certainly had not found over the winter was proof of the old king's secret. The man was a snake, she was sure. Yet she could not accuse or attack him as a Cultist until she had proof that it was so.

She passed their still-chained estate, then stopped off at the small two-room house they had been granted by Pausanias. There she washed and sat in the doorway of the home, drinking a long draught of berry water. Her gaze slid across Pitana – to Leonidas' ashlar tomb. It was almost noon, she realized. With a tired sigh she rose and walked over there.

'Why here, Mother?' She sighed absently, wondering why Myrrine had asked to meet her at the tomb come midday. Brasidas and Myrrine were to leave Sparta tomorrow also. They had arranged to travel to neighbouring Arkadia over the spring and summer, Mother having found evidence suggesting that Lagos, Archon of Arkadia was a Cultist too. If he was, then he could surely be 'convinced' to betray the identity of the rogue Spartan king.

She stepped inside the ancient tomb. Myrrine was kneeling by a lit sconce under the solemn, ascetic statue of King Leonidas, naked bar helm, spear and shield. Kassandra knelt beside her mother.

'Leonidas was Sparta's last true hero,' Myrrine said. 'We would all be under the Persian yoke were it not for his courage.'

'What has that to do with me and my journey north – where Greek will slay Greek?'

'Do you know why Leonidas went to the Hot Gates, despite the odds?'

'Because he was strong, heroic, unlike me,' Kassandra snapped.

'Hold out your spear,' Myrrine said calmly.

Kassandra narrowed her eyes suspiciously, but did as asked. 'The last time anyone asked me to do this was when Herodotos –'

Myrrine moved the spear towards the statue and a jolt of lightning shot through Kassandra.

I am in the Kings' Hall – but it seems different: the ancient thrones brighter, less worn . . . and empty.

'Sparta will not go to war. The Pythia has spoken,' screams a skeleton of a man behind one throne. An ephor, I realize. The four others bay in agreement. Some of them wear or clutch those foul masks. Kneeling in their midst is a shrivelled old hag, muttering, rocking. I recognize the diaphanous robes, the dripping trinkets. The Pythia! They have the Oracle at their heel like a dog!

The lone figure at the foot of the throne-plinth steps, back turned to me, broadens. 'All of this talk about the Pythia! The Pythia! Well the Pythia says only what you tell her to say. She has been your puppet for far too long. The time has come to cut her strings.'

'Oh Leonidas, the days of heroes are over. You think your blood makes you special? If we opened your veins it would spill to the ground and disappear through the cracks. You are no one.'

I realize where I am now, and when.

Leonidas lifts his spear and points it at the ephor. 'Nothing, am I? Step down and face me; you are more than welcome to find out.'

Now the Oracle stops muttering and lifts her ancient head. She places a gentle hand on Leonidas' spearhead, pushing it down. 'Why do you fight certainty, Son of the Lion? Xerxes will unite us. He will bring Order to Chaos.'

My blood runs cold. Why are the Oracle and the ephors asking

the Spartan King and his army to stand meekly aside for Xerxes,
King of Kings, Master of Persia, and his vast armies?

The ephor's face peels open in a gleeful grin. 'You see? Defy the
Pythia and everything you stand for will fall.'

Leonidas stares at them all for a time, then swings on his heel.
'Prepare the men,' he thunders as he strides away from the plinth. 'If
Xerxes wants Sparta then he will have to go through me.' He passes
through me like a wraith, and in a flash of white, it is over.

She found herself on her knees beside Myrrine.

'You see?' her mother said. 'Leonidas went to war to
save Sparta from Persia . . . and from the Cult.'

'They were here, weeded into Sparta's foundations,
even then?'

'Even then,' Myrrine confirmed. 'Our return to Sparta
has allowed me to find out much. All of it grim. But now
you must go north, Kassandra. Think not of Archidamos
or the past. Simply survive . . . and find the proof we
need – to tear the black roots of this vile parasite from our
homeland for once and for ever.'

The lonely clop of the gelding's hooves lulled Kassandra
into misty reveries of the past – of the recent few years
and the storm of war she had been drawn into, and of the
older times, still lodged in her heart like rusting hooks.
Suddenly she heard the beats of many hooves and looked
up, startled. But the Boeotian hills were deserted – just
grey scrap and green brush, shimmering in the early summer heat. The valleys were growing high around her, she
realized, and the ghost riders were merely echoes of her

own mount. *I'm nearly there*, she realized, eyeing the path ahead that rose into the mountains, silvery and magnificent against the cobalt sky. She smiled, seeing Ikaros gliding up there, her forward scout. No sound from him — a good sign. She slid an apple from her saddlebag and crunched through it absently, the cold, sweet flesh pleasant. She slowed a little to slide forward and feed the core to the gelding. That was when an odd thing happened. The echoes of the beast's hooves slowed in a strange way — as if the echoes behind her had taken a little *too* long to slow. Her back, slick with sweat, prickled with a sense of unease. She twisted in the saddle to look from whence she had come. But now, with the gelding stilled, there was no sound other than the frantic chatter of the cicadas, the playful gurgle of a stream and the hollow drumming of a woodpecker in a pine grove.

She sneered with a confidence she did not feel, then set off on her way again. The whole time, the echoing hooves sounded . . . wrong. For every part of the remaining journey she rested one hand inside her cloak, upon the haft of the broken lance.

But the phantom echoes never took the shape of any real threat, and by late afternoon, she beheld the argent peak ahead: Mount Helicon. She spotted a ring of spears up on a plateau, and the red-cloaked sentries and white tents within. She moved her hand from her spear and to the hide scroll, then clicked her tongue to gee the gelding into a canter uphill towards the camp entrance. When the two Spartiates flanking the gate saw her, they swung their spears level and raised their shields, murder in their eyes.

She drew the scroll as if it were a weapon. They saw the markings on it and let her through.

She dismounted, tethered her gelding near a feeding trough, then set off on foot. As she moved through the tented barracks, she combed her gaze across every detail, using her peripheral vision to take it all in. *All I need is the smallest of clues, Archidamos. All will know you are one of the masked ones, and your false reign as King of Sparta will end. The Cult will surely crumble too.* Eventually, she came to the command pavilion – an off-white tent a little larger than the rest, with the sides rolled up so the many Helots and soldiers could come and go with news and refreshments to fuel what looked like frantic talks. She saw the Spartan commander standing over a table, shoulders broad and head stooped, sweeping over a map again and again. The others around him cawed and brayed with contradictory advice. For a moment, she felt sympathy for the leader . . . and then he looked up.

She halted in her tracks. 'Stentor?'

Stentor's face paled, then his cheeks glowed red, and his lips grew thin as a blade. He stepped away from the table, swept the nearest adviser from his path and strode over to her.

'I did not realize it was you who was in command of –'

Whack!

His knuckles caught her square on the mouth and a white spark struck through her head. A moment later, she realized she was on her back, head spinning. '*Malákas!*' she groaned, then saw her attacker perched over her, his face ablaze with fury, his sword drawn. A crowd had gathered.

At once, her daze vanished and she rolled back, drawing the scroll and shaking it. 'I'm here to help you, you idiot!'

'Not after Megaris. Not after what you did, you murdering whore!'

The gathered crowd of Spartiates rumbled in anger. How much had Stentor told them?

She lifted the scroll high so all could see. 'King Archidamos sent me to aid you in securing this region.'

The thunder of voices ebbed, all eyes on the edict. Stentor, chest heaving, slammed his sword back into its sheath, then spun away and stomped over to the northern edge of the camp. 'This is how much Archidamos trusts me,' he bawled back over his shoulder. 'By putting his faith in a *fucking* mercenary?'

Kassandra touched her jaw – the lips tender and the bone aching. Carefully, she followed her step brother. She stopped behind him, seeing the view of the north: sweeping, sun-baked golden plains and in the centre, the great Lake Kopais fed by the green ribbon of the River Kephisos. Shadows rolled across the land where light cloud moved across the sky.

Stentor's ears pricked up, detecting her closeness. 'The Gods are punishing me with your presence.'

'If I were here to punish you, you'd already be dead,' she said, her patience deteriorating.

'What is Archidamos hoping to achieve by sending you – a single, traitorous mercenary – here?'

'To do what you clearly cannot,' she snapped, fuelled by the now blinding pain in her jaw.

His head spun round. 'You have no idea, have you? For

256

four years, this war has raged. You think you know all about it because you walked to battle with us *once* in Megaris?'

The pain peaked, then began to settle. Kassandra harnessed her anger. 'I have remained entangled in conflict ever since that battle, Stentor. Let us not make swords of our every word. We have a job to do. I expected to find mercenaries and allies in this place. I did not realize the main Spartan force was here. Why? Why Boeotia?'

Stentor's head dropped a little – as it had been at the map table. 'We had Athens,' he said, raising one hand and clutching at the air, shaking his fist then letting it fall. 'And then Kleon seized power there. He directs Athens with an iron glove. He has piloted many foolish land invasions, but some have been successful: when we tried to return to Attika, he drove our forces back. We find ourselves now mired in this region – a patchwork of allies and staunch enemies. The armies of Athens and their Platean allies threaten to squeeze us from this region too. *That* would be disastrous.'

'I will do what I can to ensure that does not happen,' Kassandra said calmly.

Stentor remained, staring out over the land. 'The only reason you are still alive is that writ you carry. You are no ally. You are merely a weapon.'

'There is much you do not know about what happened that night in Megaris,' she began.

He threw up a hand in demand for silence. 'I have pieced it together, since, sell-sword. You were the Wolf's lost daughter. You came in the guise of a mercenary . . . when all along you were an assassin.'

Kassandra said, daring to take a step to the mountain's edge, beside him. 'You do not understa–'

Screech. Stentor quarter-drew his sword again. 'One more word.'

She let the matter rest.

After a time, Stentor spoke again. 'We have just one lochos here. Just as in Megaris. The omens were too uncertain and so the ephors withheld the other four regiments. So the chances of victory for Sparta in these lands rests on the shoulders of her allies. Thebes.' He gestured to the east, where a pale-walled city was just visible in the weltering heat of the plain. 'And south, across the Gulf, Korinth: they have a fleet ready to land and support us – with great numbers of men.'

She beheld the city of Thebes, then ran her eye across the most direct route from there to here – over the golden flatland. But her gaze snagged on a silvery vein that stretched from the southern shores of Lake Kopais to the easterly foot of the Helicon range upon which they stood. At first she thought it was a river, and then she saw it was in fact earthworks and men. Athenian hoplites.

'Very good,' Stentor mocked. 'You see it too. That line is like a wall between us and our Theban allies – our only source of cavalry support. Pagondas and his riders cannot travel to join with us. That band of flickering Athenian steel controls the flatland like a strangler's rope. They have plentiful supplies, and more men arriving by the day. The Athenian army swells like a boil, some say; Kleon is heedless of the nearly bare treasury – so obsessed is he with appeasing the people's disquiet over his predecessor's cowardly defensive strategy.'

Kassandra's eyes shifted to the far end of the Athenian line where it met with the southern shores of Lake Kopais. She flicked her gaze across the lake to its northern edge. A way around?

'Rugged, impassable highlands,' Stentor pre-empted her suggestion. 'The horsemen of Thebes know this land better than any other, and they do not even try to take their prize steeds through those treacherous passes to come round and meet us that way lest they lose half to broken limbs.' He pointed out the strange X shapes on the ground before the Athenian line, on the side nearest Mount Helicon. Kassandra squinted for a time before she understood what they were: two dozen Spartan men, staked out spread-eagled, naked, baking in the sun. 'By the Gods, we have tried to break that wall of spears, and that is the result.'

'Then the Korinthians and their vast numbers are the key,' Kassandra mused. 'When they land, they can fall upon the southern end of that line. It would distract the Athenians enough to allow your lochos to assault them from this side, and Pagondas and his Thebans from the other side.'

'Well observed.' Stentor's shoulders jostled as he laughed dryly. 'Yet Boeotia is famed for its plains, its woods . . . and its damnable lack of landing sites. There are just two good spots for the Korinthian fleet to make shore.'

Kassandra's eyes slid shut. 'The Athenians hold them both, don't they? The Korinthian fleet is unable to land.'

'Welcome to my bed of thorns, misthios. Not so confident now, are you?'

She spent many nights planning, travelling along the Helicon range, roving south and north as far as she could go unseen, watching, searching. At last, she knew what she had to do, and she returned to Stentor's command tent.

'You are but one hired blade. What can you do that my lochos could not?' Stentor spat, rising from the stool and taking a long draught of watered wine.

'Give me a dozen men.'

Stentor glared at her with an icy half-grin. 'By all the Gods, I will give you nothing.'

'You need victory here. Sparta needs victory.'

Stentor's grin turned into a snarl as his teeth ground and he turned away from her, striding around his map table. 'I promised the Korinthian fleet a beacon before the summer was out. If they receive no such signal, they will have to return to their own city. But we cannot light a beacon until we clear one of the landing sites for them.'

'Give me men and I will make it so.'

He turned to her, his angry mien melting into a grin again. He snapped his fingers, making some signal at staff behind her. She heard light feet pattering up behind her.

'Master?' the wiry Helot croaked, his face all but hidden behind curtains of black hair and his dogskin cap.

'The misthios here has a plan,' said Stentor.

Kassandra's mouth opened to object.

'You are to aid her in her efforts,' Stentor finished before she could speak.

Her top lip twitched. 'So be it,' she spat, turning away. 'Be ready at dawn, as I explained.'

She and the Helot trekked south as darkness fell. They stopped not to sleep but to eat and rest for a short time, eating hare roasted on a spit, Ikaros picking over the bones. The Helot introduced himself as Lydos – a shy and fearful man of thirty years. Kassandra tried to put him at ease by asking him about his family, but he gave their names and offered little else. He had a nervous habit of tucking his hair behind one ear every few moments, and when he did, she noticed one of his cheeks was sunken – broken at some point in the past. More, the backs of his legs were laced with scars.

'The krypteia have been cruel to you,' she said, thinking of the young Spartan men whose job it was to torment the Helots. She felt a rising sense of pity for this poor wretch, and of loathing that her homeland was built on such cruel pillars.

Lydos shuffled in discomfort, licking his lips, refusing to meet her eye. 'It was not the krypteia.'

'Then who?'

'King Archidamos' temper is legendary. He lets his anger loose on us Helots. He had me whipped with a barbed scourge for interrupting him while he was having talks with a group of strange visitors one night. Over the years he has broken my ribs, my leg, my nose.'

'Your cheek?'

He smiled awkwardly. 'No, that was King Pausanias. He is less cruel, and that wound was deserved. I was pouring wine for him one night and I clumsily spilled some of it. I tried to mop it up with the hem of my tunic, I really did. But I just made a bigger mess – making a wine-print of my hand on the edge of a document he was writing. He rose and punched me. At least he stopped there. If it had been Archidamos, I would have been beaten to a pulp.'

She lowered her voice, as if afraid Cultic spies might be listening in this open, deserted countryside. 'You said Archidamos . . . had strange visitors one night?'

Lydos frowned. 'Travellers from afar, strange to my eye and ear. But then even Spartans are strange to us Helots. I mean no offence, of course.'

She tipped her head to one side to indicate none had been taken. 'Did these visitors wear anything odd . . . like masks?'

He seemed confused. 'Masks? No. They wore the garb of officials and traders.'

She sought another angle to question him, but could not find one. An owl hooted, breaking her chain of thought, and she realized that time was pressing. They continued southwards, spotting a low plain of ferns and a glow of torchlight on the coast ahead.

'Korsia,' Kassandra whispered. 'This is one of the two harbour villages.'

Lydos nodded hurriedly.

'So you remember everything I told you?' she added.

Lydos nodded again.

She sighed, wondering if this was a mistake, and one that might be the death of her. 'Go,' she said at last.

Lydos hitched his leather bag and sprinted off into the black hills overlooking Korsia.

Kassandra crept forward through the ferns towards the harbour village, Ikaros on her shoulder. The night was muggy and the sky treacherously clear – the moon and stars like torches, betraying everything in their veil of ghostly white. She stooped to lift earth as she went, blackening her face and arms. Toads croaked and foxes and voles darted. She came to a halt an arrowshot from Korsia. Hundreds of Athenian hoplites lined the wooden walls of the dock itself, and the rest of the garrison – two taxiarchies each five hundred strong, she counted – sat encamped in and around the village streets. She understood Stentor's reticence – assault this well-defended place with his five hundred Spartans and lose, and Boeotia would fall into Athens' hands. The war might pivot on such a defeat. She heard the bawdy roars from the tavern, saw the silent vigilance of the archers patrolling the rooftops and watching the seas, admired the rugged claws of coastline that struck out into the sea either side of this soft, short bay. There was one structure that stood out above all the others – a freshly hewn timber tower, upon which an archer captain strode, his bare chest and white cape glinting in the moonlight. Far beyond, she even saw the dark shapes of the Korinthian fleet, picked out by torches. Waiting out at sea in impotence. The Athenians had the coastline so well watched that the flotilla could not hope to make shore without losing most of their men in the initial landing.

She looked into the heart of the town, and at the archer's platform once again, then at the dark hills behind her. For all the world she was sure Lydos was right now bounding through the heights, making a break for freedom. *Too late to worry about that.* She sighed.

She shrugged one shoulder, setting Ikaros to flight, then stole through the ferns towards the town's outskirts. The landward-facing Athenian guards were less numerous, and she found one asleep. A way in. She vaulted a low fence, creeping through a private yard, then peered over a half-wall, seeing the village's main packed-dirt road, and the foot of the high timber watchtower. She waited as a pair of Athenian hoplites strolled past, then leapt up and over, rolling into a tall pile of hay just before another pair came into view. She heard their muted conversation rise then fade as they too passed. Climbing free of the straw, she came to the base of the archer's tower. Here, a stink of resin spoiled the air. She saw scores of amphorae of the stuff stacked around the tower's base. Death by fire for any Korinthian vessel that dared approach. There was a strange device too: a hollow, iron-bound beam as long as a mast, with bellows at one end and a cauldron hung with chains at the other end. A war machine of some sort? For a moment, her mind began to work on a new plan . . .

But that would matter only if she did what she needed to here. She turned her attention from the strange device and looked up. The timbers were smooth, but she saw notches and binding ropes here and there, and as soon as she had picked out a climber's path to the top, she set off. Her fingers ached with the effort, her shins burning as they slid on the ropes and wood. Near the top, she heard the archer captain's slow, deliberate strides, and the heavy breathing of another. She halted when they began to speak.

'The Korinthians will turn for home by the end of this moon. The Spartans will be forced back to their farms too, and then Thebes will fall,' the captain mused. 'The war will turn on our efforts here,' he said, 'and our part won't be forgotten.'

'But, Captain Nesaia. What you did . . .' said the heavy-breathing other. 'The families you killed here.'

'It was naught but the spoils of conquest,' Nesaia scoffed. 'You will be getting the blame, should the matter ever arise. And you –'

Kassandra leapt onto the archer platform. Both men swung to face her. 'Set your minds at rest,' she said, 'the matter is over.' She flicked out one hand, the small knife in her bracer streaking out to take the heavy-breather in the neck, her spear flashing forward to plunge into Captain Nesaia's chest. They both fell without a sound. She waited a few moments to be sure nobody down below had noticed, then set her mind to the next step of the plan.

She turned not to the sea, but to the landward side of the village, stared at the black hills, cupped her hands around her mouth and made a shrill call like that of a bird. Three times.

Then . . . nothing. Just the continued clacking of tavern

cups and rumbling laughter. She glared at the hills. *You fool*, she cursed herself.

Now she saw a few figures turning from the dock palisade and squinting up at the archer tower. 'Nesaia, all quiet?' one called.

Kassandra froze. 'Aye, nothing,' she boomed in her best attempt at the dead captain's voice.

Then she saw, to her horror, the runnel of blood oozing from Nesaia's body and spilling from the platform edge.

'Blood?' the voice of a passing guard murmured down below. 'Something's wrong. Up on the tower.'

Footsteps staggered from the nearest tavern. The warm repartee changed, the voices becoming hard-edged.

'Nesaia? What's going on up there?'

She heard the scrape of boots, felt the timbers shaking as men began to climb up. Ikaros swooped from the night to claw at the climbing men, but he could not stop their ascent.

Then the night shook with the most haunting moan of Spartan war pipes. The plaintive howl spilled from the dark hills and poured across the ferns, flooding the streets of Korsia.

The scrape of climbing men and the scuffle of boots halted, then the voices below changed, joined by hundreds more, spilling from the tents, billeted quarters and taverns. 'The Spartans come!' they roared. 'Form up, take your shields, face the land!'

Kassandra watched as the two taxiarchies shambled into formation, combing out into the ferns to face the hills and the oncoming phantom army. *Thank you, Lydos.*

She cast her eye over the shore defences, now stripped of most of its men – just a score of archers left behind on the dock palisade, and none of them had braziers or pitch nearby. She regarded the jar of pitch up here and the crackling brazier, then looked out to sea at the Korinthian fleet. *I hope you're awake*, she thought, then booted the pitch vase over. The stinking, viscous liquid spilled all over the tower top. She then moved over to the brazier. *Because here is the beacon you were promised* . . .

She kicked the brazier over, leaping from the platform as the flames rose behind her with a whoosh. Her eyes grew wide as she plummeted down for the straw pile.

Many miles north, oblivious to the goings-on at the distant coastal town, Stentor's Spartan lochos formed up near the foot of Mount Helicon. He stepped out in front of them and gazed across the Boeotian plain, streaked with dawn light, towards the huge Athenian line.

'We should not have abandoned the mountain camp,' a Spartan officer advised.

Stentor, head aching from a night of little sleep, bit his lip to cage his initial response. 'Yet here we are.'

He tried once again to spot a weak point in the earthworks and assembled Athenian troops. Some of them had boomed and roared when the dawn had revealed the Spartans' descent from the mountains: five hundred men facing some five thousand. What if this was the misthios' final joke – luring him and his lochos into a poorly defensible position like this?

Be ready at dawn, she had implored him as she set off

with her lone Helot. For a time, he had wished he had not been so mule-headed as to give her only a slave.

'Lochagos,' the Spartan by his side hissed. 'The Athenians are moving, look!'

He saw it for himself: their long line, bristling, as if readying to march forth and smash his lone regiment here. Shame and ignominy awaited. His heart plunged.

'Lochagos!' another Spartiate yelled. 'Look!'

Stentor turned towards the southern end of the Athenian line. There, he saw something strange, ethereal. It was as if a god had grabbed the land like a rug and shaken it, sending a slow, mighty ripple northwards. Dust rose. The southern end of the Athenian line became a frantic scattering of men, turning to face the south. Turning to face the armies of Korinthia, landed, marching.

'She did it,' he growled in envy and delight. 'Spartans, ad-*vance*!'

Under the red banners of Korinthia, Kassandra marched with the allied strategos, Aristeus, and his high guards. The Korinthian divisions moved like a great sickle, driving at the southern end of the Athenian line.

'Savage their flank, roll up their line,' Aristeus bellowed. A drummer thundered out a rapid tune.

Kassandra tapped her helm, causing it to slide down from her brow to cover her face. She stepped up to the closest earth mound in time with the royal guards, holding her pike firmly. One Athenian commander rose to point at her and no doubt mock her as the cur at Megaris had. He did not manage a single word before her spear punched through the centre of his face, crumpling helm, skull and brain. Dozens of Athenians fell as the Korinthian advance crunched up and over a carpet of fallen, capturing the mound. Glancing west, Kassandra saw a red swell emerge from the heat haze, coming this way from the lower slopes of the Helicon range.

'The Spartans march from the west. Now signal the Thebans,' she cried.

Trumpets blared in rapid song, whistles blew and the undying cry of war grew louder and louder as first Stentor's Spartans smashed into western side of the disrupted Athenian line, then – from the east – a vast wing of silver Theban riders exploded into view. Led by the magnificently armed Pagondas, they came in a huge wedge, faces shaded by their wide-brimmed bronze and iron helms, their huge pikes trained on the disordered Athenian line's eastern side.

'*Áge! Áge! Áge!*' they trilled, bringing their steeds into formation in perfect time, then exploding into a full charge. They speared into the Athenian mid-section with a terrific boom like a thunderstorm, the flanges of the wedge hitting home with successive peals of iron upon iron. Blood whorled above the battle line in sudden bursts. Severed limbs flew into the air, heads spun and bounced through the dust and the screams seemed to tear the very ether. Kassandra kicked away the first of a band of Athenians who tried to retake the captured mound, then braced behind her shield when more came for her. She saw the great Athenian line now coiling and thrashing, like a snake that had been bitten on its tail and both sides by dogs . . . but the moment of surprise was over – and the Athenian numbers were still more than the allies combined.

A Korinthian guardsman streaked his spear across the chest of one Athenian, opening him to his lungs. The foe fell away, yet scores more foes came for the mound. 'Protect the strategos!' the guardsman screamed. They clustered with Kassandra around Aristeus, shields interlocked. The Athenians came at them with a forest of spears, then a rain of arrows. Kassandra speared one in the guts and smashed the knee of another, but the world darkened as they surrounded her in an ever-thickening surge. Arrows rained down on her helm, the wet sighs of stricken Korinthians sinking silently into death rose around her. The circle protecting the king was growing smaller . . . smaller.

'Bring the device,' she screamed through it all, knowing not if anyone would hear above the dreadful song of war. 'Bring it!'

An Athenian giant cleaved the head of the Korinthian next to her, then ran the strategos' personal bodyguard through. Kassandra leapt into his place, throwing down her hoplite spear and drawing the Leonidas half-lance. The Athenian giant struck out at her. She blocked, but felt her entire body shake, such was the force of the blow. Two more coming in for her from the sides. Not enough time to react. And then . . . the most colossal roar.

It came with a hard slap of heat and sudden weltering of the air right in front of her. She screamed, so intense was the heat, stinging her skin, burning her eyes. The smell too – the stink of burning flesh and singed hair. As if the sun had fallen to the ground and burst across the plain, a wall of orange rose behind the Athenians fighting her. The rearmost one fell away, shrieking, his back ablaze. Behind him, hundreds more pitched over and rolled to and fro like human torches. Almost all others nearby dropped weapon and shield and ran from the flames. The giant before her, deserted by the two at his sides, now suffered the lance point of the Korinthian strategos, right through his throat.

Kassandra gasped for air in the midst of the choking tendrils of black smoke that scudded across the land. She saw the huge iron-bound copper pipe on the back of a wagon, and the three Korinthians working the leather bellows at one end. With every strained compression of the bellows, a great whoosh of air spewed from the far end of the pipe, lending fresh rage to the small cauldron of resin-fuelled fire hanging from a cradle there, sending a new breath of flame across the Athenian ranks. It had been her suggestion to take the device from the port and bring it here. *Villainous acts for a greater good*, she reassured herself.

The Athenians were in full flight before the sun had fully risen. The Theban horsemen raced after them, spearing down the most reckless amongst them. Korinthian bowmen too gave chase, raining arrows on the retreat. The day was won.

Kassandra stabbed her half-lance into the dirt mound. Ikaros swooped down to settle on her shoulder. The handful of remaining Korinthian royal guards escorted the strategos from the worst of the carnage. 'I will not forget what you have done for my army, misthios, or what you have done for my city in the past,' he called back to her. A time passed, the rising songs of victory filling the Boeotian plain, along with the hum of flies and shrieking of crows. The stink of death and burning men would never leave her, she realized. But the day was over. She tied her lance to her belt, staggered down the mound, her skin black with smoke, dirt and dried blood. She saw then the most pathetic sight: Lydos the Helot who had made this all possible. He was waiting for her, cowering, at the edge of battle. He held a bowl of water and a flask of oil – an offer to wash her. She stepped over to him. 'You have done enough for today. Gods, you have done enough to earn freedom, I would claim.'

He trembled where he stood. 'I . . . I would not dare dream of such a right,' he said, anxiously tucking his hair behind his ear.

She squeezed his shoulder. 'I will see that your part in this land's salvation is not overlooked, Lydos.'

Turning from him, she looked across the battlefield, and the many small victory stelae taking shape along the broken Athenian line. She heard a throaty cry of many Spartan voices together: '*Aroo!*' She saw the red-cloaked soldiers, spears raised in salute to their commander. She saw Stentor then, a mask of blood worn like a wreath of victory. He was coming towards her in a hurry.

'You led the lochos well. Victory is Sparta's. Victory is yours,' she said as he approached.

But he kept up that strident pace, coming right for her. 'And now King Archidamos' victory is secured, I can finally deal with my true enemy . . .'

She saw his spear flash up like a rising cobra, licking through the air. She leapt clear of it. 'Are you mad?'

'I have never been clearer in my thoughts,' he rumbled, swiping at the air as Ikaros tried to attack him. 'You will die for what you stole from me in Megaris.'

'It doesn't have to be this way,' she rasped, dodging his jabs as he circled her.

'No, it didn't. Things would have been very different, had you not marched into the war. *Ruined* the war. Slew my father, you *fucking* murderer.'

'I did what I had to,' she growled, drawing her half-lance.

'And so will I,' Stentor raged. His body tensed like a lion about to pounce . . . and then he slackened, stepping back once, twice and again, face falling, eyes fixed on a point just beyond Kassandra's shoulder.

Kassandra turned, seeing a shape walk through the injured and the clouds of scudding smoke. Dressed in a simple brown robe, he looked like neither a Spartan nor an Athenian nor anything other than a simple man of Hellas.

'She has nothing to answer for, Stentor,' Nikolaos said gently.

Kassandra's skin tingled with a shiver as he passed her, offering her a knowing nod. She realized now that she *had* been followed, all throughout her time in Boeotia. The Wolf had watched her every step.

'Father? I . . . I thought you were dead?' Stentor croaked.

'I was dead to the war, for a time,' he replied. 'When Kassandra confronted me in Megaris, I knew I could not

273

lead men with such . . . shame upon my back. I knew also that you were ready – ready to take the mantle of leadership. I did not want to leave you without saying farewell, but I knew that if I came to you that night, I would not be able to leave at all.'

'She killed you, on the bluffs,' Stentor stammered.

'She could have. Some might say she should have. But she did not. She took my helm to claim her reward but left me there, weeping. Her words, as true as Apollo's light, cut deeper than any blade. I died a thousand deaths as I walked the lands for a time. At last, I made peace with my past. And then I came back to your side: for nearly two summers I have been watching you and your forces. I have done what I could to divert enemy spies, and to leave clues for you as to the best routes to take.'

Kassandra slid her spear into her belt. She met Stentor's eye, feeling not a crumb of righteousness.

'But the truth is you did not truly need my help. My son will be a greater general than I ever was,' Nikolaos said, stepping close to Stentor.

Stentor offered his father a brisk and manly salute.

A general returns from the dead to a frosty soldier's salute from his son, thought Kassandra. *The iron shell of a Spartan is thick and cold indeed.*

But then Nikolaos replied by extending his arms.

Stentor's face sagged. His spear slid from his hand and he fell into Nikolaos' embrace.

The two remained locked like that for an age, the warriors looking on.

Kassandra felt her heart swell with a fond sadness. *The*

flame flickers, deep within the iron shell, she realized. *This was all I ever wanted for myself. Love. Between father and daughter. Mother and brother. Now, Stentor, the gift is yours. Enjoy every moment of it.*

After a time, Stentor made a strangled sobbing noise, and a rivulet of tears sped down his cheek. He momentarily opened one baleful eye to glower at all watching and swept the tear away, insisting that it was merely the smoke stinging his eyes.

Kassandra's top lip twitched in a brief and wry smile. With that, she turned from the pair and walked from the battlefield, Ikaros gliding alongside her.

14

She left for Sparta as summer faded into autumn, Nikolaos' parting words in her ears all the way: *Be careful. I once warned you of snakes in the grass, but it is much, much worse than that. Something evil hangs over the Hollow Land. I did not see it when I was in the army and in the throes of the war, but from the outside, I saw it well enough – like a crawling black shadow.*

She knew what he meant. Even to one without full knowledge of the Cult of Kosmos, there was a certain chill in the Spartan air – a sense of impending disaster. She pulled her cloak a little tighter and rode on. Nikolaos had listened as she explained that Myrrine still lived as he had hoped, and that she was now back in her homeland. He had fallen silent for a time upon hearing this, then quietly said: *Perhaps a day will come when once again I can sit with her, break bread and drink wine.* The sad look in his eyes suggested it would be a dream and no more.

She rode along the Eurotas' western banks, passing the Temple of Lycurgus and the Babyx Bridge. At a parting of the trees ahead, she saw them: her new family waiting to greet her. Myrrine stood with Barnabas, Brasidas and Herodotos. The messenger she had paid to ride ahead had brought word to them. Her mother's eyes were wet with tears. Herodotos and Brasidas beamed like proud uncles. Barnabas blubbed like an old hen.

Memories of Nikolaos and Stentor's reunion flashed through her mind as she slid from horseback and into Myrrine's arms. She drank in her mother's warm petal scent, and felt the thick bear hug of Barnabas swaddling them both.

They parted after a time, Kassandra and Myrrine both adopting tall, proud stances as if suddenly aware of their Spartan surrounds.

That night, Barnabas fell into a snoring slumber at the corner of their small abode in Pitana village while Brasidas sat in the doorway, whetting his spear. Herodotos busied himself making a sketch of Ikaros, who preened himself in an eaves-niche above the doorway. Myrrine and Kassandra – having enjoyed a bracing swim in the Eurotas and a good strigilling – sat around the hearth wrapped in freshly washed woollen blankets, drinking cups of hot black broth. She told her mother everything about Boeotia, and about Nikolaos' reappearance. 'I never told you I spared him. I wasn't sure you would forgive me that.'

Myrrine ladled more of the broth into both of their cups, breaking a second small loaf between them. 'You once told me about the flame inside, Kass,' she said quietly. 'I told you to hide it, to keep it a secret. I was wrong,' she said softly. 'We are Spartan . . . but we are more than that,' she said, clasping Kassandra's hand.

Kassandra half-smiled and supped on the hot soup, the flavour strong and warming. 'Yet it was not Nikolaos I set out to find. Of the Cultist king – the Red-Eyed Lion – I found nothing. No clues, no whispers.' She stared into the flames and dropped her voice to a whisper. 'I am due to report to the Kings' Hall tomorrow, to detail my efforts in Boeotia. I had planned to use that moment to expose Archidamos . . . but he has covered his tracks well.'

'I too found nothing,' said Myrrine. 'Arkadia is a strange land, and I was glad of Brasidas' company. He and I made use of our spears more than once, even against its archon.'

Kassandra saw the recent scars on her mother's hands.

'Yes, Archon Lagos was, as I feared, one of *them*.' She set down her broth mug as if suddenly losing her appetite. 'He had a troop of masked ones with him. Brasidas and his hand-picked guards fought like lions to slay them. Finally, I had Lagos pinned at spearpoint on the floor of his palace. He thought himself invincible: as if his wretched Cult would burst in and save him. Then I told him who I was, who my daughter was. His confidence fell like a rock. Forty-two of them, there once were,' she said, squeezing Kassandra's knee, 'and now only six remain. Mainly thanks to you.'

'But one of those six sits on the throne of Sparta,' Kassandra said flatly.

'I tried to get him to confess the traitor king's identity,' Myrrine sighed. 'Before I ran him through, he wailed and pleaded. Yet he revealed nothing. All I could discover was another script.' She shrugged, drawing from under her blanket a tattered scroll. 'From the Red-Eyed Lion, once again.'

Kassandra held it up to the firelight, staring at the same lion-head seal as was stamped on the Parian script. She rolled the scroll out and scanned the Cultic lettering, understanding none of it – again, just like the one from Paros. Worse, this document was soiled too – part of the text obscured by . . . the breath caught in her throat. Realization rose within her. She barely heard the sound of her broth cup falling to the floor, or of Barnabas waking, startled, or of Brasidas dropping his now-honed lance, or of Mother shaking her. 'Kassandra, what is it? What is it?'

The prattle of the Gerousia filled the Kings' Hall as two Spartiates yelled and remonstrated as they put their respective cases: one man claimed the olive orchard on Taygetos' lower slopes as his own thanks to his tending of the estate, the other insisted it was instead his by birthright. The pair screamed until their faces were red, and it was only when the one claiming birthright drew the loudest wail of acclamation that the matter was deemed settled. The two were shepherded from the doors by the spearpoints of the Hippeis guards. Now, all eyes settled on the trio who were up next for judgement.

Kassandra stepped forth and beheld the two kings and the five ephors.

'Ah,' grunted Archidamos, 'I heard that Boeotia was secured. You didn't die in the struggle then?'

The Gerousia rumbled with dry laughter.

Kassandra stared at him. His tousled mane and beard, his bloodshot eyes, his foul, menacing mien.

'You have Sparta's gratitude,' he muttered at last.

'And your estate,' added King Pausanias quickly. 'I will see to it that the chains are taken off and the place is cleaned for your return there.'

Two Hippeis guards moved as if to shepherd Kassandra from the chamber, but she did not move.

'Is there something else?' Archidamos spat.

'My family was betrayed,' she said. A gasp arose from the Gerousia. '*Sparta* was betrayed. We've come to expose the traitor.'

Archidamos stared at her for a time. 'Oh really? And who is this traitor? What is their crime?' He roared with laughter, rocking back on his throne to conjure more hilarity from the Gerousia too.

'On the island of Paros, I found evidence that one of Sparta's two kings is allied not to the state, nor to the Gods . . . but to the Cult of Kosmos. He goes by the name of the Red-Eyed Lion.' She heard the hall fall silent, so still that even a feather falling to the floor would have been like the beat of a war drum.

Archidamos' eyelids slid down a fraction, his gaze growing hooded. 'That is a dark accusation, shamed descendant of Leonidas,' he growled. 'You had best have proof of this, if you wish to keep your head.'

She threw him the scroll taken from the Cultists on Paros. Archidamos' face paled, and his bloodshot eyes reddened further. 'The markings of the Cult indeed. Still, this proves nothing.'

'Alone, it is worthless,' agreed Myrrine, stepping forward to her daughter's side. 'But then I travelled to Arkadia. There, I had another traitor confirm that there *is* a Cultist on the Spartan throne, and obtained another scroll with the same lion-head seal.' She held up the Arkadian document and shook it.

Archidamos trembled with ire. 'Are you blind?' He held up his meaty hand, the hawk seal-ring catching the light, then gesturing at Pausanias' hand too and the crescent-moon seal. 'There is no 'Red-Eyed Lion' on these thrones!' he hissed, raising a finger for the Hippeis guards, who positioned their spears behind the two, ready to run them through, waiting on Archidamos' finger to fall. 'I should have done this the moment you first walked in here.'

'Wait! *Wait!*' Kassandra cried, throwing the Arkadian script at Archidamos. 'Look at this second script.'

He caught it, hesitating on the brink of giving the order . . . then unrolling it.

'See the strange blotch upon it in the shape of a hand?' said Kassandra. 'In Boeotia I was aided by a Helot who spilled the wine that stained that hide, whose hand made that mark . . .'

Archidamos' bloodshot eyes rolled down to the dark stain on the document. The remaining colour in his face vanished.

'. . . when it was being written by King Pausanias.'

All eyes swung to the younger king.

'Show me your secondary seals,' Archidamos said in a low drone.

'What is this nonsense?' Pausanias laughed. 'Have them killed and be done with it.'

Archidamos glowered at his co-monarch, then lurched from his throne and grabbed him by the collar, lifting him to his feet like a toy. He grabbed the small silver chain around Pausanias' neck and snapped it, dragging it from under the folds of the younger king's robe and holding it up.

Every soul in the Kings' Hall stared, aghast, at the lion-head signet ring dangling on the chain.

'You?' Archidamos growled.

'It was always him, My Liege,' Kassandra said calmly. 'Hiding behind the guise of reason. Masked in daylight just as he is in the dark halls where he and his ilk meet.'

With a scrape of benches and feet, every single one of the Gerousia rose. Silently and solemnly, they shuffled in towards the two kings. Archidamos set Pausanias down. The younger king turned to the elders, then he backed against the ephors, who blocked any exit that way.

'You do not understand. She lies!' he said, turning to see the circle of vengeful faces around him.

'The evidence does not lie,' said one old man softly, drawing a cudgel from his belt.

'The state and the Gods demand that the Kings of Sparta must not be harmed,' Pausanias yelled, panting as the circle around him grew smaller.

'Oh, the Gods will understand,' said one of the ephors, stretching a thin cord between his hands.

Archidamos, at the circle's rear, twisted to the trio of Kassandra, Myrrine and Brasidas. 'Leave us. The matters of the past are now settled. The traitor will be a problem no longer.'

Kassandra felt a cold shudder of pity for Pausanias – despite everything – as they walked from the hall. As they stepped outside, they heard the most blood-chilling scream from within, before the Hippeis slammed the doors shut with a sepulchral boom.

Nearly all this time, she had been so sure Archidamos was the one. Pausanias' un-Spartan eagerness to help them should really have been a warning, she realized. From the mist of memory, she recalled Sokrates' wry line.

Things are rarely as they seem, Kassandra.

15

Kassandra hung over the bow of the *Adrestia*, watching the swell and the dolphins leaping alongside in the sparkling waters of the Aegean and Ikaros speeding along in time with the boat. Her mind combed over the autumn, winter and summer gone since Sparta had been rid of its poisonous king.

The autumnal and snowbound months had been spent exercising with Testikles in the gymnasium, running lap after lap of the track in driving blizzards. Barnabas and Reza helped where they could too, building a steep snow-mound for him to race up and down. Yet one day they could not find him. Only when they heard a muffled, drunken song from within the mound did they realize where he was. They dug away the snow at one side to find him in a snow cave of sorts – really just a hole he had burrowed into. He was pickled to the point of oblivion, hugging a wineskin as if it were a baby.

'To teach young Spartans never to drink neat wine, they force Helots to get this drunk and make fools of themselves,' Kassandra explained to Barnabas as they dragged the champion by his ankles out into the silent snowfall. 'Clearly, Testikles missed that lesson.'

Once Testikles had sobered up, Reza offered himself as a sparring partner for Pankration. Testikles showed flashes of brilliance, leaping, kicking, grappling and throwing the helmsman to the ground. Reza stood again, dazed, and the pair fell into a boxer's poise, fists raised and ready. Herodotos, watching from the sidelines, chanted eagerly:

> With impatient fury, in he goes,
> Foot to foot, at his foes.
> This is a Spartan's noblest praise,
> And to immortal glory he will be raised.

Testikles' head swung to him, his crown of matted hair shuddering. 'Hmm?'

'It's a poem,' Herodotos replied with a sigh. 'A famous Spartan poem.'

Reza's fist whirled round and cracked the distracted Testikles' jaw. He fell like a stone, then awoke, demanding neat wine to nurse his aching head. All groaned.

The freezing evenings were spent in the estate's hearth room, mother and daughter talking of the past, and of the strange lull in the war. No news of fresh battles. No word of Deimos. Perhaps it was thanks to the coming summer's Olympics, and the truce that all in Hellas were sworn to obey while the games took place. It felt to Kassandra like that moment on the mountain, just before Alexios fell. A strange, pregnant bubble of respite . . . but one she knew could not last.

When the spring came, news broke that a large band of Helots had slain their masters and fled from Spartan lands, heading west. A messenger brought word that they had sought refuge on the island of Sphakteria, just off the coast. Worse, they had stolen arms and provisions. The runaway slaves' boldness was a dangerous affront to the Spartan state; like a thread being pulled from the hem of a tunic, it had to be stopped lest the entire garment unravel. In an angry gathering, the ephors declared that a whole lochos would be despatched under the command of Brasidas – fast becoming a hero of Sparta – to track down and capture the runaways.

While the Spartan regiments marched off to deal with this, the *Adrestia* set sail, almost unnoticed, carrying Testikles around the Peloponnese towards Elis, for the Olympic gathering. Herodotos chronicled every step of the champion's voyage, while Barnabas was like a boy, brimming with excitement for the many events the great Testikles was sure to win. In the end, the only trophy he secured was the unofficial title of 'Greatest Idiot in all Hellas'. It happened just a day's sail away from the games, when the drunken athlete had woken with a burning need to be oiled before they landed. Reza and Barnabas had suddenly found pressing tasks to attend to high up on the ship's mast, while Herodotos had vanished into the cabin, locking himself in there. So Testikles had turned to Kassandra, a lopsided grin cracking across his face. 'You will oil me?'

'Oil yourself.'

'But there are certain regions I cannot reach.' The other half of the grin rose. 'Come on!' He laughed, spreading his arms wide . . . then lurching at Kassandra.

She deftly stepped out of his way, never expecting for

one moment that it could go so badly wrong. The fool tripped on a coil of rope and pitched overboard. A mighty splash and a plume of water brought everyone to the boat's edge.

Barnabas grabbed the coil of rope, ready to throw it down to the champion.

'Testikles?' he called in the boat's wake.

Nothing.

'Testikles?' he cried again, looking ahead.

Nothing.

Then, the tip of a black fin broke the surface adjacent to the ship's edge, before submerging again. All stared, aghast, as the water quietly blossomed red. A few air bubbles rose, then Testikles' filthy loincloth floated to the surface.

Barnabas, heartbroken for his hero, fell to his knees, hands outstretched to the waves. '*Testikleees!*' he cried out in a hoarse and interminable wail.

After that, the summer games had been a blur: days of explaining to the officials that Sparta would have no entrant, before their sneering and gleeful attitude goaded Kassandra into competing in Testikles' place. At pankration, she bettered every man she faced and took the olive-leaf crown. At running, she was swift as a deer, losing only by a whisker to Alkibiades – who seemed all too eager to celebrate with her in his usual way. At the discus, she threw well, beating the previous Spartan record, being bettered only by an islander with the shoulders of a bear.

'Ha . . . ha!' Martial yelps drew her from her reminiscence of all that had happened and back to the present.

She turned from the boat's rail to see Barnabas re-enacting the pankration victory, swinging punches at thin air. Herodotos stood atop a pile of grain sacks, narrating excitedly. 'And then she grabbed him by the waist. Threw him down.' Barnabas acted out every step and Ikaros screeched from the ship's spar like an excited spectator.

Kassandra had given the captain her olive crown, and he had worn it day and night since they left Elis. She wondered if any in Sparta would appreciate it as much as him. *Sparta.* For once she thought of her homeland without the spikes of hatred. She gazed ahead along the coastline, seeing the port of Trinisa roll into view. Skiffs and rafts dotted the calm waters near this good stretch of Sparta's coastline, men diving from the small vessels and surfacing with armfuls of porphyria shells, their bodies stained with the crustaceans' famous purple dye. She set her eyes on the land and felt her heart ache for her mother, for home.

When she saw Myrrine on the jetty, her spirits surged. But when they drew close enough to see the look on her face, she felt the strange bubble of elation burst like a thrown amphora.

'What is wrong?' she said, stumbling from the boat and onto the pier. All around the pair, soldiers shouted urgently, angry, troubled.

Myrrine took some time to collect herself and stave off the tears gathering in her eyes. 'Brasidas and his men arrived at Sphakteria and found that the armed Helots were not the greatest threat. Athenian regiments were already there.'

'A trap?'

'It seems so. But Brasidas sprung the gambit before it could snap shut. All through the summer, he and his men have battled to hold on to the island: ships groaning and circling to block the narrow bays, skirmishes on the island and on the coast of Pylos, fraught truces and talks which dissolved – every time – into angry exchanges and then battle again. The island runs red with blood. Brasidas is trapped there, but with his purebred regiment, he will not easily be beaten. Yet word has spread that Kleon has sent Athenian reinforcements to crush the Spartan brigade and secure the island. Kassandra . . .'

Kassandra saw something in her mother's eyes and knew what she was about to say. 'Deimos sails with the reinforcements.'

Myrrine nodded and buried her head in Kassandra's chest. They held each other like that for a time, the sun setting, the peace over. She heard the soldiers' frantic calls now. They were sending out the dye skiffs to find and summon the few galleys of the scant Spartan navy back to this dock. The ephors had refused to send another precious lochos in support of Brasidas, lest their homeland be left scantly protected. A band of Tegean allies had been summoned instead. One thousand men who might save the Spartan regiment trapped on the island.

Myrrine drew her head up and shook Kassandra. 'I know what you're thinking. I know there is no stopping you. If Deimos sails in support of Athens, then the Cult wants Athens to win, to slaughter the Spartans on Sphakteria. We cannot let it happen. Go, do as you must. I ask you only this: bring my boy back to me.'

Duplicitous warfare was not the Spartan way. Nor was it the way of any soldier in Hellas. But the great war had twisted the ancient rules of engagement. No longer did phalanx line up against phalanx in an honourable slash of steel. This was a new age of devious sieges – tunnels under city walls and countermines to ruin those tunnels and suffocate the diggers – of mighty contraptions like the great flamethrower, of deception, of lies, of desperation. Oaths lost their meaning and became tools of duplicity. All Hellas became a writhing bed of red-eyed beasts. And so it was on the isle of Sphakteria.

Stiff bodies of Spartan, Helot and Athenian lay twisted and unburied on the soil. The men of Brasidas' Spartan lochos were like lions, whittled down day by day but never beaten, while Athenian galleys rocked up to the shores every moon, packed with fresh troops. Only in the last days of summer – when Brasidas and his men had been pushed into the island's narrow northern peninsula – did the first relief boats from Sparta arrive. Ten triremes, brimming with Tegeans. The *Adrestia* sailed at their head.

It was night when they came, a sultry and stinking wind coming from the direction of the island. Kassandra crouched on the prow, Ikaros on her shoulder, both scouring the thickly wooded isle and the odd glow along its long spine. 'Why does the island shine? There is no village there – just an old Spartan fort.'

Barnabas' face lengthened. 'Alas, misthios, I fear the Athenians have learned much from their defeat at Boeotia.'

Kassandra blinked to moisten her dry eyes and saw it now: the glow was in fact an angry blaze. The pine and olive woods crackled and thundered with orange flame. The closer they drew, the more she saw: fire arrows streaked through the night sky like phoenix feathers. The missiles whistled and hissed, endless, countless, shooting from the isle's northern shores and raining down on the small area inland – already ablaze. There were flame pipes too, breathing great clouds of orange.

'It is like the Gates of Hades,' Barnabas whispered.

She heard the distant and forlorn wail of the Spartan pipes, and recognized the tune – a call for a last stand, just as she had heard in that vision at the Hot Gates.

'We must be swift,' Kassandra urged the crew.

'We can't approach directly,' Barnabas said. 'The shores are awash with Kleon's men. But we can draw close. Hold tight, misthios.'

As he stalked away, Kassandra grappled a rope and braced. The *Adrestia* cut close to the island's waist then sped north, parallel to the shoreline – dangerously close to the shallows, but using the overhanging cliffs as a screen from the Athenian-held coastal areas. The galley sped through a natural arch of rock and then the bluffs peeled away to reveal the Athenian efforts on one bay: a few hundred archers and a phalanx of some five hundred hoplites were stationed here. Only a fraction of the Athenian force spread around the northern shores.

The *Adrestia* crunched onto the shingle bay just as the Athenians beached there noticed her presence, the other nine galleys coming to land alongside. 'Take the shore!' Kassandra howled, leaping down onto the bay.

The Athenian taxiarchos jolted, seeing the landing enemy. He bawled at his men, who turned their fire arrows upon the relief flotilla. A storm of blazing shafts spat forth. Kassandra threw up her shield as she moved, the Tegeans clattering into place beside her. They were brave and loyal, she knew, but there was something missing – they were no Spartiates. The aura of invincibility she had felt when she had fought alongside Stentor's men was absent. It would be her task to inspire them.

The arrows whacked and spat down all around them. Tegeans slid away, shaking and clutching at the throat-piercing missiles. One ran, ablaze like a human torch, back into the shallows. The one beside her took a shaft in the eye and dropped like a sack of wet sand.

'Level spears!' she thundered, an arrow zinging from her helm. 'Walk, in time.'

She felt the Tegeans draw courage from her steady, strong orders. They marched with her in a rapid lockstep. The Athenians stood their ground for a time. Then she saw one backstep. A moment later, the archers began to melt into the trees, knowing they could not hope to face Kassandra and the newly landed hoplites. Now just the five hundred Athenian spearmen faced the Tegean thousand. 'Advance!' the taxiarchos bawled.

They closed the distance in moments, and the two forces met with a clatter of spears and shields, joining the chaos of screaming from inland and all along the shore. Kassandra prodded her spear into the shoulder of one man, driving him to his knees, pulling the lance clear then using it to shove another's shield away. 'Finish him!' she screamed at the Tegean by her side, who duly thrust his lance into the Athenian hoplite's belly. The enemy fell in droves, and Kassandra felt their corpses grind under her feet as she led the push, driving them back into the woods. After a time, the Athenians broke out in a panic, more than half of them dead, the remnant fleeing. It was as if great doors were opening onto the underworld as the way into the burning woods presented itself. She cried at her Tegeans, urging them uphill through tangled undergrowth and pitted ground. She saw silhouettes leaping and spinning through the trees in that fiery chaos, sparks blowing like rain. Spartans fought like wolves, some with their hair burnt away, others with seared skin. One man fought with half his face a mess of blisters and weeping fire wounds. The Athenians who had pushed inland surrounded them like jackals – the numbers impossible. But when Kassandra saw Brasidas, just uphill, she knew she could not give up. The Spartan general spun on his heel to run an Athenian champion through, then he took the head of another with a deft flick of his spear, before ramming the lance hard into the belly of a third.

'Misthios!' he yelled, spotting her, his face black with blood, his grin wild, eyes wide.

'Hold your ground,' she yelled up at him. 'We'll clear a path back to shore for y—'

That was when the fire parted like a pair of curtains. Behind Brasidas, a shadow walked, head dipped. For a moment, she thought it was an avatar of Ares . . . and then the figure raised its head. *Deimos?*

'Brasidas, behind you!' she cried, rushing forward with all her strength.

Brasidas' wild and confident mien faded as he swung to his rear. Deimos' spear flashed up like a lightning bolt, and Brasidas' shield crumpled under the mighty blow. With an adroit swirl, Deimos brought the lance streaking down. Brasidas' spear swung to block, but he was too slow. In the scudding smoke, she saw the two shapes shuddering . . . then Brasidas toppling to one side. His body rolled off downhill through a carpet of blazing heather.

Kassandra staggered to a standstill, her feet where Brasidas had stood a heartbeat ago, Deimos before her. Her brother cocked his head this way and that, like a predator eyeing strange prey. His gold-and-white armour was streaked with black smoke and running with blood and his face was demonic, uplit by the flames. His expression flashed with madness and he leapt for her.

Kassandra threw up her shield to take the blow. His sword bit deep, breaking the bronze coating and crumpling the timber below. She tossed the ruined shield down. Deimos' spear lashed for her again. She parried and struck back. Sparks flew as they hammered blow after blow like this until, exhausted, she caught his next strike on the tip of her Leonidas spear. The pair strained, shaking, vying for supremacy. Around them, ancient trees groaned and toppled in great whooshes of fire and smoke. When she edged his spear slightly to one side, she saw Deimos' confident glower waver for a moment. But it was like a fuel to his madness and, with a roar, he pushed back, swatting her lance aside. She rolled clear of his follow-up swipe and stood, backing away.

'You came here to die?' Deimos spat, striding towards her, spear poised to strike.

She felt her heels meet the edge of the small hill and stopped.

'Do not make it so easy for me,' he growled. 'At least put up a fight.'

'I came here to bring you home.'

She saw it again: the flicker of uncertainty in his face.

'That's right. Mother wants you to come home . . . to Sparta.'

She saw a mist pass across his eyes now, as if the words had thrown him into the distant past. But the mist faded, and his lips curled into a mockery of a smile. 'You don't understand,' he said, jabbing a finger down at the smouldering earth, sweeping his hand around the blazing cage of trees. 'Battle is my trade, and the fields of war my estate. I live only to take the heads of my enemies. This *is* my home . . . and your grave.'

She saw his body tense, saw him lunge for her, felt her knees soften into a crouch. She leapt clear of his strike and brought the lance round, the flat whacking him on the temple. Stunned, he staggered back from her, then crumpled in a heap.

She stepped forward, sinking to one knee, cradling him. When she touched his chest, his pulse thundered under her palm. 'And now, I will take you home . . . to Mo–'

Her words ended when a terrible groan sounded from above. She looked up just in time to see a huge pine, roaring in a fury of flames, swing down upon her and Deimos like an executioner's axe.

Blackness.

16

The blackness lasted for an eternity. And then she awoke to the crack of a barbed whip.

'Up, *bitch*! If you're fit enough to mutter in your sleep, then you're fit enough to walk for yourself.'

Her head ached and it felt as if she had not sipped water for a year. She felt herself being pulled upright from a stretcher of some sort, but she could not bear to prise open her eyes. A thick nausea rose from her belly and she longed to lie down again, but ropes were wrenched around her wrist, then yanked taut, hauling her along in a dazed shamble. She opened one eye now: seeing the blinding daylight of what looked like Arkadian countryside — frostbitten, the woods golden. A great serpent of Athenian soldiers marched for miles ahead, along with a wagon train and a pack of mules. It was to one of these sumpter beasts that her wrists were roped. She noticed many other Spartan prisoners tied likewise. They wore rags and bore thick scars and burn welts, their hair filthy and tousled.

'Aye, bitch, you lost,' cackled the toothless Athenian slave driver.

She had no sooner looked at him than he lashed his whip across her back. She heard just a ringing in her ears, felt her jaw lock open in a soundless scream, one knee touch the ground, before the slave driver grabbed her by the hair and pulled her up. 'If you fall again, I'll hack off your legs and leave you for the wolves.'

By her side, she saw one of the Tegeans walking, roped like her. 'We came close to saving the beleaguered men,' he whispered. 'Had we arrived a little sooner, we might have succeeded. But the island was a death trap that night. Those who were not captured were left to burn alive. It was a shameful defeat for Sparta, and one that will echo over all Hellas. Where men once feared to even speak of the Spartans, now they will laugh and mock them.' He let out a long, weary sigh. 'The worst of it is that Sparta offered peace in return for our release.' He gestured up and down the prisoner column.

'Peace?' Kassandra whispered. 'Then why do we head north, *away* from Sparta.'

'Because Athens rejected the proposal. They say that Kleon whipped the people up into a frenzy, convincing them that now was the time to drive home the advantage, to abandon the last vestiges of Perikles' defensive strategy and to crush Sparta under their heel like an insect.'

She closed her eyes. The Cult had the Athenian victory they wanted. They were back in firm control of the war . . . of the world. 'You and your men fought well,' she said to the Tegean. 'Your efforts will never be forgotten.'

'Memories won't feed my wife and three girls,' he said quietly.

On they went in silence. Kassandra heard the familiar cry of an eagle at times, and she knew Ikaros was tracking her, watching over her. *Stay away, old friend*, she thought. *It is not safe.*

After a month of marching – the Athenian army and the slave train camping with impunity in Spartan allied territory as they went – they returned to Attika, crunching over the autumnal frost to march through Athens' land gates to a storm of petals and singing. Now she understood the sheer magnitude of the defeat at Sphakteria.

All around the streets, Spartan shields were mounted like trophies. The lost shields of the fallen and captured at Sphakteria – whisked here before the prisoners themselves. The ultimate shame for the famous warriors of the Hollow Land. There were Tegean shields up there too, and the man beside her sighed in despair as he noticed this. 'Eternal infamy,' he whispered.

The whips cracked as they were led through the city streets. The decay of the plague had long since been eradicated, she realized, seeing crowds where the heaped corpses had once been. Rotting vegetables whacked down on them along with showers of spittle and torrents of jeering and cursing. As they walked through the agora, a woman ran out from her house and hurled a bucket of still-warm sewage over Kassandra and those near her.

At the agora mouth, where the Long Walls led off to the coast and Piraeus harbour, naval crewmen waited, and were given groups of Tegean prisoners. 'They'll take us to the colonies,' the Tegean said. 'To work us like dogs in the hot fields, our ankles chained. Or to live in the darkest pits of the silver mines – where men go blind and most kill themselves after a few years.'

She watched as the Tegean was dragged off with fifty

other prisoners and driven like a mule down towards the harbour. Slowly, the many hundreds of prisoners were taken away. The slave-handlers then approached her and the small cluster of Spartans remaining. He wagged a filthy finger at her. 'You . . . I have a fine fate in store for you. Every day will be worse than the last,' he enthused.

But a hand rested on her shoulder. 'Stop: the purebred Spartiates are to be kept here as prisoners. As a guarantee against a Spartan assault on the city. They will be billeted in the wheat-grinding houses and there they will work their fingers to the nub. But this one? She comes with me.'

'Yes, General,' the slave-handler agreed, backing away and bowing obsequiously.

Kassandra felt a sudden rising of hope . . . until she turned around.

Kleon grinned back at her, his red locks swept back and his beard combed to a point. His face was bent with malice, and she saw a shape under his cloak. The shape of a mask. 'You're one of them?'

'The darkest of them all,' he whispered.

Two pairs of guards' hands grabbed her by the shoulders and a sharp blade dug into the small of her back. Purposefully, they drove her away from the harbour route and towards the other side of the agora. She eyed the shadowy, sorry jail.

Where souls are sent to be forgotten, Herodotos whispered from memory.

'No,' she croaked, fighting feebly. '*No!*'

*

Months passed in that cage of stone. She could see nothing of the outside — just the moving rectangle of sunlight that hit the floor from the jail's tiny ceiling grille and crawled across the flags at an agonizing pace. She would stare for hours through the cell's iron-bar gate, watching the hay on the floor of the corridor. Every so often, a breeze would steal in from the exterior door, gently stirring the stalks on the floor. Movement. Something.

The sounds of life were an even bigger torment, the bustle of the agora fading over the winter, then rising with the heat as spring came and then summer. Sweltering days passed when she saw nothing, nobody, just the daily opening of a wooden hatch and the appearance of a filthy hand setting down a bowl of thin wheat porridge and a single cup of brackish water onto the floor of the corridor, close enough for her to reach from her cell gate.

Kleon had explained nothing when he had cast her in here. He did not need to. She worked it out the moment she heard the lock clicking and the chains settling into place. She was to be a reserve, no more. A replacement, should the Cult need a new champion. Yet why would the Cult need to change anything? They had the world all but in their palm. But what was left of the Cult? Was it not now just Kleon and a handful of others? She had lost count of the number of those masked bastards she and Myrrine had killed in these last years, but of the forty-two she had witnessed in the Cave of Gaia, almost all had been slain.

They haunted her at night, when Athens fell quiet. She dreamt of their masked faces, standing around her filthy bed of hay, staring down at her, those wicked smiles unfaltering. By day, she tried to keep her mind's worst thoughts at bay by leaping for the ceiling grille and grabbing the iron bars, then hauling herself up then lowering down, over and over, catching glimpses of clouds rolling by high above. Her shoulders, back and arms stayed strong and thick thanks to this, but she longed to run – to speed across the countryside, feel the wind on her face, smell the scent of summer meadows . . . anything but the shit-stink of the agora in summertime.

It was like a ray of sunlight when she awoke in the middle of one night to hear a new inmate being dragged into the adjacent cell. The stone wall meant she could see nothing of him, but she drank in the sound of every word as if each syllable was a treasure.

'Tell me where you found it. *Where?*' one unseen guard roared, underlining his last word with what sounded like a backhand slap across the new inmate's mouth. The sound of teeth landing and scattering across the ground was followed by a dull whimper. 'I . . . I don't know. I was shipwrecked, and so I was lost. How can I tell you if I don't know?'

'Well, we'll beat you into a pulp every day until you remember,' cackled a second guard.

When the guards had left, she whispered to the fellow. 'Who are you?'

'Please, don't speak to me. If they hear, they will come in and beat me.'

'Why?'

'Because they enjoy it. And to wring from me a secret I cannot give to them.'

'They will not hear us speaking. At night, the guards stand nearer the tavern end of the agora.'

Silence for a time, then: 'I . . . I found something they seek,' he said.

'They? You mean the Cult?'

He seemed reticent. 'Yes, the masked ones,' he croaked. 'The Athenian guards act under their orders.'

'Why don't you tell them what they want to know?'

'Because if they find the carvings, then the world will burn.' He caught his last word. 'I have said too much.'

He fell silent for the rest of that night. Days passed, and each one began with the inmate being beaten by the guards. When the guards left, she tried to comfort him with simple conversation, but he would be too busy muttering to himself, chanting over and over.

The following day, Kassandra heard the guards beating him again. 'Cough up your secrets, dog,' they sneered as they broke his fingers, one by one. Kassandra hugged her knees to her chest and closed her eyes, wishing it to be over for the poor man as quickly as possible. As the guards left, one called back at him: 'It'll be your toes tomorrow.'

He whimpered quietly to himself. 'Dear Photina, I pray you are well, that Demeter blesses the soils of Naxos to keep you well fed, that Ariadne blesses the grapevines . . . Dear Photina, how I miss your touch . . . Sweet Photina, it has been years since last we were together, but . . .'

Kassandra's eyes blinked open, realization dawning. 'Your wife is Photina of Naxos?' she said, thinking of Barnabas' brief love on the island.

Silence.

'And you are Meliton, the seafarer.'

Another short silence, then: 'The guards told you that, did they? Are they paying you to question me now?'

'You spoke with Herodotos once,' she continued, 'told him of the time you were shipwrecked on Thera . . . of the carvings there, the lost knowledge of Pythagor–'

'*Shhh!*' he hissed. 'Very well, we can talk, but promise me you will not say his name aloud – for it will be the death of us both.'

They talked that day and into the evening, Meliton recounting the story of Thera, eulogizing Herodotos and reinforcing the historian's fears that the lost wisdom be found by the Cult. That night, when they both fell asleep, her new friend was taken from her. The guards stomped into the adjacent cell in the darkness. She heard Meliton wail, heard them thrashing him, then heard the crunch of a stamping boot breaking his skull, the wet sputter of his brains bursting across the floor and finally the hiss of his legs trailing as they dragged his smashed corpse outside.

Isolation, once again.

As the seasons wore on, through heat and cold, she began to see the masked shades again. In her dreams as before, but this time in the waking hours also. Deimos too. They would stand and stare from the edge of her vision as she repeated thousands of sit-ups, leaps, squats and balancing exercises. Every so often, she imagined that she held the Leonidas spear in her hand, and she would swish round, streaking the make-believe weapon through the imagined ghosts, scattering them. This became such a habit that she took to laughing when she saw them, shrieking with delight when she made them vanish.

One morning she awoke to the sound of scratching. A rat, she guessed. No, it was coming from up above. She squinted at the small rectangle of light in the grid overhead, seeing a feathery mass shuffling about up there. For a moment, her heart skipped a beat. *Ikaros?* But with a flurry of wings and before she could be sure it was him, the bird was gone, and a small object thumped down on her forehead. She yelped, then caught the small clay disc as it bounced. Her eyes combed the surface of the disc over and over, and the words inscribed there. *Be ready*, it stated. She looked up at the grid again. *For what?*

On rolled the endless march of time, the masked visions taunting her. One day, the vision of Deimos appeared, alone at the cell gate. She pretended not to notice him for a time, before springing up, thrusting her 'lance' at his chest.

He did not vanish.

'Sister,' he said.

The word echoed through the jail like a drumbeat.

She struggled to balance, still in that mock battle pose. It was the first word she had been offered in so long. He wore his white robes, but – for once – no armour.

'I have struggled to understand what you were trying to do back in Sphakteria,' he said.

'The last thing I remember,' she replied, her own voice sounding strange after so long without speaking, 'was trying to save you.'

'The last thing *I* remember is your spear knocking me

305

unconscious,' he replied instantly. 'It wouldn't be the first time you have cast me away to die.'

'So that's what the Cult told you?'

'That's what I *know*.'

Kassandra laughed coldly. 'Then what now? Have you come to open my throat?'

'I could, any time I wanted. Right now, even,' he rumbled.

She felt a deep resignation, a will for him to do as he threatened. But then she noticed him looking back over his shoulder, an edginess in his eyes, as if checking nobody else was in the jail with him.

'But before that,' he raised a hand and clasped one of the gate bars, then pressed his face to a gap, 'tell me what you know.'

'I thought the Cultists told you everything. Sounds like you're on their side, but they're not on yours. You know that's why they keep me here, don't you? As a spare.'

Deimos' mouth flashed in a rictus and he shook the gate by the bars, causing it to clank. 'You think I'm replaceable? Just a puppet? The Cult are nothing without me.'

'Did they tell you that too?' she asked calmly.

Deimos' eyes flicked this way and that. 'Do not goad me, Sister. Perhaps I *should* kill you right now – to spoil your theory, to show that you are nothing.'

'Then open the gate, come, do it,' she said, her heart gathering pace as she wondered if her legs had the spring they might need to make a break for it.

Deimos' anger ebbed. 'First, you will tell me your

twisted version of the truth. Why was I abandoned that night on the mountain?'

Kassandra's plans of escape faltered then. All she had wanted since that night was the chance to explain. Her thoughts began to gallop like a herd of Thessalian steeds, but she drew on invisible reins, slowing them, taking a breath, remembering her discussions with Sokrates. The best way to win a debate was to gently guide an opponent to the conclusion, using simple questions and plain reasoning like oars. She knelt on the cell floor, gesturing for Deimos to do the same on the other side of the gate.

'What do you remember of it?' she said. 'I don't mean the memories the artefact has shown you. What do *you* remember of it?'

Deimos slid down the gate to sit as well, one hand wringing his hair. 'Mother, Father . . . you. Watching, all of you, as an old man lifted me.'

'An old man?'

His brow furrowed. 'An . . . ephor.'

'Aye, it was.'

'Why? I was not lame or ill, was I?'

'No. But you were kissed by the poisonous lips of the Oracle.'

Deimos' eyes searched the ether.

'And you know who feeds the Oracle her words.'

He nodded slowly, silently, staring into space. 'A baby with a fate so terrible it was thrown off a cliff. What kind of prophecy would lead to that?'

'The Oracle said you were going to bring about Sparta's downfall if you lived. So Sparta did what Sparta does.

Waiting for the outcome was too big a risk. When you survived, the Cult took you for themselves. They moulded you into a champion . . . a weapon.'

'I made myself,' he growled, his eyes rolling up to stare at her like an angered hound.

'Into what? Is this what you wanted to be?'

'The Cult think me a *God*. They worship me!'

'Do they?' said Kassandra glibly.

Deimos rose again, chest rising and falling. He began to pace before the cell gate. '*Malákas!*' he cursed. 'And your bones are made of gold, are they? Ha! They threw off the wrong child! No . . . I *was* saved that night, shorn from you and my wretched family.'

'Do you remember the last time you saw me that night?' she said.

Deimos slowed. 'I remember . . . a look. A final look.'

'Aye, it was when I rushed for the edge of the mountain. When I tried to save you, to catch you.' Her head lolled as a sob tried to grow in her chest. 'I failed. I killed an ephor instead. I was thrown from the mountain too as punishment. My life ended up there also.'

'The tragic heroine,' he growled, swiping a hand, but unable to look her in the eye.

'Nobody is to blame but the Cult, Deimos. Even Father – duty-bound and blinded by his Spartan pride – was their victim that night. It took me more than twenty years to understand his quandary. Had he not done what the Oracle demanded, we would all have been disgraced.'

'Disgraced?' Deimos raged. 'And that would have been worse than the position we find ourselves in now?'

'Mother went after you too,' Kassandra pleaded.

Deimos halted. 'What?'

'She went down into the bone pit to find you. And she did find you.'

Deimos stared at her.

'She fled Sparta and took you to a healer. But that healer was Chrysis the Cultist. She lied to Mother, told her you had died.' She wrapped both hands around the cell bars. 'Don't you see: you're being used. You wouldn't be here with me if you thought they were telling you the whole truth.' She gestured to the jail's exterior door. 'This is what the Cult do. They harness power while it is useful. They have done it with you. They have done the same with Athens. They once did the same with Sparta, planting their number amongst the ephors and even the kings. When a person or even a state ceases to be useful, they will be cast off, destroyed.'

'Kleon has the power in Athens now,' he seethed. 'He will not be letting go. And he would not be so foolish as to underestimate my part in bringing him that prize.' He grabbed the bars like Kassandra, his nose touching hers. 'The Cult will never control me. I'm winning this war for them.'

Kassandra stared into his eyes. 'At what cost ... Alexios?'

Deimos trembled. 'Whatever it takes,' he whispered. 'Is that not your very mantra, misthios?'

Both beheld each other for an age.

The groan of the exterior door snapped them from the moment.

Kleon strode in and looked Kassandra up and down as if she were a scrap of dog meat. Deimos backed away from the bars looking guilty.

'We've been searching for you, Deimos,' Kleon snapped. 'Interesting that I should find you . . . here.'

'I came to . . . it's nothing.' He shook his head, not meeting Kleon's sharp look.

'You came to kill her?' he guessed, arching an eyebrow. 'That was not your action to take, *boy*. Leave. Now!' He snapped his fingers, pointing at the door.

'I am not your puppet,' Deimos rumbled, looking Kleon in the eye, 'and you are not my master.'

Kleon held Deimos' gaze. An oily smile rose on his face. 'Of course, Champion,' he said, his tone softening. 'I merely worry for your well-being.'

Deimos shrugged. 'Do whatever you want with her,' he hissed, turning to leave. As he did so, he met Kassandra's eye one last time before swinging away, leaving the jail.

Kleon beheld her now, hands clasped over his belt like a fat man who has just enjoyed a double helping of food. She noticed the cloying scent of sweet wax wafting from his carefully groomed red locks and pointed beard, and that he wore one of Perikles' robes.

'No better fit than a dead man's clothes,' she said flatly.

Kleon chuckled. 'Perikles' strategy brought Athens to the brink of disaster.'

'So you had him murdered.'

'You can't find the perfect yolk without breaking some of the quail's eggs. He wasn't right for us. Killing Perikles then taking Sphakteria was only the beginning. Since

310

then I have heaped victory upon victory onto my glowing reputation. The neutral island of Melos rebuffed our offer to bring them under the Athenian wing. So we smashed their city and took their island for ourselves. The Aeginetans dared to side with the Spartans, and we routed them utterly. The Spartan isle of Kythera fell to us soon after. My legend grows. I can do *anything*.'

'Like raise the tax levy to crippling levels? Or lead young Athenian soldiers to their deaths? I heard the gossip of passers-by, about a crushing defeat at Delium. How many fell there?' she sneered. 'I have sensed the change in tone during my time in here. The cheers and songs of the early days have turned sour and hoarse. People now grumble about your blind pursuit of conquest and instead champion talk of truces and armistices. You are no longer the hero you were once mistaken for, and –'

'And my next move will be the finest yet,' he interrupted. 'There are rebels on the isle of Lesbos, in the city of Mytilene. It is rumoured that they have opened talks with the Spartans with a view to defecting to the Peloponnesian League.'

'What have you done?' she said, spotting the evil in his eyes.

'Me? I've done nothing,' he laughed. 'The vote has been cast, and the fleet has set sail. The soldiers and citizens of Mytilene will have a hard time revolting once they're all dead!'

'Another atrocity? When they mocked you, called you the screaming ape – I thought it was because you were loud and repugnant. Well you are, but now I know that

that is exactly what you are inside as well. You scratch every itch, paint over every crack, snap every rope to cling to power at any cost. That is tyranny defined. Perikles sought not to appease the animal whims of the masses, but to guide them to better ways of thinking, to understand democracy and reason.'

'Democracy?' he smiled. 'Well, only one man sits at that much-vaunted table now. And that man . . . is me.' He pointed to his chest with a huge grin.

'Now I must be going. Trouble stirs in the north, near Amphipolis. The Spartans simply do not know when they are beaten. Right now they try to secure the north as their own – to steal the gold, silver and good timbers of those lands. I smell a further triumph in the offing. Once I have crushed them, the gates to the north and to Thrakia will be mine to control. You know what lies up there, don't you?'

Kassandra felt a chill pass over her.

'King Sitalkes once promised his vast Thrakian army to the Cultic cause: one hundred thousand spears and fifty thousand horses – fierce, brutish warriors. Sitalkes has since died, but his barbarian army is still very much at large. They will answer my call and they will descend upon and shackle all Hellas. An age of order and control awaits.'

Kassandra stared at him, her heart plunging.

He clicked his fingers. 'The Cult wins, Kassandra. You lose. You lost the moment you rejected the chance to join us. And now . . . it ends for you.'

He left, and two guards entered, armed with axes, faces

set hard. They clicked the cell gate closed behind them, locking it. One twirled his axe and grinned. 'He told us to make it hurt.' He flashed a look at the other. 'Hack off her feet.'

The other swung his axe at her ankles. Kassandra felt instinct take hold. She sprang up, catching the ceiling grate. The axe sped through the space her legs had occupied. She kicked down hard on the top of the first man's skull. A crack of vertebrae echoed through the cell and he slumped to the ground. She landed and grabbed the dead man's axe, slicing it upwards to catch the strike of the other before driving him back against the wall, pirouetting on her heel and slamming the axe blade into his grinning face, chopping his head off from the lips upwards. The top half of his head rested on the wall-embedded axe and the rest of his body slid to the ground below a trail of wet, black blood.

Shaking, she turned to the first fallen one, fishing the keys from his belt. She unlocked the cell door, tasting sweet freedom, almost there . . . until she heard the thunder of more approaching feet. That frantic fight had taken almost every trace of energy from her malnourished body. No more . . . no more.

'*Charge!*' a familiar voice roared. Two figures burst into the jail and staggered to a halt, back to back. One was armed with a shovel and the other with a broom. Both looked first a little bemused, then crestfallen when they saw her standing by the open cell door.

Her heart surged with joy. 'Barnabas, Sokrates?'

'Misthios!' Barnabas wailed, dropping his war-shovel and seizing her in a tight embrace.

Sokrates eyed the two butchered guards. 'You asked me to stay alive.' He raised his arms aloft like an Olympic champion. 'And here I am.'

'We heard rumours that you were here,' Barnabas panted. 'We weren't sure. We sent Ikaros so you would know to –'

'– to be ready,' Kassandra finished for him. Her ears pricked up when she heard yet more scuffling feet. 'And we must remain alert. These two guards will soon be missed. But where can we hide? This city is Kleon's.'

'All is in hand,' Sokrates assured her. 'Come, we will take the alleys and the hidden tunnel back to Perikles' old home. It has been abandoned since his death. There, we will plan our next move. Hope is not lost, but it fades . . . and fast.'

In the noon heat of the sweltering Athenian summer, she stood on the balcony of Perikles' old home, twisting the half-spear in one hand in gentle repetitions of old combat training moves. It felt good to have the lance in her grasp again. Herodotos had salvaged it from the ashes of Sphakteria. Barnabas had brought her good leathers too – a warrior's shell. She swirled the spear once more then slid it into her belt, feeling strong. Many days of rest, good bread, honey and nuts had recharged her body once again.

Ikaros floated down to rest on the balustrade and she stepped over to preen him, kissing his head. He was an old bird now, she realized sadly. She looked out into the silvery heat of the east, seeing the Athenian fleet setting to sea, sails bulging as more than thirty vessels cut north towards distant Amphipolis. Kleon was gone to claim his glory. But the city was still his and the Cult's. Or more accurately, given Sokrates' update – that four more members of the Cult had been killed during her stint in jail – it might be Kleon's alone, if he was the last of them.

The last and the darkest, he had said.

Behind her, voices rose and fell as the survivors of Perikles' retinue squabbled about this grim truth. She plucked a grape off of a vine dangling from the balcony trellis and popped it into her mouth. The explosion of cool juice could not sweeten the scene as she turned to look upon them. Sokrates, the ever-underdressed Alkibiades, Herodotos, Aristophanes, Euripides, Sophocles and Hippokrates stood around the dead leader's dusty planning table, faces wracked with tiredness and indecision.

'Call upon Thucydides,' Herodotos insisted. 'There are boats and regiments who are loyal to him. They will stand against Kleon.'

'Not enough,' Herodotos sighed. 'And he languishes in exile, far from here, for his part in Amphipolis' original fall from Athenian hands.'

'We are here, in Athens, in her pulsing heart. She needs us now,' Hippokrates bleated, chapping the table.

'What do you suggest?' Sokrates scoffed. 'That we form a brigade armed with shovels and brushes and seize control? We would look ridiculous. Worse, it would make us tyrants.'

'Kleon wrested power by sheer force. It is his way,' argued Aristophanes. 'But there are other ways – more refined and lasting – with which to win the hearts and minds of Athens' people.'

'He's going to suggest a play,' Sophocles said, his eyelids sliding over in exasperation. 'And let me guess: only *he* is witty enough to compose such a work.'

Aristophanes shot him a sour look. 'Nonsense. I'll let you hold my tablet, and fetch me drinks.'

Sophocles exploded in outrage. Sokrates wheeled away from the table with a sigh, only to bump into Alkibiades, who helpfully offered to massage his shoulders and alleviate his stress . . . then began to nibble on his ear. When Sokrates shrugged him off, exasperated, Alkibiades threw out his hands in innocence. 'What? Is it not the purpose of a loved one to exude love?'

Sokrates melted into a throaty chuckle. 'So you *have* been listening to me? Perhaps it is, yes, but not now,' he said, gesturing back to the table.

Kassandra watched, longing for these great minds to produce a jewel of a plan. But days passed with no resolution. One day, Barnabas came to her side as she watched.

'I feel it too, misthios. An itch that cannot be scratched by standing here.'

She turned to him. 'Even after all the strife you have been through with me, you yearn to travel to Amphipolis?'

'They didn't tell you, did they? About the Spartan garrison there.'

She frowned. 'There are thousands of Spartiates there, I hear. Kleon will gather up nine thousand of his own along the way. He will have a tough fight on his hands. He will not seize the gateway to the north easily.' She thought again of Kleon's boasts about the Thrakian horde beyond those gates, and mouthed a prayer in support of the Spartans.

Barnabas shook his head. 'There are little more than one hundred Spartiates there, and a few allied hoplites.'

'What?'

'Since the disaster at Sphakteria, the ephors refuse to allow the purebred regiments to march to war. To defend Amphipolis, they commissioned just a knot of Spartiates and filled out the ranks with masses of Helots.'

'Helots?' Kassandra gasped. They were effective support skirmishers and baggage handlers. But to make up an army almost entirely of them was madness. 'May the Gods be with them. Who leads them?'

'General Brasidas,' Barnabas replied.

She stared.

'He was rescued from the ashes of Sphakteria too. All this time while you were incarcerated, he has led his Helot army around the north, seeking allies, searching for cracks in Kleon's iron empire.'

She heard the group inside reciting the lines of the play they had concocted in these last days. Euripides stood on a crate, playing the part of Perikles, imperious, solemn, plainspoken. Aristophanes then entered the scene, skipping, waving his hands as if picking flowers, then squealing like a tortured pig. 'No, listen to me, listen to *me*! Look, there is a dark cave. Come with me, let us leap blindly inside!'

Alkibiades roared with laughter as he sucked on a wineskin. Herodotos clapped. Sophocles beamed with delight, tapping the tablet, reading along with the script as the two acted it out.

'The assembly gathers tomorrow,' said Sokrates, coming over to Kassandra's side. 'This play will show the people Kleon's cynical ways, and that he is no champion or hero. His reputation will be left hanging in ribbons.'

She noticed his sideways gaze resting on her.

He arched one eyebrow and smiled. 'I can see words burning behind your lips. Say what you feel.'

'Destroying his reputation alone is not enough,' she mused. 'We cannot merely wound him, for he has the means to wreak a terrible revenge. We must destroy him utterly.'

'Exactly,' Sokrates said, his smile fading.

'Then my part in this affair will be on the stage of battle,' she said, standing straight, looking to Barnabas.

'The *Adrestia* is ever ready, misthios.' Barnabas half-bowed fondly. 'We await your command, as always.'

17

A hot wind furrowed Brasidas' hair as he rested one foot on Amphipolis' sun-bleached southern parapet, staring across the parched grass outside. The River Strymon forked around the city's northern walls, and a hill lay an arrow-shot to the south. The morning before, the hill had been a pleasant, quiet mound and no more. Then Kleon's boats had arrived at Eïon Harbour, a small Athenian-held dock where the Strymon spilled into the Aegean. Now, the hill was capped in the silver, white and blue of first-class Athenian hoplites. Thousands and thousands of them. Ironclad riders and a sea of allies too. They sang bold songs, mocking the Spartans' defeat at Sphakteria. The chorus was unending, humiliating.

'There are too many of them,' said Clearidas, his deputy.

Brasidas saw from the corner of his eye the jumble of men down inside Amphipolis' walls: the army he had been granted to take and hold this vital northern city. The hundred and fifty Spartiates stood like statues near the gatehouse below. But the rest? The Helots had served him well in this northern campaign – standing their ground and attacking bravely, but never against a foe such as this. They wore their dogskin caps in place of helms, and shabby brown capes instead of Spartan red. He glanced to the north, across the river, seeing nothing but a warping band of heat. The Thrakians lay somewhere out there. Woe betide Hellas should the red-haired bastard on that hill win this land and throw open the doors to them. But the darkest danger stood with Kleon on the hill. The beast who had almost killed him at Sphakteria.

Deimos. The invincible dread.

'What are we to do?' Clearidas pressed. 'We have little grain left, and Kleon knows this.'

'What can we do?' Brasidas replied. 'On one of the rare occasions when the Athenians dare to face us in the field, we have not the means to meet them. I value every Helot in my ranks as much as any one of the Spartiates . . . but they will be massacred if we face those Athenian elites on the plain in pitched battle. Our only option is to wait, and to pray that the Goddess Tyche will shine favour upon us.'

Clearidas left him and went off to address and encourage the men. Brasidas stared at the huge army outside the city, and felt the strangest, most un-Spartan of emotions.

Fear.

The sun burned on the back of Kleon's neck, and the saddle had turned his buttocks numb. But it would not do for him to dismount and be on the ground at the same level as the wretches around him – at the same level as Deimos. He eyed the champion, standing nearby on the hill's brow. *I do not need you, dog*, he mused. All the way here on the galleys, the soldiers had cheered Deimos' every appearance from the cabin. At Eion Harbour, they had sung songs of his heroics at Sphakteria. Yet most shrank as he passed them. *Fear and respect, that glorious blend,* Kleon seethed, the hand beneath his cloak clutching in futility at thin air, forming into a fist and shaking. *Well, when battle comes, perhaps you will find the greatest honour, Deimos.* He smiled, the clutching hand settling around the upper limb of his bow. *To fight as a hero . . . and to die in the fray.*

Just then, an explosion of laughter rolled across the hilltop. Behind his foremost, serried ranks, the allied hoplites from Korkyra had set down their spears and shields and were drinking water and sharing bread. One amongst them pranced in circles around another. 'Look at me! Look at *me!*' the prancing one chirped. More laughter. Hot fingers of disgrace crawled up Kleon's neck. *The play . . . the damned play!* Rumours of the goings-on back in Athens had reached them that morning in Eion. He had heard whispers, seen men's laughter-red faces quickly turn away from his. One messenger confirmed it: in his absence, Perikles' orphaned rats had crawled from their holes and spread a plague of lies about him to the people. *Well,* he seethed, *I will send word to my powerful friends back there, and they will . . .* The train of thought halted when he thought of the last Cult gathering. He and one other masked figure. The rest? All dead. *When I return, I will have the rats hung from the city walls by their ankles. The crows will peck out their eyes.*

The re-enactors were in full sway now. His chest stung with anger, but now was not the place to deal with them, in full view of the rest of the army. They would respect punishment, yes, but not the horrible death he had in store for the offenders. He thought of his dogs back in Eion, and glanced south to that small harbour. Those hounds would feast upon these actors' open bodies, while they still breathed.

'General,' asked one of the Athenian taxiarchs, snapping Kleon from his dark thoughts. 'What say you? Do we assault the city walls?'

Kleon eyed Amphipolis, and the lonely figure of Brasidas watching him up on the city walls. Some of his officers had claimed the Athenian hoplites were growing restless, and whispering that after so many years of bombast against Perikles' conservative strategy, now the great Kleon was afraid to attack what was no more than a shower of Helots. A hot spike of pride shot through him, and he made to grab his sword, imagining hoisting it aloft and booming out the order for the advance – a heroic moment that would be talked about for ever, trampling the irksome gossip of the play . . .

'Because I'm not so sure we should,' the taxiarchos added. 'See the trees beyond the city – there could be horsemen in there. Remember the carnage the Theban riders wreaked at Boeotia? If such a force was to fall upon us here then . . .'

Kleon felt his guts twist and turn, and a loud gurgle of distress rumbled from his abdomen. He heard little more of the taxiarchos' advice. 'Send scouts to reconnoitre the woods. Establish a watch up here. The army will return to Eion.'

Grumbles and gasps of frustration rose from the Athenian ranks. Kleon's neck burned with indignation. 'We will return tomorrow,' he howled. 'By then the Spartans will have had another day of dwindling bread and growing dread. Tomorrow we will parade their heads on our spears. Tomorrow . . . for *victory!*'

The speech stirred a few cheers, but the barked orders of the many officers quickly drowned it out, as they shouted for their regiments to turn and descend the hill's southern slope. A thunder of boots rose from the hilltop as the Athenian army shuffled round, turning away from the city of Amphipolis, kicking up a thick plume of dust. Kleon saw the Korkyraean allies forming the left wing of the pivoting force. In theory they were supposed to be leading the march back to Eion. Yet they were slow and shambling, out of line – some still snatching up their helms and spears, putting corks back in their drinking skins. His fury rose like a burst of molten bronze.

'Move!' he roared, heeling his horse over towards them, drawing a wooden baton to whack the slowest of them on the back of the head.

Brasidas felt the hot wind fall still at that moment. 'They withdraw?' he whispered to himself. Through the dust-obscured sunlight he saw the shambolic manoeuvre. Memories of childhood in the Agoge exploded across his mind: of the tacticians teaching him and the other boys how to identify a weak spot in an enemy force. *Backs and flanks*, the hoary old expert had implored them, arranging lines of polished pebbles on the dirt floor to demonstrate. His neck lengthened and a shiver scampered up from the base of his spine and across his scalp.

'Spartans,' he boomed down to his hundred and fifty. 'Be ready.'

They stiffened, holding their spears aloft. '*Aroo!*'

'The shame of Sphakteria has burned in my heart for too long. Is it not the same for you?' he roared as he sped down the battlement steps to come before them. They thundered in agreement, beating their spears on their shields.

He turned to the mass of Helots, led by Clearidas. 'And you, brave warriors, throw off your dogskin caps, take up your spears and prepare to stride with us . . . into *eternity*!'

The *Adrestia* sliced into the sands of the bay by the mouth of the River Strymon, halting with a violent judder. Kassandra leapt down into the coarse sands. Silence reigned. Until she heard a distant sound, carried on the hot breeze: a low groan of timbers. Gates swinging open, and the colossal roar of men. She looked up the long, low ridge – a grassy wall blocking her from the source of the sound. She sped up the slope, slipping in the scree, skin slick with sweat. Ikaros circled and shrieked madly, already high up there and seeing it all. When she came to the ridge's brow, she staggered to a halt, struck by a hot blast of wind and frozen by the sight ahead.

A round hill dominated the flatland. Down the southern slopes, the Athenian army washed in a perilously loose formation. Streaking round the hill's faraway eastern side was a tiny knot of red-cloaked Spartans, and she knew at once who led them. Yet the small Spartan force was dwarfed by the Athenian army.

What are you doing, Brasidas? she mouthed. *You know you cannot win this fight.*

But when those one hundred and fifty smashed into the unprepared Athenian left, they gouged deep and without mercy. With a thunder of shields and clatter of spears, a din of screams and a crackle of breaking bodies, Brasidas' Spartans laid waste to the Athenian left, pinning the centre too. It was like that vision at the Hot Gates: Brasidas leapt and spun amongst the enemy, he and his comrades cutting them down in scores, but she knew he could not win owing to sheer lack of numbers. When the Athenian trumpets blew, she saw Kleon's right swing in to support the stunned left, and felt a great sadness rise within her, knowing this was the end for Brasidas.

But then new Spartan pipes blared from the slopes of the hill's obscured western side. From the haze, a great wave of armed Helots spilled into view. Kassandra shivered at the Helot war cry as they sped around the hillside and into the unprotected backs of the Athenian mass.

The hillside became a riot of flashing silver and geysers of crimson. Kassandra saw Brasidas now deep in the fray, the front-line Athenian hoplites crowding around him, Kleon himself yelling and cajoling them, demanding Brasidas' head. The vision of the Hot Gates pulsed in her mind, the fall of the Spartan hero. *No, not this time.*

She lunged down the ridge, leaping over a brook and speeding to the edge of the fray. She ducked an Athenian spear, sliding through the blood-wet earth and leaping up, barging aside a Korkyraean who tried to attack her. There was no enemy on the field today but Kleon.

A gawping head bounced across her path, and a shower of hot blood and innards slapped on her back as she ran. At last she came to the heart of the fray. Athenian champions hacked at Brasidas. She grabbed one foe by the shoulder, twisting him to face her then ramming the Leonidas spear up and under his ribs. A second lashed his spear across her belly, slitting the skin and coating her thighs in blood. She dodged his second strike then sliced off his hand. Now Brasidas pounced upon the momentary upturn in fortunes to headbutt a third Athenian champion, then rip a fourth from face to groin. Swaying, shaking, face striped with blood, eyes and teeth white in a manic battle-grin, he raised his spear to salute Kassandra. 'I knew I had not seen the last of you! And your timing is perf–'

He spasmed, and then the tip of a lance burst through his chest with a gout of red.

'No!' Kassandra cried, reaching out.

The spear rose, taking Brasidas up with it like a fisherman's catch. The general twitched, vomiting blood. Deimos raised the spear like a banner of triumph, his muscles bulging with the effort, before he cast Brasidas down.

Deimos stared at her. 'So Kleon could not organize your execution?' he spat. 'Perhaps he should have left it to me after all.' With that, he flew for Kassandra, drawing his sword and swishing it for her neck. She backstepped and threw up her half-lance to cage the blow. Pressed together, the two blades shook madly – just as they had at Sphakteria – and both roared with effort, the battle raging on around them. 'This is it, Sister,' Deimos rasped, his

326

sword gradually edging her weapon towards her own neck. 'One of us must die.'

She felt a shudder of strength and forced her spear back against his blade. Like an arm-wrestler turning a contest, she grew as he shrank, his blade began to slide, her spear tip now edging towards his neck. Deimos' confidence began to crumble. She saw his eyes widen. Here she was again: on the precipice, with the chance to save her brother or let him die. And then he convulsed suddenly with a harrowing scream.

He fell. Kassandra backed away, staring at her lance. Had she done this? No, her blade had not touched him and had no fresh blood upon it. How then? Who? Then she saw the arrow jutting from Deimos' back, saw him slump to his knees and slide to one side. The battle swallowed up his body in a frenzy of struggling men, thrashing limbs and whirling spears. Her eyes traced the path the arrow had taken – to a small wart of rock behind Deimos. Up there stood Kleon, his bowstring still vibrating, his face lengthening as if in disbelief. His lips flickered up into a crazed and fleeting grin of triumph, and then he hurriedly nocked a fresh arrow. But before he could even draw, Kassandra lurched towards him.

'*Skatá*!' he squealed, fumbling the arrow, his arms becoming entangled in the bow.

As she speared for his chest, he threw himself to one side, tossing the bow down, then plunging into a reckless sprint through the battle. She raced in pursuit, fighting off a maw of gnashing spears just to cut through the chaos and keep sight of Kleon. Arrows whizzed and slingshot bullet-stones spat overhead as she leapt over the groaning wounded, splashed through puddles of blood and vomit and the contents of loosed bowels.

Only when she reached the edges of the fray did the battle start to thin. Eventually, the din of war was but a buzz behind her. All that mattered was the sprinting, flailing Athenian ahead. He stumbled and rolled, his blue cloak rapping and snapping in his wake. She ran like a deer, feeling her soles scrape on bare earth and then wet sand. The crash of waves surrounded her as she chased Kleon onto the beach. Clumps of wet sand flicked up in his wake, then plumes of foam as he thrashed out into the shallows. He waded out until water rose to his chest, then halted, gasping, panting, head flicking back to her and then to the sea. His face was white as the moon. 'I . . . I can't swim,' he garbled.

Silently, Kassandra waded out to him. He raised his sword. She grabbed his wrist and twisted it until he dropped the weapon, then seized him by the collar of his robe, dragging him back to the ankle-deep shallows. There, she cast him to his knees. He began to wail and plead. She heard not a word of it. Planting a hand on the back of his head, she pushed him down, prone, driving his face into the sand. His arms and legs thrashed and muffled screams shook the sand. At last, he fell still.

She fell back to sitting, her breath coming in great rasps. The last and most dangerous member of the Cult was dead. Behind her, she heard the moan of Spartan pipes, the solemn cry of victory. '*Aroo!*' they cried, spears raised, forming a circle around the body of their adored leader. Brasidas was dead, but against all the odds, Amphipolis was saved, the north too.

From within Kleon's robes, something floated out into the waves. A mask, she realized, notched on the brow from the strike of a sword. Ikaros came and settled on her shoulder as she watched it drift along the shoreline. The eagle shrieked at the shrinking piece of flotsam.

'Aye,' Kassandra said, stroking his feathers, 'it is over.'

18

They said that Brasidas died with the song of Spartan triumph in his ears. They said that he died with a wistful smile. Few had really seen his terrible end on the tip of Deimos' spear. As the *Adrestia* peeled away from the bay of Amphipolis, Kassandra gazed over the hinterland, shining red in the dying sun, pocked with funeral pyres and trophy mounds. The hill upon which the fray had turned was clear of bodies now, but the dead would never be forgotten. More, in Brasidas, Sparta had a new hero. Already they talked of his polyglot army as 'The Brasideans'. Even now those Spartans and Helots were camped together – for once classless and brotherly in victory.

Despite the triumph, the voyage south was a sombre one, with Barnabas and his crew subdued, spending the nights quietly drinking and chatting about their adventures with Kassandra. They stopped at Athens, where a new general had been elected. Nicias, championed by Sokrates and the set who had held on to Perikles' principles in the darkest days of Kleon's rule, had even opened talks with Sparta. A peace treaty was in the offing, some said – a fifty-year oath of harmony. It seemed fitting, Kassandra thought. Both Sparta and Athens had been ravaged by this war. Neither side had gained anything but an army of widows and orphans. She spent a moon in Athens, sitting by the graves of Phoibe and Perikles in silence before she set sail again, for home.

They reached Sparta in early August. Barnabas walked alongside her horse as she ambled north from Trinisa port and into the Hollow Land on a bright, late summer morning. So much time had passed since the disaster at Sphakteria, since she had last seen her mother. It felt like that moment approaching Naxos, years ago. Did Myrrine even know she was still alive? Was she still well? Her heart thumped as they entered the Spartan villages. Helots stopped what they were doing and stood, staring at her.

'The misthios,' one whispered.

'The heroine of Boeotia,' said another.

'Is it her? She who fought alongside Brasidas at Amphipolis and won the north?'

Spartiates too, braying and mock-sparring in the gymnasium, looked over at her, falling silent. They beheld her with evil scowls, as always. Then, as one, they began to lift their spears. For a moment she thought they meant to come at her, but the spears continued to rise, one-handed, pointing skywards in salute. As one, they issued a cry that stirred her to her soul.

'Aroo!'

Beyond them, she saw the gates of her family home creak open. Myrrine slipped through the gap, one hand on her chest as if to control her heart. Kassandra slid from her horse, staggered over and fell into her mother's arms.

They sat up most nights around the hearth, drinking well-watered wine, eating olives and barley cake. It took many nights to explain it all: the disaster at Sphakteria, the long maddening moons in the Athenian jail and the day when it had all changed. Freedom, Aristophanes' play, and then the journey north to Amphipolis.

'News of what happened there reached these parts last moon,' Myrrine said, supping her wine. 'They talked of a great number of deaths, but a glorious victory. About the fall of Brasidas.'

'He was an example to us all,' said Kassandra. 'The ephors granted him scraps to work with, and he saved the north from Kleon. I hear they plan to erect a cenotaph for him, near the Tomb of Leonidas. Fitting company.'

'I wept when I heard of his passing. But then I heard people talking of another who was present at the battle – a she-mercenary. At once I felt great hope in my heart that somehow, *somehow*, it was you. Since that moment I sent you to Sphakteria, I had not heard a thing – just tales of blackened corpses on that burnt island. But I never allowed myself to truly believe it was you at Amphipolis. At times, I prayed it was not . . . for they said Deimos was there too.'

A stone rose in Kassandra's throat. 'He was.'

Myrrine slowly looked up from the fire, her face half lit, eyes glassy. 'Aye, and so the whispers that it was he who killed Brasidas must be true also.'

'You . . . you asked me to bring him home,' Kassandra whispered. 'I could not.'

Myrrine seemed to shut down then, her gaze returning to the fire, staring, lost.

'I tried, Mother. But Kleon of Athens struck him down out of envy.'

After a time, Myrrine nodded. 'Then another of our bloodline is gone,' she said quietly. She rose, coming to slide down into Kassandra's seat, wrapping an arm across her shoulders. 'So few of us left,' she said, brushing Kassandra's loose hair with her fingers, staring into her eyes. 'I feel I should answer the question that you asked me once, long ago.'

'I don't understand.'

'Your father, Kassandra. Your *real* father.'

Myrrine leaned in, putting her lips to Kassandra's ear.

The name she whispered echoed through Kassandra's body. It was like a bell pealing inside. Now she understood . . .

The season turned, and autumn brought with it gales and rainstorms. One morning Kassandra awoke in the warm comfort of her bed, fresh of mind and her body for once devoid of the aches and pains that had accompanied her for years. She saw the sullen sky outside, framing the heights of Mount Taygetos. Perhaps it was the closeness of sleep, or the exact hue of the clouds, but something stroked her heart then, conjuring the memories of that night from her childhood. For the first time, she let the memory play out without fear. Since her return to Sparta, she had visited each of the five ancient villages, attended feasts and poetry evenings, trained in the gymnasium and swum in the bracing waters of the River Eurotas at dawn most days. Today, she had planned to take Ikaros hunting in the woods, but she realized now that there was one place she had yet to tread.

She went alone, not telling her mother or Barnabas. Carrying just a drinking skin and a round of cheese, she set off, taking deep breaths to clear her head, the air fresh and scented with pine and damp earth. Walking uphill, she unroped her famous half-lance and tried to use it like a walking cane. She smiled sadly, realizing just how inadequate it was for such a purpose, and just how small she had been all those years ago. As she climbed the mountain path, she imagined the ghosts of that lost age walking before her: the wretched ephors and priests. Nikolaos, Myrrine. And in her arms . . . little Alexios.

Tears stung behind her eyes, and she hardly noticed Ikaros' cries up ahead. When she reached the plateau, she gazed upon the sad, weather-worn altar where it had all taken place. For a moment, it seemed as if all her misery was set to swell up and explode. She almost let it happen. Only one thing stopped her.

The other figure standing up there.

He stood with his back to her, gazing out over the abyss.

'A . . . Alexios?' she stammered.

Ikaros' warning cries were all too clear now, the eagle circling and screeching above.

Alexios did not reply.

'But you fell, at Amphipolis.' She stared at her brother's bare shoulders, seeing the angry welt of a recent scar from an arrow wound, part masked by his long coils of dark hair.

'The wound is merely a decoration.' He turned to her, his face impassive. 'I have been waiting for the last moon on these heights. I knew you would come here eventually.' There was a terrible steel in his gaze. And she realized he was looking not at her, but at someone behind her.

'My lamb, my boy,' Myrrine said, stepping up to Kassandra's side.

'Mother?' Kassandra hissed. 'You followed me?'

'The mountain drew us all here,' Myrrine replied, placing a gentle hand on Kassandra's shoulder as she stepped past her. 'You promised to bring him home, Kassandra, and you have.'

Kassandra grabbed her wrist, halting her. 'It is not safe, Mother.'

But Myrrine's eyes brimmed with tears and she extended a hand towards him.

Alexios' brow pinched and he looked away. 'On the edge of the world, a mother reaches out to her child. Touching.'

'Alexios, please,' Myrrine whimpered.

'You use that name as if it means something to me,' he growled.

'It is the name your father and I gave you.'

His head twitched, cocking to one side to behold her in mistrust. 'Was that before you brought me up here to die?'

Myrrine clutched her chest. 'It was the Cult who brought us all up here that night. I did everything I could to save you.'

Alexios clenched his fists and shuddered where he stood.

Kassandra saw the fire rise within him. 'Alexios, it is over: the war, the Cult. Let their clouds clear from your mind. Remember who you are.'

He shook his head ever so slowly. 'The Cult sought to bring order to the world. *I* was their chosen one, and now I will be the bringer of order.'

'We are of the same blood, Alexios,' said Kassandra. 'All I have ever wanted is my family. I feel it in you too.'

Alexios' head lolled. He fell silent for a time. 'Once, when I was a boy, under Chrysis' care, I found a lion cub trapped in a snare. My friend tried to free it . . . and that's when I heard the deadly growl of its mother.' His head began to rise again. 'I watched as the lioness tore my friend to shreds. In the world of beasts, a family protects its young.' His head rose fully now, his eyes dark and wet with emotion.

'I loved you, Alexios,' Myrrine sobbed. She grimaced for a moment, as if quarrelling with herself. 'To the pits with Spartan ways, I *loved* you . . . and I still love you.'

Slowly, Alexios reached up to his shoulder scabbard and began to draw his sword. 'My name is Deimos. The one you love is dead. My destiny is clear and you will not stand in my way.' He stepped towards Myrrine and tore his blade free in a flash.

Clang! Kassandra's spear met his strike, saving her mother. Myrrine did not flinch – his blade edge a finger's-width away from her head – but her face flooded with fresh tears.

'Alexios, no!' Kassandra cried.

Spittle flew from his cage of teeth as he tried to force the blade upon his mother.

Kassandra yelled and summoned all her strength, throwing him back then pointing her spear at him. 'I don't want to fight you.'

'I told you at Amphipolis, Sister. One of us must die,' he drawled, then leapt for her.

Their blades clashed in a fury of sparks and the terrible song of steel rose from the mountain.

'No. *No!*' Myrrine cried, backing away, sinking to her knees.

Deimos launched a flurry of strikes, ripping at her arms, cutting her forehead, nearly driving her from the precipice, and were it not for her quick thinking and a kicked-up puff of dust, he would have run her through. The angry clouds gathered and rumbled above, and Kassandra felt a great anger rise within her. Rain fell as she battered and battered at his sword, saw his demon's glower crumble away, watched his weapon spin from his hand and off over the abyss, looked on as her brother crumpled to the ground, hands thrown up like a shield, felt her spear arm tense, then her whole body convulse as she sank to strike.

The spear tip halted right before his breastbone.

They both panted, staring into each other's eyes, she cradling him, holding him on the edge of death. The sky growled with nascent thunder.

Myrrine crawled over to them, clutching at her hair. 'Please, no.'

'I have done terrible things,' he whispered. 'Sister, it could have been so different.'

Kassandra felt that warm flicker of flame inside her heart. 'It still can, Brother.'

He shook his head. 'I told you that one of us must die here. None possessed the strength to better me . . . until

I fought you on Sphakteria. You were my equal there. And then at Amphipolis. Had Kleon not struck me down, you would have beaten me.'

'It matters not,' she pleaded. 'Think of what could lie ahead for us. A family as we were meant to be.'

They shared a look then – just like that moment of their shared childhood, when Kassandra had nearly caught him. A fresh tear spilled down Alexios' cheek, mixing with the rain. 'I cannot be what you want me to be.' His head shook slowly, his lips trembling. 'The weeds burrow too deep.'

She saw his hand move towards the edge of his greave, saw him draw the hidden knife from there, saw him strike towards Myrrine's neck. Time slowed. Kassandra felt her body spasm, as she drove the Leonidas spear deep into Alexios' chest. The knife tumbled from his grip, and then he stared into the sky with a long, slow, final breath.

Myrrine let out a plaintive wail, and Kassandra sobbed long and loud. The thunder rolled overhead, and only as it faded did Myrrine's weeping fall silent.

'I tried to save him, Mother,' Kassandra croaked as the rain began to ease.

'I saw what happened,' Myrrine whimpered. 'He is free now.'

They embraced each other and Alexios' body for hours. Eventually, the clouds parted and shafts of deep orange light stretched across the heights of Mount Taygetos.

Epilogue

I walked through the darkness, and I was not afraid. I was a Spartan, a misthios, a war hero. My footsteps sounded so lonely in that dark old place. As I went deeper underground, the summer heat behind me faded. I struck a flint hook to light my torch, and passed the now-empty rock-cut chambers. The chains were still there, and the long-dried bloodstains of the Monger's victims. I passed the forgotten hall with the grim snake statue. The trough below its fangs had long run dry of blood, and so the snake would starve. The altar where I had first met that twisted soul, Chrysis, now languished under a thick coating of dust. On I went.

Part of me dreamt, like a child, that I might find my brother deep in these old caves, just as I had found him that night when the Cult had gathered here. But the memory of splitting his heart with my spear was still too close and raw. It had been almost a year since his death. We buried him and we wept. None had expected any others to attend the ceremony, but when Nikolaos and Stentor appeared to watch from afar, I gave them both a solemn look, inviting them to come closer. That night we dined in the old family estate. It was desperately awkward at times. When Nikolaos, at one end of the table, asked for a cup of wine, Mother, at the other end, poured one . . . then drained it in one gulp herself before carrying on eating. Stentor chuckled in amusement, before disguising it with a cough. Aye, those wounds did not heal with that feast, and they most probably never will. But there was an understanding now — the hatred of the past was buried, the Cult with it.

It was with Mother's blessing that I set out once more the following spring, on one last voyage that I knew I could not avoid. As the Adrestia *cut across the seas, Barnabas and Herodotos were inseparable, recounting the tales of our adventures together, the captain acting out and wildly exaggerating events on the deck, while Herodotos tapped away with his stylus at woodpecker-like speed to record it all, tongue poking out in concentration.*

We came to the broken island of Thera on a serene day – the sea like a teal silk and not a breath of wind in the air. Herodotos offered to accompany me into the black mountains, but I declined. This was a journey I had to make alone – well, with Ikaros on my shoulder. I walked around that crescent – that barren husk of blown-apart volcano – wondering if Meliton's claims of elaborate carvings high up on the rocks had all been a hoax, a wild jest. What was there on this forsaken isle but ash and stone?

I trekked into the heights. I spent days searching the rugged land. One day, I came to a sheer wall of rock – blank to the eye. It was only when I slid my hand along the surface for balance that I felt the fine etchings. When I stood back I saw the strange inscriptions – betrayed by the merest hint of shadow. I stayed there for days, exploring, reading the symbols again and again, watching them at night in the hope they might light up as they had done for Meliton. One night they did, and a section of rock peeled back to reveal a hidden gateway into the mountain. I stepped inside, and that was where I found him. My real father.

The legend, Pythagoras.

Alive some sixty years after most thought him dead – many, many more years older than men should live. His eyes were bright, his mind golden. His words changed everything. He showed me things that I knew I could never explain to another soul . . . except maybe Barnabas. The island of Thera was a smashed husk, yes, but beyond that rocky gateway, golden wonders lay. The strange carvings were only the beginning of it. He gave me an ancient staff — a fine piece that felt strange to the touch just like my spear — and showed me many other such marvels. Yet as if tragedy had shadowed me here, I spent only a few days in his company. The brightness in Pythagoras' eyes began to wane, his gait became shambling and his breath shallow. He explained it was because this was meant to be, that the staff had granted him his extra years and now I was to be its bearer. It was on the third day that I awoke to hear him wheezing, saw his lips had turned blue. I tried to help him, to give him back the staff, yet he refused and insisted it was his time. He died in my arms, just like Alexios.

I burnt his body on a pyre as he insisted I must, and watched the smoke carry his shade away. After that I chiselled at the stone around the hidden gateway, causing the cliff to slip and bury the entrance for ever. Again, Pythagoras had insisted on this, and I knew why. For those few days inside that place had shown me that all in this world was truly not as it seemed — just as Sokrates had insisted. Yet there were still so many secrets, so many questions unanswered. With his dying breaths he had told me that we would speak again. And that was why I knew I had to come back to the Cave of Gaia.

My footsteps echoed like the flapping wings of disturbed doves as I entered the great cave, and set eyes upon the circle of polished stone, and the red-veined plinth in the centre. No Cultists, no Deimos . . . no Alexios. My throat thickened, achingly sad for all that I had lost. Then I set my eyes on the dust-coated pyramid atop the plinth, and felt my heart begin to soar.

I stepped forward, sucked in a lungful of air and blew the dust from the pyramid. Its golden lustre returned, and I felt that low hum strike through the cave, saw the strange glow from within the piece.

And then it spoke to me.

'Come closer,' it whispered.

My heart froze. The voice . . . it was Mother's voice. That was one secret my real father had explained to me: 'The artefacts of the ones who came before are enchanting . . . but devious. They search within you, they know what you are, what you love, what you fear. They twist your heart, shape your soul, fog your mind. Be careful, Kassandra.'

I reached up, my hand hovering over the pyramid, feeling the heat emanating from it.

'Touch me,' it begged.

I wet my lips, spread my feet as if about to go into battle, then placed my palm upon the smooth surface. It was as if I had been struck on the head with a boulder. White lights, golden flashes, an aria of shrill song. Something seized me, shook me, wrung me. It was like great hands pinning me, then hammering at my spirit as a smith might try to shape a blade. This unseen force was trying to steal from me my very essence . . . or to slay me. I felt a scream rise in my chest.

Then a force like a stiff gale hit me, and the wicked energy was gone. I felt safe now, in this strange netherworld of soft light, where I had neither weight nor form. Now I heard another voice.

'You have witnessed in full what this artefact and the others like it can do to men,' Pythagoras said.

'Father?' I croaked.

'The voice you heard beckoning you was not your mother's. But this is me, of that you can be sure. I told you we would speak again.'

'How, how can it be? I set your body on the pyre.'

'Charon the Ferryman is waiting for me to cross the Styx. My bond with the artefact is the only thing holding my soul on the banks of the living, but that bond is coming to an end. And so I must tell you the truth about the pyramid, before it is too late. It was created

342

by the ones who came before in order to see through the webs of time. Past, present and things yet to come . . .'

'That is why the Cult revered the pyramid so much,' I said, suddenly realizing. 'It is a key to control and order.'

'They never understood.' Pythagoras sighed. 'Many decades ago, a group of people gathered together to uphold a theory which they believed could bring stability to the world. That everything functioned in equal parts, order and disorder. Discipline and freedom. Control and liberty. Like a set of scales in perfect harmony.'

The soft light around me warped to form a hazy image of a gathering. Amongst them, I saw a younger Pythagoras, guiding, teaching. Many heads nodded and some debated. Then I saw some, to the rear, whispering amongst themselves.

'But some of this group could not resist the temptations of boundless power. They fell into the arms of chaos . . . and the Cult of Kosmos was born.'

Images flashed across the soft light: of the masked villains gathering, chanting, of the tendrils of their wicked schemes – armies dying needlessly, citizens butchered, innocent men executed . . . and a child being tossed from a mountain.

'They abused their power, casting the Greek world into eternal war.' The images ceased abruptly. 'A war you were destined to stop.'

I felt my heart thud. 'I? And . . . Alexios?'

'Aye, but the Cult took your brother and made him one of their own. Mortal blood runs in your veins, Kassandra, but so too does the crimson elixir of the ancient ones. Leonidas was of their line. So was I, and so too your mother. That was why she and I came together. In doing so she might have betrayed the Spartan, Nikolaos, but . . .'

'But better that than betraying the world to the Cult,' I finished for him.

'Aye. They hunted you, me, your mother and your brother because we were the keys to truly harnessing these artefacts. The pyramid only speaks to those who carry the blood of its creators. That's why the Cult needed Deimos, even when they realized they could not control his chaotic nature.'

'But now the Cult is gone. I destroyed them. I succeeded,' I said.

His face sagged. 'I wish I could tell you it was so, Kassandra. But in destroying the Cult, you have swung the scales too far. The world can know harmony only if there is balance. Don't you see? It is the one lesson I should have imparted before I passed: by obliterating the Cult, you have merely cleared the earth for a darker, stronger weed to rise. Balance must be restored.'

A chill struck through me. 'How can I restore balance? Where . . . where do I begin?'

'The staff is the key. It will grant you the gift of time. Time is everything. With it you can . . .' He fell silent.

'Father?'

'No . . . it is too late,' he said, his voice tight. 'The dark weed has taken root already.'

'I don't understand.'

'You must go, Kassandra, now!'

'Father?' I cried.

But with a whoosh, the visions were gone. I found myself in the quiet, deserted Cave of Gaia once more. The pyramid was cold and silent now. I heard my rapid breathing slow and felt my heart fall into a steady rhythm again.

'You saw it too?' a voice echoed through the cavern. 'It was beautiful, wasn't it?'

I now saw the pale hand resting on the other side of the pyramid, the arm reaching out from a well of shadow. Dead fingers crept over my skin. 'Who's there?'

She stepped forward from the shadows like a creature crawling from a dream. 'Aspasia?'

'You're surprised to see me?' she said.

I did not reply – my demeanour surely was answer enough. I beheld her: beautiful, elegant, draped in a white stola. And then my eyes came to rest upon the shape underneath the garment. A hideous, hook-nosed, wickedly grinning theatre mask. Aspasia took a step towards me and lifted the mask out. I stared at her. 'How? Why?' I stammered.

'The Cult is gone, Kassandra,' she said, dropping the mask on the floor. She stepped upon it with her sandaled foot, cracking it in two. 'I played my part as one of them, but only to aid my own designs.'

'Which are?'

'You heard the legend speak, did you not? Of the need to bring a new order to the world.'

'I don't know what you heard or saw, Aspasia, but that is not what my father said. He showed me that extremes of order or chaos are not the answer, that balance is crucial.'

'Pythagoras was not strong enough to bring true order to the world,' Aspasia continued as if I had not spoken, 'nor was the Cult. You were a useful ally in sweeping them from the board of this great game.'

'But . . . you let them kill Perikles.'

'I would have stopped it if I could have,' she said, her face impassive. 'But you were there that day; you saw what happened. Deimos and his men would have slain us all had I tried to intervene. In any case, Perikles would have gladly died to bring about the Cult's end.'

Silence.

'And now?' I asked, dreading the answer.

'Now, the dream.' Aspasia said.

I could not tear my gaze from her eyes – glinting like ice crystals.

'The dream of all Hellas as a republic – no more squabbling city-states. An end to the competing ideologies of democracy and oligarchy. No more blue and red. No more fractious leagues. One realm, controlled – utterly – by a true leader: a philosopher-king to guide us all – a helmsman who will bring order to the world. It will be a lengthy process, like the growth of a new forest, and one best seeded in a bed of ashes . . . after the fires have raged.'

'Ashes? Fire? Aspasia . . . Hellas is at peace,' I said.

'This sham of an accord? I will see that it does not last,' she purred. 'In what forge but that of war can we otherwise hope to craft the dream?' Her face quirked with emotion: the traces of a cold smile. She shrank back into the shadows, and her next words came from the darkness.

Instinctively, I stepped after her, but found nothing in those shadows.

'The dream of true, complete, unspoiled order . . .' she whispered from somewhere, the sibilant words fading with an echo. Then I heard the distant patter of departing feet. Gone.

Alone, my mind rocked like a boat in a squall, my hand itching to tear the Leonidas spear from my belt. To chase and challenge Aspasia? And then what – strike her down and fire the vengeance of her well-placed minions? After all that had happened, all I had been through, I realized that it was not over.

It had only just begun.

Glossary

Abaton A hall in the Sanctuary of Asklepios where the sick slept.

Adyton The innermost shrine of a Greek temple.

Agoge Sparta's famous school for boys, which forced them to weather extreme hardship and foster a great love of the state from the age of seven. Boys would remain tied to the school in many ways until they were thirty, when they would finally be considered full-blooded Spartiates.

Andron The main room in a Greek home for entertaining.

Archon Leader.

Auloi (sing. aulos) Spartan war pipes.

Bakteriya The distinctive T-shaped staff held by Spartan officers.

Enomotia A 'sworn band' of thirty-two Spartan soldiers who were often related or had close ties. They would camp, eat and march together.

Ephors A group of five elected Spartan statesmen. It was the ephors' responsibility to declare war, to determine how many of the rare Spartan regiments would march to battle, and to hold the two kings of Sparta to account.

Exomis A single-shouldered tunic, usually worn by men.

Gerousia The Spartan council of elders.

Hetaerae Esteemed courtesans who served the goddess Aphrodite.

Himation An old-style garment worn by men that left most of the chest bare.

Hippeis The Spartan royal guard.

Hoplite The heavy infantryman of classical Greece.

Keleustes The rowing master aboard a trireme.

Khaire Welcome.

Kothon A mug from which Spartans used to drink their beloved black broth.

Kybernetes The helmsman on a galley.

Lochagos The officer in charge of a lochos.

Lochos A Spartan regiment. Ever more rare in the time of our story.

Malákas! Asshole!

Misthios A mercenary.

Navarchos Admiral.

Pankration A sport similar to modern boxing and wrestling.

Peltast A lightly armed infantryman who would carry a supply of javelins and harry the enemy from the edge of battle.

Porpax A leather or metal sleeve inside a shield. The wearer would slide their arm into this and their shield would effectively become part of them.

Skatá! Shit!

Skiritos A special Spartan levy of free but non-citizen subjects who lived near the Skiritis Mountains. They excelled at scouting and serving as outlying night watchmen, as well as performing a vital role as support troops in battle.

Stola A long pleated dress.

Strategos A military governor.

Strigil An implement used to exfoliate the skin after bathing.

Symposiarch The person in charge of orchestrating a symposium.

Taxiarchos The officer in charge of a taxiarchy.

Taxiarchy An Athenian regiment (in our story, though in reality probably all Greek city-states used the term at some point).

Thorax Body armour.

Triearchos The captain of a trireme.

List of Characters

Alexios Kassandra's younger brother who was cast off Mount Taygetos as a baby, following a damning prophecy by the Oracle of Delphi.

Alkibiades Cunning and hedonistic ward to Perikles, the most powerful man in Athens.

Anthousa The senior Hetaera at the Temple of Aphrodite in Korinth.

Archidamos The senior of Sparta's two kings.

Aristeus The Korinthian strategos.

Aristophanes Perhaps Athens' most famous comic playwright.

Aspasia A brilliant thinker and speaker, and partner to Athens' leader Perikles, Aspasia enjoys a place at the centre of Athens' vibrant intellectual community.

Barnabas Loyal friend to Kassandra, a well-travelled seafarer and one-time mercenary with a passion for tall tales.

Brasidas One of Sparta's greatest and bravest generals, Brasidas was also an accomplished statesman with the noble objective to help end war.

Chrysis A Cultist priestess who raised Deimos to become a weapon of the Cult of Kosmos.

Cyclops, The Powerful criminal tyrant of Kephallonia.

Deimos Raised within the Cult of Kosmos to become their hero and champion, Deimos is a brutal, living weapon whose extraordinary powers give him a fearsome reputation.

Diona A Cultist from Kythera.

Dolops Son of Chrysis and a priest at the Sanctuary of Asklepios.

Elpenor A rich, powerful businessman from Kirrha.

Erinna One of Anthousa's Hetaerae.

Euneas Navarchos of the Naxian fleet.

Euripides Famous Athenian tragedian.

Hermippus A playwright and poet ... with dark connections.

Herodotos 'The Father of History', a chronicler of facts and events, and yet a fine storyteller, who decides to accompany Kassandra on her journey.

Hippokrates Widely thought of as the father of modern medicine, Hippokrates is famous for his important and lasting contributions to the field.

Hyrkanos An Athenian-hired mercenary, operating in Megaris.

Ikaros Kassandra's most loyal companion since he was a mere eaglet.

Kassandra A hardened and formidable misthios.

Kleon The staunch power-hungry rival of Perikles who believes Athens needs to take an aggressive stance in the war.

Leonidas Sparta's legendary king, and Kassandra's grandfather, best known for leading his three hundred warriors into the battle of Thermopylae.

Lydos A Helot slave in the service of Sparta's two kings.

Markos A shady Kephallonian 'businessman'.

Monger, The A Cultist who leads the underground business market, feared for his torture methods.

Myrrine Kassandra's mother; a fierce Spartan.

Nikolaos Kassandra's father, a fierce, ruthless general unshakeably loyal to Sparta.

Oracle of Delphi The Oracle, consulted by commoners and the most powerful people of Greece alike, delivers prophecies and insights that can turn the tides of history.

Pausanias The junior of Sparta's two kings.

Perikles The elected leader of Athens.

Phoibe A young Athenian orphan adopted by Kassandra.

Pythagoras Legendary philosopher, political theorist and geometrician.

Roxana One of Anthousa's Hetaerae.

Silanos A Cultist who rose to power in Paros thanks to his great naval skill and wealthy supporters.

Sokrates Famous Athenian philosopher patronized by the intellectual elite of Athens.

Sophocles Famous Athenian tragedian.

Stentor Nikolaos' adopted son and a Spartan officer of some repute.

Testikles The talented and inebriate pankration champion of Sparta.

Thrasymachos Sokrates' intellectual sparring partner.

Thucydides One of Athens' key generals during the Peloponnesian War and one of the first historians to record an objective account of the struggle.

Special Thanks

Yves Guillemot, Laurent Detoc, Alain Corre, Geoffroy Sardin, Yannis Mallat, Thierry Dansereau, Jonathan Dumont, Melissa MacCoubrey, Susan Patrick, Stéphanie-Anne Ruatta, Etienne Allonier, Elena Rhodes, Aymar Azaïzia, Anouk Bachman, Antoine Ceszynski, Maxime Durand, Sarah Buzby, Clémence Deleuze, Julien Fabre, Caroline Lamache, Anthony Marcantonio, François Tallec, Salambo Vende, Elsa Fournier, Virginie Gringarten, Marc Muraccini, Cécile Russeil, Michael Beadle, Dominic DiSanti, Kimberly Kaspar, Heather Haefner, Joanie Simms, Aaron Dean, Tom Curtis, Annette Dana, Grace Orlady, Stephanie Pecaoco, Sain Sain Thao, Giancarlo Varanini, Morgane Frommherz, Valentin Hopfner, Valentin Meyer, Aline Piner, Clement Prevosto, Trevor Horwood, Joel Richardson, Elizabeth Cockeram, Thomas Colgan, Miranda Hill.